WISH UPON A STAR

Trisha Ashley was born in St. Helens, Lancashire, and gave up her fascinating but time-consuming hobbies of house-moving and divorce a few years ago in order to settle in North Wales.

For more information about Trisha please visit
www.trishaashley.com

By the same author:

TRISHA ASHLEY

Wish Upon A Star

avon.

Published by AVON
A division of HarperCollins*Publishers* Ltd
1 London Bridge Street
London SE1 9GF

www.harpercollins.co.uk

This paperback edition 2018

First published in Great Britain by HarperCollins*Publishers* 2013

A catalogue copy of this book is available from the British Library.

ISBN: 978-1-84756-278-4

This novel is entirely a work of fiction. The names, characters and incidents
portrayed in it are the work of the author's imagination. Any resemblance to
actual persons, living or dead, events or localities is entirely coincidental.

Typeset in Minion by Palimpsest Book Production Limited, Falkirk, Stirlingshire
Printed and bound in UK by CPI Group (UK) Ltd, Croydon CR0 4YY

MIX
Paper from
responsible sources
FSC C007454

This book is produced from independently certified FSC™ paper
to ensure responsible forest management.

For more information visit: www.harpercollins.co.uk/green

This book is dedicated to all my wonderful readers – my stars to steer by.

Acknowledgements

Although I mention Boston Children's Hospital, I have never been there and have no knowledge of the staff members, so all characters and medical procedures in the book are wholly the product of my own imagination.

On the other hand, the scenes set in Honey's Haberdashery shop were entirely based on fact, for my Grandmother, Edith Long, started up such a shop in the early years of the twentieth century, and all manner of treasure-trove came to light when it was cleared.

Prologue: 2001,
The Return of the Native

It was early evening in the village of Sticklepond and the bar of the Falling Star was almost empty, apart from a couple of locals who'd dropped in on their way home from work, and the shoe salesman in the corner who had booked a room for the night and was now studying racing form in the paper as if his life depended on it.

As Florrie Snowball slapped a hot, limp, microwaved sausage roll and a pint of Middlemoss Brown Ale in front of Pete Ormerod, who farmed up by the edge of the Winter's End estate, she said, 'I hear there's an Almond moved back into the village.'

'That's right,' he agreed, poking the middle of the sausage roll with the end of a gnarled finger as if unsure what might pop out. 'News gets around fast.'

'Someone saw her – there's no mistaking an Almond, and anyway, we've seen Martha come and go over the years, right up till her mother died, haven't we? Not that she didn't keep herself to herself, just like her parents did.'

'They had cause enough, didn't they?'

'I'm not one to think the sins of the fathers should be visited on the children, poor innocent mites, and only us old ones remember the whole story now,' Florrie snapped. 'And anyway, Martha's parents were no more than cousins, so it wasn't really anything to do with them.'

'They still felt the shame, though,' Pete Ormerod said heavily, 'and went off to Australia with the rest of the family, even if they were back within the year.'

'Well, you did all right out of it, didn't you?' she pointed out tartly. 'Buying Badger's Bolt farm gave you twice as much land and they were in such a hurry to get away, I bet you paid less than it was worth.'

'It was enough to buy them a sheep holding in Australia and that's what they wanted – though the sheep were what Jacob couldn't abide. But there was never a better cattle man than Jacob Almond and I was more than glad to give him his old job and cottage back.'

'I always thought the whole clan of them upping sticks and emigrating was a bit of an over-reaction myself,' Florrie said. 'Came of them being Strange Baptists from that chapel that was over in Ormskirk, I expect. The young ones these days'd think nothing of what happened – they see worse on the soaps every night. So now Martha's back living in the very same cottage she grew up in, it's surely time to forgive and forget.'

'Not *exactly* the same cottage,' Pete said through a mouthful of sausage roll, 'the last people who had it built a big garden room at the back with a bedroom over it and tarted the place up no end.'

'Well, you should know, you were the one who sold it off to them in the first place. And it's just as well it's been done up, because it was no more than a hovel before, and after being married to that London doctor Martha must be used to something different – and come to think of it, she's not an Almond now, she's Martha Weston.'

'She'll always be an Almond as far as some of us are concerned, there's no getting away from it,' Pete said, shaking his head, and seeing he was set in that conviction she said no more, though she did severely admonish him for having the bad manners to talk with his mouth full, before leaving him to the rest of his sausage roll and pint.

It had been sheer serendipity that the house where she was born should have come up for sale just as Martha Weston had started her search for a new home. Now, unpacking books in the almost unrecognisable cottage, she neither knew nor cared whether the locals were talking about her or not – she was just glad to be back where she felt she belonged.

Although she didn't know all the ins and outs of it, Martha was well aware that one of her relatives had somehow blotted his copybook and been expunged from the family records in the dim and distant past ('Never mention Uncle Esau to your father,' her mother had always said), an event that had precipitated the entire Almond clan taking flight like a flock of startled birds.

She barely remembered Australia, except that it had been hot and smelled of sheep, but her parents had been even more insular on their return and she became a solitary child, happy in her own company, who could often be seen sketching in the countryside.

She'd gone to grammar school in Merchester and then, after being taken up and encouraged by Ottie Winter from the big house (who was even then getting a name for her sculptures), went off to art school in London.

Marrying a doctor and staying there hadn't been any part of her plans, but love plays tricks on us all. Still, as soon as his death released her, she had flown like a homing pigeon back to the village where she was born.

She belonged in Sticklepond, but since both nature and nurture had made her solitary she often walked in the gloom of the evening when few were about and did most of her shopping in the nearest town instead of the village.

But strangely and without her being aware of doing it, whenever her way took her past the war memorial on the green, she would avert her eyes and quicken her step, just as her mother had always done.

Chapter 1: A Star is Born

While the consultant was explaining the complexities of my baby's heart condition to me in a hushed, confidential tone, I stared fixedly at his yellow and red-spotted bow tie, half expecting it suddenly to spin round like a joke one: that's how spaced-out with fear, anaesthetic and shock I was after my emergency Caesarean.

I don't know why he bothered to lower his voice anyway, since I'd been shunted off into a room of my own . . . or maybe that should be a *store cupboard* of my own, because it was a tiny slice of space with one high window and a wall lined with boxes of equipment. They were probably as surplus to requirements as I seemed to be, now that my baby was sustained by the resources of the intensive care baby unit instead of my own.

'Can I see her?' I interrupted.

Ma, whose ample frame was squeezed into a tubular metal chair on the other side of the bed, with her elbow resting on a pile of cardboard cartons, said, 'She can't come up here, Cally, when she's in an incubator attached to all those bleeping things, and you certainly aren't up to going down there yet. But she's perfect – hands like tiny pale pink starfish.'

'You said she was so blue she looked like a Smurf,' I said accusingly, tears welling.

'I thought you were still asleep when I was talking to that nurse, and anyway, it was just a glance in passing right after she was born. She looks pink now.'

'She *was* a little blue at first, but now she's stabilised and a relatively healthy colour,' the consultant said soothingly. 'You will be taken down in a wheelchair to see her as soon as you are recovered enough.'

'She is going to be all right, isn't she?' I pleaded. 'Only there was an angel hanging around when I woke up and I thought it might have come for her.'

'That was a nun,' Ma said. 'She had a white habit on and flapped past the trolley when you were being wheeled out of theatre. Thought she looked more like an albatross, myself.'

'Why would a nun be on a maternity ward?' I asked.

'I don't know, but it's a damned sight more likely than an angel.'

I focused on the consultant again and he looked back at me and frowned. 'Your baby's heart problems should really have been picked up on a scan . . .' He paused and then added with false brightness, 'Still, there is *one* good thing.'

'There is?' Ma asked incredulously.

'Yes, the majority of female babies with similar malformations also have Turner's syndrome, which can lead to other side effects, but your baby doesn't.'

'Thank heaven for small mercies, then,' my mother said drily, without removing the jade cigarette holder that was clenched between her teeth. Having tired of repeating to hospital staff that she'd no intention of lighting up inside the premises, she'd removed the pink Sobranie from it and

6

placed it carefully in a silver case in her vast red Radley handbag. The consultant eyed the empty holder in much the same way I'd been looking at his bow tie, and then his gaze moved to the colourful splashes of oil paint on the legs of her black slacks and across her tunic where her bosom tended to rest on her palette while she painted. She looked like a walking embodiment of Jackson Pollock's Dark Period – if he'd had one.

Still, it was a measure of her love that she'd rushed down on the first train once my friend Celia had called her, despite her oft-repeated statement that she never wanted to set foot in London again.

'Never mind Pollock: this is *my* dark period,' I muttered.

'I think our Cally's a bit delirious,' she said, laying one small, cool, plump hand on my forehead. 'Though she often talks daft.'

'I'm not – and I understand about Stella needing an operation right away. Will she be all right afterwards?'

'She certainly won't survive if we *don't* operate,' the consultant said evasively, still in that low, confidential voice. 'She's not quite full term and of course there are always risks involved in operating on such small babies. But you do understand that her long-term outlook is at present obscure, don't you? She will definitely need more treatment later, possibly including further operations.'

'There seems no option but to agree to this operation,' Ma said, shifting the jade holder to one side of her mouth. 'It will give her a fighting chance, at least.'

He nodded, though he didn't look as if he'd have placed any money on it.

But I clung to that idea, for of course the advances of

modern medical science would ensure that my baby would make a full recovery and live a normal life. She'd be one of the lucky ones: my Stella, my little star.

Having been fathoms deep in a bottomless ocean of anaesthesia when Stella came into the world, I worried that I might find it difficult to bond with her. But the moment I set eyes on my baby I was consumed by a blinding flash of such instant besottedness that I could spend an hour or more just marvelling over the perfect convolutions of her tiny ears, or the minute crescents of her fingernails, like those fragile pale pink shells I used to pick up on Southport beach.

Celia, the friend who had so luckily been staying with me when I was rushed into hospital, was equally enthralled and enchanted, but Ma, who is not the type to dote on babies, only said the poor mite looked like a skinned rabbit. Then, this obviously having triggered a thought train in her head, she went out and bought Stella a white plush rabbit that was bigger than she was.

When we got the hospital chaplain to christen Stella, Ma suggested we have the rabbit as a godparent, after Celia, though I *think* she was joking . . . But there it was in the photographs, along with the special cake iced with the baby's name that I'd sent Celia out to buy. If all had gone to plan, of course, I would have made it myself at a later date. For me, important occasions must always be accompanied by cake, since it earned me a living as a cookery writer, as well as being my comfort food of choice.

'Go to Gilligan's Celebration Cakes off Marylebone High,' I told her. 'If it has to be shop-bought, they're the best and they'll ice her name on it while you wait.'

'Oh, yes, I remember you going there to research an article on traditional wedding cakes for *Good Housekeeping* and bringing me a chunk of fruitcake back,' Celia agreed. 'And you said one of the staff was dead sexy and looked just like Johnny Depp.'

'Did I? Oh, yes, but Johnny Depp as Captain Jack Sparrow,' I said, a sudden flash of recollection bringing up the undeniably attractive image of a thin, dark, mobile face with high cheekbones and a pair of strangely luminous light brown eyes meeting mine across a work table, while the heady scent of dried fruit and spices mingled with the sweet smell of sugar.

'That seems like another life,' I sighed. 'It happened to a different person.'

Chapter 2: The Night Watch

During the long night watches after Stella's first operation, as the lights flashed on the machinery and the hospital hummed faintly along to the tired buzzing in my head, there were way too many hours in which to think.

Her arrival had instantly turned my life upside down, so that everything I'd once thought important had run right to the bottom of my hourglass of priorities. My hard-fought-for career as a cookery writer, for instance, which paid the mortgage on the shoebox-sized basement flat within walking distance of Primrose Hill, where I lived with my little white dog, Toto.

Toto was a Battersea Dogs and Cats Home stray and looked like a cross between a whippet and a Skye terrier, if you can imagine that: all bristly white coat, with a terrier head but slender body and long legs. Ma and Celia were both staying on at my flat and looking after him, as well as taking it in turns to come into the hospital, though Ma spent most of her visits drawing a series of starfish-like little hands and winged creatures that appeared to be some kind of nun/angel/albatross hybrid. Her paintings are already very Chagall-with-knobs-on, so I could barely imagine the turn they would take when she got back home again.

Toto was an excellent judge of character and although he adored Celia and Ma, he'd never taken to my ex-fiancé, Adam, a tall and charismatic marine biologist who'd proposed to me after a whirlwind romance. In retrospect, I only wished I'd trusted my dog's instincts more than my own.

Adam had swept me off my feet and we'd planned to get married in the lovely ancient church of All Angels in the village of Sticklepond, where Ma now lived . . . the minute he got back from the eighteen-month contract in Antarctica that he'd already signed up for, that was.

I'd suggested he cancel it, but he'd explained that he'd always dreamed of going there and needed to get it out of his system before he settled down.

'It'll be cutting it fine for starting a family by then, though,' I'd said. 'I don't want to leave it too late, or it might not happen at all.'

'Mmm,' he'd agreed, with much less enthusiasm than he'd shown while talking about the Antarctic; but by then I'd discovered his acute phobia about hospitals and illness of any kind, and put it down as some general squeamishness to do with that.

Still, I'd been convinced he'd be bored out of his skull stuck in the Antarctic for eighteen months with a lot of other boffins, examining the local frozen seafood. But no, it turned out that there was a whole community there, with everyone from cooks to dentists laid on, which I supposed made sense when most of the year you couldn't fly in or out.

They made their own entertainments too, and going by the pictures on Facebook of Adam messing about on Ski-Doos and in the snow with his new friends, he'd found a few ways to occupy his spare time.

Of course, we'd constantly emailed and chatted via Facebook, and sometimes he could call me, though not the other way round. But as time passed he seemed to become less and less interested in anything outside the base . . . I suppose that's a bit like hospital, where your real world shrinks to your immediate surroundings and everything else seems remote and unimportant.

I expected that would change once he came home, even if I did feel nervous about our reunion. And there *was* a sticky moment at the airport, when he looked like an unshaven stranger as he came through into the arrivals hall. But when he spotted me and smiled there was that instant feeling of connection, just like the first time we'd met, and I ran straight into his arms. He'd kissed me, then said, looking genuinely startled, that he'd forgotten how pretty I was!

We went back to my flat and that evening everything was all right between us – in fact, it was more than all right. He *was* tired and abstracted, not helped by a call from a colleague, though what could be that urgent about Antarctic pond life I couldn't imagine at the time. His end of the conversation was a bit terse.

I should have smelled a rat right then, because next morning it was like Jekyll and Hyde revisited: right after breakfast he suddenly announced he'd already signed up for another eighteen months in Antarctica *and*, moreover, he'd met someone else up there and she was going back in April, too.

Of course I was devastated and furious. I told him to get out of my flat and my life and he'd packed up his stuff and left within the hour, with my parting shot that I hoped they both fell down an Antarctic crevasse on their next tour of duty ringing in his ears.

Toto, gleefully grasping that the hated interloper was out of favour, managed to sink his teeth into Adam's ankle at the last minute, which would give him something to remember us by till all the little puncture wounds healed up again.

It was only much later that I realised that Adam had left me a much longer-lasting and life-changing memento.

Once Stella was out of immediate danger, Celia needed to get back to her husband, four rescue greyhounds and six cats in Southport, who were all pining for her.

I would also pine for her, though she'd promised to return when Stella was finally allowed home.

Ma was staying on for a few more days, though I was sure she was dying to head straight back up north, too. In fact, I was surprised she'd stayed as long as she had.

When I was growing up in Hampstead I'd thought she'd seemed happy enough, though she was always fairly reclusive and preoccupied with her work, of course, but she sold up and moved back with alacrity to the Lancashire village where she was born after Dad died.

'Ma' is not some cute contraction of 'Mum', but a relic of her early attempts to get me to call her by her Christian name, Martha. She was never much like any of my school friends' mothers, delegating most of her maternal responsibilities to a series of foreign au pairs, but I'd never doubted that in her way she loved me. And Anna, the final and most beloved of the au pairs, a tall, blonde, Swedish domestic goddess, had instilled my love of cooking and baking, so it worked out brilliantly for me.

I emailed Anna the news about Stella and received a warm, reassuring reply straight away: she'd always had the power to make me feel comforted, an effect that has also rubbed off onto the cakes she taught me to make.

I decided that for Stella's first birthday I would make her a *prinsesstårta*, that most splendid of Swedish celebration cakes.

'You *are* going to tell Adam about Stella at some point soon, aren't you?' Celia asked, just before she finally set off home.

'No! Why should I, after he accused me of getting pregnant on purpose when I told him she was on the way and then suggested I get an abortion?'

'I know he didn't want the baby, but now she's arrived he might feel differently,' she suggested. Having an incredibly generous heart she was always looking for the best in everyone, even my absent ex-fiancé, Adam Scott – or 'Scott of the Antarctic', as Ma generally referred to him.

'I don't think so. Anyway, he's changed his email address and I couldn't phone him in Antarctica even if I wanted to, which I don't.'

'Facebook?'

'I've blocked him.'

'I still think he ought to know,' she said stubbornly. 'He has a responsibility to support you, too.'

'I don't want his support and I'm sure he still wouldn't be interested – even less so in a baby with health problems, because he's got that phobia about illness and hospitals, remember?'

'Oh, yes, I'd forgotten about that. So perhaps you're right, but if he hears about the baby from anyone, he may contact you when he comes back to the UK.'

'I doubt it, and it wouldn't be till October of next year, when Stella—'

I broke off, swallowing hard, and she said quickly, 'Stella will be walking and saying her first words by then, you'll see. The operation went well, didn't it?'

'Yes, but they made it plain they couldn't fix everything in one go and would have to wait and see how her condition developed. She *seems* to be making progress.'

'The body has great powers of self-healing,' Celia said firmly.

I clung to that thought after she'd gone back to Southport: once I finally got her home, Stella and I would take the future one step at a time, savouring each moment like a special gift.

Chapter 3: Lardy Cake

Long before Stella's due date I'd stockpiled articles for my two regular publication slots: the 'Tea & Cake' page in *Sweet Home* magazine, which are quick, easy recipes, and my Sunday newspaper supplement one, 'The Cake Diaries', which have more complicated recipes along with some quirky background history, or stories about where I first came across a particular cake, thrown into the mix.

I usually work months in advance for magazines anyway, filing my Christmas articles in summer and my summer articles in winter, but this time I had almost a year's worth in reserve. This foresight proved to be a very good idea, given the distractions and alarms of Stella's first weeks, because the pieces all came out just as if nothing was going on in my life but baking and eating cakes.

Of course, I'd missed out on all the extra articles and assignments that would normally have come my way during this time, which usually put a bit of icing on the gingerbread of life. Once Stella was home, I knew I needed to get back into the groove as quickly as possible, even though this wasn't going to be easy with a brain occupied entirely with worried thoughts wrapped in a thick fuzzy blanket of hope.

I hadn't even lost any baby-weight, either – in fact, due to lack of activity and comfort eating, I'd put more on – so when I inadvertently caught sight of my stolid, stodgy pale nakedness in the bedroom mirror soon after Stella finally came home, I thought I looked just like a lardy cake.

Oh, lardy me!

I sat down on the bed and wept, and once I'd started I found I couldn't stop for ages, which I expect was all the hormones still whizzing about in my system. But at least it was cathartic. It finally shook me out of the zombie trance and set me back onto the researching, experimental baking and writing track again, even if I did tend to shoehorn most of it into the times when Stella was asleep.

I'd kept on the expensive dog walker I'd had to hire for poor Toto while I was spending so much time at the hospital, and she took him out in the mornings. Eventually, when Stella was well enough, the three of us would head for Primrose Hill every afternoon for a bit of fresh air. (It's as about as fresh at the top of the hill as you will find in London.) Toto, thank goodness, had taken to the baby immediately and didn't seem in the least jealous, so slowly we all settled into the new regime.

And – waste not, want not – at least the lardy cake revelation inspired a new 'Cake Diaries' recipe.

Lardy Cake is a wonderfully stodgy, bready cake that originates from Wiltshire. It's made with yeast and dried fruit – plus, of course, lots of lard, but I thought I would try to devise a slightly different version, replacing some of the lard with butter and adding a little spice . . .

Stella's first three years were as up and down as a ride on the Big Dipper at Southport fun-fair, and while I struggled to persuade my changeling fairy child to eat and put on weight, *I* went from a curvy size twelve/fourteen to a Rubensesque sixteen/eighteen. This is what happens when your comfort food of choice is cake, and the nature of your work means the oven wafts the sweet smell of temptation at you every day.

The proof of the pudding was in the eating and I *was* that pudding.

I said so to Celia, who had come down to stay with me so she could do some early Christmas shopping, pop into the *Sweet Home* office (she did their 'Crafty Celia Pull Out and Make' section – if you could stick it, knit it, or stuff it, Celia was your woman) and, most crucially, support me through the next meeting with Stella's hospital consultant, when he would outline her care plan for the next year.

'The extra weight suits you, though,' Celia assured me, 'because you're quite tall and still in perfect proportion, while I've never had a waist to start with and now gravity's pulled me into the shape of a squishy pear. Just as well that Will likes pears,' she added, grinning.

That was a bit consoling, but I'd have to accept that I was now never going to be an airy confection of spun sugar, only a solid Madeira sponge. My smart clothes had been packed away for so long I feared the creases were permanent and I was living in jeans, trainers and sloppy T-shirts. I'd also given up any attempt to straighten my curly fair hair, or cover the freckles across the bridge of my nose with makeup. In fact, I'd entirely resigned myself to looking wholesome, it just didn't feel that important any more . . . though I might still grind cake in the face of the next person to remark brightly that I looked like a young Hayley Mills, because I'd Googled her films and no, I *didn't*.

What would I have done without Celia? Other friends had slipped away since I had Stella, but she had remained constant since the day I first moved out of the family home and we shared both a flat and the struggle to make a living. She met her husband, Will, when *Sweet Home* commissioned an article about his driftwood sculptures and we happened to be in the offices when he came in to ask about getting a regular column. Love at first sight. Will is so nice, he almost deserves her.

'What does Stella want for Christmas – or need I ask?' she said now. 'More of those Sylvanian Families?'

'Yes. I'm afraid the addiction might be permanent, and it's all my fault,' I said ruefully. I'd been too old really for the little fuzzy animal toys when they first came out, but I'd loved them anyway and, over the years, added a few more to my collection. Now Stella, at three, had taken them over and I'd bought her even more.

'I know she's scarily bright, but isn't she a bit young for them?'

'Perhaps, but she's never put things in her mouth, apart from her thumb, and she plays quietly with them for hours. She wants a house for the mouse family to live in next, but there are a few other things that I know she'd like. There's a Father Christmas mouse too, with a little tree and parcels – that looked fun.'

'You can show me on the internet, and I'll order something. You're coming up to Sticklepond to stay with Martha for Christmas, aren't you?'

'Yes, and bringing all the ingredients for festive fun with us, as usual, because Ma wouldn't bother otherwise. I do love going up there and I know that Ma, for all her reclusive ways, loves Stella.'

'We *all* love Stella, she's bright and delightful – *she* read her *Meg and Mog* book to *me* last night,' Celia said. 'And then she said if she knew a witch she would get her to do a spell to make her heart better.'

'I only wish *I* knew one. She's so tiny for nearly three and a half and she gets tired so easily that we still have to take the buggy everywhere. She doesn't eat enough to keep a bird alive and any slight infection is dangerous . . .' I sighed. 'Well, we'll see what the treatment plan they've drawn up for her at the hospital for next year is.'

'They did say she might need another operation, didn't they? Perhaps it will be the final one, so she can live a normal life,' Celia said optimistically.

But there didn't seem to *be* an ongoing treatment plan – or not one leading in a positive direction. I was shocked when the consultant told me there was nothing more they could do and gave me to understand that Stella's long-term outlook was poor and she was likely to go slowly downhill as her condition increasingly put a strain on her body, until finally she succumbed to some infection.

'Of course, we would like her to gain weight so that she has the reserves to fight infections, but then again, as she grows, that will also put a strain on her organs . . .' he explained.

'When I asked him if they couldn't operate again, he said no, because no one in the UK was doing the kind of complex surgery she needed,' I reminded Celia later, back in the flat, when Stella had gone for a nap and we were talking it all over. I was still shell-shocked and tearful, but Celia suddenly seized on what I'd just said.

'So he did! But maybe that means they *are* doing it in another country, like America? I saw a newspaper article about a child who'd gone to America for life-saving surgery, though it cost thousands and thousands of pounds, so they'd had to do a lot of fundraising to pay for it.'

I stared at her blankly. 'But – wouldn't the consultant have mentioned it, if there was anyone else capable of helping Stella?'

'Not necessarily, I don't think, if it was another country. Come on, it's worth a go – Google search.'

And that's how we found Dr Rufford Beems' experimental programme over in Boston, and a fresh spring of hope.

We emailed the hospital in Boston straight away and after that things just seemed to snowball, so by the time Stella and I finally set out for Christmas with Ma in Sticklepond, I'd had Stella's medical information sent over to Boston, a very kind and detailed response from the surgeon, and a reluctant agreement from my consultant that it was currently Stella's only option, other than settling for palliative care.

'Dr Beems says it would be best to do the operation before Stella's fifth birthday, but the sooner the better,' I told Celia when I called her to give her the latest update. 'I'll need as much time as possible to raise the money, though, because it's going to be phenomenally expensive.'

'Nothing is too expensive if it can cure her,' Celia said. 'We can do it.'

21

'The surgeon is going to waive his own fees, since it's still experimental surgery . . . and when he says *experimental*, my heart goes cold,' I confessed.

'Yes, but his success rate is already excellent and the alternative isn't to be thought of,' she pointed out. 'It's the best option. So now we need to work out a fundraising plan over Christmas. I'll bring Will across and we'll put our heads together.'

'I . . . am doing the right thing?' I asked her.

'You're doing the only possible thing,' she assured me, but it suddenly felt as if Stella and I were drowning and someone had thrown us a lifebelt: I wasn't quite sure how I could get my arms through it without letting go of her, but I'd have to give it my best shot.

Chapter 4: Christmas Pudding

I drove Stella up to Sticklepond a few days before Christmas with a boot full of hidden presents, the cake, turkey, mince pies and pudding – in fact, most of the ingredients we'd need for the festive season. Left to her own devices, I'm very sure Ma wouldn't treat the day any differently from the rest of the year, but she went along with it all.

As usual, I had the emergency numbers for Ormskirk Hospital and Alder Hey (the big children's hospital in Liverpool) just in case – but I hoped we wouldn't need them, because I was determined that this was going to be the best Christmas yet.

'Toto has very sharp elbows,' Stella said from her child seat in the back, as the dog adjusted himself into a sort of meagre fur lap rug. 'Did you remember to bring his presents, Mummy?'

'Yes, they're in the boot.'

'Will Father Christmas remember we're staying with Grandma?'

'I'm sure he will: he knows everything by magic.'

'Like God,' she agreed sagely. 'Hal says God knows everything.'

Hal is under-gardener at Winter's End, the historic house just outside Sticklepond, and lives in a cottage on the edge of the estate, across the lane from Ma. A taciturn man with a bold roman nose and a surprising head of soft silvery-grey curls under his flat tweed cap, he's been moonlighting as Ma's gardener ever since she moved up there, and they seemed to have become increasingly friendly . . .

'I like Hal,' she added. 'He makes me sweet milky tea in a special blue cup when he brews up in his shed and last time we came he showed me a dead mole he found in the woods.'

'That was kind of him,' I said. Hal had created a cosy den in the old shed next to Ma's studio in the garden, with a little Primus stove where he brewed up endless enamel pots of sweet tea for them both. Just like Dad, Hal seemed to wander in and out of the studio, or sit reading the paper in the corner, without appearing to bother Ma in the least.

Despite looking so morose he was really a very nice man – and what's more, he'd slowly brought Ma out of herself a little bit, to the point where, as well as the library, she went with him to the monthly Gardening Club, and the occasional game of darts at the Green Man with the other Winter's End gardeners.

Ottie Winter occasionally visited her too, because over the years her early patronage and help had turned into friendship. I'd often met her at our house in Hampstead, and Ma had taken me to one or two exhibitions of her sculptures, which are bold and figurative . . . sort of. You could say the same about Ma's paintings.

Her only other regular visitor seemed to be Raffy Sinclair, the Sticklepond vicar, despite her not being a churchgoer.

'Are we nearly there yet? I wish we lived in Sticklepond. It's much more fun than home,' Stella said from the back seat.

'Do you?' I asked, startled and glancing at her in the rear-view mirror. 'Wouldn't you miss Primrose Hill and the zoo?'

'No,' she said firmly.

Sometimes it was hard to remember that she was only three and a half going on a hundred . . . But I was just grateful we'd left the tricky subject of God behind and were not again pursuing the question of where people went when they were dead like we had the previous week, after I'd had to tell her that she wouldn't be seeing one of her little friends from hospital again . . .

While I chatted to Stella as we trundled north up the motorway, part of my mind was occupied with how I was to raise the astronomical amount of money it would take to get her to America and to pay for the operation. It seemed near impossible – but how different her life would be if I pulled it off and the operation was a complete success . . . which it surely must be. If only she stayed well enough, till then . . .

But if she didn't, if things took a turn for the worst and the need for the operation became urgent – which, please God, they wouldn't – then I had a contingency plan to raise the money quickly, one that I'd need Ma's agreement to. It would be a *big* ask and even though I'd already declined her generous offer to mortgage the cottage to pay for the oper-ation, I wasn't quite sure how she'd react to it.

Will had already started the process of setting up a fund-raising website, Stella's Stars, having had experience of doing something similar with his and Celia's greyhound fostering one.

It proved to be quite a complicated affair: I'd never have managed it on my own. He'd promised it would be up and running by the New Year, though.

Turning off the motorway as the short winter's day grew towards dusk, I clicked on the Bing Crosby *White Christmas* CD that was Stella's surprise favourite and resolutely turned my mind to having a merry little Christmas with a bright yuletide and jingle bells all the way.

Ma's house was a long, low building made of slightly crumbly local sandstone, once a tied cottage on the Almonds' farm, Badger's Bolt. From what I'd gleaned, Ma had a fairly solitary childhood there, with parents who didn't mix much with the local people. But it sounded like the Almonds had always been clannish before they emigrated after the war, so I suppose when Ma's parents came back, they *would* feel isolated. Ma didn't like to talk about the Almonds much, but that could be because, apart from her father, she didn't really remember them.

I do dimly recall visiting Grandma Almond: a small, plump, silver-haired woman, who only ever seemed to have a real conversation with her hens. The cottage had still belonged to old Mr Ormerod, the farmer who'd bought up the Almonds' land and buildings, so it was a very different place now from how it was originally. A few years before, he'd sold off the buildings he didn't need, including this cottage, and the new owners extended upwards and out at the back, giving Ma an upstairs master bedroom with ensuite over the light airy garden room, as well as a garage at the side.

The big barn nearby has been converted into a smart house, but the old Almond farmhouse at the top of the lane was currently uninhabited and for sale, since there had been some trouble with the last owner a year or two back and it had lain empty ever since.

Stella and I had the two small downstairs bedrooms just off the old sitting room and next to the family bathroom, and Toto and Moses, Ma's cat, fight it out for the rag rug in front of the wood-burning stove in the kitchen.

Ma seemed mildly pleased to see us, but it was just as I thought: she hadn't remembered to get a tree, or find the decorations, and was even hazy on which day of the week Christmas Day fell. But we quickly settled in and next morning I decided to leave Stella with Ma after breakfast while I went into Ormskirk to do a huge supermarket shop for basics: anything else I needed I intended to buy in the village, which has a good range of shops now.

I would take Toto with me, since he was always happy to go anywhere in the car and it took him and Moses the cat two or three days of wary circling and jostling before they settled down happily together, so time apart was good.

Ma and Stella were going to go up to the studio and, since it was a Sunday, I was sure Hal would also be about to keep an eye on her. Stella, though, saw things differently and promised to look after Grandma while I was out.

'I'll tell her off if she puts her paintbrush in her mouth,' she assured me. 'And Grandma, you shouldn't smoke.'

'I'm down to two Sobranies a day now, so have a heart, love,' Ma said, guiltily laying down the jade holder she had removed from her mouth for long enough to eat her breakfast and which she'd been about to replace. It seemed to be a comfort thing, a bit like the thumb-sucking Stella still resorted to in times of stress. Today's Sobranie was the same green as the holder.

Stella made a tut-tutting noise and shook her head, so that all her white-blond curls danced.

'You leave Grandma alone,' I told her. 'I'm sure she doesn't breathe the smoke in.'

Ma looked even guiltier, and Stella unconvinced, but I left them to it and went to brave the pre-Christmas shops: with only a few days to go a kind of feeding frenzy was taking place in the aisles and a near-fight erupted over the last family-sized deluxe Christmas pudding.

There was no sign of anyone at the cottage when I got back so I put away all the shopping in Ma's almost empty fridge, freezer and cupboards – though she was big on packets of coffee, Laphroaig whisky, Plymouth gin and frozen microwave dinners – and then went up to the studio, where I found Stella and Ma painting at adjacent easels. Hal was sitting in an old wooden chair reading the Sunday paper, which in her painting Ma had origamied into a newsprint winged creature trying to escape from his hands.

Stella's painting seemed to be an angel of a more traditional sort. 'Look, Mummy – this is a dead person's angel from the graveyard. Me and Grandma went there to draw and there are lots more.'

'I hope you fastened your coat up, because there's a cold wind out,' I said, admiring the picture.

'They went in the car and she was wrapped up warm. They were only out half an hour or so,' Hal assured me. 'They both had a hot cup of tea when they came back, too, and a couple of garibaldi biscuits.'

'Oh, thank you,' I said gratefully. It was certainly warm enough in the studio, where an electric stove in the corner radiated fake flames and heat.

I went off to get lunch ready, but Toto jumped onto Hal's knee, so I left him there. He'd probably be immortalised in oils too, winged or otherwise.

Stella's health usually seemed better in Sticklepond and, as always on our visits, we soon settled into a pleasant routine. I pushed Stella in her buggy to the village most days, sometimes with Toto when he would deign to come with us, since he always ungratefully attached himself to Ma. We would do a little shopping and feed the ducks on the pond by the village green, or go on a longer walk up towards the Winter's End estate and back round the right of way used only by locals.

It was all very familiar from previous visits, though it had changed a lot in the last few years since the discovery at Winter's End of a manuscript purporting to have been written by Shakespeare. The village had flourished and turned into a thriving tourist destination and now there was an almost cosmopolitan hum about the place. Several long-empty shop fronts had suddenly sported new signs and opened their doors for business.

I'd been visiting the village for so long that many of the inhabitants were also familiar and it suddenly occurred to me that Sticklepond now felt more like home than London ever did, what with everyone so friendly when I was out and about with Stella.

Ma might keep to herself, but of course she knew who everyone in the village was, and they knew who she was before she married. And *I* couldn't hide who I was even if

I wanted to, because just like Ma I have inherited the typical Almond looks: very fair curling hair and slightly wide-apart clear blue eyes, with a tiny gap between my front teeth.

Occasionally some elderly villager would look at me closely and then tell me I was an Almond and, when I told them yes, my mother was Martha Almond before she married, he would nod and walk away; but though I knew that my distant cousin Esau had blotted his copybook, no one ever told me how, and my mild curiosity remained unsatisfied.

Stella still needed a long nap every afternoon, she got tired so easily, but once awake again we had a lovely time preparing for Christmas: sticking together paper-chain garlands, setting up the Nativity crib, decorating a quick chocolate Yule log, and baking star-shaped spiced biscuits, which we threaded with red ribbon and hung on the modest Christmas tree we'd carried home from the Spar in the village, partly wedged down the side of the buggy.

Later, I wrote up the Yule log for my 'Tea & Cake' page.

To whip up a quick and easy Yule log, cut out the fiddly task of making your own Swiss roll and instead buy a large one – the brown kind with a white creamy filling looks best. Cover with a thick coat of chocolate butter cream, roughly spread with a knife to give the effect of bark. Decorate with a robin and some holly, or whatever takes your fancy and keep in the fridge until you need it.

While we were back in the Spar buying the hundreds and thousands and little edible silver balls to decorate the trifle with, Stella told the friendly middle-aged shop assistant that we'd just been to visit the angels in the graveyard again (which was unfortunately becoming a habit, though at least it didn't seem to be a morbid interest). The assistant asked if we'd been into the church to see the Nativity scene, which was apparently well worth viewing.

Stella remembered this later, and badgered Ma into agreeing to go and see it with us next morning. I hoped Stella wouldn't be disappointed, because I was expecting no more from the Nativity than the usual dustily thatched crib and battered plaster or plastic figures, but they turned out to be the most beautifully carved wooden ones. Stella was enthralled by every tiny detail.

'The Winter family brought them from Oberammagau before the war. It's where they have that there Passion Play,' said a voice behind us, and when I turned round I saw a small, wrinkled, lively-looking woman regarding us with sparrow-bright eyes full of curiosity.

'This is Florrie Snowball, who has the Falling Star at the other end of the village,' Ma introduced us. 'She was at school with your grandfather.'

'Oh, yes, I've seen you about,' I said, 'but I didn't know who you were.'

'And I've seen you – and I'd have recognised you for an Almond, with that hair and those eyes, even if I hadn't already known you were Martha's girl.'

'Yes, everyone says that.'

Her eyes rested on Stella who, ignoring us, was still rapt with enchantment by the Nativity. 'And your little girl, too – the Almond blood is clear in her veins.'

'Well, we're not trying to hide that we're related to the Almonds,' Ma said slightly snappishly.

'And why should you?' Florrie demanded. 'I said to that old fool Pete Ormerod that what's past is past and it's only us ancient relics that remember what happened. And in any case, it was nowt to do with *you*, was it?'

Ma looked at her. 'I suppose you're right and no one cares much about the old stories now.'

'You should come to the pub,' she invited me. 'We have a coffee machine what makes any kind you fancy, and my son, Clive, will show the little 'un the meteorite.'

'The meteorite?' I repeated.

'That's how the pub got its name,' Ma said.

'What's a meatyright?' Stella put in suddenly, having finally torn her gaze away from the Nativity scene.

'It's a big rock that fell out of the heavens,' Florrie explained.

'God threw a *rock* at you?' Stella gasped, impressed. 'You must have been *really* naughty.'

Florrie gave a wheezy laugh. 'Not me, lovey – this was last century . . . or maybe the one before that. But there it sits in the courtyard now, right in the way, but bad luck to move it.'

'I'd like to see it,' breathed Stella, and I had to promise to take her next day.

'Good. I'll make you a charm, poppet, too,' Florrie promised obscurely.

On the way home, I asked Ma what old stories Florrie knew about the Almonds. 'Is this Granddad's cousin Esau that you never want to talk about? Did he do something very bad?'

'Nothing that matters now,' she said, and wouldn't be drawn. I'm not sure if she even knew exactly what it was.

'And what did Florrie mean when she said she was going to make a charm for Stella?'

'Rumour has it that she's a witch, one of Gregory Lyon's coven that has the witchcraft museum opposite the Falling Star.'

'Really? How do you know?'

She shrugged her plump shoulders. 'Hal tells me stuff, and anyway, there's always been a history of witchcraft in the village. Ottie says the Winter family are distantly related to the Nutters, and her sister, Hebe, dabbles in the dark arts, though really I think she's more of a herbalist.'

'The *Nutters*?' I repeated.

'A famous witch family, further north. Didn't you read the information boards at Winter's End when you visited?'

'No, mostly we were in the gardens, but maybe I should.'

'Well, you'll have to wait till it reopens for the season at Easter, if you can come up then.'

'That would be lovely,' I agreed, then ventured tentatively, 'I . . . don't suppose Esau's disgrace was anything to do with witchcraft . . .?'

Ma gave a derisory snort. 'Don't be daft! Strange Baptists, the lot of them.'

Chapter 5: Falling Star

Stella gave me no rest until I took her down to the Falling Star next morning where Mollie, the barmaid, asked me to sign her copy of the last *Sweet Home* magazine at the top of my 'Tea & Cake' page where, as always in this edition, there was a variation of my Christmas tree biscuits: 'Crisp ginger and spice biscuits are quick to make and you can hang them on the Christmas tree or have them as a festive treat with coffee . . .'

Then Clive, who was Florrie's middle-aged son and the landlord, took us outside and proudly showed off a rather unimpressive grey rock sitting squarely and inconveniently in the middle of the small courtyard that was now a car park.

I took a picture on my phone of Stella poised on top of it, looking a bit like a well-wrapped-up fairy about to take flight, and then we went into the snug out of the icy breeze, where Florrie expertly produced a cup of cappuccino for me from a large, hissing, stainless-steel monster of a machine, and then a hot chocolate for Stella.

I still couldn't quite believe that she was a witch, but when she put a little leather bracelet on Stella's wrist and told me to let her wear it night and day, it didn't seem quite so far-fetched. It was a bit lumpy, which she explained by saying that normally she put her charms in a little pouch, to be hung around the neck.

'But that's not safe with childer, so I've bound it into the bracelet instead.'

I noticed her use of the old Lancashire word 'childer' for children, something I remembered from my grandmother, whose speech patterns had also been peppered with 'thees' and 'thous', though that might have had something to do with the Strange Baptist religious sect the Almonds used to belong to.

'Is it magic?' Stella asked seriously, fingering the leather band and, when Mrs Snowball nodded, she looked pleased.

'It'll help get the roses back in your cheeks and a bit of flesh on your bones, so the wind doesn't blow you away,' she said.

It seemed kindly meant, so I thanked her, but later Stella threw a typical three-year-old's tantrum when I took it off before she had her bath, even though I put it right back on again afterwards.

The next afternoon I left Ma minding Stella while I went for a rummage round the Sticklepond shops. Chloe Lyon's was my first port of call. I bought a box of Chocolate Wishes for Christmas Day, which were a sort of chocolate fortune cookie, and a little milk chocolate angel lolly for Stella's stocking. Chloe made all the chocolates herself and the smell had lured me in a few times before, so she recognised me. She was the vicar's wife, too, which was odd, seeing as her grandfather was Gregory Lyon, who ran the next-door witchcraft museum and Ma said was a self-confessed pagan.

While she was putting my purchases in a glazed paper carrier bag, she absently handed me a pack of cards to hold. Then she took them back and laid them out on the counter. 'These are angel cards. Pretty, aren't they?'

'Yes, lovely,' I agreed, admiring the pictures on the backs.

She smiled, turned some of them face up, then shuffled them back together and lifted down a large chocolate angel from the shelf, which she insisted was a special present just for myself, refusing any payment. It was extremely kind of her because her chocolate is very expensive, so I thanked her and said I would save it for a special treat on Christmas Day.

I popped in and out of the village shops, buying Stella the latest *Slipper Monkey* children's book in Cinderella's Slippers, the wedding shoe shop, since the owner, Tansy Poole, is the author and keeps a rack of them next to the till. I didn't dare even to glance at the gorgeous shoes, since spending money on myself for something so impractical was totally unthinkable when I had Stella's fund to think of.

I crossed the road and bought Ma the latest Susan Hill crime novel from Felix Hemmings in the Marked Pages bookshop, and had a nice chat with him about my cookbooks. I hadn't realised before quite what a literary hotbed the village was, but apparently Ivo Hawksley, Tansy's husband, writes crime novels, Gregory Lyon at the Witchcraft Museum writes supernatural thrillers and even Seth Greenwood from Winter's End has had published a gardening tome called *The Artful Knot*.

When I got back to the cottage and went up to the studio I found that Ottie had visited in my absence. She divided her time between her house in Cornwall and Winter's End, where she lived in the converted coach house, but of course she came back for Christmas. There was always a huge party up there for all the staff, family and friends, and I knew Ma had been invited a few times, but wouldn't go.

I was sorry to have missed Ottie (as a little girl, I had attempted to call her Auntie Ottie, but it had been too much of a mouthful), who had always been kind and prone to arrive with unexpected presents.

Stella was fast asleep on the battered old chaise longue, with a fistful of pheasant feathers from the collection she kept in the studio loosely splayed around her, but woke as soon as she heard my voice.

She was still pretty sleepy, though, and after lunch went willingly off for her nap just before Will and Celia arrived for our fundraising session.

Will had put the finishing touches to the Stella's Stars website and it was about to go online, which was exciting.

'The fundraising will really get going then,' Celia said.

'I only hope you're right, because it's such a lot of money to raise quite quickly. I mean, Dr Beems wants to do the operation before she's five, so the latest date she'd have it would be spring of the year after next . . . and he did warn me that if her condition suddenly deteriorated, it might have to be much sooner.'

'We'll hope it won't; that's just the worst-case scenario,' Celia assured me.

'I know, but I've had some sleepless nights thinking about what I'd do if it came to it and I've come to the conclusion that the only way I could raise the money in time would be by selling the flat.'

'Sell the flat?' echoed Celia. 'But you still have a mortgage on it, don't you?'

'Yes, but because Dad gave me a good deposit and I bought it just before prices went through the roof, I'd make a *huge* profit,' I said optimistically.

'But then you'd still have to rent somewhere for you and Stella to live,' Will pointed out, 'and that's likely to cost more than your current mortgage payments.'

'Well, that's the thing – we'd have to move up here and live with Ma for a while.'

'I think that would be a bit hard after having your own place – and would Martha think it was a good idea?' asked Celia. 'I know she loves to have you visit, but that's a bit different from your being here all the time.'

'I don't know, but I think she'd do it because she loves Stella – they seem very alike in some ways. And it would be only until Stella had had the operation and recovered, then I'd move back to London and pick up my career again.'

We talked through lots of fundraising ideas and drafted a standard email that we could send out to everyone we could think of who might help, with a link to the website. 'And everyone in your address book,' Celia suggested, 'even if you haven't heard from them in years. If you give people a positive way of helping, I'm sure they'll do it.'

'Yes, everyone loves to support a good cause, especially where a child is involved,' Will agreed.

'I'll organise a couple of events too. My knitting circle can have a sponsored knitathon, perhaps, and in the spring we could have a Crafty Celia garden party. I'm having lots of ideas,' Celia said enthusiastically. 'Will could put one of his sculptures in if we had a selling exhibition, too.'

He nodded, 'Good idea. And maybe Martha can get some fundraising going in the village?'

'She isn't really tuned in to village life,' I told him. 'She's been to one or two sessions of the Musical Appreciation Society and she goes to the monthly Gardening Club, and to the library, but that's about it. She did suggest mortgaging this house and giving me the money, but I wouldn't let her: she isn't that well off.'

We tossed ideas around a little more, while eating warm mince pies, then Ma came down from the studio and Stella woke up, so we all had an expedition to the gatehouse at Winter's End to buy bunches of the mistletoe they grow there, a local tradition.

Later, I asked Ma the important question.

'I mean, I really hope that Stella stays well and it won't come to it, but I wanted to ask you now, just in case . . .'

'I see what you mean,' she said, 'but I hadn't thought of that possibility.'

'Well, do, but don't answer me now, have a think about it, because I know you like your own space and so it would be a big ask.'

'It's not so much that, but I think you'd find it very difficult getting back on the property ladder in London when you moved back.'

'I know – impossible, in fact; we'd have to rent. But at least Stella would be well again . . .'

'Let me sleep on it,' Ma said.

Ma wasn't much of a churchgoer, except to admire the architecture, monuments and windows, but she'd attended every

Midnight Carol Service at All Angels since moving back to the village. I think it was the music: her tastes were very eclectic and she often said that Mr Lees, who was the organist there, had to be heard to be believed.

And actually, I *had* heard him, because he often played the organ at the strangest times, and a fugue distantly haunting you in the dead of night when the wind was in the right direction certainly got the hairs standing up on the back of your neck.

I'd never been to the services with her, because taking Stella out in the freezing cold night hadn't seemed like a good idea, so that evening Ma went off with Hal, who called for her. While she fetched her voluminous black cape, which made her look like a smaller and more rotund version of the woman in that Scottish Widows advertisement, I asked Hal why he didn't fly out to New Zealand and spend Christmas with his daughter and her family and he said he wouldn't go in an aeroplane ever again for love nor money, but he'd be off up to his sister's in Scotland for Hogmanay instead.

'I couldn't miss the Winter's End Christmas party,' he added. 'I'm the Lord of Misrule and we have a grand time.'

'I don't know about Lord of Misrule, but you're an old fool, getting dressed up and prancing about at your time of life,' Ma said, reappearing.

'There's nowt about my time of life to stop me prancing, and anyway, you never come to the party so you don't know what goes on.'

'I've heard things, though.'

'I'd love to go, and Ottie invited us, but it would be a bit much for Stella,' I said.

Stella was already overexcited by the thought of Father

Christmas arriving during the night and it had taken me ages to get her settled down that evening. Still, finally she'd gone to sleep and later I'd tiptoed in and hung her stocking on the bedpost, then arranged the presents beneath the little pine tree, before eating the gingerbread and carrot left out for the great man and his trusty reindeer.

Ma had already put her presents under the tree, roughly wrapped in brown paper and tied up with green garden twine, so they looked strangely trendy.

When she came back from the service she looked cold and the tip of her nose was scarlet. Once she'd divested herself of her woolly cape, I handed her a warm mince pie and a glass of Laphroaig, her favourite whisky.

'How was the service?'

'Very good – all the old favourite carols and hymns, sung to the right tunes, although Mr Lees played us out with "Nearer, My God, to Thee", which was a slightly odd choice. It was worth going, just for that.'

She put her feet up on a red Moroccan leather pouffe, sipped her whisky and said, 'Well, our Cally, I had a good think about things while Raffy was doing his sermon, all about the Nativity. And, of course, there's always room at *this* inn.'

'You mean . . . we can come and stay, if I have to sell the flat?'

'Of course you can, you daft lump. I was hardly going to turn you down, was I?'

I got up and went to give her a hug. 'If it happens, I promise we'll keep out of your hair as much as we can, and then as soon as Stella's well again, leave you in peace.'

'You can have too much peace,' she said surprisingly.

* * *

41

Ma's reply was not unexpected but it was a weight off my mind.

Of course, part of me still hoped for a miracle to happen before the operation became necessary – or at least that some new treatment would become available over here. But logically, I knew that it was unlikely that the cavalry would come riding to my rescue over the brow of the hill, and the most I could hope for was that Stella's condition didn't worsen over the coming year.

Since she was born I'd learned to live in the present, but nothing could stop me dreaming of a future.

Chapter 6: Hasty Pudding

After a magical Christmas, when Stella seemed to be eating well and growing stronger, as she always did in Sticklepond, it had been quite a shock when she became ill with breathing difficulties and a rocketing temperature right after we got home, and was rushed into hospital.

What would be a minor sniffle cured by a dose of Calpol in a normal child became a near-miss with pneumonia for Stella, and though luckily they quickly got her stabilised and her temperature down, it was a week before she could come home, clingy, pale and exhausted by the least exertion.

It was another setback but – more than that – I'd seen the writing on the wall. Even before the consultant suggested contacting Dr Rufford Beems in Boston about bringing forward the date of the operation, I'd told Ma I was putting the flat on the market.

The operation had been booked for the coming autumn. All I had to do was raise a vast amount of money, and keep my darling child from catching any more infections between now and October, when we were to leave . . .

To say I was stressed out was an understatement, and after comfort-eating four microwave-in-a-mug chocolate cakes in quick succession, when it got to the fifth I started thinking of ways to jazz them up a bit and came up with Black Forest gateau variation.

I sent the recipe off to *Sweet Home* magazine with some others I'd stockpiled, and the editor liked it so much she slipped it into the April edition (which of course, as is the way with magazines, came out in March) instead of a raisin roll one.

In the same April issue, Celia was showing the readers how to create friendship bracelets from old buttons, and Will had an article about making found-object pictures using an old frame he found in a skip, bits of driftwood, sea-washed fragments of glass, and shells.

A lot of the stuff you find these days washed up on beaches after high tide you wouldn't *want* to stick in a picture, but Celia and Will never seem to notice anything ugly, only what is good and beautiful.

You know, before we met him, when Will had only just started sending articles about his driftwood sculptures into the magazine, we used to jokingly call him Wooden Willie. But once we'd met him we liked him so much we never did again.

When Celia went to live in Southport with him I really missed her, so at least once the flat's sold and we've moved in with Ma I'll be living near her and I can file my *Sweet Home* articles from Lancashire like they do. Stella always seemed both happier and healthier in Sticklepond, too.

I was pretty sure Ma was dreading it even more than I was, so it was with mixed feelings that I picked up the phone on the same brisk March day that the *Sweet Home* magazine came out, to tell her I'd had offers on the flat at full asking price – luckily two people had wanted it – and accepted the one who could complete quickest.

'I'm flabbergasted you've sold it so fast,' she said. 'Fancy someone paying all that money for a space no bigger than a shoebox, and down a hole, too.'

Ma had never been a big fan of basement living . . . and come to think of it, neither had Toto, since we only had the little paved area at the front for him to go out into, the garden belonging to the flat above.

'It's still not going to be quite enough,' I said. 'The expenses for the trip seem to go up all the time – lots of things I hadn't thought of before, like finding insurance and paying for somewhere Stella can convalesce before coming home.'

'What about those people at the magazine – weren't they supposed to be doing some fundraising?'

'Yes, and they raised quite a bit, but now they've moved on to the next Big Cause,' I said. 'Celia and Will are planning some fundraising events, and there's been a steady trickle of small donations into the Stella's Stars website – that had quite a boost when the evening paper did a story about us – but once we're in Sticklepond I'll have to come up with a few new ideas for the rest.'

'And when do you think that might be?' she asked.

'Well, that's the thing: it's a cash buyer who just wants a *pied-à-terre* in London, so it should all go through very quickly.'

'Well, I don't know, he must have more money than sense,' she said, slapping down the flat vowels like so many wet fish onto a marble slab.

She sounded more Lancashire every time I spoke to her. Despite her cottage being on the outskirts of the village, and her reclusive streak, when she moved there she'd slipped straight back into the fabric of Sticklepond like a hand into a glove.

'Ma, I can't help thinking it's a major imposition,' I confessed. 'And I feel so guilty, because you've made everything just how you like it and are enjoying your life up there.'

'Well, you're not going to put the dampers on that, are you? We all get on fine when you and Stella come up to stay, and the studio is separate so you won't affect my work. And if I want a bit of peace, I've got my garden room at the back of the house to escape into.'

This was true: and when we stayed she often vanished in there in the evenings, where she read old crime novels or watched endless battered and slightly fuzzy Agatha Christie videos.

But it was very much my mother's house and besides, both of us were used to having our own space. I would so miss my little flat . . .

'Oh, well,' I sighed, 'at least you know it won't be for ever.'

'True. I expect when Stella's had her operation and is well again, you'll want to move back to London and pick up your career. But I won't be putting you out on the street, however long it takes.'

'Yes . . .' I paused. 'Ma, we do seem to have a lot more possessions than I thought we did, once I started tidying up the flat to show buyers around. Perhaps when we move up I could rent a storage unit somewhere nearby.'

'There can't be that much in such a little flat.'

'You'd be surprised,' I told her.

'My car can live outside then, and we'll store some of your things in the garage. It's dry in there and we can cover it all up with dustsheets.'

'That's true: it must be the only carpeted garage in Lancashire . . . and possibly the *country*.'

'Don't mock my garage,' she said severely. 'I happened to have the old carpet when I had the sitting room one replaced and it seemed like a good idea.'

'I'll buy your car one of those waterproof covers,' I promised, because I knew she loved her little black Polo hatchback.

'It's only a car, love – you save every penny for Stella's fund. I got the librarian to show me the Stella's Stars webpage when I was down there earlier. She wanted me to sign up for the Silver Surfers First Wave course, so I could check it myself, but I told her there was nothing else on the internet I wanted to look at.'

My mother is not much past sixty and her short mop of curling hair isn't silver, but hennaed a red so vibrant that she practically fluoresces in the dark, but I suppose they have to call the course something. This was the first sign of interest in computers that she'd ever shown.

'I can show you anything you wanted to look at on the internet anyway – and we could do with having broadband put into the cottage quickly.'

'Could we?' she asked vaguely. 'I'll leave that to you. When do you think you and Stella will be moving up here?'

'The end of April, I should think, if all goes well. They said Ormskirk Hospital could carry on giving Stella her regular check-ups, though if there are any problems she might be referred to Alder Hey.'

'We'll hope there aren't any problems then, and soon she'll be on that plane to Boston for the operation,' Ma said stoutly.

'If I can raise about another twenty thousand pounds, or so.'

'That's a drop in the ocean, compared to the amount you've already raised from selling the flat. I could take out a loan against the cottage for that much, if we need to.'

'You know I won't let you do anything like that,' I said firmly. 'One of us needs to have her own home and be financially secure.'

She had a good widow's pension from Dad, but income was falling along with everything else. Still, her paintings sold modestly well and her retro exhibition a couple of years ago had been a sell-out.

'We'll see how the fundraising goes, but one way or the other we'll get Stella to America and then she'll be as right as rain, you'll see. After that, I expect you'll be fretting to get back to your career full time. I know how important it is to you.'

'Actually, none of that seems important any more,' I confessed. 'I mean, I love making cakes and writing about baking, but I don't miss all the urgent deadlines for the freelance articles.'

'Priorities change a bit when you've a child to consider, especially a poorly one. Nature seems to have preprogrammed we mothers to put our offspring first – or most of us. Even me,' she added, 'to the extent where I knew I'd be rubbish at the maternal stuff, so I made sure you always had someone motherly looking after you.'

'Moses is going to be disgusted when Toto moves in permanently,' I said.

We'd been out for a Boxing Day walk two years previously when we'd fished a picnic basket out of the river at the edge of the Lido field and found the black kitten inside. Toto had made it abundantly clear then that he'd thought we should just toss it back. His opinion didn't seem to be much changed since.

'They'll shake down together: we all will,' Ma said, though with more hope than conviction in her voice.

Jago

Before the staff syndicate at Gilligan's Celebration Cakes struck lucky on the lottery, Jago Tremayne and his friend David had been happy enough working there.

Besides the traditional iced wedding cakes that Gilligan's were most famous for, both men had developed a speciality of their own. David created tall cones of beautifully coloured macaroons, which were in high demand for all kinds of events, while Jago was an expert in making the perfect croquembouche: the fabulous French wedding cake made from an airy pyramid of patisserie-cream-filled and caramel-dipped choux pastries, a skill he'd learned during a year spent working in Paris.

The lottery win opened new possibilities, because although the winnings were not enormous once their jackpot had been shared between twelve of them, it was still enough for Jago and David to start up a new business of their own, if they wanted to.

And they certainly did. David, like his fiancée, Sarah, came from West Lancashire and they yearned to move back nearer to their families; while Jago, who no longer had a fiancée and whose parents had taken early retirement and gone to live near his brother in New Zealand, was equally desperate for a fresh new start outside London.

Jago intended setting up a specialist croquembouche wedding cake business and at first thought of moving to Cornwall (where his ancestors came from) ... until David persuaded him that there was a big opening up north and he ought at least to consider the idea.

'You'd probably do really well in one of the wealthy areas, like Knutsford or Wilmslow in Cheshire,' he suggested.

'Then why aren't *you* buying a shop there?' Jago asked drily.

But he knew the answer, for when he and his friend were searching for suitable properties on the internet, David had fallen in love with an old bakery in Ormskirk, even though he realised starting up a specialist shop in a small Lancashire market town would be quite a gamble.

Jago hadn't yet found his ideal property. Unlike David, he didn't want a shop; since his orders would mainly come from the internet and magazine adverts, he just needed a large kitchen/preparation area. So he offered to move up with David and help him get started, while continuing his own search and, perhaps, testing the waters with his cakes.

He suspected that business in David's shop would be slow to pick up, but he was proved quite wrong, for when the doors of the Happy Macaroon opened for the first time, they were practically trampled to death in the stampede.

David said it was probably due to the free macaroons on offer to the first twenty customers – but then, he'd been born and raised not so far away and knew how much Lancashire folk loved a bargain.

There was also a lot of interest in the model macaroon

party cones and croquembouche they put on display in the window, which looked realistic enough to make the mouth water, and the two patissiers both soon got their first orders.

But the macaroons themselves were to be David's bread and butter, and their enticing rows of many colours proved irresistible to the local population, even though they were quite expensive. Every purchase, from a single macaroon to a dozen, went into a distinctive silver card box, a sweet treat that would probably never make it all the way home.

Certainly the many students who came into the shop tended to stand outside and eat them then and there, but David and Jago considered that a kind of free advertising.

They soon began to bake a tray of gingerbread pigs every day, too, which were more to children's taste (and less expensive) than the macaroons that lured their parents into the shop.

In his free time, Jago stepped up the search for a place of his own: he liked working with David, but once his fiancée, Sarah, gave up her job and moved into the flat above the shop as they planned, three would *definitely* be a crowd. He was fond of them both, but when your heart had been broken, it was a little hard to be around two people as much in love as David and Sarah were . . .

Of course, he'd always known that his ex, Aimee, was out of his league, and he had been amazed when she'd said she would marry him. But in retrospect, Sarah (who was a hairstylist in a smart Mayfair salon and seemed to know everything about everyone) had probably been right when she'd said Aimee had only grabbed him because Daddy had just put his little princess's nose right out of joint by getting engaged to his very young PA.

'I mean, you're a good-looking bloke, Jago, don't get me wrong,' Sarah had said kindly but bluntly, 'but she organises events for her seriously rich friends, while you earn peanuts making cakes and only met her because you were delivering one to a party venue.'

'We don't have a lot in common,' he'd agreed, 'but she loves me and wants to settle down.'

'Well, it's time enough; she must be *years* older than you.'

'Oh, no – she's younger,' he'd protested. 'Only thirty-two.'

'Is that what she told you?' Sarah had asked pityingly. 'In her dreams!'

But, blinded by Aimee's beauty and charm, he'd been as mesmerised as if she'd hypnotised him . . . which in a way she had. In fact, she must have done, because although he was a quiet man who hated parties, he seemed to be out every night. And being introduced to her friends as a chef was embarrassing, since he was a baker, or a cake maker, or a patissier – but definitely *not* a chef.

When Aimee had run off after a man she'd secretly been having a fling with, just before the wedding, Jago's heart and his already low self-esteem had taken a knock, but he was horrified to find there was also a tinge of relief that he wouldn't have to live her lifestyle any more. He was exhausted, partying late and then getting up early for work.

Still, he'd loved her, and he'd certainly never run the risk of seeing her with someone else if he lived up in the north, because the Cotswolds were about the limit of civilisation as far as Aimee was concerned, unless she was organising a country house party in Scotland.

So he looked for a suitable property in Knutsford and Wilmslow, where David had first suggested, but they were very expensive . . . and anyway, he'd begun to fall in love with the area around Ormskirk, with its lush farmland and friendly people, and the long golden beach of Southport only a short drive away. And he wasn't that far from his original search area. After all, croquembouches didn't travel huge distances, perhaps four hours maximum, but that was still a good range.

A little more research showed that no one else was supplying them locally and, making his mind up, he switched his search to the villages surrounding Ormskirk.

Chapter 7: The Cult of Perfection

Stella was excited by the move to Sticklepond, and Celia looked after her and Toto while I was in the final throes of the packing, so they were spared the worst.

But I was so exhausted that it took me a couple of days to bounce back, before I resumed getting up with the larks. I'm an early morning person, as you've probably gathered, and I enjoy baking away to the sound of the radio while everyone else is still asleep . . . except Toto, of course, who was usually hanging around my feet hoping for fallen scraps as soon as he'd been out into the garden.

In London my view of the sky had been limited to the small patch above the paved area, but here I could hardly wait to see the first light coming up behind the copse of trees at the back of the house, while the village below us still slept in darkness.

That morning's skies were streaked with pink, blueberry and silver, like a very special Eton mess. I wondered if I could devise a blueberry Sticklepond mess . . .

But that would have to be another day, for this one was to be devoted to macaroons and I wanted to get two articles out of it – a simple recipe for *Sweet Home*, and a longer piece all about this new macaroon shop that Ma had told me about, for my 'Tea & Cake' page. I'd already made a start on that one.

Since moving up to rural West Lancashire I've heard tell of a magical macaroon shop in a nearby market town, though it seems a bit of a mythical beast to find so far from London. I'll let you know when I have investigated further, but meanwhile, here's my own very good macaroon recipe.

Ma had gladly relinquished the kitchen to me, since she'd rarely done more than microwave a ready meal or slap a sandwich together in there herself, and already it had taken on a new and familiar persona, being now full of my mixers, bowls, implements, cookbooks and notebooks, with a laptop area in the pine breakfast nook in the corner.

I made plain macaroons and then some chocolate ones, which were delicious, and then typed some notes into the laptop. I was trying to build up an even bigger hoard of articles than I had before Stella was born, seeing I'd be occupied with other things in autumn and winter . . . and I still couldn't quite believe that we were committed to flying across the ocean for a risky operation. My fear that she would fall ill before then was almost as extreme as my fear of the operation itself – even thinking about it made me eat four macaroons straight off, one after the other.

The magazine and newspaper were fine about my filing my articles from Lancashire (or they would be, once broadband had been installed in the cottage next week), and would send a photographer round as necessary, when they couldn't use illustrations from stock. Actually, I prefer it when they use pictures of my baking, because I get loads of despairing mail from readers saying the things they make never look perfect, like in the cookery books, but they can see that most of mine don't look like those either. Food needs to look good enough to eat, but it doesn't need to win a beauty competition. I hate this cult of 'food presentation' where someone fiddles around with the food, adding a scoop of this and a dribble of that, and mauling it about, or the magazine hires a food stylist, which is a bit like airbrushing a naturally beautiful fashion model, setting an unattainable standard because it *isn't real*.

Not me: I'd so much rather have a chunk of crumbling apple pie with a dollop of cream, or a delicious fruit fairy cake with slightly singed edges.

It's probably just as well for my figure that I now have someone else to help me eat all my baking, though not so good for Ma's. Not that Ma *cares* about her figure: she says she was born to be a dumpling and why fight nature?

Stella wandered into the kitchen in her pyjamas just as I was arranging a pyramid of chocolate macaroons on a plate, her silken hair in a tangle and dragging Bun, the large plush rabbit that Ma had bought her when she was born, by one ear. She looked at the cakes and removed her thumb from her mouth long enough to say, sleepily, 'Awesome.'

'I think I've been letting you watch too much TV while I've been unpacking and sorting out,' I said ruefully.

Stella seemed no worse for the move now we'd settled in. We went to Alder Hey Children's Hospital in Liverpool later in the week, where she was checked over thoroughly, though she was to be monitored regularly by Ormskirk Hospital, which was nearer, and only referred back in future for any problems . . . which I sincerely hoped there wouldn't be.

The vicar, Raffy Sinclair, came to call one afternoon – he often visited Ma, but this time he came specially to see me.

I'd never met him to speak to before, though I'd seen him about sometimes. He was a tall, handsome man, an ex-rock star who moved to the village a couple of years ago and married Chloe Lyon. When I went to her chocolate shop to buy the chocolate angel lolly for Stella's Christmas stocking she'd said they had a little girl too, called Grace, though I think she is much younger than Stella. (And that big chocolate angel she gave me before Christmas had a most inspiring message inside, telling me not to fear the future. As I ate the delicious chocolate, I felt I was ingesting hope with it.)

Stella was having her afternoon nap when the vicar arrived so we were able to have a good talk. He knew about her problems, of course, because Ma had told him.

'Martha says you've sold your flat and moved in here, in an effort to raise enough money to take your little girl to America for a life-saving operation,' he said, when I'd made coffee and fetched in a plate of macaroons (I was still experimenting with flavours).

'Yes,' I said, and told him all about the operation and Stella's medical condition – I really opened up and poured it all out, but he was the *kindest* man.

'I still need about another twenty thousand pounds, I think, because all kinds of extra expenses keep cropping up. Someone advised me to take a qualified nurse on the plane there with me, for instance. And insurance – well, that's difficult too.'

'How long have you got to raise the money?'

'The surgeon in Boston has pencilled her in for the start of November so we need to be there by the end of October. I ought to start booking the plane tickets and the hotel and so on . . . I've just waited to see how far off the target I was after selling the flat. My best friend, Celia, and her husband, Will, have been a huge help, setting up the Stella's Stars fundraising site, which is getting lots of small donations, too.'

'I'm sure you'll make it – and I and the rest of Sticklepond will help you,' he promised.

'That's kind of you, but I'm really a stranger here. I mean, we've only visited before, we aren't really part of the community . . .'

'Oh, that won't matter,' he said, and assured me that the villagers would all unite to support a good cause.

Ma, who'd wandered in at that moment still holding a fully loaded paintbrush, taken a macaroon and begun to leave again without seeming to notice the vicar, stopped and focused at that.

'They may not for this one, because my family were never well liked in the village: I told you,' she said to Raffy, taking the jade cigarette holder from her mouth and gesturing with it. A half-smoked red Sobranie dropped out of the end and Toto, who'd followed her in, sniffed at it before making friendly overtures to Raffy. I'd have warned him about getting white dog hairs on his black jeans if he hadn't already got a liberal sprinkling there from his own little white dog, which I'd seen him out with sometimes.

'I've heard the odd rumour about the Almonds,' he admitted, 'but it was something that happened so long ago that I think only the most elderly parishioners know the details. But when it comes to helping a child, I can't see any of them thinking twice about it.'

'Why *exactly* aren't the Almonds well liked? You've never actually told me,' I said, emboldened to press Ma by the presence of the vicar.

She straightened with the Sobranie in her hand, shoved it back in the holder, and then shrugged her plump shoulders. 'It's as the vicar says, an old story, and I don't know all the details. Let's let sleeping dogs lie.'

'The important thing is to raise the money,' Raffy agreed, 'and we'll soon do that – so trust in the Lord and make all the bookings. There's nothing the village likes so much as uniting to fight for a good cause – only look how we saw off those property developers in the village itself, and then managed to have planning permission for turning the Hemlock Mill site into a retail park overturned.'

'True,' Ma said, and then she suddenly seemed to become aware of the loaded brush in her hand and, without another word, went out again.

'I wish she'd put a coat on, because that wind is cold, even if it is May,' I said, watching her through the window as she started back up the garden towards the studio. Then Hal suddenly loomed up next to her from behind a clump of Fatsia japonica, draped his tweedy, shapeless jacket over her shoulders, and they turned and went up the steps together.

'Hmm . . . I don't think I've ever seen Hal smile before,' Raffy said thoughtfully. 'He usually looks like Indiana Jones on a bad day, crossed with just a hint of the Grim Reaper.'

'They do seem to be good friends,' I said noncommittally, 'and he's here quite a bit . . . though weekends and evenings, mostly. Perhaps today is his half-day from the Hall.'

'I don't think it is, actually,' Raffy said, 'but with the estate coming right up to his cottage on the other side of the lane, I expect he just popped back for something.'

He smiled at me. 'Chloe said she'd had a nice chat with you before Christmas in the shop. She loves your "Cake Diaries" in the newspaper and says that you also write about cake in a magazine – I don't know where you find the time,' he said, taking another macaroon.

'To be honest, sometimes I'm not too sure myself,' I confessed. 'Things have been slightly easier as Stella's got older and stabilised, though she's prone to infections and then we have to get her treatment straight away. Each bout seems to sap what energy she has . . .'

'Yes, I don't suppose she has a lot of resistance to things and it must be a huge worry to you.'

'It is, and I really don't want any more complications till we leave for Boston. She needs to put a little weight on before the surgery too. You'd think with all the cakes around she'd quickly do that anyway, but she's the pickiest eater in the world.'

'Unlike me,' he said, ruefully eyeing the macaroon plate, now almost empty.

I asked suddenly, 'You *do* think I'm doing the right thing, don't you? Only the operation is experimental and although Dr Beems has been very successful with it, there are no guarantees . . .'

'Of course you are. You've had to make the decision with your head, not your heart, because logically there's no other course of action you can take, is there? If she doesn't have it, you've been told that she doesn't have a long-term future, it's as simple as that.'

I felt better for hearing him spell it out. Then Stella woke up sounding a little fractious and I fetched her in to meet Raffy. She seemed to like the look of him – and who wouldn't?

'I nearly forgot,' he said, digging out a Cellophane-wrapped chocolate figure from his pocket. 'Chloe sent you a gift. Are you allowed chocolate now, before tea?'

'I don't see why not,' I said, 'it's very good chocolate.'

'An *angel*,' breathed Stella raptly, taking it.

'Stella's very into angels at the moment,' I told Raffy. 'I think it's Ma's fault for pointing out all the angels in the graveyard.'

'And the funny little men with horns and tails in the window,' Stella said.

'Oh, yes, the Heaven and Hell window is great,' he agreed.

'Grandma paints angels in her pictures,' Stella confided. 'Flying ones with bird faces. Moses and Toto are flying round in her new one and Hal is holding on to the angel's leg to stop it flying right off.'

'I'd like to see that!'

'I thought I saw an angel when I was having Stella,' I told him, 'and though Ma said it was a nun going by in a white habit, it seems to have stuck in her head. The oddest things do.'

'You saw an angel? I must tell Chloe,' he said, interested. 'We're both great believers in guardian angels. Get her to tell you about the time she saw one when she was a little girl.'

Stella announced that she was going to show the chocolate angel to her Sylvanian Families and vanished off back into her bedroom.

'Transylvanian?' Raffy asked, looking mildly surprised.

'No, *Sylvanian*. They're collectable toys, little fuzzy animals.'

'Oh, right.' He passed on an invite from Chloe to take Stella to her Mother and Toddler group, which met on Monday mornings up at the old vicarage.

'If she's well enough, it would be nice to go and meet other local mothers and children,' I said, 'though so far I've tended to avoid that kind of thing in case coughs and colds are going round.'

'I'll ask Chloe to warn you if there are,' he promised. 'But if not, I should give it a try and if Stella finds it too tiring, you needn't stay long.'

'You're right, and it would get us out of Ma's way for a bit too . . . Though actually, she doesn't seem to mind Stella hanging around her, because in many ways they're kindred spirits. Ma's already said that she'd much prefer to keep an eye on Stella while I go into Ormskirk on Saturdays and do the big weekly supermarket shop than do it herself.'

'Let me think about fundraising for the rest of the money, and I'll get back to you with some ideas as soon as I can,' Raffy said, getting up and shrugging into a long black leather coat. 'We need an organised push to raise it quickly, but it will come,' he assured me, and with a smile left me feeling hopeful, comforted and cheered.

When I got back after seeing him out, the last two macaroons had vanished from the plate and Toto and Moses were lying innocently before the stove.

'You have crumbs in your whiskers,' I told them coldly, before going to see what Stella was up to.

Chapter 8: The Happy Macaroon

On Thursday morning it was Stella's first check-up at Ormskirk Hospital and although she is amazingly stoical about these things, I could gauge how stressed she was by the rate of the thumb-sucking.

But actually, when we got there it was not too bad. She was seen very quickly by a friendly consultant who was already up to speed on her condition and the projected operation in America.

She was quite pleased with Stella, but said she'd like to see her gain more weight – and so would I, though of course not *too* much, since that would also add strain to her heart and other organs . . . it's a fine balance.

Afterwards, since Thursday was a market day, I drove into town and parked, so we could have a walk around. It was an ancient market and very good, though the part selling fruit, eggs, cheese and foodstuffs had vanished a few years back, which was a pity.

Ormskirk now had a huge and increasing student population, since the university on the edge seemed to be expanding like a mushroom every night, but it did give the place a new buzz.

I knew Stella was tired, but she still insisted on getting out of her buggy as soon as we'd got to the top of the hill from the car park. Ma had given her some money to buy a treat with, which I suspect was going to become a habit, and she'd also asked us to get her a new tube of yellow ochre oil paint from the art shop up a side street, so we went and did that first. Stella spent most of her money in there on a new watercolour paint box and a Hello Kitty pencil case, which reminded her of the mummy cat from one of her toy families.

After that we had a look in the bookshop and I was pleased to see they had both my cookbooks, though I didn't tell them who I was since, as usual, I looked like a bagwoman down on her luck and I didn't think they'd believe me. Then Stella climbed back into her buggy and we went to find the macaroon shop.

It was called the Happy Macaroon, according to the smart deep red and gold signboard and about fifteen different colours of macaroons were on display in the window, laid out in trays like so many rows of giant gaming counters. It looked upmarket and expensive, like a smart London shop in one of the arcades where I'd occasionally pressed my nose to the glass and stared at the culinary perfection within. I did much the same now: if Ma hadn't already told me about the place, I'd have thought I was imagining it.

On one side of the window was a large cone with pink and white macaroons stuck all over it, the sort of thing I've seen before at parties. On the other, to my amazement, was a tall pyramid of caramel-dipped choux buns, the wonderful French wedding cake called the croquembouche or *pièce montée*. Of course, like the macaroon pyramid, it was a model, but they were both very realistic.

'Cakes,' Stella said, admiring the macaroons.

'They're special macaroon biscuits really, darling, like the ones I made the other day.'

'I didn't like those,' she said, my own little food critic. 'These look prettier.'

She had a point: the colours were certainly a lot brighter. 'See that big pyramid of buns?' I said, pointing to the croquembouche. 'It's a French wedding cake.'

'And there are gingerbread piggies.'

'No, I don't think there are—' I began, then broke off, following the line of her pointing finger, and found she was quite right, there *was* a tray of gingerbread pigs at one side of the window, with raisin eyes and curly iced tails.

Then something made me look up and my eyes met and locked with those of a man standing behind the window display. My first thought was that he looked like Johnny Depp in *Pirates of the Caribbean*, since he had the same angular sort of face and he'd tied a black scarf pirate-style over his hair, presumably instead of one of those little white hats bakers usually wear. The second thought was that his eyes were of a very unusual soft, light caramel brown, fringed with long black lashes . . . and impossible to remove my gaze from . . .

Then suddenly we both smiled simultaneously and the trance was broken.

Stella had clambered out of her pushchair and now tugged at my hand and asked if she could have a gingerbread pig and when I looked up again a moment later, he'd vanished.

'Of course you can, darling,' I told her, so pleased she'd

shown an interest in something to eat that I would happily have bought her a hundred gingerbread pigs . . . and anyway, I wanted to ask the pirate baker a few questions to add to my 'Cake Diaries' article.

He was standing behind the counter as if waiting for us, his smile warm. 'Hello,' he said, his voice as caramel as his eyes. 'Has our window display lured you in?'

'We *were* admiring the croquembouche,' I told him. 'Or at least, *I* was. I'm afraid Stella only had eyes for the gingerbread pigs.'

'Piggies with raisin eyes and curly-wurly tails,' agreed Stella.

'It's not everyone who recognises a croquembouche; they're still a bit of a novelty, especially up here,' the man said.

'I'm a cookery writer, specialising in cake – I have a page in *Sweet Home* magazine and a Sunday supplement,' I explained. 'I *love* cake.'

'Mummy made me a pink princess cake for my birthday,' Stella piped up.

Jago's interpretation of this as some kind of Barbie princess cake was written clear across his expressive face, but instantly dispelled when I said, 'It was a Swedish prinsesstårta – you know, those domed sponge and confectioner's cream cakes, with a marzipan covering? It's my party piece.'

'Wow! Now it's *my* turn to be impressed.'

'Oh, I'm sure they're nowhere near as fiddly as the croquembouche, just time-consuming. Yours needs real skill, not only to make the choux buns, but to put it all together.'

As I spoke to him I was increasingly sure that we'd met before, for there was something very familiar about him.

He was in his mid-thirties like me, I guessed, with a light olive skin and treacle-dark hair showing under the black bandanna.

'We've met before, haven't we?' he asked, obviously feeling the same way. 'Didn't you come to Gilligan's Celebration Cakes, when I worked there?'

'Of *course*, that's it. I've been racking my brains wondering where I'd seen you before. I did an article about wedding cakes . . . but I don't remember seeing the croquembouche.'

'I think you only wanted to feature the traditional cakes,' he said. 'I helped with those as well, but the croquembouche is my speciality. We weren't introduced, but I'm Jago Tremayne.'

'That sounds very Cornish?'

'It is – that's where my father's family came from.'

'I'm Cally – Cally Weston.'

We shook hands across the glass display cabinet and he asked curiously, 'What's Cally short for?'

I grinned, because I get that a lot. 'Nothing. My mother just had a thing about an old TV series called *Blake's 7* and called me after one of the characters. And this is my daughter, Stella.'

'I'm nearly four and I'm a *star*,' Stella told him.

'You certainly are,' he agreed.

'And I want a piggy,' she added, seeming to feel we'd lost the point of why we were there.

'Of course.' Jago lifted out the tray of gingerbread pigs so that Stella could select her own, which was obviously going to involve a lot of deliberation.

'So . . . are you visiting the area?' he asked me. 'I suppose in your line of work, you need to be London-based.'

'We *did* live in London, but we've recently moved to live with my mother in Sticklepond, a village a few miles from here. It's about as far from the bright lights as you can get, so it was quite a surprise to find a specialist shop like *this* in Ormskirk.'

'It was my friend's idea to open it here and I came to help,' he told me, then added as a slim, fair man appeared from the back room to serve a noisy gaggle of students who'd just come into the shop, 'that's David.'

'Oh – right. I wanted to mention the shop in an article for "The Cake Diaries", though it probably won't come out for months – do you think that would be all right? They'll send a photographer.'

'I'm sure David will be delighted. All publicity welcome. Look, here's his business card with his email address on, so you can send him any questions.'

'Thank you, that's great,' I said, pocketing it.

'I want *that* pig,' Stella said, having made her mind up and pointing at the one with the biggest curly icing tail.

'Please,' I prompted.

'*Please*,' Stella repeated and Jago put the chosen pig into a little paper bag and gave it to her. She took it straight out again and bit off its nose.

I paid him and he handed me a little silver box with my change. 'These are a couple of macaroons for your mum to try,' he explained to Stella. 'It's the bait to lure you both back in again.'

'I don't think you'll be able to keep us out anyway,' I said. 'We'll have to come here to the hospital most Thursdays, so this can be our special treat afterwards, can't it, Stella?'

She nodded, her mouth full of gingerbread.

'I don't know why it is, but the head always tastes better than the rest,' Jago said gravely and Stella nodded again, very seriously.

'It's wonderful to see her *eating* something voluntarily,' I thought, then realised I'd said it aloud, and Jago was looking sympathetically at me with his soft, light brown eyes.

Of course, I'd often made her gingerbread men, but obviously they didn't have the magic of the shop-bought pigs.

I drove back to Sticklepond with Stella fast asleep in her seat in the back of the car. In one hand was clutched the limp rear end of the gingerbread pig, saved for Grandma.

It was odd how I'd felt an instant connection with Jago when our eyes met through the shop window, though I supposed that was partly because I'd previously met him, even though I hadn't remembered at first. And how could I have forgotten those unusual eyes?

He seemed very nice and I think we simply instantly recognised each other as kindred spirits and perhaps were destined to become good friends? That was all I needed from a man these days, all I had the spare time and emotion left over for . . .

I checked again on my frail sleeping child in the rear-view mirror, turning over in my mind what they'd said to me at the hospital after Stella's check-up, about the country air soon putting some roses into her cheeks and improving her appetite, searching for any faint crumb of comfort.

When we got home and Stella, revived, had gone to present Grandma with the soggy gingerbread pig's bottom, I put Toto in the car for five minutes to hoover up the crumbs: dogs have a multitude of uses.

Jago

When Cally and Stella left the shop, Jago had the strange feeling that they'd taken all the May sunshine with them.

He'd liked everything about Cally: her no-nonsense manner, her pretty face with wide-apart harebell-blue eyes, the disarming sprinkle of freckles across her nose and her dishevelled, silky, pale gold curls.

'Pretty woman,' David said, since he'd finished serving the customers and there was a temporary lull. Then he added hastily, 'Not as in the film *Pretty Woman*, of course. I'm not insinuating she's a hooker.'

'I should think not! And she is pretty, though she's obviously under a lot of strain. I think it must be about the little girl, because she mentioned she would be having regular hospital check-ups and she looks as if a puff of wind would blow her away.'

'Poor little thing,' David said kindly, but somewhat absently, arranging a fresh batch of macaroons into neat rows of pink, red and green. Then he looked up curiously at his friend and grinned.

'You found out a lot in a short space of time.'

'She's on the same wavelength as us, that's all – and anyway, we've both seen her before at Gilligan's, don't you remember? She's Cally Weston, a cookery writer, and she was researching an article about traditional wedding cakes.'

'Really? No, I can't say I do remember that, but of course I've seen her articles,' he said, though his friend obviously *had* remembered her. Since this was the first hint of real interest in another woman Jago had shown since his fiancée ran off to Dubai to be with that sports car salesman she'd had a fling with, he thought it was a healthy sign.

'She wants to write you and the Happy Macaroon up in her "Cake Diaries" page in the Sunday supplement, so I gave her your card so she can email you questions,' Jago said. 'The paper will probably send a photographer.'

'Great, I'm all for free publicity,' David said enthusiastically. 'I like her even more!'

Chapter 9: The Blue Dog

I went back into Ormskirk on the Saturday morning to do the big supermarket shop while Ma minded Stella . . . or perhaps that was the other way round? Anyway, they intended going to the studio to paint and Hal had promised to come over later with an old wasp's nest as big as a football to show her, so it looked like being a red-letter day.

I only hoped Ma would remember the sandwiches I'd left them for lunch and not just share endless cups of sweet tea and biscuits with Stella. I wanted her to have more energy, but not a permanent sugar high!

Somehow I found my steps taking me past the Happy Macaroon, but this time Jago Tremayne wasn't looking out of the window, probably because it was so busy in the shop that the queue came right out of the door.

For the first time I noticed a sign for the Blue Dog Café next door to it and went up a steep, narrow flight of stairs into a busy room humming with conversation and the rattle of cutlery. It was obviously very popular and after I'd looked about fruitlessly for a vacant table I was just about to give up and go away again when suddenly I spotted Jago Tremayne sitting at a table in the far corner. He looked up and waved, smiling warmly, and I looked round to see if someone else had followed me up: but no, he was waving at me, so I made my way across.

'I just spotted you – do please join me,' he said, nudging out the chair next to his. Then he looked at me diffidently. 'I mean – you do *remember* me, don't you? It's Jago, from the bakery next door.'

'Of course I remember you, and it's very kind of you to let me share your table. I was just about to give up and go away again.'

I sat down and he handed me the menu. 'It's all cold food apart from the soup of the day, but they do a great beef sandwich with horseradish sauce.'

'Sounds good to me – I'll have that,' I said, as the waitress came to take my order, 'and a large Americano with some cold milk.'

I felt guilty spending any money on myself like this, when it might go into Stella's fund, but Celia had made me promise to be nicer to myself after I told her I'd been taking a flask of coffee out with me everywhere to save money. She said treating myself to coffee and a bun once in a blue moon might mean the difference to my staying sane or completely losing it, so it would be worthwhile in the long run. She was probably right, but it still felt a bit guilt-inducing.

'Stella not with you today?' Jago asked.

'No, I've left her at home with my mother and come in to do the big supermarket shop on my own. She tires easily, but she hates sitting in the trolley and I can't carry her *and* push it at the same time. Ma would rather keep an eye on her than shop, but she's an artist, so when she's wrapped up in her work she tends to be a bit forgetful . . .'

'I'm sure Stella will be all right,' he said reassuringly. 'She seems like a child who'll say if she wants anything.'

'Oh, yes, she can be a real bossy boots – and she was certainly determined to get one of those gingerbread pigs, wasn't she? And she ate most of it. I offered to make her some, but no, she says yours are special, so I suppose I'd better take one back with me today.'

'I'll send you the recipe, if you give me your email address?' he suggested.

'I'd love the recipe, but I don't think even then I can compete with the lure of yours.'

'I've left David in charge of the shop while I have my lunch,' Jago said. 'It's really busy on Saturdays, but his fiancée, Sarah, comes for the weekends to help out. In fact, I tend to feel a bit of a spare part and I'll feel even more so when Sarah gives up her job and moves into the flat over the shop with us permanently.'

'I suppose three *is* a crowd, even if they don't mean to make you feel left out.'

'It doesn't help that I got *dis*engaged about the same time David proposed to Sarah,' he said, and his thin, handsome face became gloomy. '*Very* disengaged.'

'I'm so sorry,' I said sincerely.

'Don't be, because she went off with another man a couple of weeks before the wedding, so it was better she did it then than after we were married.'

'That's true, I suppose, though it doesn't stop it hurting, does it? I was engaged before I had Stella, but my fiancée signed up for a second long contract abroad without telling me and then dumped me for someone else he'd met out there.'

Jago raised his coffee cup. 'Here's to a fresh start for both of us, then,' he said, and smiled at me. His mouth went up a bit at the left corner when he smiled and so did the corner of his eyebrow on that side. I found myself smiling back.

'So, how did the Happy Macaroon come about?' I asked. 'I've only just emailed David my questions for the article.'

'It was literally a stroke of luck. We both worked for Gilligan's, as you know, and we were in the lottery ticket syndicate when our numbers came up.'

'Wow!' I said enviously.

'It wasn't *millions*, nothing like that, but our shares were enough to change our lives, if we wanted them to. Some of the older members of the syndicate just paid off their mortgages and took holidays, or bought new cars, but David and I decided we wanted to get out of London and set up our own businesses.'

'Great idea.'

'David found his premises first, so I came up to help him start off and fell in love with the area. Now I'm hoping to find somewhere nearby to run my croquembouche wedding cake business, and the sooner the better. We thought it would take quite a while to get the Happy Macaroon off the ground, but actually business took off like a rocket from the first day.'

'But what made him choose Ormskirk? When I heard about the shop, it seemed the most unlikely place – yet I can see it's a huge success.'

'David comes from Southport and fell for the old bakery after he spotted it on the internet, and luckily there was an empty flat above it, too. What about you,' he asked tentatively, 'why did you move up here?'

'I sold my flat near Primrose Hill and we moved in with my mother because I needed to raise some capital quickly to fund treatment for Stella.' I took a sip of coffee, which was strong and good. 'Perhaps you noticed how small and frail she looks for her age?'

He nodded, his eyes soft and sympathetic.

'It's because she was born with a heart condition, a serious and complicated one.'

'Hence the hospital appointments you mentioned? I'm so sorry – it must be an enormous worry to you and she's such a bright, lovely little girl.'

'Yes, it is,' I confessed. 'The hospital here has taken over monitoring her progress, but they'd really like her to put on some weight before she goes to America in autumn for an operation . . . It's very risky, you see, experimental surgery, but without it the consultant in London said that eventually her organs would begin to suffer under the strain of coping.'

I don't know what came over me, but I found myself describing in detail Stella's problems and what the consultant said, just as if I'd known Jago for ever. It felt that way.

'But surely she could have the operation here, on the NHS?' he demanded. 'You shouldn't have to go abroad for it.'

'They can do so much these days with surgery, but in Stella's case, they'd reached the end of the road over here. But Celia and I – that's my best friend – researched on the internet and found a surgeon who'd pioneered the operation she needed in Boston, but he's the only one who can help. I got the hospital in London to send him all the X-rays and her notes and stuff, and he's willing to do it, but of course it'll cost an absolute *fortune*.'

'So you sold the flat and moved here? I see . . .'

'We thought we'd have longer to raise the money, but Stella was ill back in January and they advised us to move the operation date forward to this autumn, so I put the flat on the market. I've put the profit I made into the charitable fund that Celia and her husband, Will, helped me to set up and run, called Stella's Stars. Donations are coming in all the time, though not big ones – people are so kind, even strangers.'

'Stella's Stars? That's a good name.'

'She's my little star,' I said, feeling better for telling him all about it. 'Some of the people I know in London have fundraised, but even after selling the flat I'm still around twenty thousand pounds short, even though the surgeon has generously offered to waive his fee for doing the operation. But the operation is booked for the start of November and we need to fly over at the end of October, so I'll have to find the rest of the money quite quickly somehow.'

I smiled at him ruefully. 'It looks like we've both taken a gamble in moving up here – you and David on the success of your new businesses and me on being able to raise the rest of the money.'

'Your gamble is much more important than mine . . . but couldn't Stella's father help?' Jago asked tentatively.

'Stella's father is my ex-fiancée that I told you about. He'd left me by the time I found out I was pregnant and he wasn't remotely interested in being a father when I told him. In fact, he suggested I have an abortion, and when I refused, he cut off all contact with me – changed his email address and everything. He was back in the Antarctic by then, which made him even more uncontactable.'

'The *Antarctic*?'

'Yes, he was working out there as a marine biologist. I don't know where he went after that. He could still be there, for all I know.'

'He doesn't sound much of a loss.'

'No, I think he probably comes under the heading of "lucky escapes".'

'That's pretty much what David said when my fiancée ran off with someone else,' he said wryly. 'Sarah works in a Mayfair hair salon so she'd heard lots of gossip about my ex, Aimee, and she was pretty blunt about telling me what she thought of her. Aimee organised events for her rich friends for a living, and she was beautiful, smart, classy and connected – way out of my league, but I did think she loved me . . .'

They sounded an unlikely combination: a rich social butterfly and a hard-working baker, even if the said baker was the quietly handsome sort that you might pass in the street, but then turn round and go back to have another look at.

He shook off his fit of abstraction. 'Well, at least the lottery winnings gave me the chance of an exciting new start somewhere where I'll never come across Aimee again.'

'Stella had already turned my life upside down before I moved here. I had this idea that babies just slotted into your life, especially if like me you do most of your work at home. But even if she hadn't been born with so many health problems, everything would have changed once she'd arrived anyway, I can see that now.'

'Children do have a way of turning lives upside down,' Jago agreed. 'But I'm sure you've never regretted having her for an instant.'

'No, my only regret is that she has to suffer the effects of the heart problems – and even if I manage to raise the money for the operation, there's no guarantee of success . . . so I worry about that, too: but it's her only hope of living a normal life.'

I finished off my very excellent sandwich and Jago ordered two madeleines to go with another cup of coffee, which he said was his treat.

'They do perfect madeleines. I don't think I've tasted such good ones outside Paris.'

'I used to make them years ago, but had sort of forgotten about them,' I said, distracted as usual, even if only temporarily, from Stella's problems. 'I still have a madeleine baking tray, though . . .'

'I'll send you my recipe for them, if you like?' he offered. 'It's a genuine French one and usually turns out well. I worked for a year in Paris, that's where I learned how to make the croquembouches.'

When they came, we dunked our madeleines in the coffee, companionably.

'Madeleines would be a really good thing to feature in one of my articles,' I mused. 'I'm trying to stockpile as many as possible, to leave me free for several months later in the year. I've been thinking about doing a feature on proper Eccles cakes for "The Cake Diaries", too.'

'It must be difficult constantly coming up with ideas when all the Stella stuff is going on?'

'It is, but I have to keep them coming and bringing in the money – and anyway, I find baking cakes a sort of a comfort . . . and eating them too.'

'Yes, so do I,' Jago agreed.

'At least yours hasn't hit your hips,' I said wryly. 'I must have put on stones in the last couple of years.'

'I think I'm just the type who burns it off. And you don't look overweight to me, but just right.'

I'm sure that was a kind lie, but even so, I warmed to him even more.

'So, have you had any more ideas for fundraising the rest of the money you need?' he asked.

'Nothing major. The Sticklepond vicar visited us the other day and when I told him about Stella he said he was sure the whole village would get together and help me, and he'd think of how best to organise it and get back to me . . . and you know,' I added ruefully, 'I suddenly seem to have gone from being one of the most buttoned-up women in the world, to one who tells everyone her whole life story on first meeting. I'm so sorry to unload on you, when you just wanted a quiet lunch.'

'I'm glad you did.' He laid his warm hand momentarily over mine on the table and squeezed it. 'I *want* to know all about you, because the moment I saw you, I felt as if we'd known each other for ever. We're obviously on the same wavelength and I hope we'll become good friends.'

'I felt much the same,' I admitted, and our eyes met and held, just like the first time . . . His wrinkled up around the edges as he smiled.

'We do have so much in common, don't we? Broken hearts, a love of cake . . .'

'I don't suppose you also love watching rom com films?' I asked, laughing.

'I certainly do! *Love Actually* is my all-time favourite and I've put it on so many times that David has hidden the DVD.'

'That's my favourite too . . . or maybe it's *Pride and Prejudice*.'

'Or *Mamma Mia!* Oh, and *While You Were Sleeping*.'

'Yes! In fact, I like anything with Sandra Bullock in, but that is one of her best.'

We discussed rom coms for a few minutes and then I said, 'Do you think we were separated at birth, or simply knew each other in a previous existence?'

'I don't know, but I'll settle for knowing you in this one.'

'Me too, and I certainly need a *friend* – especially one who understands that Stella's needs must come first right now, and that I can't think beyond getting her to the USA for the oper-ation,' I said directly and honestly, just in case he *was* thinking about anything in the romantic line. Though actually, given the weight thing and that I'd stopped bothering much with makeup and what I was wearing, I should be so lucky even if he wasn't clearly still carrying a torch for his beautiful ex.

'I not only understand that, but I'll help you,' he offered. 'In fact, I'd *give* you the money if I thought you'd take it, but already I know you well enough to be sure you'd turn me down.'

'Quite right, I would, because that's the money you need to buy your own premises, isn't it?'

'Yes, but I could always rent for a while, or get a small mortgage.'

'No you couldn't. But thank you for the offer . . . And don't try doing it anonymously through the site, because I'll guess it's you,' I warned him, then paused. 'The vicar said I should trust in God to provide and go ahead and book the tickets and the hotel and everything, so I'm going to take his advice, even if finding the rest of the money does give me sleepless nights.'

'The vicar was right,' he said encouragingly. 'It is a lot of money to raise in a small amount of time, but it's not impossible, by any means.'

His mobile rang just then and when he finished the call he said it was David sarcastically asking if he planned on going back to the shop that day.

'I'll have to go. He and Sarah want to have their lunch too, and the shop's still busy.'

We exchanged mobile numbers and email addresses, and then I went back with him to the shop to buy a gingerbread pig for Stella, though he refused to charge me for it. I only hope he isn't as generous to all his customers or he won't be making much of a profit . . .

Driving home from Ormskirk, I thought how amazingly easily I'd opened up like that to a man I'd only just met. But then, we had so much in common and he was so sweet and sympathetic that he'd instantly felt like an old friend. We were comfortable together.

I liked his thin, mobile face and the way it reflected every passing emotion, something he probably wasn't aware of, his unusual light brown eyes and the way his dark hair, released from the pirate scarf, was just a little too long and trying to curl around his ears . . .

When I got home Ma and Stella were in the garden – Ma sketching and Stella sitting in her blue plastic clam-shell sandpit, carefully arranging a pattern of bits of sand-washed glass that we'd picked up on Southport beach into an intricate pattern. Toto wagged his tail but didn't get up from under the lavender bush.

The May sun was quite warm, but there was still a bit of

a chilly breeze, so I was glad to see that Stella was wearing her little purple corduroy coat. She must have put it on herself, because only one of the big buttons was fastened and it was in the wrong hole.

Ma's ample derrière rested on her ancient and ingenious fold-up sketching stool, which incorporated an easel in front, and she had obviously been working for some time, for oil pastel and charcoal sketches of Stella littered the grass around her. Toto and Moses featured in some of them, though I don't think Moses was feeling very co-operative since I could see the tip of his tail from underneath one sheet of paper, where he must have decided to go to sleep.

'Mummy!' Stella exclaimed, and Ma looked up.

'Had a nice time?' she asked.

'Yes, and I'm sorry I was a bit longer than I expected,' I said guiltily. 'I did the shopping and got the flake white paint and the linseed oil, and I've brought you a vanilla slice from Greggs and a gingerbread pig for Stella from the Happy Macaroon.'

'Lovely . . .' Ma said absently, adding a touch or two to the sketch in front of her.

'I had a sandwich in a café and shared the table with Jago from the Happy Macaroon – remember I told you about him? He makes croquembouches and we'd met before, when I went to Gilligan's Celebration Cakes where he used to work.'

Now I was closer I could see that Ma's current sketch was of Stella, who seemed to have sprouted little white feathered cherub wings, as had Toto, and even Moses the cat, and were all three whirling about among a lot of clouds.

Ma finished edging the bottom of the picture with giant

foxglove spikes and started to collect her stuff together. 'Yes . . . I remember,' she said vaguely. 'I expect it was nice to meet an old friend.'

'Hardly that, because I only saw him that once very briefly in London, but I got to know him a bit today while we were chatting and he's *such* a nice man.'

Stella looked up and asked, 'Can I have my gingerbread piggy now, Mummy?'

'Did you eat the little dinosaur sandwiches I left you for lunch?'

She shook her head. 'We haven't had lunch, have we, Grandma?'

'Haven't we?' Ma looked surprised, but when I checked the fridge the sandwiches were untouched under their cling film, as were the two little dishes of chocolate mousse.

I went back outside. 'Come on in, Stella, and eat a sandwich, and then you can have your gingerbread pig. Ma, do you want your sandwiches out here, or are you coming in?'

'I'll be in in a minute. I'll just take everything back up to the studio and fix the charcoal drawings.'

Stella got out of the sandpit and I closed the lid in case Moses took it into his head that it would make a super cat litter tray, and we went in the house holding hands. Ma wandered off up to the studio and I knew she would forget to come back, so I took her lunch up there after we'd had ours, along with the vanilla slice. There was a steaming mug of tea next to her, so Hal must have been around somewhere.

'I should have got another cake for Hal, shouldn't I?' I said. 'Does he like vanilla slices?'

'I don't know. He likes Nice biscuits, garibaldi, gingernuts and fig rolls, though,' she said, taking a big bite out of a ham sandwich. 'I'm ravenous,' she added, sounding surprised.

'Well, it's after two. Stella's eaten a dinosaur sandwich and she started on the gingerbread pig, but got too sleepy, so she's gone for a nap. I expect she'll eat the rest when she wakes up. Her appetite really seems to be picking up since we moved here.'

'There's magic in the air in Sticklepond,' Ma said.

Jago

David's eyebrows had gone up when Jago and Cally walked into the Happy Macaroon together chatting comfortably like old friends, and Jago knew he'd be in for a bit of merciless teasing later, when the shop was quieter.

He was right, too, because David told him he was glad to see his broken heart was on the way to being mended.

'Don't be stupid, Cally's just really nice and we're interested in similar things, but mostly we've been talking about her little girl. She was born with a very serious heart condition and Cally's trying to raise money to send her to America for an operation in autumn.'

'Oh, poor little thing,' Sarah said.

'She's set up a charitable website, called Stella's Stars. I'm going to have a look at it later.'

'Well, I hope you're not going to give them all your lottery winnings, Jago,' David said forthrightly, because he knew his friend's soft heart. Being bullied at school because of his dyslexia, and being always in the shadow of his older and academically gifted brother, had dented Jago's self-confidence, so that he always felt for the underdog.

'She's already raised the bulk of it by selling her flat in London, so she only needs about another twenty thousand . . . and I *did* offer,' he confessed, 'but she turned me down, because she knew by then I'd only just won enough to set myself up in my own business. She told me not to try anonymously donating it either, because she'd guess it was me and give it back.'

'She's certainly got your measure in a short space of time,' Sarah said admiringly. 'I like the sound of her.'

'Yes, and she's much more your type than Aimee ever was,' David agreed. 'I can't imagine why she ever agreed to marry you. Unless it's like Sarah says, that it was just to pay her dad back for getting engaged to his PA.'

'Oh, once she was the wrong side of forty she probably found good-looking straight single men willing to settle down were thin on the ground. I expect panic had set in by the time Jago proposed and that was part of it too,' Sarah said airily.

'I keep telling you, she's younger than me,' Jago protested.

'No way: you only had to look at her knees.'

'Her *knees*?'

'Baggy, saggy knees.'

'She has the longest legs in the world . . .' Jago sighed reminiscently. 'I can't say I noticed her knees. And gee, thanks for the confidence boost, by the way.'

Still, it was true that he hadn't been able to believe his luck when the tall, elegant, beautiful, sophisticated Aimee had accepted his proposal . . . which actually he would never have had the courage to make if she hadn't prompted him into it.

'You're a good-looking guy, don't get me wrong,' Sarah said kindly, 'but you had absolutely nothing in common.'

'I know,' he said humbly.

'All that late night partying followed by the early starts for work ran you ragged and made your friends worry about you,' David said.

'And while we're speaking of the devil who wore Prada,' Sarah said, 'you had a phone call when you were out. She's back.'

'Who's back?' Jago demanded, startled.

'Aimee.'

'*Aimee*? Aimee's back in the UK?'

'Yes, she's been back a while, but she's only just tracked you down. I expect she heard about our winnings,' David said drily.

'Her new stepmother uses the salon and she told me weeks ago that Aimee was back. She's pregnant, too, because she didn't want to have her hair coloured, in case it harmed the baby.'

'Aimee's *pregnant*?' Jago exclaimed.

'No, you idiot, it's her new young stepmother who's pregnant.'

'Right . . .' He looked at his friends. 'You both knew all this time she was back and didn't tell me?'

'You said you were over her and wanted a fresh new start in a different part of the country,' Sarah pointed out. 'Anyway, she's bad news.'

'Yes, we didn't want her messing you around again,' David said.

'I think I'm old enough to decide for myself,' Jago said

with dignity. 'And of course I'm over her . . . Anyway, I expect she just wants to get back in touch to be friends.'

'Yeah, right,' Sarah said acerbically, but Jago wasn't listening. He'd thought he was over her, and his friends were probably right that breaking up had been a good idea, but still . . . knowing she was back unsettled him.

'Did she leave a number? Or did you give her my mobile number?'

'Neither, because we were a bit busy at the time. You were having an extended lunch, if you recall?'

'Oh, yes . . . Did she say anything else?'

'Something about things not working out with that bloke she chased off after to Dubai, so I expect she's been dumped and now you've won all that money you're a much more interesting prospect.'

'You're such a cynic,' Jago said. 'But I can't believe you didn't even get her *number*.'

'She said she'd ring you again and why the interest? Didn't you just tell us you were over her?'

'I *am* over her,' Jago insisted, though he suspected that a few embers of his love still smouldered deep in his heart and might just reignite at the sight of her.

In the late afternoon, just as they were clearing up the shop ready to close, the phone in the back room rang and Sarah stuck her head in the door and said it was for Jago.

He went past her into the back room and returned ten minutes later looking sheepish.

David and Sarah exchanged glances.

'Don't tell me,' David said, 'it was Aimee again. She really doesn't let the grass grow under her feet, does she? So, what happened to the new life with what's-his-face in Dubai?'

'She said she knew it was a mistake almost the minute she got there and Dubai was a tricky place if you weren't married – and he certainly didn't want to get married. And she missed me.'

'Not enough to look for you as soon as she got back,' Sarah put in.

'She didn't know I'd left London and it took her a while to track me down,' Jago explained.

'Your post is being forwarded on, and anyone at Gilligan's could have given her your new mobile number as well as the one for this place,' David said.

'Yes, someone at Gilligan's did give her our number eventually, but they were a bit reluctant.'

'Considering that after she took off we all ate your wedding cake and commiserated with you, it's hardly surprising,' David said drily. 'And she could have asked Sarah in the salon.'

'She did come in, but I expect she'd forgotten about me,' Sarah said mendaciously, crossing the fingers of both hands behind her back.

'I think she was nervous about contacting me in case I was still mad at her, but it's like I told you: she just wanted to say she was sorry about what happened and she hoped we could be friends now she was back.'

'I'll bet she did,' Sarah said. 'I suppose whoever she spoke to at Gilligan's told her you'd won the lottery?'

'No, not until I mentioned it, so it was a complete surprise to her – she'd wondered what we were doing up here. I explained about helping you set up the Happy Macaroon and then that I was going to start my own wedding croquembouche business.'

David flipped the closed sign over on the door and lowered the window blind.

'And how did she take that?' he asked, turning.

'She thought it was a great idea and she'd love to meet up with me to hear all about my plans. Only that won't be for a while, because she can't leave town at the moment and I haven't got time to go down there.'

'Thank heaven for small mercies,' muttered Sarah, starting to cash up the till.

'I'm not stupid enough to fall for her twice over,' Jago said with dignity. But still, it had shaken him to hear her soft, contrite and honeyed voice.

'Good, because she's like Julia Roberts in that *Runaway Bride* film and she'd just keep dumping you for a better option,' Sarah said frankly.

'That's a bit harsh,' he said, wincing, but her words dispelled a little of the enchantment that Aimee had managed to cast over him again.

'We're only saying these things because we're your friends and we don't want you to go through the whole thing twice,' David said.

'I know.' Jago sighed, and then smiled wryly. 'Maybe I've watched too many romantic comedy films where it's all turned out right in the end.'

'It *will* turn out right in the end,' Sarah assured him. 'Only not with Aimee Calthrop. She belongs in an entirely different kind of film.'

Luckily she didn't say exactly *which* kind, but mention of romantic films had made Jago remember his earlier conversation with Cally and gave his thoughts a different direction.

'You know I was telling you about Cally trying to raise money to take her little girl to America for that life-saving operation? Well, I've just had an idea for how *we* could help . . .'

Chapter 10: Sweet Perfection

Later, while Stella was still asleep, having gone down for her nap so late, and I was doing a little research on the history of madeleines (I thought I might get a long piece for my 'Diaries' page, as well as a quick and easy recipe for 'Tea & Cake' out of it), my phone buzzed and it was Jago.

'We've just closed the shop, so I've emailed you the madeleine recipe I mentioned.'

'Oh, great – thanks,' I said gratefully. 'Funnily enough, I was just doing a bit of research into them.'

'I hope I'm not disturbing you?'

'No, not at all. My mother's working in her studio and Stella's still asleep, so I thought I'd make a start. She was so tired she only managed to take one bite out of the gingerbread pig, but she's still holding it.'

'It's strange how many children love gingerbread,' he commented, then added, 'I just got my third wedding croquembouche order.'

'Oh, well done!'

'They want it to be flanked by two of David's white and pink macaroon pyramids too, so expense no object.'

'I can imagine how good that would look at a wedding reception. You know, I think your croquembouche business is going to be a huge success.'

'I hope you're right, but maybe it will because, David's has taken off so well, and macaroons are another expensive luxury.'

'People are prepared to pay for a special cake for a wedding,' I assured him. Then I added tentatively, 'Are you all right? Only you sound a bit . . . I don't know – stressed?'

'Knocked for six, more like,' he confessed ruefully. 'Aimee, my ex, just rang me at the bakery. Things didn't work out with the other bloke and she's back. In fact, she's been home for a while and my friends knew and didn't tell me.'

'I suppose they were just trying to protect you,' I suggested.

'So they said, but they needn't have bothered because she only wanted to say sorry and to be friends.'

'Right,' I said, though I thought I detected a hint of uncertainty in his voice. 'Well, that'll be lovely then, won't it?' I added, with a brisk cheerfulness I didn't feel, because my heart had suddenly sunk like an undercooked sponge at the possibility that he might be snatched back to London by the horrible-sounding but glamorous Aimee when I'd only just got to know him.

When Stella was in bed that night, and Ma off in the garden room watching old Agatha Christie films, I made some madeleines to Jago's genuine French recipe, which were delicious, and then started to write the articles.

The 'Tea & Cake' one was quick and easy.

Here's a simple recipe for madeleines, those wonderful little buttery French biscuits, usually baked in deep shell-shaped moulds. Perfect with coffee at elevenses, but a lovely treat at any time . . .

But the other one took time, and I finally finished around midnight, when even Toto and Moses had gone to bed, both in the same basket. They seemed to have buried the hatchet and while I'd been typing at the kitchen table I'd seen Moses give Toto a very thorough washing, especially around the ears.

I'm not sure that Toto exactly appreciated it, going by the long-suffering expression on his furry face, but it's surprising what you'll put up with from your friends.

The house had long been silent except for the clicking of my fingers on the keyboard and the ticking of the clock, and although I offered to let Toto into the garden, he didn't even bother opening both eyes. Mind you, I caught him crawling through the cat flap earlier in the day, so if he has cracked that, then he can let himself in and out whenever he wants to.

I looked in on Stella on my way to bed and she was fast asleep, hugging Bun. His plush is a bit worn and I'd sewn my mobile phone number onto the sole of one foot, after we once left him behind on a park bench and had to dash back to find him, luckily still there.

Stella looked angelic, a sleeping cherub, dimly illuminated by the faint light from her nightlight, which was one of those porcelain ones like a toadstool with a little mouse family inside. She had added one or two of her fuzzy toy mice to the scenario too, I noticed.

I looked down at her, so small and delicate that she reminded me of those old stories of fairy children exchanged with ordinary ones at birth – but if she had been, they weren't having her back.

The next day Hal popped round to stretch a canvas for Ma. It seemed like a very un-gardener-like thing to be doing.

'Hal spends a lot of time here, doesn't he?' I said tentatively to Ma later.

'I suppose he does, but it's evenings and weekends, mostly. Some of the Winter's End gardeners work Saturdays over-time, especially when the place is open to the public, but Hal says he'd rather take things a bit easier at his time of life.'

'What about his family?'

'He's a widower and his daughter married a New Zealander, so he's only seen the grandchildren twice in eight years, when they came over here. He won't fly, he's scared. I've told him he should go on one of these courses to get over it.'

'That's a coincidence: Jago's parents moved to New Zealand when they took early retirement – his older brother lives there. He didn't say a lot about them, though. It's a small world.'

'It is if you fly, as I keep telling Hal.'

'He keeps your garden this side of total jungle,' I said.

'He does that, and I don't mind him about: he doesn't fuss me.'

This didn't sound to me as if there was any big romance going on there, just an odd friendship of opposites. Jago and I, on the other hand, were clearly destined to be friends because we were so very similar . . . unless Awful Aimee lured him back to London again, of course.

I texted him that the madeleine recipe came out perfectly, and to thank him again, but he replied not to mention it because he always loved to talk cake.

Aimee

Aimee Calthrop pondered her phone call to Jago, and the surprising comfort it had given her to hear his soft, mellow voice. I could get him back, if I wanted him, she told herself.

In retrospect, it had been such a big mistake to dump a handsome, kind man who adored her . . . But then, he'd earned peanuts at Gilligan's and seemed to have no aspirations to do anything other than bake cakes.

Cold feet had set in, which was part of the reason she'd run off to Dubai just before the wedding. But Vann Hamden had seemed a lot less enthusiastic about her arrival when he met her at the airport than he'd been during their brief affair in London, and positively blanched when she tried to kiss him.

They didn't do that kind of thing in public over there, he'd explained, and immorality was a big no-no, so he was too afraid it would affect his business to step out of line.

Dubai had to be the most boring place on earth: no one seemed interested in having her organise their parties for them and, in any case, she wasn't part of the fashionable in-crowd there. She couldn't even shop, because Daddy, who'd liked Jago, had been so cross with her that he'd stopped her allowance. So she spent her days drinking too much (privately; that was also frowned on) and sunbathing none too wisely, between Vann's visits, and when he said things weren't working out too well and suggested he buy her a plane ticket home, she accepted the offer.

The whole fiasco was really Daddy's fault. It was his sudden decision to marry his young PA that had made her nudge Jago into proposing in the first place. And now her place had been taken by a new baby girl for Daddy to dote on just as he'd once doted on her . . .

He refused to reinstate her allowance, too, saying that since she was in her forties it was time she was earning a proper living, which was another nasty shock, because she'd been totally in denial about her age for so long that she'd forgotten what it really was. So what with that and the realisation that she was never going to oust the two new contenders for her father's affections (and wallet), she'd plunged into a bit of a panic.

He'd finally relented to the point where he agreed to pay her a reduced allowance for six months while she got on her feet, but her friends and the party crowd had moved on in her absence and now she was struggling to pick up the threads of her old life. She was out of touch . . . and suddenly starting to feel old.

When someone told her the rumour about the big lottery win at Gilligan's, she wondered . . . and even tried pumping that snotty, red-headed fiancée of Jago's friend David, while she was having her hair done, but got nowhere. Sarah had pretended she had no idea what Aimee was talking about and then insinuated that her hair extensions were giving her a bald spot on the crown, which had to be a foul lie.

She wished she knew just how much he'd won on the lottery . . . No one at Gilligan's had been prepared to tell her – in fact, they'd been really reluctant even to give her his new contact details. Maybe that meant it had been squillions? She certainly hoped so!

She tried ringing him again, but still couldn't get hold of him on his mobile, because he must have been so flustered at hearing her voice that he'd given her the number wrongly. She thought that was a good sign, but it was annoying that the shop number now rang through to voice mail and that friend of his was quite probably wiping her messages as fast as she left them . . .

Chapter 11: Flaky

On Monday morning I was up so early again that the sky was still a deep blueberry with only the tiniest hint of single cream seeping into the east. The sparse streetlights of Sticklepond glimmered like tired fireflies below me and were answered by the sharp, minute diamond sparkle of a star overhead.

Twinkle, twinkle . . . I thought of next Christmas and how much I hoped that Stella would be running round, fit and well and excited about Santa's bumper crop of presents for a special little girl . . .

That sky made me want to try out blueberry fairy cakes, but apart from the fact I didn't have any blueberries, I'd got up expressly to have a giant baking session for the new articles, so I got on with that. I'd produced Eccles cakes, Chorley cakes and even a few Sad cakes, before anyone other than Toto and Moses was awake, and I added a recipe to my 'Cake Diaries' outline.

Although there are several variations on the same theme as Eccles cakes, there's nothing else quite as delicious as a proper one, made with thin, flaky, crisp pastry and

stuffed full of juicy currants. If you've never tasted the
real thing, follow my recipe and be amazed!

The kitchen air smelled so good it could have been cut up
and sold by the slice, and I munched on a warm Eccles cake
as I wrote. When Ma came down she said she was becoming
accustomed to waking to the smell of baking, because even
if I don't cook first thing, I still pop some kind of loaf into
the bread maker the night before and she can smell that.

'You're like a sort of culinary Pied Piper, luring me into
the kitchen. Just as well I took to elastic-waisted trousers
and baggy tops years ago,' she remarked, deciding to try one
of each pastry for breakfast. 'I'm sure otherwise I'd be
exploding out of my clothes like the Incredible Hulk.'

'I think I already am,' I said ruefully.

'Oh, I don't know, you look about the same as when
you got here,' she assured me. 'I expect those long walks
in the afternoons with the buggy and Toto are keeping it
down a bit.'

'Yes, that's true, I must be getting fitter even if not thinner,
because apart from Primrose Hill, which is more of a grassy
bump than anything, there weren't really that many nearby
open spaces to tempt you to have long walks in London.
Stella says she misses the zoo, but that's all. It's a pity the
little one at Southport closed down.'

Chloe hadn't rung me to warn of any pestilential disease
laying the local children low, so mid-morning Stella and I
went to the Mother and Toddler group at the old vicarage
for the first time, and I felt a bit nervous, not really knowing
anyone.

It was held in the drawing room, which was vast enough

104

to hold most of the footage of Ma's cottage, and had lots of toys for the little ones to play with scattered over its acreage.

There were nine or ten other mothers there and the children ranged in age from tiny babies upwards. Stella was the oldest, but she was by no means the biggest. In fact, she looked worryingly fragile next to some of those sturdy, rosy-cheeked toddlers . . .

Chloe introduced me to everyone, though of course I knew several of them slightly already from my shopping expeditions into the village, like Poppy, who was married to Felix Hemmings, proprietor of Marked Pages, and Tansy Poole from Cinderella's Slippers, and many others by sight. They all made me very welcome, anyway, though I immediately forgot several of their names. I don't think the warmth of the welcome was entirely due to the three cake boxes I'd put down on the coffee table . . .

'I've already told everyone about Stella's Stars and the fundraising,' Chloe said. 'We've decided to think up some ways to raise money.'

'That would be wonderful,' I said gratefully.

'I know Raffy's got some ideas, too,' she said. 'He's going to come and see you again soon to discuss them, so perhaps we'd better see what he suggests first and then fit our fundraising around it?'

'Or we could just have a jumble sale in the village hall; that's always good,' someone suggested, and they all seemed keen on that idea. Poppy, who was also a member of the parish council, said she would find out what day the hall was free in June, to give everyone time to get their jumble together.

That was a great start, but I hoped Chloe was right about

Raffy having come up with a plan, because time seemed to be galloping by and I still had so much money to raise.

'Cally's kindly brought us some Eccles cakes she's made, to have with our coffee,' Chloe announced.

'Yes, I'm writing an article on the differences between the traditional Eccles cake, Chorley cakes and Sad cakes for my next "Cake Diaries",' I explained, 'and I thought perhaps you could tell me which you prefer?'

'Oooh, lovely, a taste test,' said a tall, attractive dark girl who I think was called Zoë . . . or maybe her friend was called Zoë and she was called Rachel? It was one way or the other.

'I did mention that Cally is a well-known cookery writer, didn't I? She writes the "Tea & Cake" page in *Sweet Home* magazine, and "The Cake Diaries" for a Sunday supplement,' Chloe said, and several of them said they got the magazine, even if they hadn't seen my pieces in the Sunday paper.

A tall, grim and alarmingly Mrs Danvers figure in a black apron brought in a tray of coffee to have with my cakes, and left without saying anything, her rat-trap mouth firmly shut, though I heard Chloe thank her and call her Maria, so she must be some kind of housekeeper.

Once everyone was munching on Eccles cakes the conversation turned to nice local places to visit with children and they told me about the new nature reserve that had been created on the site of a former mill, and how the Victorian mill manager's house was being turned into a museum.

'Oh, yes, the vicar mentioned that when he was telling me about how everyone in the village always came together to fight for a good cause,' I recalled.

'They were going to build a retail park on the site, but

we were all against that, so in the end it was sold to a charity, Force for Nature. Luckily there was a huge anonymous donation, so already they've put up an eco-friendly wooden café and information centre and boardwalks around the site,' Poppy said.

'Now they're starting to convert the mill owner's house to how it would have been in Victorian times,' Chloe put in. 'There's a courtyard with some outbuildings at the back, where I think they might have a couple of craft workshops eventually, or something like that.'

'I'll have to take Stella out there; it sounds lovely,' I said.

'We have an annual teddy bears' picnic, and we've decided to have that there this year,' the tall, dark girl said, then nudged her friend. 'Rachel, Betty Boo's put an entire Duplo figure in her mouth.'

'She's got a mouth like a letterbox, that child,' Rachel said with a long-suffering sigh, going over and casually hooking it out again. 'She doesn't get it from me.'

Betty Boo roared loudly for five minutes, then stopped suddenly and crawled off towards something else. I hoped it was larger than the plastic figure.

Stella tired after a bit and came and sat quietly on my lap, thumb in mouth, so I carried her home, glad I'd taken the car because of carrying the cake boxes. They were now much lighter, containing only the odd crumb.

'Did you enjoy that?' I asked her.

She nodded. 'I liked all the toys, especially the pink castle. Could I have one of those, Mummy?'

'Do you want a Barbie doll to go with it?' I asked cautiously, because she'd never shown any interest in dolls to date, and I'd hoped if she was going to start, it wouldn't be with something so strangely mutant-looking and unnatural, so it was a relief when she shook her head so the fine silvery-gold curls danced.

'No, I want it for all my *families*,' she explained.

'It's pretty big, so you could certainly fit them *all* in. Do you want it more than that tree house we saw?' I asked. 'Or the camper van?'

She pondered. 'Not *more* . . .' she said finally. 'The same.'

'You could ask Santa if he'd bring you one, when we get a bit nearer to Christmas,' I suggested. 'I expect he'll feel you deserve a *big* present after we've been to America to get you made better, so you never know.'

I emailed Jago when I got home and told him the verdict on the cakes: Eccles cake was definitely favourite, Chorley cake was all right, but Sad cake was a bit more shortcakey, so that fingers of it would go well for elevenses with a cup of coffee. That could be my next recipe on the 'Tea & Cake' agenda – more crossover of my two different regular columns.

He emailed back and said maybe biscuits like garibaldi would make a good follow-up article, because it was only one step from an Eccles cake to a garibaldi really, when you thought about it.

That was a great idea! It's so wonderful having someone on the same wavelength that I can bounce baking ideas off, because it's clearly going to spark all kinds of useful things.

Celia came over on the Wednesday for another fundraising discussion, though without Will, since he had to deliver one of his larger sculptures, a group of driftwood birds on a sea-smoothed log, to a customer.

Stella was in her room with the door open so I could see her playing on the carpet with her fuzzy ginger cat family and I could just hear the murmur of her voice as she talked to them, too. She looked up long enough to wave at Celia, before vanishing back into her game.

She kept an eye on Stella while I went to make coffee and fetch in some Sad cake, which I'd made into bar shapes this time, rather than rounds. 'See what you think of these.'

'Are they fattening?' she asked, picking one up.

'Yes, very.'

'Good,' she said, taking a great bite before unrolling her ideas.

The Crafty Celia circles had taken the fundraising bit between their teeth and were planning all kinds of events. They were all up for a sponsored Knitathon, to start off with, producing as many squares of an afghan blanket as possible in a day.

'That sounds like a lot of knitting.'

'It's going to be crochet really, only "Crochetathon" didn't really sound right. Afterwards we'll sew all the squares into blankets and sell *them* to raise money, too,' she explained. 'Then we'll have a selling exhibition of craftwork in the coach house in summer, maybe combined with a garden party. We could lure people in with the promise of coffee and cakes, with entrance to the exhibition included in the admission charge.'

'I could make the cakes for that,' I said. 'Oh, Celia, you and Will have already done so much more than all the rest of my friends put together.'

'Will says if you have a fundraising auction, you can have one of his bird sculptures as a lot.'

'He is so kind. Chloe Lyon said the vicar had some ideas and was coming to see me again to discuss them,' I said. 'She's the vicar's wife, did I say? It's very odd, because her grandfather is a self-professed warlock and runs the Museum of Witchcraft.'

'Really? It seems a rather odd village altogether,' Celia said. She'd usually come over to visit me when I'd been up here staying with Ma, and so had got to know it a bit.

'It is – but in a good way. Everyone has been very nice to me, considering how Ma has always kept to herself, though that seems to have been an Almond family habit, so I expect they're used to it.'

'From what you've told me, the Almonds all sounded a bit *Cold Comfort Farm*,' she said frankly.

'Yes, and I think they had their own version of "something nasty in the woodshed" too, that they didn't talk about, but no one will tell me what it is. Mind you, it must have been so long ago that not many people know what it was, anyway.'

'Martha seems to be getting about a bit more than she used to, though, from the sound of it,' Celia said.

I considered it. 'She is a bit, though even now she rarely goes into the village for shopping. However, she does like the bookshop, Marked Pages, and she'll go in the Spar if she's run out of anything vital, like tea or whisky. You know, I have to buy huge amounts of granulated sugar when I do the supermarket shop, because when Hal is here, he brews up endless mugs of sweet tea for them both.'

'Is that the gardener you mentioned, who seemed to be here a lot?'

'Yes, he's a bit of a fixture now. He's really the under-gardener up at Winter's End, so he's moonlighting when he does Ma's garden.'

'Maybe it's a romance?'

'Well . . . he's not bad-looking, I suppose, in a morose older Indiana Jones sort of way, and he's pretty fit,' I said thoughtfully. 'Ma doesn't seem to mind having him around either. He comes and goes, and hangs out in the new shed she had put up behind the studio . . . But no, I haven't really seen any sign of romance, and when I sort of prodded her about him, she said they were just good friends.'

'Then that's probably all they are,' Celia said, and went back to the vital matter of the fundraising. 'Did you see there have been a few more donations to the site? Nothing big, though.'

'Apart from you and Will, I don't think anyone else is fundraising at the moment. Certainly no one we knew in London.'

'Well, you know what it's like with that crowd: they'll be on to the latest trendy charitable cause, preferably something involving a fashion show or a party,' she said.

'You were the only real friend I made down there.'

'And vice versa. Well, except for Will, of course.'

'He's not so much a friend as a soul mate.'

She gave a happy sigh. 'I know, I was so lucky to meet him and I love living in Southport. The Crafty Celia classes in the coach house gallery are going really well, and of course Will has his studio and gallery upstairs and customers can use the outside staircase, so it's all worked out really well. If I'm not in the coach house I'm in the attic workshops in the house, so there's always one of us around for the dogs and cats, too.'

'That Mother and Toddler group I went to on Monday have promised to hold a jumble sale in June.'

'Oh, yes, you said on the phone – and I want to hear all about this Jago you kept mentioning, too. Jago is a weird name. Very *Poldark*.'

'*Poldark*?'

'Some novels set in Cornwall I read years ago: I think there was a TV series too.'

'He *is* Cornish by descent – his surname's Tremayne. But his parents are both academics and he was mainly brought up in Oxford.'

'He sounds really nice – you obviously clicked straight away.'

'I do feel like I've always known him,' I admitted, 'but not in a romantic way, just a friendly one, and I'm sure that's how he sees me, too. I mean, I really haven't got enough time or spare emotion to invest in a romance until Stella has had her operation and is on the road to recovery.'

'I suppose not.'

'Jago was jilted and I'm sure he isn't over his ex yet: we have that in common too.'

'Except that you were totally over your ex ages ago,' she said.

'Jago's ex rang him up out of the blue the other day and I think she wants him back. I hope she doesn't succeed, but it's quite selfish of me because I love being able to talk cake with him and I'm sure she'd persuade him to go back to London.'

'Let's hope she doesn't manage it, then,' Celia said, and then we got out the notebooks and discussed plane tickets and Googled budget hotels in Boston. We'd need a room for a few days before Stella went in for her operation, but once she was in hospital, I didn't suppose I would be anywhere except by her bedside for a lot of the time . . .

We found one through the hospital's helpful website eventually, situated nearby, which looked the best option.

'Ma is going to go with us, which is good, but I feel I'd really like a trained nurse on the plane with us too, just in case . . .'

'I'm sure Stella would be fine,' Celia said. 'Didn't your consultant say that if there is no radical decline in her condition by autumn, the journey shouldn't be a problem?'

'Yes, but even so . . .' I said stubbornly, and then sighed. 'I suppose it's out of the question anyway, because it would be extra expense.'

'Perhaps we'd better just concentrate on raising the twenty thousand for the moment, and see what suggestions the vicar makes,' she said. 'If he comes up with some brilliant ones, we can see about finding a nurse to go out with you then. Meanwhile I'll get Will on to sorting out the flights and hotel reservations because they really need to be booked soon.'

'I know,' I said. I'd been putting it off, though I'm not sure why. The operation was booked, after all, and I'd go through hell and high water to get Stella there.

Chapter 12: Fruitful

Chorley cakes look a little like a flat, thin Eccles cake, but are less sweet and simpler to make, basically consisting of a layer of currants spread between two thin rounds of plain shortcrust pastry. Traditionally they were eaten buttered on top and with a slice of Crumbly Lancashire cheese on the side.

Cally Weston: 'Tea & Cake'

You know, I could be mining this seam for ever, it's so fruitful (pun intended). It was great being able to bounce ideas off Jago by way of texts, calls and emails, too, but as Thursday approached I found myself looking forward to actually *seeing* him again.

Stella was, too, and after the hospital check-up, when they were quite pleased with her and said she'd put on a tiny bit more weight, it was a toss-up which of us was the most eager to go to the Happy Macaroon. So we were quite disappointed to find only David in the shop when we arrived, serving a customer.

But then I caught sight of a tray of iced gingerbread stars on the glass counter, with a sign saying that all proceeds from their sale would go to the Stella's Stars fund, to send a local little girl to America for a life-saving operation!

'They're Jago's idea,' David explained when his customer had left and Stella had wandered off to the other glass counter to show the gingerbread pigs to the mummy penguin she'd brought with her.

'A pound each and all the money goes into the Stella's Stars box here. We've already sold over a hundred and they're going like hot cakes. Or maybe that should be hot biscuits,' he added with a grin.

'That's *so* amazing of you both,' I said gratefully, so moved by this act of kindness that tears came to my eyes.

'Jago's an amazingly nice guy, with a heart soft as butter. He was really broken up when his fiancée dumped him, though actually, we all thought she was poison anyway,' he confided. 'None of his friends want to see him hurt like that again,' he added, which I took to be a friendly warning.

'Yes, he told me about his fiancée, and since mine dumped me, too, we have that in common. I hope we'll become good friends, because that's all I have time for when my time is so taken up with getting Stella well again.'

'Right . . .' David said thoughtfully. 'Then I hope *your* ex isn't trying to weasel back into your life, because it looks like Aimee's not letting Jago go that easily.'

'He *did* mention she'd been back in contact,' I said. I'd really have loved to have pumped David for all the details, but I didn't want to seem nosy . . . even if I was. And anyway, at that moment Stella spotted Jago coming in from the back room, carrying a tray of green macaroons.

She let out a squeal of delight. 'Jago!' she cried, as if she'd known him for ever, and his thin, dark face, which had worn an abstracted and slightly sad look, suddenly lit up in a grin.

'She practically dragged me in here so she could get a gingerbread pig,' I told him, even though there hadn't been any need to drag me. 'And I can't thank you enough for raising money with the gingerbread stars. Stella, look – Jago's selling these stars to raise money to get your heart mended in America.'

Stella looked at them, then up at Jago and nodded. 'I'm going in a big plane and when I come back, I'll be all better.'

'That will be great, won't it?' he said encouragingly. 'And it'll be exciting going in a plane to America.'

'Yes, but I have to go into *hospital* again when I get there,' Stella said gloomily. Then she perked up. 'But Mummy says when I get back it'll be nearly Christmas and Santa might bring me a big pink castle and a riverboat and a tree house and maybe even a hotel!'

Jago blinked. 'I'm sure he'll do his best.'

'The pink castle is the Barbie one she saw at the playgroup,' I explained. 'But the rest are for those little animal toys she collects. I made the mistake of showing her the range on the internet and her Santa list suddenly grew by several feet.'

'Here's Mummy Penguin,' Stella said, waving the toy at him. 'Say hello to Mummy Penguin.'

'Hello, Mummy Penguin, I'm very pleased to meet you,' he said gravely.

'Me too,' David said. 'It's not every day you meet a penguin. Look, Jago, it's gone quiet,' he added 'Why don't you all go for a coffee next door and see if you can think of any more good fundraising ideas? I can ring if it suddenly gets busy again.'

'Good idea, and I can snatch a quick lunch before things hot up again,' Jago agreed, then said slightly diffidently to me, 'That is, if you and Stella have time to join me?'

'That would be lovely.'

'Gingerbread piggy,' Stella said pointedly.

'Of course! Here we are: you choose one. I don't suppose the café will mind if you eat it while your mum and I have a cup of coffee.' Jago held the tray within reach. 'I have lunch there every day; I must have regular customer status by now.'

It was busy in the café, as always, which I suppose showed how good the food was. But we found a table, next to one occupied by three very elderly ladies who all smiled at Stella and commented on how pretty she was.

'I'm nearly four and I can read books,' she told them gravely, though the first was a lie since she's only three and a half. She eyed the enormous cream meringues in front of them and added, impressed, 'Are you going to eat all that?'

When they said they were, she was so taken by her new admirers that she decided to join them, climbing onto the empty chair at the table and putting her gingerbread pig down on a clean plate.

I was going to remove her, until they assured me they were delighted, so I left them to it. She was hauling Mummy Penguin out of her pocket ready for introductions, but if she started asking them difficult questions, like whether they minded being really old and if they would die soon, I would whisk her away.

Jago glanced at Stella. 'How did the hospital visit go?'

'Quite well. She's put on another tiny bit of weight so they said unless there were any problems, she could next go in a fortnight.'

'That's great!'

'We'll probably still come into Ormskirk next Thursday anyway, though, because it seems to be becoming a habit and we both like a mooch round the market.'

We drank our coffee and chatted and I asked him, 'How did you get into baking? Didn't you tell me your parents were academics and your brother is some kind of biochemist?'

'Yes . . . they thought I was a bit of a dunce at school and I never quite fitted in – my brother was so clever, but my parents didn't understand me at all. My granny – the Cornish one – came to live with us when I was five and I spent most of my time in the kitchen with her. I'm sure that's how I came to love cooking, and especially cake making, so much.'

'You don't seem at all stupid to me!'

'It turned out I was dyslexic,' he explained. 'I don't know why no one thought of testing me for it sooner, but once they did and I got some help, I learned to cope with it. Though my spelling is a bit random and anything longer than a recipe can take me a while to get through. But I do. How did you get into the cookery journalism?'

'A bit like you. I wasn't academic or arty, and although Ma loved me, she was never very maternal and her painting engrossed her. "Ma" isn't even a version of "Mum" – she always called herself Martha, and Ma was all I could get my tongue around when I was tiny. Dad adored Ma, but he was clever and remote, so not very good with children. So I had foreign au pair girls, and the last one, Anna, was a really keen cook and taught me all kinds of things. I came to the cookery writing through journalism, though.'

'We have such a lot in common,' he said. 'Baffled parents, early cookery influences and jilting fiancés.'

I laughed and agreed. 'And cake, don't forget! We've turned out all right in the end, haven't we?'

'Or we're heading that way, at least,' he said.

'Does the dyslexia still make things really difficult?'

'It's OK now that I've found ways to manage it, though when I have my own business I'll have to get some help with the paperwork, I expect. But my dyslexia is a minor hurdle compared to what Stella's been going through.'

'Did I tell you how grateful I am about the gingerbread stars?'

'About a million times – it's getting embarrassing,' he said with a grin.

'OK, I'll stop now,' I said laughing.

He hadn't mentioned his fiancée again, so I'd no idea what was going on with that . . . but now we were friends I really hoped they *wouldn't* get back together, even if that was selfish of me, because I was certain she'd whip him straight back to London again.

When I got home with a tired but cheerful Stella, she awarded Ma the chewed remains of the gingerbread pig as usual, and told her she'd met three ladies much older even than Ma was.

'Nearly three hundred years old!' she elaborated. 'And they're all called Grace.'

'I think they meant their combined ages, and they were exaggerating slightly,' I explained.

'That's a relief and I'm glad I don't look three hundred years old,' Ma said. 'What do you mean, they're all called Grace, Stella?'

'They're the three Graces, they said so.'

Stella went off for a nap as usual after lunch and the vicar arrived soon afterwards. Luckily there was a freshly baked fruit loaf, so I buttered that and made a pot of tea, and while we had it I told him about Jago and the gingerbread stars and how it had given me hope that the rest of the money could be raised in time.

'I mean, we've barely met and he's done so much for Stella already.'

'He makes me ashamed I've only just got started on helping,' Raffy said ruefully.

'Not at all, I understand you must have other calls on your time.'

'I do, but Stella's fundraising is urgent and I've popped in today because I've had some ideas – and first of all, I've called a meeting in the village hall on Saturday to get things rolling, with a fundraising committee in charge. The posters are going up all over the village today; Hebe Winter is organising all that. I hope you'll come?'

'What, *this* Saturday – the day after tomorrow? Is that possible at such short notice?'

'Oh, yes, the Sticklepond grapevine works almost instantly. I suspect some of my parishioners of telepathy,' he said gravely.

'Of course I'll come, but I won't have to speak, will I?' I asked, alarmed by the idea.

'Not if you don't want to. I'll outline why we need to fundraise and introduce you to everyone, but you'll know most of them by sight at least by now, I should think and they'll already know all about you and Stella.'

'I suppose that's living in a village for you. But since we don't really belong in Sticklepond, I still don't think we count as a local cause.' Ma did, of course, but she could hardly be said to be a part of village life.

'That doesn't matter, you're all part of the fabric of this village now, and in any case, they'd unite to support a sick child wherever it came from. I'm a father myself, so I can imagine what you're going through and I'll do everything in my power to help you. God will provide – so get on and finalise the arrangements to take Stella to America and leave the rest to us.'

'You're very kind,' I told him gratefully, and then we discussed all the arrangements I'd have to make.

'Will, my friend Celia's husband, is very good at sorting out details and he'll make all the bookings for me. The costs keep going up all the time, though, so I think twenty thousand is the minimum extra I need,' I said ruefully. 'I mean, I'd really like to take a nurse with me on the plane, but that would be an extra expense, so it's out of the question.'

'Let's see what we come up with at the meeting, and go from there,' Raffy suggested. 'Chloe said you went to the Mother and Toddler group meeting and you took some wonderful Eccles cakes – though actually, they couldn't have been nicer than this tea loaf,' he added, taking about the tenth slice. 'She's expecting again, though she wants to keep it quiet until she's past the three-month stage.'

'Congratulations!' I said, though I felt a pang of jealousy, because I'd have loved a big family . . . though of course, not a big single-parent one. But I knew I was lucky to have Stella, and getting her fit and well, then resuming my career so that we could have our own place again and leave my poor mother in peace as soon as possible, had to be my current priorities in life.

When he got up to go, Raffy said again, 'So, you will come to the meeting on Saturday?'

'Yes, if Ma will baby-sit . . . and I really don't have to make a speech?'

'Absolutely not, if you don't want to.'

'I could manage to thank everyone for coming and say I would be grateful for any help, because I don't want to seem churlish or ungrateful.'

'Great, that's really all it needs.'

'Can I invite my friends Celia and Will? You'll remember I told you they're already fundraising.'

'They really should be there, then, and the more the merrier,' he said.

I rang Celia up later and told her that Jago's friend David had said Jago's ex was trying to get him back. I don't know why that nugget of information slipped out first, but it just did. Celia had never met him, so she wasn't likely to be that riveted by the news.

'And I think he's still carrying a torch for her, because he didn't mention her while we had coffee in the café next to the shop, so it wouldn't surprise me if he ends up getting back with her and then going to London to start his business up.'

'That would be a pity,' she said. 'You'd think he'd be once bitten, twice shy.'

'Yes . . . but actually that's not why I phoned you up. The vicar came and he's already called a meeting in the village hall for Saturday.'

'What, this Saturday?'

'Yes, that's just what I said! When he gets the bit between his teeth, he certainly doesn't hang about. When I took Stella up to feed the ducks after he'd gone, there were already posters up everywhere and two people stopped and said they were going to be there. You know, everyone's suddenly much friendlier now I'm doing lots of shopping in the village, and I already know the dog walking crowd and some of the local mums.'

'That's the good side of living in a small place,' she agreed. 'Of course, the downside is that sometimes you don't actually want everyone to know your entire business.'

'I suppose there is that,' I said. 'I'm sure they know everything there is to know about me and Ma – and maybe even more about how Esau Almond blotted his copybook than either of us!'

'You really ought to investigate the family mystery sometime. It's intriguing,' she said.

'I suppose so, but I don't suppose it's really anything that terrible – or nothing that we would consider terrible these days. So, will you both come to the meeting?'

'I'll certainly come and I'll see what Will's doing,' she assured me.

When Jago emailed me later I was tempted to tell him about the meeting, too. But then I thought he was already doing more than enough and he might feel obliged to come, when he would rather be doing something else. He'd have been busy in the shop anyway, it being a Saturday, so he'd probably also be tired. Bakers have such long days! He told me he starts work at four or five if he has a croquembouche to make, because he creates the whole thing on the day it is required.

If he'd let me, one day I'd like to go and watch the whole process . . . and then get a stupendous 'Cake Diaries' piece out of it!

Jago

On Friday, when trade was going quiet just before lunch, a very tall, dark-haired man wearing a black T-shirt with a white clerical collar walked into the Happy Macaroon.

'Aren't you Raffy Sinclair, the front man of Mortal Ruin?' David said, staring at him hard.

'I was, but now I'm the vicar of Sticklepond,' he said, and Jago recalled reading about Sticklepond's vicar's ex-rock star past somewhere, though he didn't remember Cally mentioning it, or how good-looking he was . . .

'I came in to see Jago.'

David indicated his friend. 'There's your man.'

Raffy shook Jago's hand and smiled warmly. 'I'm really pleased to meet you. Cally told me how much money you'd already raised by selling gingerbread stars and I wanted to invite you – both of you – to come to a fund-raising meeting at the village hall in Sticklepond tomorrow night.'

'Not me,' David said hastily, 'it's all Jago's idea, and though I'm more than happy to help, my fiancée's coming up for the weekend and we don't get much time together.'

'I understand. Then I'd really like it if *you* could come,

Jago? I'm hoping for a good turnout and lots of ideas, and your good start will inspire everyone.'

'I'll be glad to come,' Jago said, though he still felt strangely jealous of the tall and charismatic vicar, until he bought a gingerbread star for his little girl, Grace.

'My wife would probably love some macaroons, because she's got quite a sweet tooth. Those pale pink ones look wonderful,' he added, and Jago warmed to him.

'I'll give you some for her to try, a free sample.'

'That's very kind of you!'

'It's how we lure new customers in,' Jago said, putting some into a silver box, then asked, 'Do you really think we can raise the money in time?'

'Oh, yes, I'm quite sure the whole village will unite to help us,' Raffy assured him. 'Now they know it's the life of a child hanging in the balance, there'll be no stopping them.'

When he put it like that, Jago couldn't see how they could fail, either.

Aimee walked into the Happy Macaroon, then did a double take and stared after the tall, dark and stunningly handsome man who'd just passed her on the way out.

Then she got a grip on herself and, refocusing on the mission in hand, looked round for Jago, but only David was to be seen.

She waited until he'd served two students, and then said, 'Hi, David. Where's Jago?'

'*This* is a surprise, Aimee,' he said, though not as if it was a good one. 'He didn't tell me you were coming.'

'He didn't know, but since I was on my way up to the

Lake District to organise a weekend party, I thought I'd pop in and take him to lunch.'

'You just missed him. You're looking . . . *tanned*,' he added.

'Why, thank you.' She batted her mascara-lagged eyelashes at him.

'Like leather. The last dewy bloom of youth must have got burned off in the desert.' David thought that was pretty poetic: he must have watched too many of his friend's rom com films!

A look of fury crossed Aimee's face, swiftly transformed to one of melting delight when Jago suddenly appeared from the back room, pulling on his jacket. He stopped dead at the sight of her, feeling his heart leap and then start to thump.

'There you are, darling! David just told me you'd gone out.' She gave his friend a dirty look.

'I *was* on my way out . . .' he stammered, still thrown off balance by her sudden appearance.

'Come on – I'll take you to lunch, that's why I'm here. You *have* to come,' she wheedled, 'to show you forgive me.'

'Oh, right,' David put in helpfully, 'if you buy him a sandwich and pout a few times, he's bound to completely forget you jilted him just before the wedding.'

'Butt out, David!' Aimee snapped with a face like a Fury, then did another quick change to her sweetest expression and said to Jago, 'Do come!'

But by now Jago had recovered from his initial shock at seeing her and he wasn't sure quite how he felt about it *or* her assumption that he'd forgive her for what she clearly considered some trifling little misjudgement.

'I'm only going next door to the café for a quick bite to eat. Half an hour at most.'

She pouted. 'I'm sure David could manage without you for a bit longer than that. We've got so much to catch up on.'

'Fridays are busy; I'll need to get back quickly so he can have his break, too.'

'I suppose half an hour is better than nothing, I'll come with you,' she said, and, with another dirty look at David, followed Jago out and up the stairs of the café next door. It was not exactly the ambience she'd had in mind for making it up with Jago.

Sitting opposite, Jago looked broodingly at her. In the shop he'd seen her in exactly the way he had when he was still blinded by love: tall, very slender, with long blond hair, green eyes and endless legs shown off by a short, tight skirt.

But now, suddenly, the scales seemed to fall from his eyes and it was like looking at a stranger. Her time in the hot sun of Dubai had hastened the slightly shrivelled and leathery look that comes to all sun worshippers in the end, and her hair seemed as dead and artificial as a doll's. Apart from the ability to pout and bat her eyelashes, her face seemed remarkably immobile, so she'd probably been at the Botox, too . . . and Sarah had been right about the baggy knees.

His mind conjured up another and much more natural beauty: Cally, with her white-gold hair springing from a central parting in crazy curls to frame a broad forehead, lovely deep blue eyes and the entrancing dusting of freckles across her nose. She was sufficiently plump to hug without being pierced by sharp bones and looked wholesome enough to eat, though he'd got the message that she'd kill him if he said so.

He smiled, which unfortunately encouraged Aimee.

She smiled back beguilingly, confidently, with those lovely

green eyes sparkling as she tried to cast her spell of enchantment over him once again. 'I've missed you so much, Jago – and you *are* pleased to see me, aren't you?'

His smile vanished and he muttered, 'Just take a bite from this lovely poisoned apple.'

'*What?*'

'Sorry, I was just thinking about dessert.'

'Then I wish you'd think about me instead! I was just saying how much I'd missed you and . . . well, really, I wanted to say sorry.'

'I think it's a little late for apologies, Aimee. By the way, what happened to all the wedding presents and the arrangements? I mean, I cancelled everything my end, but when I left a message for your father, he never replied.'

'Oh, Daddy cancelled everything else. He was a *teeny* bit cross with me, because once he'd met you he said you were a good, honest, hard-working man, and I couldn't do any better.'

'Did he? I thought he'd have told you that you were throwing yourself away by marrying a bakery assistant, even one who could make his own five-tier fairy-tale wedding cake,' Jago said, surprised. 'Mind you,' he added, 'running off with a car salesman probably wasn't what he wanted for you, either.'

'He wasn't some kind of *used* car salesman, Jago! He's got the dealership for top-of-the-range sports cars in Dubai. That's entirely different.'

'He's still a car salesman, though, isn't he?'

'What did you do with our wedding cake?' she asked, ignoring that. 'Fruitcakes keep, don't they? I expect you've still got it.'

'No, actually, after you ran off we had a bit of a party at Gilligan's and ate most of it, then we shared the last two tiers to celebrate our win on the lottery.'

She looked faintly indignant, though why she should when she was the one who had run off just before the wedding was anyone's guess.

'Daddy had all the wedding presents sent back,' she said regretfully.

'So, how is . . . what was he called – Dan?'

'Vann,' she corrected coldly. 'So far as I know, he's fine. Things . . . didn't work out between us.'

'So you said on the phone. And there was me all this time thinking you'd be living happily ever after in Dubai, among the palm trees and concrete. I'm sure I saw they even had an indoor ski run with fake snow – there's surely everything there you could want, if you don't mind it hot and artificial.'

'The shopping would have been wonderful if Daddy hadn't cut my allowance off but actually, apart from that I hated Dubai because Vann wasn't really in with the top people and so we never got invited to the best parties,' she said, dissatisfaction and disappointment in her voice. 'And it was tricky not being married, because they're really hot on immorality over there and he was afraid to put a foot out of line.'

'So he was a bit of a washout from the social-climbing angle,' Jago said with mock sympathy. 'I'm gutted for you.'

'Jago, darling, you make me sound like such a shallow bitch and you know I'm not . . . *really* I'm not.' She put her hand over his on the table and he noticed for the first time that she was still wearing the engagement ring he'd given her – one he'd still been paying for even after she'd run off – but on her right hand. The diamond flashed at him like a warning signal.

'I think I got cold feet. Getting married seemed such a big step to take.'

'So does running off to Dubai with a car salesman,' he said drily.

'I realised almost at once it was a mistake, that it was you I really loved and wanted to settle down and raise a family with.'

'I think you may have left having a family a little late,' he said, and a look of fury crossed her lovely face.

'That bitch David's engaged to told you how old I really am, didn't she? I knew she recognised me when I went in the salon!'

'Aimee, it wouldn't have bothered me that you were a few years older,' Jago said. 'There wasn't any need to lie about it.'

'I know that now . . . and that you're the only man who's ever truly loved me . . .' she said, with a break in her voice.

'It's a pity you didn't figure that out earlier then, isn't it?' he said, but more gently.

'But I realise it now and that's all that matters, surely?' she said softly, squeezing his hand. 'Please forgive me! I'd so love to wear my ring on the proper finger again.'

He stared at her, his light brown eyes startled and wide. 'Aimee, you can't just swan back into my life after living with someone else for a year and expect to pick up where you left off.'

'But I still feel the same about you . . . and I know I hurt you, but you still love me, don't you? I promise this time it will be different. You can start your own business in London and I can help you with all my contacts,' she suggested, though truth to tell the whole party scene had moved on and changed while she was away and she no longer seemed quite to fit in.

'Set up my business in London? Using what for money?' he demanded.

'Your lottery winnings, of course! You told me the syndicate at Gilligan's had a big jackpot.' She paused. 'Though come to think of it, when I went there to try and get your number, I recognised quite a few of the staff, so why were they still there?'

'Apart from the fact that they all love their work, we didn't win that much by the time it was divided between us. The rest of them just paid their mortgages off or bought new cars or whatever, then carried on working. David and I were the only ones who wanted to set up our own specialist businesses.'

'You didn't win that much . . .?' Her mouth went tight.

'No. I haven't even got enough to buy premises somewhere trendy in the North-west, like Knutsford or Wilmslow, where I first looked. Though that's a blessing, as it turns out, because actually I love it round here and I want to settle in one of the villages near Ormskirk. I'll be near David and Sarah, and I've already started to make friends locally.'

'But – if we got married and started up a business in London, I'm sure Daddy would help us,' she suggested.

'But we're not going to get married and nor am I coming back to London,' Jago said wearily. 'You can't just come back and expect to pick up where you left off, Aimee. I've moved on and things have changed.'

'You've found someone else?' she said quickly.

'I – no, of course not, David and I have been too busy,' he said, but he must have sounded unconvincing because she eyed him suspiciously. 'Like I said, I've made friends locally but that's all.'

'Good, because I'll be back and I intend to make you change your mind and give me another chance.'

'That's not going to happen, Aimee. We can be friends, but there's no way we're ever getting back together.'

'We'll see,' she said with a confident little smile. 'I've just accepted a job with the Corporate Party People, starting next week, but I'll keep popping up to see you when I can.'

She gave his hand another squeeze and the sparkling diamond, having slipped right round her bony finger, dug painfully into his hand.

Chapter 13: Sad Cake

Another, more frugal, relation of the Eccles and Chorley cakes is the Sad cake, which originated in East Lancashire. Basically pastry sprinkled with currants or raisins, it can be baked in a large round or square and cut into wedges or fingers to go with morning coffee.

Cally Weston: 'Tea & Cake'

Since I talked to Jago on Thursday he'd instantly become my sounding board for questions, ideas and interesting foodie stuff, and messages by text, phone and email constantly flew to and fro between us. But he was much more than just a sounding board, because he was so interested and knowledgeable that he constantly sparked off new ideas.

The one thing he hadn't mentioned again was his ex-fiancée, so I hoped David was wrong and he wasn't about to kiss and make up with her. Then latish on Friday we were chatting on the phone and I thought he sounded a bit subdued, so to cheer him up I told him the story of Ma losing the hammer and my finding it in the fridge.

'It was the one from the studio she uses to make her

canvas stretchers with, so she must have been carrying it when she felt hungry and came down to make a sandwich. It was where the ham had been, so I went up to the studio and looked in the toolbox and there it was. It's lucky I know the way her mind works by now.'

'That is seriously absent-minded,' he said, impressed.

'It's because her mind is usually focused on her work. She's always done things like that.'

'My mind's been a bit preoccupied this afternoon,' he confessed. 'Aimee dropped by unexpectedly on her way up to the Lake District and it was really odd to see her again.'

'Yes, I can imagine,' I agreed, though wondering whether it had been odd in a good or bad way.

'We were very busy in the shop, so I didn't have long to talk to her.' He sighed heavily. 'She was a bit upset and kept saying she'd made a big mistake and would I forgive her.'

'And – did you?' The question tumbled out, despite myself.

'Oh, I've long forgiven her, because I think it was all for the best and it wouldn't have worked out if we'd married. I hated all that partying and clubbing, so I'd have bored her senseless.'

'You're not boring in the least,' I assured him, surprised.

'Not to you, perhaps, because we're both interested in the same things, but I don't think I'm that exciting to most women.'

He can't ever have looked at himself properly in the mirror! But actually, it was quite engaging that he had no idea just how attractive he was.

'Maybe she's had enough of exciting and she's ready to

settle down now?' I suggested. 'So . . . are you going to see her again?'

'She said she'd keep dropping in, though she's about to start a job in London so maybe that won't be so easy,' he said. 'I told her I was looking for somewhere to buy up here and there was no way I'd ever get back together with her or live in London now.' He sighed again. 'I hate it when she cries over me.'

That sounded like emotional blackmail to me and I hoped he hadn't fallen for it. But he brightened up and told me something funny one of his customers had said and I capped it with Stella rapping on Ma's head earlier when she was trying to get her attention and asking her if she was in there.

That made him laugh, so at least I'd cheered him up a bit, but I wished this Aimee would leave him alone because she sounded like bad news on all fronts. In fact, if I'd known Gregory Lyon or Florrie Snowball a bit better, I'd have asked them for some kind of vanishing powder to toss at her if we ever came face to face.

I got up early as usual next morning, to a blackberry-dark sky with one pale Promethean spark of light, and from sheer habit let Toto out into the garden, even though he'd totally mastered the cat flap and could let himself in and out any time he liked.

I thought of David and Jago, probably even now baking the first batch of the day's macaroons . . . and I had had a good idea in the night for a new Christmas recipe – filling a traditional Eccles cake with mincemeat! If it worked I thought I'd call them Christmas puffs. I need to file a few more seasonal recipes fairly soon, so that would make a good start.

First, though, before I started baking, I checked the Stella's Stars fundraising website, for often there had been small random donations from kind strangers. But to my incredulous amazement, this time someone had donated the whopping great sum of ten thousand pounds! And I thought I could guess who it was, despite what I'd said . . .

Feeling cross, I rang Jago up on the shop line and I was right about their being up and working already because he picked up almost immediately.

'Jago? It's Cally. I've just spotted that there's been an anonymous donation of ten thousand pounds to the fund. It was *you*, wasn't it?' I said accusingly.

'*Me*? No, honestly it wasn't,' he answered, sounding genuinely surprised. 'But that's wonderful, isn't it?'

'Do you *swear*, on a first edition of Mrs Beeton, it wasn't you?' I demanded, still suspicious.

'I swear,' he assured me solemnly. 'I admit to thinking about it, but I was sure you'd guess it was me, so I decided I'd just put some money aside in case there was any shortfall at the end of the fundraising. You'd have had to take it then.'

'I suppose I would, and it was a kind thought, but you really need all your winnings to start your croquembouche business.'

'Well, you may not need it anyway now, because you should be able to raise the rest easily.'

'Yes, ten thousand pounds does seem more do-able in the timescale,' I agreed.

'Piece of cake.'

'Biscuit?' I suggested.

'Biscuit. I don't suppose you'll be in the Blue Dog at lunchtime today, will you?'

'I'm afraid I'll just be dashing in and out to the supermarket this time. I probably could next week, though.'

'Then I'll see you at the fundraising meeting tonight in Sticklepond village hall instead,' he said, to my surprise.

'How do you know about that? There are posters about it all over the village, but I'm sure not as far as Ormskirk.'

'Raffy came in yesterday and introduced himself, and then he invited me. It slipped my mind to tell you when I was talking to you last night, because Aimee's visit had knocked me for six. It must have slipped your mind too,' he added pointedly, 'since you didn't mention it.'

'I felt you'd done more than enough already, with the gingerbread stars. You really don't *have* to come.'

'I want to come. In fact, wild horses couldn't keep me away,' he said. 'And anyway, I welcome anything that gets me out of the flat at the weekends when Sarah's up here, so the lovebirds can be alone for a bit.'

I heard David say something rude in the background.

'Ma says she'll baby-sit Stella while I'm at the meeting.'

'Do you want me to pick you up?' he offered.

'No, that's all right, I'll walk. It's only ten minutes and it'll do me good.'

Stella wanted to see the angels in the graveyard again later, so Ma really has given her angel mania. I'm not entirely sure how wholesome an interest in visiting graveyards is in a three-year-old, but we walked down there anyway, with Toto. I hoped no one would object to his coming into the graveyard with us, since he would bark his head off if I left him tied to the lych gate.

We admired all the angels, though the one to Susan Winter was her favourite, because it's such a lively carving that it seems to be taking off vertically in a swirl of drapery.

I'd always assumed that the Almonds would be buried elsewhere, since they belonged to some obscure Baptist sect, but when I'd said so to Ma recently she'd replied that no, they were in the All Angels churchyard, because the Ormskirk Strange Baptists hadn't had their own burial ground.

So for the first time I actually went looking for the Almond family graves and found them clustered round an austere granite obelisk in the corner nearest the village green. The stones featured lots of biblical Amoses, Elijahs, Marthas and Marys, and even a very Thomas Hardyesque Bathsheba, so I think Ma lucked out on *her* name. My grandparents had a modest modern granite headstone, but the rest of the graves were much older ones of local stone, which of course they would be, because of the entire Almond clan emigrating to Australia after the war.

Stella wanted to see inside the church again, and it was unlocked, so I parked the buggy in the porch and tucked Toto under my arm – the advantage of having a small dog – before we went in. While Stella was gazing raptly at the Heaven and Hell window behind the altar, I wandered up and down looking at the memorial brasses and stone plaques and discovered one or two more Almonds there – including one that seemed to have had an additional name chiselled out of it, for after saying, 'And to the memory of', there was just a roughly hacked space.

Strange . . . I wondered if perhaps the missing name was that of Esau Almond, the black sheep of the three brothers up at Badger's Bolt, the one that Ma didn't want to talk about. What little I knew about them was that the eldest, Saul, had stayed on the farm during the war, since food production was vital, while the other two brothers, Amos and Esau, had enlisted. I'd asked her once if they'd both survived and she'd just said she thought the past was best left behind us, and then clammed up.

On the way home, as an afterthought, we detoured for a quick look at the war memorial. There were two Almonds listed as killed in the First World War, but none in the Second . . . though again, someone had roughly chiselled out a name in the As.

It was all very mysterious.

When we got back I didn't mention it to Ma, though Stella told her all about the angels when we took her some sand- wiches and a couple of the Eccles cake-style Christmas puffs I'd made earlier, which were a great success.

When I arrived there early that evening I was both surprised and touched by how full the village hall was. In fact, I spotted Celia and Will, squeezed into the far end of the back row, only because Will, a tall, cadaverous man with a lantern jaw, stood up and waved at me.

A paper banner bearing the hand-lettered words 'Stella's Stars' hung over the stage, which was set with a row of chairs and a small table with a jug of water on it. I would have tried to squeeze myself in next to Celia and Will, but the small, wiry woman at the door detached a plump Brownie from a group of hovering helpers to usher me to a seat right at the front of the hall instead, though at least, to my huge relief, it wasn't actually on the stage.

Someone – probably the wiry woman – had efficiently reserved the front row by placing named slips of paper on them and mine was right next to Jago, who was already there. Beyond him, Mrs Snowball was unwrapping a stripy mint humbug.

Jago grinned at me. 'Thought you'd be up on the stage,' he whispered.

'I'm so glad I'm not! I asked Raffy if I could leave it all to him and take a back seat. I feel a bit too close to things to be objective, and I don't know how interested people will be in the idea when she isn't a local child.'

'Of course they'll be interested, look how many are here tonight! And where she's from won't matter a bit,' he assured me. 'Anyway, your mother comes from the village, didn't you tell me?'

'Yes, but she's not exactly part of it and I don't think her family, the Almonds, were much liked.'

Florrie Snowball had evidently got ears like a bat, despite her advanced years, for she leaned forward and, adjusting the humbug so that it bulged in her cheek, said, 'The three lads used to come into the village to the pub and to dance – just before the war that was. They were all tall, with very fair, curly hair and blue eyes just like yours. They were good-looking, even if they were a bit close-mouthed. The eldest, Saul, he married a land girl.'

'Lots of people have commented I've got the Almond colouring – but only the older ones, who remember the family before they emigrated.'

'That's right, and so has Martha – you'd know either of you for an Almond straight away.'

'Except I'm not close-mouthed.'

'True,' she agreed. 'And that little girl of yours seems chatty enough.'

'Did all three of the brothers survive the war, Mrs Snowball?' I ventured.

'Ah, that would be telling,' she said annoyingly, then moved the humbug out of her cheek and sat back.

Several people, including Raffy, now took up their places on the stage and Jago whispered, 'Who's that scary-looking tall, elderly woman with the hawk nose, sitting next to the vicar?'

'Hebe Winter, the twin sister of Ma's friend Ottie. She lives up at Winter's End with her great-niece Sophy and her family, and apparently she's always had a finger in any Sticklepond pies going. The man behind her is her retired steward, Laurence Yatton – I know that because he was in the bookshop once and we got talking. Sophy Winter is married to the head gardener, Seth Greenwood – see, they're sitting over there, on the other side, next to Raffy's wife, Chloe, who runs the chocolate shop. And *her* grandfather's that man with long silver hair and a blue velvet cloak. He's Gregory Lyon and has the Witchcraft Museum—'

'Whoa!' Jago said, before I could carry on listing all the more notable – or infamous – of the village characters that I knew.

'Sorry,' I apologised, 'that was a bit of an information overload! In fact, I hadn't realised quite how many people I know, or how much I know about them!'

The wiry elderly lady who'd been manning the door now slipped into the empty aisle seat next to me and I saw that Raffy was getting to his feet and nudged Jago.

'Here goes,' I said nervously.

Chapter 14: Stella's Stars

When Raffy Sinclair got to his feet everyone immediately fell silent. He looked around the packed village hall and said, 'Welcome, everyone, and I'm delighted to see so many of you here tonight. The people of Sticklepond have a tradition of coming together in times of adversity and need, but this time the cause is, quite literally, one of life and death. Let me tell you about little Stella Weston.'

He did so, clearly and concisely outlining the situation and then, with a gesture towards where I was sitting, introduced me. 'I know Cally just wants to say a couple of words to you before we go on.'

Clearing my throat nervously – and there was already a lump in it from what Raffy'd said – I got to my feet and turned to face the packed hall with its pale swimming sea of faces. 'I . . . I'd just like to thank you all for coming tonight and to say that I'd be deeply grateful for any help you could give me. The operation in America is Stella's only chance of leading a long and normal life and I'm determined to give her that hope of a future, whatever it takes.'

There was a spatter of applause and I sat down again more abruptly than I intended, due to my knees giving way.

Jago took my hand and squeezed it, murmuring, 'Well done!'

'Thank you, Cally,' Raffy said. 'So, everyone: little Stella needs to go to Boston in America for the operation, leaving the UK around the end of October. Now, I've already told Cally that we're a caring, sharing village, so she should go ahead and book the flights, the hotels and the procedure while we – all of us – will raise the rest of the money needed.'

'Hear, hear,' a chorus of voices called from the hall.

'Poor little mite,' exclaimed Zillah Smith, who kept house and helped in the Witchcraft Museum for Gregory Lyon, who she was sitting next to. 'I've seen her about and she looks as if a decent gust of wind would blow her away.'

'How much do we need to raise?' asked Hebe Winter practically, turning her bright blue eagle gaze from the audience to Raffy.

'It *was* around twenty thousand pounds, but I'm told that an anonymous benefactor has just donated half of that.'

'Well, I'm sure we can't imagine where *that* came from, then,' said Florrie Snowball sarkily, but quietly.

I glanced at her across Jago and mouthed silently, 'It was the *vicar*?'

She nodded and whispered, 'And all the local charities have had anonymous donations since he moved here, so it doesn't take a genius to figure that one out.'

'The remaining ten thousand pounds will still be quite a lot to raise in such a short space of time,' Hebe was observing.

'Ah,' Raffy said, 'but if you break it down so that a hundred groups or individuals each raise a hundred pounds of that, it sounds much more do-able, doesn't it? I'm sure there must be that many people here tonight. Miss Yatton, who has kindly been on the door, might be able to tell us. Effie?'

He looked towards the wiry whippet of a woman with pepper-and-salt hair, who'd slipped late into the front seat next to me on the end of the row.

'One hundred exactly,' Effie said efficiently, 'including the child's mother and yourself, that is.'

'Really? Then that has to be a sign from God that the event will be a stellar success,' he joked and there were several good-natured groans from the audience.

'There you are, then – I'm sure we can do it. Some people will raise more than a hundred pounds and some much less, but it'll all come to the right amount, you'll see, and with a contingency fund for any unforeseen expenses.'

'There are bound to be some of those,' said Laurence Yatton, nodding his handsome, silver-haired head. He was sitting just behind Miss Winter and seemed to be scribbling down notes of the meeting.

'I think we could all take our inspiration from the great start at fundraising made by Jago Tremayne,' Raffy continued, and I felt Jago, who was still holding my hand, give a galvanic start.

'As some of you might know, he's recently helped a friend to open the Happy Macaroon shop in Ormskirk, but he's already raised over a hundred pounds for Stella by selling gingerbread stars. I'm happy to say he's here tonight.'

There was more enthusiastic clapping and when I glanced at Jago he was looking self-conscious. I think because there were so few strangers there, he'd already felt he stuck out like a sore thumb up in the front row.

He half-rose to his feet, made a sort of bow and sank

down again. The tips of his ears under the curling dark hair turned pink.

'I'm indebted to him for making me realise that if we all do one small thing to help, we'll get a big result,' Raffy continued. 'Are you all behind me?'

'No, we're all in front of you,' called Hal, in his usual deadpan way. He was sitting in a row further back with the other Winter's End gardeners and most of the rest of the Winter family (though not Ottie, who was away at her cottage in Cornwall).

'Smart arse,' Raffy said amiably, but there had been a chorus of assent from the body of the hall and Hebe Winter, after quelling her under-gardener with an icy glare, volunteered her supposedly retired steward, Laurence Yatton, to register the names of all the fundraisers.

'And his sister, Effie, can help him,' she added.

'Of course, I'm glad to,' Effie agreed from her seat next to me. Florrie Snowball, evidently feeling this needed a reward, passed her across a mint humbug.

'And further,' continued Hebe, 'I suggest we hold a summer fête in the hall and on the adjoining green, to include a raffle. What do you think of the idea, Vicar?'

'It's a very good one. And perhaps we could also have an auction as a separate event, if we can get some good prizes donated?'

'Or promises,' Hebe suggested. 'For instance, I and the rest of the Elizabethan Re-enactment Society could promise to come and perform a dance at any event or celebration that the bidder wanted and –' here she fixed her piercing bright blue eyes on a man quietly sitting a few rows back and raised her voice, 'if *Ivo Hawksley* were to offer his services reading an excerpt from Shakespeare, I should certainly be among the bidders for that.'

There was a heartfelt masculine groan and some laughter.

'Ivo Hawksley's a retired Shakespearian actor, almost as reclusive as Ma,' I whispered to Jago. 'He's married to Tansy Poole who runs Cinderella's Slippers, the specialist wedding shoe shop in the village.'

'I could read the tea leaves for the highest bidder,' Zillah Smith was offering, with a glinting gold gypsy smile. 'And Gregory, you could name the next new ley line you discover after someone.'

'*I'll* put myself up to do something, too,' Raffy said. 'Anything.'

'*Almost* anything,' Raffy's wife, Chloe, qualified, to more laughter.

'I don't mind collecting and cataloguing the auction prizes,' Effie said, 'and doing the raffle at the fête.'

'And Laurence and I will collate all the fundraising endeavours,' stated Hebe, without consulting him.

'My Mother and Toddler group will be a team, won't we?' Chloe asked, turning to the room at large, and a chorus of agreement echoed back. 'In fact, we've already got a jumble sale organised for June.'

'I could hold a book-signing event, if some of our local authors would oblige?' Felix Hemming, the proprietor of the Marked Pages bookshop, suggested. 'I know Cally Weston is the author of *Around the World in Eighty Cakes* and *The Cake Diaries*, but we also have Ivo's *Nicholas Marlowe* crime novels, Tansy's *Slipper Monkey* children's books, Gregory Lyon's supernatural thrillers and Seth Greenwood's very popular gardening book, *The Artful Knot*.'

'Gosh, the place is a hotbed of literary talent,' Jago muttered.

'The Sticklepond knitting circle has a large stock of items ready for sale,' someone called out. 'We'd already started building up to the Christmas fair, but there's plenty of time to make more for that.'

'And I'm having a Knitathon and a Crafty Garden Party with a selling exhibition at my house in Southport,' I heard Celia's clear voice announce. 'You're all welcome to come.'

'Brilliant,' Laurence Yatton said, scribbling busily. Then he looked up and added, 'There are opportunities to sell all kinds of home-made items on the internet too, these days.'

'That's right,' piped up Florrie Snowball unexpectedly. 'My barmaid Molly's always going on about selling that weird jewellery she makes on Ditsy and Bitsy.'

'Etsy and Folksy?' suggested Chloe tentatively.

'Them too,' Florrie agreed. 'I could easily make up a hundred of those little protection charms on leather neck thongs that I sell through the Witchcraft Museum and Molly can flog them on the interweb for me.'

'It's called the internet, Florrie, and I already sell my knitted tea cosies on Etsy,' a woman corrected her.

'You big know-all, Josie Pucket!' Florrie told her, turning round. 'What are *you* going to do for little Stella?'

'I'll donate a month's profits to the fund.'

'I should cocoa!' Florrie said, and then, satisfied, turned back to face the stage. 'Go on then, Vicar,' she urged.

'I think we've about wrapped it up for the evening, actually,' he said. 'Well done, everyone, for the great ideas – and keep them coming. I'm sure we'll hit our target . . . and in fact, I confidently expect we'll exceed it. There are one or

149

two things that Cally has already ruled out, because of the expense. For instance, she would prefer to have a qualified nurse with her on the flight.'

'Here, did you say the hospital was in Boston?' Mrs Snowball interrupted suddenly.

'Yes,' I said.

'Well, then – our Jenny's boy, Kevin, and his family live near there and she goes to visit all the time. She can go with them, and no need to buy her a ticket.'

'That's a very kind offer,' Raffy said warmly. 'I'm sure you all know that Jenny, Florrie's daughter, is a retired nurse? We can discuss the arrangements later, but I feel we should certainly pay her return air fare.'

A strange, dragon-like hissing emanating from the door of the annexe, which had been growing ever louder for the last ten minutes, suddenly subsided and a woman stuck her head out and shouted, 'Tea's up!' before vanishing again.

'The ladies of the WI have kindly made us some refreshments, if you'd all like to go through to the annexe,' Raffy said.

'And perhaps you could all write down your names and contact details and give them to Laurence or Effie while you're having your tea,' Hebe suggested.

'Including email addresses, if you have them,' Laurence added quickly. He sounded like a bit of a silver surfer.

We let the first stampede go, then I led the way to where Celia and Will were waiting by the door. Effie Yatton was already there, taking down the contact details for anyone attempting a quick getaway.

'Sorry we have to dash, only one of the dogs has been a bit off colour and I don't want to be out too long,' Celia

150

said, giving me a hug and Jago an appraising look, followed by a warm smile. 'But it was a great meeting and I'm positive the money will be raised now.'

'I'm just really grateful you could both come,' I told her, before introducing Jago to them and to Miss Yatton, who was hovering interestedly.

'I've heard about your macaroon shop,' Will said. 'No free samples on you, I suppose?'

'Afraid not,' Jago replied, grinning. 'But I'll give some to Cally to pass on next time she comes to the shop and then you can try them out.'

'You are *so* cheeky,' Celia chided Will.

'I bought some and they're delicious,' Miss Yatton put in. 'Everyone was talking about them, so I simply had to.'

'I thought I'd seen you before,' Jago said to her, 'I'm glad you enjoyed them. They're my friend David's speciality really and it's his shop. I'm just helping him set up, but once his fiancée can move up here, I'll be able to find premises for my own business.'

Miss Yatton was clearly soaking all this news up like a sponge. 'Around here, I hope?' she said. 'What is *your* speciality?'

I left him describing the intricacies of croquembouche to her, which was likely to take some time, while I saw Celia and Will off. Then, when I got back, luckily someone else tried to escape without leaving their details and Miss Yatton abandoned Jago and leaped away in pursuit like a sprightly but elderly whippet, so we seized our chance to make for the annexe.

Hebe Winter and Laurence Yatton cornered Jago in a pincer movement when we came in and were probably interrogating him to within an inch of his life, just as Effie Yatton had done. I expected strangers were a novelty, and Will and Celia would have got the same treatment if they'd been able to stay.

'That went well, didn't it?' Raffy said, smiling benignly down at me when I paused to graze at the cheese sticks next to where he and Chloe were standing. 'But I knew it would – and we'll soon have the rest of the money raised, so don't worry any more about that, Cally.'

'Yes, we're all fired up and ready to go now,' agreed Chloe, who was small, dark, pretty and not yet obviously pregnant.

'I'm really, really touched that so many people have said they'll help Stella,' I said gratefully. 'You're all stars.'

'Stella's stars,' Jago agreed, having made his escape from Hebe and come to find me.

Chapter 15: What the Dickens?

Jago walked me back, which he'd insisted on, even after I'd assured him that villages didn't get safer than Sticklepond. Anyway, half the other residents were also heading home from the meeting, though most had set out a little before us.

'Yes, but your mother's cottage is quite secluded, isn't it?' he said. 'You have to go up a narrow, dark lane to get to it.'

'It is a bit, though it's not isolated, because the lane leads to the Ormerods' farm, and her friend Hal lives right opposite. There's a converted barn just beyond Ma's, too. Ma likes to be quiet and her own company, though actually lately she's been coming out of herself a bit, which I think is all due to Hal. She's joined the Gardening Club and even goes to the Green Man for the occasional game of darts in the evening.'

'A riot of dissipation,' he observed, grinning.

'Ottie Winter from the hall pops in sometimes too. She's older than Ma and a well-known sculptor, and she was instrumental in Ma going to art college in London. They've been friends ever since.'

'Ottie Winter?'

'Hebe Winter's identical twin sister, I told you earlier.'

'You mean there are *two* of them?' he demanded, looking alarmed.

'Ottie's not at all scary,' I assured him. 'She lives part of the year in Cornwall and the rest of the time in a converted coach house up at Winter's End, so she wasn't there tonight.'

'There seemed to be enough Winters without her.'

'I suppose there are,' I said, thinking about it. 'As well as Ottie and Hebe, there's Sophy, their great-niece. She inherited the estate fairly recently and then married Seth Greenwood, the head gardener. He wasn't there tonight, but Sophy was. Seth also runs his own gardening company; he's a knot garden specialist.'

'I have only the vaguest idea what a knot garden is,' Jago confessed.

'I'll have to take you up to Winter's End one of these days and show you the famous knot garden terraces then. And things get even more complicated with the Winter family relationships, because Seth Greenwood is Ottie's stepson. The other Winter there tonight was Sophy's daughter, Lucy. I haven't actually met her, but Ottie's told us a lot about her. She's taking over the management of the Winter's End estate and she lives in one of the lodges.'

'How do you know all these things?'

'I know all about the Winters because of Ottie being Ma's friend – and I did mention that Hal is under-gardener at Winter's End, didn't I?' I asked, and he groaned.

'Please, no more! Is everyone in the village linked in some way?'

'It does seem like it sometimes,' I admitted. 'I'm surprised

154

how many people in the area I actually know, or know *about*, considering I've only been here on holidays and the occasional weekend, till I moved in. But people do talk to you when you have a dog or a child with you, especially in the local shops.'

By now we were walking up the main street and fewer people were about. Ahead of us were Ivo Hawksley and his wife, Tansy, and beyond them the unmistakable figure of Gregory Lyon escorted Florrie Snowball up the stone step of the Falling Star and then turned and crossed the road to the square-fronted Victorian house attached to the Witchcraft Museum, where he lived. The door opened and shut twice, letting out a bright pool of light, because I think he'd got a fold of his long velvet cloak trapped in it.

Ivo and Tansy entered a patch of dense darkness between the sparse streetlights and suddenly vanished.

'Hey, where did they go?' demanded Jago, puzzled.

'Up Salubrious Passage. It leads to a little courtyard where they live behind Tansy's specialist wedding shoe shop, Cinderella's Slippers – see, there's the sign over the passageway,' I pointed out as we got near enough to make it out. 'Ivo used to live next door but once they married, they made it all into one cottage. She has *lovely* shoes,' I added wistfully.

'Did you say she specialised in wedding shoes? Sticklepond seems a small village to support a wedding shoe shop, not to mention a specialist chocolate shop,' Jago commented thoughtfully.

'I suppose so, but people will come for miles to a specialist wedding shop. And anyway, Sticklepond is booming like a gold rush town. Ever since they found evidence that Shakespeare was connected to Winter's End, the village is a tourist hotspot, especially in summer.'

I told him the story of all the exciting discoveries that Sophy Winter had made and that there was a history of witchcraft in the area. 'So now, more and more of the old shops are reopening – and then there's Gregory Lyon's Witchcraft Museum, and a tourist trail leaflet called the Sticklepond Saunter.'

'Tourists won't impulse-buy wedding shoes, though, will they?'

'Perhaps not, but there are an awful lot of weddings held at All Angels church. Apart from it being a beautiful old building, I think the idea of being married by Raffy Sinclair is quite an attraction.'

'Yes, I suppose that would be something special in the wedding album.'

'Tansy sells vintage shoes and all kinds of shoe-shaped gifts, too, not to mention the *Slipper Monkey* children's books she writes, which Stella adores. I've chatted to her quite a bit when I've looked around the shop and she said she advertises in all the wedding magazines and also on the internet. She'd started going to wedding fairs too, before she had Prospero.'

'*Prospero*?'

'Their baby. Unusual name, isn't it? It's from *The Tempest*, and since Ivo was a Shakespearian actor, I suppose that had something to do with it. You know, Prospero is one of the few boy babies I've seen around the village; they mostly seem to be girls.'

'Perhaps he's the start of a whole run of boys, then?'

'Maybe.'

'So, the wedding shoe business is doing well?' Jago said, reverting to the topic.

'Yes. Brides will travel for *miles* for the right shoes, and they can buy wedding favours there too, because she stocks specially made Chocolate Wishes shoes from Chloe Lyon's shop next to the Witchcraft Museum.'

'That's the vicar's wife, did you say?'

'Yes, and she's very nice, though since her grandfather is an avowed pagan and warlock, not to mention being the author of a lot of lurid Dennis Wheatley-style black magic novels, their engagement apparently caused a bit of a kerfuffle.'

'I expect it did,' Jago agreed, fascinated.

'Her Chocolate Wishes always have special messages in them, like a sort of lovely fortune cookie, and she does special chocolate angels to order with an angel card reading inside. She gave me one at Christmas and the message was very positive and uplifting.'

'I must go there and buy one: I've never heard of them before. In fact, I'd like to see both shops. They sound very enterprising.'

'Tansy has some really sweet little enamelled silver bluebirds, to sew inside wedding dresses for luck: for something blue,' I explained wistfully, because when I'd seen them I'd really wanted one. 'A bluebird means happiness too, so they're extra special. I think all the shoe-related odds and ends pull in any passing trade but most of her customers find her through the bridal magazines and the internet.'

'Yes, that's how I thought I'd get orders for my croquembouche, so I don't need to be in a town and I really don't want to have a shop too, like David. There's no one making them in the North-west and though I could only deliver them within about four hours' travelling time, maximum, that's still a wide catchment area.'

'So you could be based anywhere? It would be lovely if you were not too far away,' I added.

'Would it?' he asked, seriously.

'Of course, because without you there would be no one to talk *serious* cake with,' I said lightly, but truthfully. It was amazing how quickly I'd come to rely on both his friendship and support . . .

'That's true,' Jago agreed. 'I feel just the same and I can't believe I've only known you for less than a fortnight.' He slipped his arm through mine companionably and smiled down at me as we passed one of the sparse streetlights.

'What sort of premises are you looking for?' I asked, smiling back.

'I need a large preparation area for baking and creating the cakes, and a separate packing room would be good, too. I don't need a shop front, though if there was one I could use it for display purposes. Oh, and ideally I'd like to live on the premises. Those early morning starts are so much easier if you're already on the spot.'

'That's true! Has no local property caught your eye yet?'

'I haven't seriously looked so far, because I've been too busy helping David with the Happy Macaroon. The plan was that his fiancée would give up her job in a London hair salon and move up here to help him as soon as the business seemed to be taking off, by which time *I* should have found my own place and moved out – but it took off like a rocket so Sarah's already handed in her notice.'

'So you need to get a move on and find somewhere quickly?'

'Even more so now, because David's mother, who's worked as a shop assistant in a bakery in Southport for more than thirty years, has just been told they're closing down and all the staff will be made redundant. So she's going to be working in the shop full time soon and they really won't need me any more.'

'We'd better get looking quickly then, and find you somewhere of your own!'

'I think I'd like to be in a village,' he said thoughtfully. 'David will keep my model in his window and take any orders, so I'll still have that connection when I start up, and if he is run off his feet with macaroon orders, I can help him. In fact, he's been asked so many times if he does traditional iced wedding cakes, he's thinking of offering those, too, so he probably will still need a hand with the baking from time to time.'

'Perhaps you should look here in Sticklepond,' I said, half joking, because it would be nice to have him nearby. 'Only I'm not sure there's much for sale here.'

He nodded ahead. 'I can see a For Sale sign right over there . . . though *what* it's selling is a mystery,' he continued, because we'd now left the last lamppost behind us and the sign was pointing to a tall and very narrow slice of building set well back in the dense darkness between two much taller and more substantial ones.

Jago had taken out a thin, credit-card-sized torch and the pale beam roamed over a minute shop front overhung by an upper storey set with a very Dickensian diamond-paned window.

'You know, I've never even noticed that was here before,' I exclaimed. 'Maybe it just sprang up this minute, like something in *Harry Potter*?'

'"Honey's Haberdashers",' he read, moving the torch beam over the faded shop board. Even in that weak light the paint around the door and windows was clearly peeling and the place looked as if it had been sleeping, or perhaps *rotting*, undisturbed for a century.

'Whatever it was, it doesn't look like the sort of place you need. It's a tiny frontage.'

'No, I expect you're right, but I'll see if there's anything else for sale in Sticklepond tomorrow.' He switched off the torch and put it back in his pocket. 'After all, if there's so much already going on in Sticklepond, it seems the ideal spot, doesn't it? I think I'm sold on the idea. And Aimee would hate it . . .' he added thoughtfully.

'Is that good?' I questioned cautiously.

'Oh, yes, because when she turned up yesterday she seemed to think she and I could just pick up where we left off, and I'd hightail it back to London. Once I've bought a place up here, she'll see that I'm making a new life without her.'

'Doesn't she like the North?'

'No – not that it matters what she likes or not, because there's no way we're getting back together, even if she cries over me for a week.'

He sounded pretty definite, and from what David had said, I found myself hoping he meant it and wouldn't fall for this Aimee's charms all over again.

'She used to be big on the London party scene, but since her father's cut off most of her allowance she's had

160

to take a job with a London-based corporate events firm now – all the more reason for me to stay up here in Lancashire,' he added lightly, though I still wasn't sure quite how he really felt about the sudden reappearance of his lost love.

We were walking up the dark lane now, nearly home, and I said gratefully, 'Thank you again for all you've done, Jago. You gave me hope and started the ball rolling with the fundraising.'

'The only thanks I need is for you to meet me for lunch in the Blue Dog next Saturday,' he suggested.

'I will if Ma and Hal will keep an eye on Stella,' I agreed. 'We'll probably come to Ormskirk for the market on Thursday too, even though the hospital don't want to see Stella till the following week. We like having a wander round it and she's bound to want to come and get another ginger-bread pig.'

'The hospital must have been pleased with her, if they don't want to see her for a fortnight?'

'Yes, and I'm sure the country air is doing her good. She's even put on a little weight.'

'It's bound to be better for her, though *you* must miss the bright lights?'

'Oddly enough, not at all! I suppose since Stella arrived my life had entirely changed anyway. Even Toto's a lot happier here, with a big garden and lots of long walks.'

We'd arrived at the garden gate by then and he would have declined my invitation to come in, because he said he could see I was tired and drained after the evening's events, except that Ma opened the door before he could get away.

'If that's this Jago you keep on about, then bring him in,' she ordered.

In the sitting room she subjected him to one of her penetrating though abstracted stares, as if he was a possible subject for one of her paintings, which he withstood pretty well.

'Tell Ma all about the meeting, Jago, while I go and make us some tea – unless you'd like something stronger?'

'No, tea would be fine. I have to drive back.'

I looked in on Stella on the way, who was fast asleep clutching Bun, as usual.

When I went back with the tea and some garibaldi biscuits I'd made earlier to a slightly different recipe, Ma seemed to be getting on well with Jago – this, with Ma, being measured by the fact she didn't immediately head for her garden room when I came back, but took a cup of tea and a biscuit.

So I asked her if she knew about the shop for sale we'd seen and she said she remembered it open in her childhood, but had no idea what had happened to the last of the Honeys.

She seemed a little perturbed by the question, murmuring, 'And is there Honey still for tea?' as she drifted out of the room carrying her tea, with the garibaldi balanced on the saucer.

'Oh dear,' Jago said, taking this as his cue to leave. 'Perhaps I'd better go.'

'It's all right, Ma prefers to go and watch TV on her own in the other room, and I watch TV or work in here in the evenings. Unless you have to rush away we could put a film on? That's what I'd do tonight anyway, because I'm too tired to do any work. I could make popcorn.'

'That's the clincher,' he said, sitting down again. 'It would give David and Sarah a bit more time together, too.'

We decided on *Love Actually*, though he said he always felt so sorry for Emma Thompson he wanted to hit her screen husband.

'That secretary who seduces him reminds me of Aimee,' he said.

'Why, is she dark and pretty?'

'No, she's tall, very slim and fair. I meant the amoral bit,' he said slightly morosely.

After we'd watched the film, sitting cosily together on the sofa with the bowl of popcorn between us, he said he'd better go since I was pretty sleepy by then: it had been a busy and quite emotional day.

'That Winter's End you mentioned, with the knot gardens – I'd love to see it. I don't suppose you fancied going with me tomorrow?'

'I would have, but it doesn't open on Sundays.'

'Oh? They must lose a lot of trade closing then.'

'I expect so, but that's how they like it. They're closed Mondays too, unless it's a Bank Holiday. Do you like visiting old houses?'

'Yes, very much – and gardens, though I know nothing about them.'

'So do Stella and I. But tomorrow I was thinking of taking her to see the new Hemlock Mill nature reserve over towards Ormskirk that everyone keeps telling me about. I don't suppose you'd like to come with us there instead?'

'I'd love to. Shall I pick you both up?'

'Better if you leave your car here and come in mine, because otherwise we'll have to move the child seat, which is fiddly.'

'Good thinking.'

We arranged a time and then, with a jaunty, 'See you tomorrow,' he kissed my cheek and walked off into the starry night.

Jago

Walking back, the village silent under the dark, velvety, star-studded night sky, Jago felt he would have sensed the sparkle of magic in the air even if Cally hadn't told him the history of the place was bound up with witchcraft.

It certainly wasn't the kind of village he could imagine Aimee living in, so perhaps it would protect him from falling under her spell again? Though actually, that didn't seem possible any more, since that moment in the café when he'd suddenly lost the rosy-tinted glasses of love and seen her as she really was, an ageing, petulant Daddy's princess. It had been a bit of a shock.

It was all very well for David to tell him to give her her marching orders, but he felt sorry for her and he just didn't have it in him to be that brutal. No, he'd try and let her down gently, while hoping she found someone else, someone more on her wavelength.

He'd never been to Sticklepond before, but even after only a couple of months in the area he'd certainly heard a lot about it, some of it a little odd . . . and now he'd observed some of the villagers in action, he was more inclined to believe the rumours.

The place was undeniably attractive and would be great to live in, but if it was an up-and-coming tourist hotspot, then he might already be too late to find the right property at a price he could afford.

He was level with that For Sale sign again and on impulse stopped and sent the small beam of his torch searching out Honey's Haberdashers. He half-expected the narrow, bow-windowed frontage beneath an overhanging upper storey, set slightly back between the large windows of a café and the Witch Craft Gallery, to have vanished again.

But no, there it was, surely too small and totally unsuitable for his purposes, but he made a mental note of the estate agent's name anyway.

Chapter 16: Puffball

At breakfast on Sunday Ma told me a little more about how the villagers had united to fight off a business consortium who wanted to turn the old Hemlock cotton mill site into a retail park. I did vaguely remember her telling me at the time, but I expect I was too occupied with Stella to take a lot of notice.

Force for Nature, the animal rights group, had backed them and then, thanks to the generosity of an anonymous benefactor, the site had been bought and was in the process of being made into a nature reserve.

'There turned out to be lots of wildlife of various kinds on the site – it's quite a big area, river and a bit of woodland – and some of it was endangered,' Ma went on, buttering her toast lavishly. 'I went over there with Hal last autumn, because the colours of the foliage were really something.'

That perhaps explained where the inspiration came from for the series of paintings of angels with fish faces whirling about in the water instead of the sky, though I think portraying innocent little red squirrels as devilish imps is a bit mean.

Stella had eaten most of her boiled egg and soldiers and

was now drinking orange juice and watching in fascination as Ma prepared her toast. 'I do love you, Grandma! You're funny.'

'Thank you, darling, I love you too,' Ma said, then took a bite of toast. A look of surprise crossed her face. 'Cally, I think this jam has gone off.'

'You put Marmite on top of lemon and lime marmalade,' Stella pointed out. 'And your cigarette's in the coffee.'

Ma fished out the soggy pink Sobranie and put it on the edge of the stove to dry out, before rinsing her cup and pouring herself another coffee.

'You shouldn't smoke, it's bad for you,' Stella said severely. 'Your insides go black, because they're covered in treacle. I saw a picture at the hospital.'

'Don't start,' Ma said. 'I told you, I'm down to two a day now. Everyone's entitled to a little pleasure in their lives.'

Stella looked disapproving, but didn't say anything else and Ma drank her coffee down, then got up, stuck the empty jade holder back in her mouth and went on up to the studio, taking the Marmite and marmalade toast with her.

When we got to the Hemlock Mill nature reserve and I'd looked on the big information board with a map of the various paths, I thought it would be tricky with the buggy, so we left it in the car.

After what Ma said, I wasn't entirely surprised at how much progress they had made. A prefabricated wooden tourist centre had gone up practically overnight and walk-ways were partly laid through the grounds, which ran up the side of the river Ches to woodland.

There were lots of things for Stella to look at, from puffball toadstools to the red squirrels, boldly and gracefully bounding between the trees, and it was nice to have Jago with us – especially once she tired and he carried her the rest of the way.

She wound her arms around his neck and looked at him adoringly from time to time, even when he floundered while answering classic Stella questions like, 'Why are trees up and not down?' and 'Why are clouds?'

'Trees are down as well, you just can't see them,' he said. 'Their roots spread out under the soil as wide as the branches do at the top of the tree trunk. And clouds carry water vapour about from one place to the other . . . sort of.' He looked down at her. 'How old did you say you were? Ten?'

She giggled. 'Nearly four. If we saw a dragonfly close up, would it look like a dragon?'

'No, it would look like an insect,' I told her. 'They might have a picture of one in the nature centre . . . and I hope they've got a café too, because I'd love a cup of coffee. Why don't we have a very quick peep into the old house and then go and see?'

The former mill manager's house was in the process of being renovated and restored to how it would have looked in Victorian times, according to the notice in the tiled hall. The main rooms were freshly painted in period colours, or papered in William Morris patterns and matching curtains had been hung. There wasn't much furniture yet, so there wasn't a lot to look at.

A back door from a large, bare kitchen led to a cobbled courtyard with substantial outbuildings round three sides where, according to another sign, they hoped to recreate an authentic Victorian shop or two.

'I've seen something similar in Ironbridge,' Jago said. 'That idea could work well here, too.'

'They seem very enterprising,' I agreed. 'They've already done so much in such a short space of time.'

But by now we were *all* flagging, so we went into the tourist centre, where we diverted into the gift shop area long enough for Jago, who was now putty in Stella's hands, to buy her a stuffed toy red squirrel. Then he insisted on paying for lunch in the tea room.

'I'll buy lunch next time,' I said. 'I mean . . . if you'd like to come out with us again, that is?'

'I'd love to, I've really enjoyed today.'

'We could go and look at Rufford Old Hall next Sunday, then, if you fancy it?' I suggested. 'It's a National Trust property, over near the Martin Mere bird reserve, and there are rumours that Shakespeare stayed there during the lost years . . . except that now, of course, after finding that document up at Winter's End, they think it might have been there instead.'

'I didn't even know he *had* lost years,' Jago confessed. 'Stella, do you like going to see very old houses?'

She nodded. 'They're where princesses live.'

'Right. It's a date then, Princess Stella,' he said, and she giggled.

The walk had done her good, for there were faint pink roses in her cheeks. Over her head my eyes met Jago's light brown ones and we smiled, like conspirators.

When Stella was getting ready for bed that evening, she insisted that her toy white mouse family should be ranged on her bedside table to listen to her bedtime story. After I'd fetched those and she was tucked up under her pink duvet, with Bun on one side and the red squirrel that Jago had bought her on the other, and I was finally about to open the Moomins and start reading, she asked out of the blue, 'Is Jago my daddy?'

'What?' I said, taken by surprise. 'No, darling! I've told you, your daddy lives at the North Pole, because he has to count all the penguins. But one day when he's finished counting them, I expect he'll come and visit you.'

'Is he a penguin, too?'

'No, of course not. If your daddy was a penguin, you'd have webbed feet and a beak, wouldn't you?'

'Would I?' she murmured drowsily. 'I don't think I want a penguin daddy. I like Daddy Jago best . . . '

I thought it better not to say any more about it at that point, because although phenomenally bright for nearly four, she was clearly too tired to take in any explanations. I opened the Moomins and began to read.

Jago rang me on Monday morning, just as I was getting Stella ready for the Mother and Toddler group again. I was in the kitchen with Ma, putting my shoes on, and Stella had dashed off to fetch her scarlet mack, because it was a gloomy, rainy day.

Jago said how much he'd enjoyed the day out and then added, 'You know that old shop in Sticklepond we saw on the way back from the meeting on Saturday night?'

'If you can call a frontage about five feet wide, hidden between two bigger buildings, a shop, then yes.'

'I popped round to the estate agents as soon as they opened

this morning – they have a branch here – and I've got the details.'

'That was quick work.'

'I thought they might have something more suitable in Sticklepond, but that was the only thing in my price range. Apparently prices there are going up and up. Anyway, Honey's Haberdashers sounds bigger in the leaflet than it looks, so I've got an appointment to view it this afternoon at two thirty. I'm meeting the estate agent there. I don't suppose you'd like to come too, out of sheer curiosity?'

I wavered. 'Stella usually has a nap around then . . . and I'm really curious to see it.' I covered the receiver and asked Ma, who was sitting pensively staring out of the window at the heavy rain, coffee cup in hand, if she would be in this afternoon and could listen out in case Stella woke.

'Yes, I'll be here. Ottie's back at Winter's End and she said she'd drop in this afternoon. We're thinking of a joint retrospective exhibition in the autumn and need to discuss it.'

'Oh, thanks, Ma. I'll make you something nice for you both to have with your coffee,' I promised, and then uncovered the phone again.

'I heard that, that's great,' Jago said. 'Shall we meet outside the shop just before two thirty, or would you like me to pick you up? It looks like the monsoon has struck.'

'I like walking in the rain. I'll see you there.'

When I'd put the phone down, I said to Ma, 'I do love looking at other people's houses. Jago's got an appointment to explore Honey's Haberdashers.'

'Honey's?' she said, and a brief unease seemed to pass across her face. The unlit lilac Sobranie at the corner of her mouth wavered in its holder.

'Yes – remember we said the other night that we'd spotted that it was for sale? You know the place, don't you?'

'Of course I know it. It was still in business when I was small, though mostly it was the older people in the village who favoured it, because I don't think some of the stock had changed much since Victorian times.'

'I'll tell you all about it afterwards,' I promised.

'I heard the last of the Honeys was in a care home somewhere,' she said. 'Perhaps she's died and that's why it's finally for sale.'

'It's odd it hasn't been sold long since to pay the care home bill then, isn't it?' I said, thinking about it. 'I mean, practically everyone seems to lose their homes if they go into care. It seems very unfair.'

'Yes: no inheritance for the offspring. If that happens to me, Cally, then you won't get anything at all, because your father's pension will go with me. There'll just be this house and maybe a few paintings.'

'I wasn't counting on it anyway, Ma, especially since you're not much past sixty, which is the new middle age!'

'Tell that to my knees,' she grumbled. Then she went out to the studio, holding an enormous, vividly striped golfing umbrella with two broken spikes over her head and I went to find out where Stella had got to.

Inspired by the big puffball toadstools we'd seen at the nature reserve, I'd made microwave meringues that morning and written them up for 'Tea & Cake'.

Microwave meringue – how great an invention is that?
All you need is icing sugar and egg white to create

173

mouth-watering morsels of deliciousness that magically puff up in seconds.

I'd intended to take some to playgroup with us, but when I opened the box Ma had beaten me to it and there were only a few crumbs left.

Chapter 17: Honeyed

Stella was so tired after playgroup that she was falling asleep over her lunch, but there was no sign of Ma, so after I'd tucked Stella up in bed for a nap I had to fetch her down from the studio. She'd forgotten both that she was listening out for Stella and that Ottie was coming over.

I showed her the covered plates of fruit fairy cakes and some egg and cress sandwiches. Ottie always had a very healthy appetite, despite being as thin as a lath.

Life was unfair like that. *I* was now starting to feel like some strange mutant cross between one of those puffball mushrooms and the microwave meringues they'd inspired.

I thought all this would make me late meeting Jago at the shop, but actually he and I and the estate agent all arrived more or less at the same time, each with our own umbrellas, which we folded and stood in the small, open porch. They instantly formed pools on the red quarry tiles.

The young estate agent ('Call-me-Charlie') looked like a pale and acned version of Brad Pitt, though he wouldn't have lasted five minutes with Angelina Jolie. He seemed gloomy as he inserted a large key into the door and then put his shoulder to it, moving a small Everest of junk mail out of the way.

'Haven't had a viewing for a couple of weeks,' he said apologetically, though I thought months was more like it, if at all. 'Usually Conrad from the Merchester office does Sticklepond viewings, because his family come from round here.'

He didn't say why that was a good thing, but gestured us past him into the darkness of the shop. Our feet thudded dully on the wooden floor and the air was so fogged and thick with dust particles that our lungs were probably instantly flocked.

The blinds were down over the shop window but no one suggested pulling them up to let in more light, because clearly there was a more than even chance that the cord had rotted and the whole thing would come crashing down.

It was a narrow shop, though Jago was right and it was wider than it had first appeared. It also seemed to stretch back an awfully long way. An L-shaped counter loomed in the gloom and above it to the left were glass-fronted display cabinets that were too shrouded in grime to make out the contents.

'The electricity's off, I'm afraid – pity it's such a dismal day,' the estate agent apologised. 'Still, I've got my torch.'

He sent the beam darting to and fro, illuminating a jar of knitting needles, an old wooden till drawer, some mannequin busts still draped with fifties-style blouses and a lot of hand-lettered signs on metal stands in pounds, shillings and pence – and one in guineas.

'Wow!' said Jago.

'Good heavens,' I exclaimed. 'It's like a time warp.'

In fact, the shop looked just as it must have done for many years before it was shut up, somewhere around the late sixties, but with the addition of a ton of dust and the cobwebs that hung like bad macramé from the light fitting and added an extra layer of darkness to the ceiling corners.

I was pretty sure some of the cobwebs must still have their occupants in residence, so I inched closer to Jago, in case one of them made a sudden move towards me.

Call-me-Charlie coughed hollowly. I'm not sure if the dust was getting to him, or it was simply the preface to the estate-agent speak he was about to come out with. Probably a bit of both.

'Obviously the place has been a *little* neglected since the last of the Honeys was taken to a nursing home, after breaking her hip.'

'What century was that in?' asked Jago. He had taken his own small credit card-shaped torch from his pocket and was casting it about in a fascinated sort of way.

'The last one. I suppose it was about thirty years ago,' Charlie confessed with a sudden grin. 'She's a hundred and two now, and still going strong.'

'So it's just been locked up and left ever since?' I asked, surprised.

'I think she expected to return one day, but never did. But there was a lodger in the flat over the shop until fairly recently so the roof and guttering have been maintained annually.'

'It smells dry enough in here, too,' Jago observed.

'I'm surprised the place wasn't sold to pay for the nursing home fees,' I commented.

'I think she's quite well off, because the nursing home she

lives in is *very* expensive. Of course, she was getting rent for the flat at one time, too, and I suspect it was the lodger leaving that finally prompted her to put the property on the market.'

'It says in the details that the shop will be sold as a going concern, with stock,' Jago said, flourishing the brochure.

'Y-eees . . .' Charlie said apologetically. 'Of course, that's not possible, which I've done my best to explain to Miss Honey, but she hasn't been back here, and in her mind I think it's just as it was when she was young.'

'Since it clearly *isn't* a going concern, though, the price seems a little high,' Jago said. 'That must have put people off.'

'Of course, though these things are always negotiable and it *is* a good village. Prices in Sticklepond are rising and new businesses opening all the time.'

'I don't particularly want a shop, but a display window would be nice,' Jago said. 'I make a particular kind of wedding cake, so I need a preparation area and also a packing room and perhaps office space.'

'Ah, not any kind of drapery or haberdashery then . . .' Charlie said, seeming to be musing on some knotty problem. Then he got back into agent mode: 'Come on, I'll show you the rest.'

There was a door at the back, half-covered by a thick, moth-eaten curtain with a once-gold bullion fringe, which led into a living room containing more cobwebs, an open fireplace with a pretty art nouveau tiled surround, a large and ugly dark dresser and a small organ with a rotted ruched pink silk front.

'It says in the particulars that the house is to be sold

part-furnished,' Jago said, straight-faced. 'What with the shop a going concern and some furniture thrown in, I'm only surprised no one has snapped the place up before now.'

'Try explaining that to Miss Honey,' Call-me-Charlie muttered morosely. Then he readjusted his agent's expression and led the way upstairs to the front bedroom, which had old wooden panelling and the window that overhung the shop.

'Most of this room is as it was in the seventeenth century,' the agent said, 'but the rest of the house has been rebuilt and extended over the years.'

There were two more good-sized bedrooms and a bleak bathroom, but once we'd seen those, Charlie seemed reluctant to go up the final flight of stairs to the small flat under the eaves.

I could see the reason for his reluctance once the door was open, for every wall was lined with a towering stack of yellowing newspapers to waist height or higher. You could smell the old newsprint in the air.

'I'm afraid the lodger went a bit strange during the last few years . . . but it's a good flat, it just needs a *little* updating.'

'Just a little,' agreed Jago, drily.

We trooped back down again. Charlie led the way through the bare kitchen into a smaller room that contained nothing more than an old galvanised washtub with a wooden dolly standing in it, and unlocked the back door. Across a strip of old stone flags a long, low building faced us.

'This must be the "attached outbuildings providing further self-contained accommodation",' Jago suggested, and Charlie nodded. The last of his assumed enthusiasm had long died and I don't think he expected anything to come of this viewing other than a dry-cleaning bill for his now-grubby suit.

'Yes, and it was also let for several years, though not as recently as the flat. It would make a perfect granny annexe.'

'I haven't got a granny,' Jago said.

'Or holiday let,' Charlie suggested hastily.

The annexe was minute, with a bathroom that had obviously been created by knocking through into the outside toilet and coal house and inserting into the resultant space the smallest bath I'd ever seen. It was occupied by the largest *spider* I'd ever seen, too.

'Oh my God, it's moving!' I cried, grabbing Jago's arm tightly.

'I'll save you,' he said, grinning.

'My hero!'

Charlie glanced at his watch and then quickly ushered us outside into a bramble-smothered wilderness. 'The garden, with vehicle access at the rear and garage. Well, there we have it,' he added, and then abandoned us the moment he'd locked the shop door to dash off to what he obviously hoped would be a more fruitful viewing.

We brushed ourselves down and I got Jago to check there weren't any spiders on the back of my coat.

'At least it's stopped raining,' he said. 'Have you got time for a quick cup of coffee in the café next door?'

'I think so. Ma's friend Ottie Winter is coming round and we haven't been out all that long. Call-me-Charlie didn't exactly let us linger in the house, did he?'

'No, he abandoned hope pretty quickly, for an estate agent.'

Over coffee and a cake apiece, we discussed the house and shop.

'There's lots more accommodation to it than I expected, though it's spread out a bit,' Jago said, examining his Florentine with the eye of a connoisseur.

'Yes, it's so narrow, yet it goes back for miles. I love the seventeenth-century bits at the front.'

'It may be big, but the price is still way too high, considering it *isn't* a going concern and the whole place wants painting, decorating and generally dragging into the twenty-first century.'

'I don't really think it's what you had in mind,' I agreed, licking icing off my fingers in an unladylike way. I'd had a vanilla slice, Ma's favourite, and very good it was too. 'There were some lovely authentic period features, though, like that cast-iron fireplace in the downstairs living room, with the pink and turquoise tiled surround.'

'You're right, it's *not* what I had in mind at all, but there's something about it I really like . . .' he said thoughtfully. 'And the shop is certainly big enough for a kitchen and preparation area, if it was properly arranged.'

'You're not seriously considering it, are you?' I asked him.

'Well, not at *that* price, obviously, because it's right at my limit so I wouldn't have enough left to renovate and equip the business. But the village does sound perfect, especially since there's already one specialist wedding shop.'

'You could always make Miss Honey a really cheeky offer and see what happens,' I suggested. 'If you got it, I could help you do it up. It'd be fun, and it would be nice having you living nearby.'

He smiled. 'I might just do that – but a really low offer. I got the impression she was a bit of a battle-axe, though, didn't you?'

'Yes, but you're a cash buyer, after all, so that might tempt her. But it would need a lot doing to it before you could move in, let alone start up your business there, and you want to move quite quickly, don't you?'

'Ideally. The Happy Macaroon has taken off so much faster than we could have ever hoped for that David's fiancée's going to move up to Ormskirk at the end of June. His mother, Dorrie, started working in the shop today too and I think she and Sarah will be able to handle it between them. It's just as well, really, because David's getting a surprising number of orders for his macaroon party pyramids and I've had a few more for my croquembouches, too, so we can't be serving in the shop and doing those at the same time.'

'And I suppose you're competing for space in the bakery, if you both have orders?'

'Yes, and in the flat.'

'Then Honey's wouldn't be ideal, would it, because you'd have so much to do first.'

'Oh, I don't know. If I could buy it at a reasonable price, then I'd be able to afford to get workmen in to sort it out quickly. And as soon as part of it's habitable I can move in and oversee the installation of the preparation area, which is the important thing. There's a steady trickle of orders now, so I'll probably be run off my feet with them by next spring, when we move into the wedding season.'

'I'll apply for the post of assistant then,' I joked, but then, with the sudden dread that could strike chills up my spine at any moment, added, 'though who knows what will have happened by then? Stella will have had her operation and . . .'

Jago took my hand in his and looked down into my eyes, his caramel ones sympathetic.

'Everything's going to be fine, you'll see,' he said in his soft, comforting, mellow voice. 'By Christmas Stella will have had the operation and she'll be home again, well on the way to total recovery.'

I clung to that thought.

Jago

'I've just been through a time warp into the late sixties,' Jago told David when he went back to the bakery behind the Happy Macaroon, where his friend was packing three hundred little silver boxes with macaroon wedding favours while Dorrie, his mother, minded the shop.

Jago washed his hands at the sink in the corner and then went to help his friend.

'What, this shop you were viewing in Sticklepond?' David asked. 'I thought you said it looked tiny.'

'It does have a very narrow frontage, but it goes back forever, so it was like stepping into the Tardis. There's a house behind the shop with a small separate flat in the attic storey and a minute annexe at the back.'

'What sort of nick is it in?'

'Neglected, but basically sound, I think. The décor in the main part of the house is Victorian, but the flat and cottage are sixties style, so the wiring to the whole house might have been updated,' Jago said optimistically.

'Or then again, it could all be Bakelite two-pin plugs,' David pointed out. 'But even if it was rewired in the sixties, it'd need doing again and that's expensive.'

'I know, and then it would need replastering once that was done.' Jago inserted a pink and a white macaroon into a tiny silver box and pushed the lid closed, before reaching for another. 'The whole place would need a lot of money spent on it. You should see the shop, for a start. It might have been closed up and abandoned in the late sixties, but most of the stock dates back to just after the war, I should think . . . and some of it well before.'

He told David about the elderly owner, Miss Honey, who thought it could be sold as a going concern. 'She must be deluded, because I shouldn't think there was much of a turnover even by the time it shut.'

'Well, even if it was a viable business, you don't want a haberdashery shop,' David said. 'Though I wouldn't have thought you wanted it at all – didn't you say viewing it was a very long shot?'

'I did,' admitted Jago, 'but now I can see its potential. But although it's cheap for Sticklepond, the asking price is still right up to my top limit, so there wouldn't be any money left to do it up.'

'I've heard it's a bit pricey out there. I think it's quite a thriving tourist village now.'

'Yes, and there are lots of shops, including a specialist wedding shoe one, oddly enough. Although most of my orders will come through the website or the adverts in wedding magazines, I might still get some passing trade.'

'You're really keen on it,' David said, then added, 'I can't see Aimee settling down in a small Lancashire village!'

'No – but then, she won't be asked to,' Jago said. 'Come to think of it, she hasn't rung, has she? So maybe she's found someone new.'

David gave a slightly guilty glance at the answering machine. 'Perhaps she has,' he agreed. 'So, are you going to put in an offer for the shop?'

'Yes, but a really, really low one, so I can afford to do it up.'

'What did Cally think?'

'The same as me: it grew on her. She said she'd like it if I was living out there, too.'

'That sounds keen! Who knows what will happen if you're living right on her doorstep,' David teased.

'Come on, you know we're only friends,' Jago protested, though he went slightly pink. 'It may feel as if I've known her for years, but it really isn't any time at all.'

'No, but considering how often you talk on the phone, or text or email or—'

'Even if I *did* want more,' Jago interrupted him, 'talking cake with me is just a distraction for Cally – she's too focused on Stella and the fundraising to think of anything else. And I know that when Stella's well again, Cally will be hightailing it back to London to pick up her career.'

'I suppose you're right. Pity, though, because she's so much nicer than Aimee . . . and speak of the devil, she *did* ring again while you were out,' David confessed (though not to all the other calls he'd deleted). 'I told her you'd gone out with a friend. A female friend.'

'Did she say what she wanted?'

'She didn't have to, because it's obvious. I'm hoping you won't be a soft-hearted pushover and let her muscle back in on your life, or you'll find yourself back in London, in a flat mortgaged to the hilt and competing with Gilligan's for business from rented premises.'

Jago shuddered. 'No way! She's crazy if she thinks that

saying, "Oh, whoops, I made a teeny mistake running off before our wedding, but never mind, it's all on again, isn't it?" is going to work.'

'Good. I'd settle for a place of your own up here and friendship with Cally. You've got much more in common. And *you're* almost as focused on the fundraising for Stella as she is now, so you couldn't let her down.'

'No, I think she's going to continue to need a lot of support,' Jago said.

David had been worried at first that his friend might fall for Cally and have his heart broken all over again, but he'd quickly realised that the attraction between them was mutual, even if Cally seemed unaware of it. In fact, when Sarah saw them coming in from the Blue Dog that first time, she'd said they seemed so comfortable together they might have been married for years. Then there were the constant texts, emails and calls between them, as if they needed that tenuous link of contact. It seemed to David that Jago talking cake with Cally was both a comfort and a kind of courtship, and though he wasn't sure how it would all turn out once the little girl was – please God – better again, if that bitch Aimee didn't scupper things, they just might get together . . .

'I just want Stella to have her operation and be well again. I'm fond of her already, she's such a lovely, bright little girl, and she says the funniest things,' Jago said with a grin.

'So, you're going to make an offer for the shop in Sticklepond?' David asked, getting back to the original subject.

'Yes – in fact, I'm going to ring the estate agent as soon as we've finished boxing these up. I'm a cash buyer, after all, so Miss Honey might take a low offer.'

'If it's been on the market for ages, there should be room for negotiation,' said David.

'If I bought it, I'd be spending a lot of time out there overseeing the renovations and I'd move in as soon as part of it was habitable, though if you don't mind, I'd have to keep doing my cake making here for quite a while.'

'Of course I don't mind, and Sarah, Mum and I can easily manage the Happy Macaroon between us, so long as you carry on giving me a hand with rush orders?'

'I'll always do that. You know, this could all work out really well – if they accept my offer!'

'Then you'd better go and ring the estate agents and make it, while I finish these,' David said, thinking it would be great if his friend was living nearby – and even better if that meant he managed to get rid of the leech-like Aimee.

He wondered if he'd been right or wrong to hint earlier to Aimee that Jago had a new love interest up here. And he also wondered if Jago had actually told her *exactly* how much he had won on the lottery, or if perhaps she was still under the delusion that they had become millionaires with modest aspirations. Perhaps, if he got a chance, he'd tell her himself.

Chapter 18: Pinker's End

'I put in a really low offer on that shop in Sticklepond yesterday when I got back to the Happy Macaroon,' Jago said when he rang me next morning.

'You *have*?' I was so surprised I almost choked on the mouthful of brandy snap I was taste-testing. 'You don't hang about, do you? I mean, you said you liked it, but it wants a huge amount doing to it.'

'I know, but if Miss Honey accepts the offer so I've got enough money left, then I'm sure I could at least move in there pretty quickly, even if getting the cake preparation area sorted would take a lot longer.'

'It certainly would,' I agreed, thinking about all that ancient, moth-eaten stock in the shop, not to mention a few drawbacks in the rest of the house, like the dodgy wiring, ancient plumbing, or the hermit's skyscraper stacks of old newspapers in the attic.

'If the offer is accepted, I'll have to see what the surveyor's report says, so let's hope it's mainly cosmetic.'

'It smelled dry, and I didn't notice that it was falling down a hole, or you could see through the roof or anything,' I said helpfully.

How lovely it would be having him living in the village, even if by the time the renovations were done and he'd moved in, I'd probably be thinking about going back to London . . . if everything went well, that was.

As always when I thought of autumn and what it would bring for Stella, I felt shivery, even though I knew I was doing the right thing . . .

I shook off the negative thoughts and got back to the subject in hand. 'When will you know if she's accepted your offer or not? I assume it *is* down to Miss Honey? She isn't gaga or anything?'

'Well, that's the thing – she may be a hundred and two, but she sounds sharp as a tack and she insists on meeting me before considering my offer. She's still under the illusion that the shop can be sold as a going concern, so I'll have to convince her otherwise. The estate agent says mine isn't the first offer; he's already tried and failed more than once.'

'Mmm, tricky, then.'

'She's asked me to go and see her at her nursing home, at three this afternoon, though it was more by way of a royal summons, really, and I wondered . . . could you possibly come with me? *Please?*' he begged. 'Only I'm terrified and I need you to hold my hand.'

'I'm sure you don't, really. Weren't you mainly raised by your grandmother?'

'Yes, but she was the cosy sort, while Miss Honey sounds anything but as sweet as her name. Please come with me,' he wheedled.

'Oh, I don't know . . . I'm already feeling guilty at leaving Ma baby-sitting so often and I'm always worried she'll forget and go up to the studio. But actually, I suppose Stella will have woken from her nap by the time we leave, so she could go up there with her.'

'Could you ask her? It would make me feel better if you came with me.'

'All right. I'll get back to you in a bit.'

Asked, Ma said I was welcome to take Stella up to the studio when she woke, because she was no trouble. Hal had started making a village for her animal toy families on an old coffee table in the corner, with moss and a couple of broken plant pots, so she would probably quite happily play with that.

When I left Stella with Ma, along with sandwiches and chocolate apricot flapjacks, she'd already begun adorning her table-top village with a jar of seashells, while her rabbit and mouse families stood at the edge, waiting to move in. Ma was engrossed in her latest canvas – yet more bird-angels and another red squirrel-imp thing. Very odd.

'Are you two going to be all right?' I asked, turning at the door. 'Will you remember to eat the sandwiches and cake?'

'Don't worry, Mummy,' Stella said seriously. 'I'll look after Grandma.'

She probably would, too.

Jago's car was waiting to pick me up in the lane and we set off for Pinker's End, though any name with End in it seemed an unfortunate choice for a retirement home.

Jago had an ancient Saab estate car. I'd never seen one quite that shape and I was surprised he hadn't swapped it for something glossy and new when he won the lottery, but when I asked him he seemed surprised and said actually, this *was* the car he'd chosen with his winnings.

'I've always liked these old Saabs, and it's been completely renovated.'

'It is a nice car,' I agreed. 'Chloe's grandfather at the Witchcraft Museum has one a little bit like it.'

'Has he?' Jago asked, interested. 'I'd like to see that. But I think I'll have to buy a little van soon too, and rig out the back to make transporting the cakes easier.'

'Yes, that would be much more practical and you can advertise on the sides too, so that would be a bonus.'

'I'm really glad you could come with me. Was your mother OK about looking after Stella?'

'It was more the other way round, because Stella promised me very seriously that she'd look after Ma. Still, I'm starting to think I should look for an occasional baby-sitter.'

'You could probably find someone locally.'

'Chloe and Poppy are sharing a nanny, so they can do some work as well, a young local girl. Chloe said the nanny might be able to take Stella out in her double buggy sometimes, because Poppy's baby is too small for it yet, but really I could do with someone I could call on when I need them.'

'And not just a teenager with no experience, who might panic if Stella wasn't well or let her overtire herself,' Jago agreed.

I brooded a moment as he headed up the small roads between Sticklepond and Merchester, passing the Hemlock Mill nature reserve on the way.

'Did you get another email from Laurence Yatton this morning?' I asked. 'That makes three! Hebe seems to be throwing herself into organising the fundraising with a vengeance.'

'I did. In fact I think all of Stella's Hundred must have

got the same one, though at the bottom of mine she'd put that I was already doing my bit with the gingerbread stars, but I might be called on to help with later fundraising activities, like the fête.'

'And mine said I'd already done as much as I could, and should just help out generally, but I'd really like to think of ways to raise more money myself.'

'I'm sure we'll both be roped in to other things. You'll be helping with the playgroup jumble sale in June, for a start, won't you?'

'That's true. Celia said she emailed Hebe back with ideas for her Knitathon, which will also probably be in June, then her Crafty exhibition and garden party later on, when the weather's warmer.'

'We don't know when the fête will be yet, do we? That should be a big fundraiser.'

'I suppose that will be summer, too. Hebe said she'd list more of the upcoming fundraising activities in the next newsletter, so we'll have to wait and see what that one says.'

I pointed out a sign to Pinker's End and we turned off onto an even narrower road.

'I'm getting nervous now,' Jago confessed. 'I've really fallen for Honey's, and the more I think about it, the more ideal it seems.'

'The village location is pretty perfect too, what with a church wedding every five minutes,' I said. 'There has to be a local demand for wedding cakes.'

'And the house behind the shop could be made back into a really nice family-sized home, with maybe the cottage as a guest suite,' he suggested. 'It would be easy to glaze over that bit of paving between the kitchen and the annexe and turn it into a conservatory with a view of the garden and a sliding door through into the living room.'

'I think *garden* is a bit of an optimistic term to use for that wasteland,' I said. 'Goodness knows what's in there.'

'True, and the estate agent might call that rotting heap of wood at the end a garage, but I think it's only the ivy and weeds keeping it standing. It probably needs replacing.'

'Don't count your chickens,' I warned him, amused by his enthusiasm. 'And here we are, ready to beard the dragon in her den.'

Pinker's End Residential Apartments were reached via a long, well-kept gravelled drive through acres of wooded garden in which I glimpsed a red squirrel (there are lots of surviving enclaves of them dotted about West Lancashire) and a small lake. It ended at a large, square, Victorian mansion with a courtyard surrounded by mews-style cottages. I'd glimpsed other roofs set in the grounds as we drove up, so there were probably a lot of residents in differing kinds of accommodation, according to their needs, and it was all obviously hugely expensive.

Miss Honey had a ground-floor apartment, furnished in a minimalist, easy-to-clean Scandinavian style. Or that had evidently been the *intention*, anyway, but Miss Honey had defeated any attempt to make her rooms low maintenance by cramming every surface with souvenir knick-knacks, most of them decorated with the unmistakable shape of Blackpool tower. There was a bit of a china donkey thing going on, too.

The overalled assistant ushered us in and said cheerily, 'Here are your visitors, dear.'

'I'm not your dear,' Miss Honey snapped acidly. She was

a small woman with silver hair in a feathery urchin cut and a surprisingly sharp expression on her elfin, age-spotted features, and was regally seated in a high-backed wing chair with her feet on a tasselled hassock.

'And I was only expecting the one visitor,' she added, leaning forward slightly and screwing up her eyes, as if trying to bring us into focus.

'I've brought a friend with me. I hope that's all right, Miss Honey?' Jago asked nervously.

'I suppose so,' the old lady conceded. 'Joan, you can bring tea now: and I want the full works, mind – none of your one cup and a biscuit each.'

'Cook's got it all ready, I'll fetch it in.'

'Go on, then, and after that see if you can find my damned glasses. I must have put them down somewhere again.'

The assistant scuttled off and we sat down, but Miss Honey had only just started to grill Jago on what she called his foreign-sounding name, when Joan returned, pushing a trolley with squeaky wheels, laden with chintz-patterned china, plates of small sandwiches and a sliced fruitcake.

'That looks fine, thank you, love,' Miss Honey said, mellowed slightly by the sight of refreshment. 'I'll ring if we need fresh tea – now, you go and find my glasses.'

She fixed her faded grey eyes on me and said, 'You can pour. I like a spoon of sugar and a dash of milk in mine. And pass me a sandwich – egg and cress.'

I did that while she carried on interrogating Jago about where he came from, his family, age and education. Then she asked him how he came to have enough brass to buy her shop outright and when he told her, she exclaimed over his story of the lottery winnings.

'So you decided to set yourself up in business?' she said approvingly. 'That shows good sense, lad, even though I don't hold with gambling.'

She contemplated us over the rim of her teacup as she took a couple of slurps. 'I expect you're wondering how I'm paying for a posh place like this, but my sister married a wealthy man and then she left it all to me: she'd no one else. I came here to convalesce after I broke my hip and somehow, I just never went back to the shop. I thought I would, but I didn't . . .'

She fell silent and I said gently, 'It seems very comfortable here, and the grounds are beautiful.'

I didn't mention the fruitcake, which was a dreadful shop-bought thing, light on the fruit and sickly sweet: I was not impressed. Fruitcakes are so easy to make, and I'd expected the food to be good here.

'Yes, it's certainly that – and just as well, because the only way I'll be leaving it now is in a box. I can see it's time to pass Honey's on to someone else and the only relative I've got left is my cousin's girl, Natalie. She's some kind of actress down in London, so she won't be interested.'

She took another sip of tea and ruminated. 'I like the idea of a young couple taking the shop on and raising a family under the roof,' she said finally.

'Oh, we're not married,' Jago said quickly.

'I don't hold with people living together under my roof unless they *are* married,' she said severely.

'That's all right, I can safely promise you we won't do that,' I assured her.

'We're just friends,' explained Jago. 'Not a couple at all.'

'Best way to be before you wed: start as friends with shared

196

interests,' she said approvingly. 'In my day you walked out together for years, went for bicycle rides or perhaps on the bus to Southport on a summer Sunday . . .'

She lost herself to happy memories for a few moments before resuming her interrogation. 'You seem to be doing it the right way round, but have the children *after* the wedding. I don't know what the world's coming to, with everything topsy-turvy.'

I was about to try to explain the real situation again and mention Stella, when Jago got in first.

'If you sell Honey's to me, I'd be moving in on my own as soon as I had some of the house habitable, then renovating the shop.'

'As a haberdasher's?'

He shook his head. 'No, I'm afraid not. I make wedding cakes: a special kind of French one, called a croquembouche.'

'Never heard of it.' A shadow seemed to cross her face. 'I don't like anything French, neither. Never have, never will.'

Jago described the elaborate choux bun edifices he created, but she seemed rather confused by the idea.

'A wedding cake should be a good, solid fruitcake, a lot better than this stuff they give me, and covered in white icing,' she said. 'I prefer a nice sticky bun with my tea, an iced one, so next time you both come you can bring me one.'

Jago looked slightly startled, but I said, 'We'll certainly do that.'

'Pour some more tea,' she told me, 'and cut me a piece of that apology for a cake and a slice of crumbly Lancashire to go with it.'

While I did that, she said to Jago thoughtfully, 'So . . . you won't need the stock in the shop? I thought someone could just take it all on and reopen.'

'I'm afraid the stock is a little out of date . . .' Jago said gently. 'It would be hard to sell any of it.'

'Is it? I suppose time does fly past . . . but Honey's were always a haberdasher's . . .' she said sadly. Then she perked up a bit, reaching out for the piece of fruitcake I'd put on her plate, together with the slice of cheese. 'Still, I like the idea of wedding cakes, even if they're a funny foreign sort. I didn't marry myself – but then, that was because I lost my young man in the war: so many did. But I love a good wedding.'

'If you didn't object – if you sell the place to me, that is – I'd like to carry on calling my new business Honey's,' Jago said, though I was pretty sure he'd only just thought of the inspired idea. 'It's such a nice name.'

'That would be something, at least,' she said. Since I'd leaned forward to hand her the cake and cheese she'd been trying to focus her faded grey eyes on me and now she suddenly said, 'There's something familiar about you, lass. I wish I could find my damned glasses.'

'I can see the top of a pair sticking out of your cardigan pocket. I don't suppose those are the right ones, are they?' Jago suggested tentatively.

'Oh, yes, there they are.'

She jammed them onto her nose and scrutinised me. The glasses had huge blue frames and her eyes were enormously magnified. 'Are you a local girl?' she demanded.

'No, though my mother was born in Sticklepond. She moved back about ten years ago, after my father died. She remembers your shop being open.'

'What was her maiden name?'

'Almond,' I said, a little nervously, because she was certainly old enough to remember the ins and outs of whatever skeleton was in the Almond family cupboard. 'Martha Almond.'

She obviously remembered only too well, for a shutter seemed to slam down over her face and her small mouth shut like a trap. 'I thought as much – you can't mistake the Almond look! And to think, I've been sitting here taking tea with an Almond all this time and never knew it.'

'I'm so sorry,' I said, seeing how upset she was, 'but I'm not really an Almond, my name is Weston.'

'I thought they'd all cleared off to Australia,' she said accusingly.

'They did, but Ma's parents came back again within the year and worked for the man who'd bought the family farm.'

'Ormerod,' she said. 'I think I remember young Martha and them coming back – her father's Jacob Almond, one of the cousins, isn't he?'

'He was, but both my grandparents are now dead.'

'They barely showed their faces in the village after they came back – and who can blame them?' she said severely.

Then she looked inimically at us both. 'If I'd known, I'd have told you you were wasting your time. I won't be selling up, if it means having an Almond living in Honey's.'

'But I won't be – we've explained that we're only friends, and that's the truth,' I protested. 'I'll never live there.'

'I'm not having the wool pulled over *my* eyes,' she declared, and though Jago tried to calm her down, she began to get so upset and agitated that we thought it better to leave.

'I'm so sorry, Jago,' I apologised as he drove me home. 'I knew that an Almond relative blotted his copybook around the end of the war, though no one will tell me how, but I really didn't think it was of any importance – I mean, not nowadays.'

'Most families have some skeleton in their cupboards and you weren't to know it would upset Miss Honey. Whatever the mystery is must involve *her* family too.'

'I always wondered what made the entire Almond clan emigrate to Australia like that,' I said. 'I'll have another go at Ma, though I'm not sure she knows the whole story. And even if I find out, it's too late now, isn't it? I'm so sorry I went with you, because it looks like I've lost you the opportunity of buying the place.'

'Oh, I don't know,' he said optimistically, 'she may cool down and think it over. All is not yet lost.'

But I thought he was just being nice to me and must be every bit as disappointed as I was.

Chapter 19: Gone, but Not Forgotten

I went straight up to the studio as soon as I got back. Stella had decorated her moss and plant pot village with shells and was now standing at a small easel engrossed in a painting, with Toto curled in a fuzzy white ball underneath. He was the first to spot me and got up, lazily wagging his tail.

'Don't strain yourself with an effusive welcome,' I told him, and Stella looked round.

'Mummy!'

Ma hadn't appeared to notice I was there before, but now she stepped back from her painting and laid down the palette and brush with a sigh. 'That dog's moved again,' she complained.

'They will do that,' I agreed, looking at the painting, where Toto had been transformed into a kind of sleeping hairy cherub-creature with a black nose and round dark eyes.

'You're back,' she added belatedly. Then her eye fell on Stella. 'Where's Hal? Didn't he go to make tea?'

'That was ages ago, Grandma and we drank it. He had to go to Ormskirk and get his medicine from the chemist. He told you.'

'Did he?' she said vaguely. 'Did you have a nice time?' she added to me.

'No,' I said shortly. 'I went with Jago to the nursing home to see Miss Honey, if you remember, so he could persuade her to let him buy the shop?'

Ma's blue eyes stopped looking vague and a wary expression came into them. 'Oh, yes . . . didn't it go too well?'

'It was a *disaster*. It started out all right, with Miss Honey accepting that she wasn't going to sell the shop as a going concern and seeming prepared to discuss Jago's offer. But that was before she found her glasses and got a good look at *me*. Once she realised I was an Almond, the whole deal was off and she got so upset we had to leave.'

'Ah,' said Ma. 'That's a pity.'

'And *that's* an understatement,' I snapped. 'It's cost Jago the property and he's set his heart on it. Ma, don't you think it's time to tell me what this is all about? Did the Almonds and Honeys have some kind of giant fall-out in the dim and distant past?'

'You could say that.'

'If you'd warned me Miss Honey might take against me, I'd never have gone with him in the first place.'

'I didn't think she'd realise. Your name's different, after all, and anyone can be fair and blue-eyed.'

'But there's obviously a family look that's very distinctive, since everyone comments on it.'

'Still, I don't really see why Miss Honey should get upset about it anyway, because it's Jago who'd be buying the place, not you. Didn't you explain that?'

'We tried, but she'd got the idea in her head that Jago and

I were an item, and no matter what we said we couldn't convince her otherwise.'

Ma sighed. 'What happened was all such a long time ago, Cally. But then, to elderly people, the past is often clearer than the present, isn't it?'

'She's a hundred and two and sharp as a tack: *everything* seems pretty clear to her,' I said. 'I only wish I could say the same, so I think it's well and truly time for you to come clean and tell me what all the mystery is. What happened? What made the whole family emigrate to Australia? Is it something to do with that Esau Almond we're not supposed to mention?'

Ma began to carefully clean her brushes. 'It all happened during the war, long before I was born, when they thought differently about things. Esau was the middle son from the three at Badger's Bolt, and he jilted a Honey girl. I think it must have been your Miss Honey's younger sister.'

'There has to be a bit more to it than that,' I said shrewdly. 'I mean, no one ever wants to talk about Esau, that's why I guessed it was to do with him, but I thought perhaps he'd been an army deserter, or something like that.'

'Look, I'll tell you everything I know later,' she said. 'It's not a very nice story.'

'OK,' I agreed, seeing that Stella was now listening in. 'Little pitchers have big ears.'

'Pictures don't have ears, do they, Granny?' Stella said. 'Mummy, you are silly!'

'That's me,' I agreed. 'Come on – and Toto, too – let's go back to the house.'

As soon as I had a minute, I wrote a letter to Miss Honey apologising for upsetting her and saying that I now realised there was some family history I hadn't been aware of previously that would make the idea of my living in her former family home distasteful. Then I assured her that Jago and I were just friends, adding that in fact I'd only known him a couple of weeks and, in any case, my time was entirely occupied with my daughter, who had serious health problems. I ended by hoping she'd perhaps discuss the shop sale again with Jago on his own.

It was the best I could do, so I hoped it was enough. Stella and I popped down to the village green with Toto to post it and then feed the ducks, though today they were reluctant to get off their little island, so everyone else had probably had the same idea.

Stella was more than half asleep and we were on the way home when we met Raffy with his little white dog, which could have been Toto's sibling, they were so similar, except for Toto's legs being about a foot longer.

They skirmished round each other while I found myself telling Raffy about the Miss Honey fiasco and what Ma had said.

'I knew there was some old mystery about Esau Almond; I've heard enough hints since I moved here,' he said. 'But none of my parishioners would tell me what it was. I'm pretty sure he didn't come back here after the war, so perhaps he didn't survive, though he's not on the war memorial.'

'Unless his name was the one chipped out in the As?' I suggested. 'A name's been hacked out of the Almond memorial plaque in the church, too.'

'Yes, and no grave for him in the churchyard, so he may have been killed and buried abroad,' he agreed.

'I expect they were very strait-laced, but Esau jilting Miss

Honey's sister doesn't seem crime enough for them to erase all memory of him, does it? It seems a bit harsh . . . unless perhaps Miss Honey's father did it?'

'I suppose that's a possibility.'

I sighed. 'If I find out any more, I'll tell you. I've just written to Miss Honey explaining my situation with Stella and stressing that Jago and I are only friends – and *recent* friends at that, though I must say it feels as if I've known him for ever.'

'I expect you've a lot in common and he seems a genuinely nice man.'

'Yes, he is,' I agreed, and I don't know why that should have made tears rise to my eyes, but it did. I blinked them back. 'Well, we'll see what revelations are to come, but for now we'd better get back and put the dinner on.'

When Stella was asleep that evening I went into the garden room where Ma was sitting sketching and eating Jaffa Cakes straight from the packet with a fuzzy Miss Marple video on in the background. Hal must have given the biscuits to her, because they hadn't been on any of my shopping lists.

As I expected, she'd entirely forgotten she'd promised to explain the Honey Mystery, but when pressed said she didn't know all the ins and outs of it anyway, only the little her own mother had told her, before warning her never to mention her uncle Esau again.

'Not that he was really an uncle,' she added.

'Then just tell me what you *do* know,' I persisted, and she sighed and laid the Jaffa Cakes aside.

'My father was a cousin to the three boys at the farm,' she said. 'The oldest, Saul, stayed there during the war, because farming was a reserved occupation so one of them had to. They got land girls on to help later. That's how my mother came here and met my father, when he was home on leave, and Saul married one of them, too. Anyway, the two younger brothers, Esau and Amos and my father were all called up and went off to war.'

'I know that,' I interrupted, 'it's what happened to Esau I want to know.'

'I'm getting to it, I just need to set the scene a bit first,' she said. 'The three brothers were all tall, handsome men with fair, curly hair and blue eyes, so despite them being typical taciturn Almonds, the local girls were mad for them. The boys did sometimes go to dances in the village and church socials, that kind of thing.'

'So, the middle one met the younger Miss Honey?'

Ma wrinkled her brow. 'You know, I have a feeling Mum said she was called Gladys. And they must have met *somewhere*, because they were engaged when he went off to war. He got back after Dunkirk, but that was the last time he came home. After D-Day he was reported missing, presumed killed in action.'

'Right . . . and they never found him?'

'Not then, they didn't. After a bit, his name was put on the war memorial with everyone else's and the family memorial plaque in the church. The vicar held a service, too. But then Esau turned up a few years later.'

'You mean . . . his body did?'

'No, he was alive and kicking. His father and older brother had gone over to France on a kind of pilgrimage to the battlefields, with a few others from Middlemoss who'd lost relatives over there, and by a sheer fluke they spotted him sitting outside a village café, dressed like a local and obviously very much at home.'

'Good heavens! That must have given them a bit of a shock.'

'I think it gave Esau a shock too. He'd been wounded and taken in by a local farmer, and when he came round, he seized the chance to begin a new life under another name. He married the farmer's daughter, started a family and had been living there ever since.'

'Wow! Sounds like some kind of novel, or a film,' I said. 'But didn't they all wear dog tags with their names and details on?'

'I think he'd lost his when he was wounded.'

'Right . . . and perhaps he'd had a blow to the head, or something, and really didn't know who he was?'

'Oh, apparently he knew all right, because he tried to run off when he saw his father and brother. They had a huge row, and then when they came home the first thing they did was chisel his name out of the memorials and ban any mention of him.'

'So how did the Honeys know what had happened?' I asked.

'The other local people in the party had witnessed it all and rumours got out, but the family felt in honour bound to tell the Honeys anyway.'

'I expect it made a bit of a stink,' I said thoughtfully.

'Yes, and being Strange Baptists seemed to make the Almonds feel the shame and humiliation very keenly, which is why they all emigrated to Australia. But my parents couldn't take it – my father was a cattle man and he hated sheep, so they came back. I don't really remember Australia.'

'I know it must have been pretty scandalous at the time, but surely mass emigration was taking things a bit too far,' I commented.

'I don't think they could face the Honeys. Gladys was away working for relatives up north when Esau was reported missing, but Mum said she came back for the memorial service and was heartbroken. It must have been even more devastating to learn he'd been alive the whole time.'

'Poor thing,' I said sympathetically. 'What happened to her?'

'You know, I've no idea, except that she moved away and presumably eventually married someone else. Of course, when we returned from Australia we never went near the Honeys' shop – in fact, my parents barely went into the village. I was taught never to talk about it and to keep to myself.'

'That accounts for a lot,' I said.

'Of course, it wasn't anything to do with my parents in the first place, really,' Ma said, 'they just happened to be related, so most local people would have been OK with them. But that's the Almonds for you. They did their shopping in Ormskirk or Middlemoss, and I had to trail all the way to the grammar school in Merchester, so I never got much chance to make local friends, apart from Ottie. Still, I always liked my own company best anyway.'

'You still do.'

'You've turned out differently, Cally. Apart from the curly hair and the colour of your eyes, there's nothing Almond about you.'

'Where did you get the arty stuff from?' I asked curiously.

'My mother liked to draw flowers and animals; she was

quite good. But of course she was never trained; it was just a hobby and one she was generally too busy for.'

'Well,' I said, sitting back. 'You knew quite a bit about the great family scandal, after all!'

'I've surprised myself, actually. Some of it I only pieced together from Mum's ramblings right at the end, when she was confused and going back over the past. It all seemed much ado about nothing.'

'I can see now why seeing a distinctive Almond face was such a shock to Miss Honey, though,' I said. 'It must have brought everything back. I can only hope that now she's had a bit more time, she'll accept that Jago and I are just friends and not moving in to her old home together.'

'Depends how acute her faculties are,' Ma said, absently reaching for her discarded sketchbook and a stick of charcoal. Her fingers were already black with it and there was a smudge across her nose. I expect she'd ingested some with the Jaffa Cakes too, but it would probably do her digestion good.

'Yes, you may manage to pull the wool over her eyes, who knows?' she murmured ambiguously, but her mind was on her drawing and I'm sure she didn't realise what she'd just said.

Chapter 20: The Proof of the Pudding

I hadn't heard a thing from Jago after we'd got back from Pinker's End, which made me suddenly realise quite how often we were usually in contact. Next morning, I tried first his mobile and then the shop number, which rang through to the message machine, so I supposed he and David were baking.

A little later I texted Jago's mobile again and this time got a brief reply, saying he was out but would get back to me as soon as he could. When he didn't, I thought perhaps now he'd had time to think about it, he might be cross with me for scuppering his chances of buying the shop, so finally I emailed him, saying that I'd written to Miss Honey explaining we weren't in a relationship. Then I added that Ma had now told me all she knew about the family mystery, so I understood exactly why Miss Honey was upset. I thought that might pique his interest . . .

Then, belatedly, it occurred to me that perhaps the Abominable Aimee was visiting again and *that* was why he'd gone quiet. Maybe by now he no longer cared whether Miss Honey forgave him and let him buy the shop or not!

*　*　*

Stella went up to the studio with Ma for a bit and I tried out an idea I'd had while making brandy snaps, when it occurred to me that you could bend Parmesan crisps round a wooden spoon just as easily and they'd make rather sophisticated snacks or hors d'oeuvres.

I was quite right, too, and I wrote the recipe up for 'Tea & Cake'.

Parmesan crisps make a sophisticated snack or first course with a dip, and are very simple to make. Line an oven tray with baking paper and then thinly sprinkle grated Parmesan cheese into roughly circular shapes, well spaced. Bake in a low oven for just a few minutes, until the gratings have joined together into a lattice, then remove and leave to cool and go crispy. While they are still warm, you can also curl them round the handle of a wooden spoon into a cigar shape, just like brandy snaps.

Florrie Snowball had suggested at the fundraising meeting that her daughter, Jenny, should come to America with us, since she was not only a retired district nurse, but her son and his family lived near Boston. I'd had no idea what Jenny herself might have made of this offer, but right after lunch she popped in to introduce herself and seemed perfectly amenable to the idea.

'Kevin lives out towards Salem, but it's the same airport for Boston – Logan International. I visit them at least twice a year, so I can just as easily go when you need me, in late October,' she said and didn't even want me to pay for her ticket, though I insisted on it.

'I'll get Will, my friend's husband, on to organising the extra ticket; he's doing all the bookings on the internet,' I said. 'He says we need to fly in better seats than tourist class, too, so Stella will be more comfortable.'

'Oh, luxury!' she said enthusiastically. 'If you give me the date we fly out, I'll arrange my other little jobs around it. I do some home nursing, baby-sitting, granny and granddad minding, that kind of thing, but I've a friend who covers for me when I'm away.'

She was a comfortable, competent-looking woman and I knew I'd feel happier for having her with us. More to the point, Stella got on really well with her and I immediately asked Jenny if I could call on her for baby-sitting occasionally too.

'I don't like to ask my mother all the time, because she has her work to do,' I explained.

'Of course! And it will give Stella and me a good chance to get to know each other properly, won't it, poppet?'

Stella, who'd been fetching relays of little fuzzy creatures from her bedroom and filling Jenny's ample lap with them, nodded seriously.

'Jenny's going to come in the big plane to America with us,' I told her.

Stella turned her huge blue eyes onto Jenny and said, 'Mummy says I can only take two of my families with me. Which ones do you think it should be?'

I left them discussing this crucial decision while I made coffee and sliced some Battenburg cake I'd made so early this morning (because I hadn't been able to sleep properly, worrying that Jago was blaming me for losing the shop), that the sky had still been darkest indigo set with a flashy great silver nugget of moon.

Over the coffee I told Jenny where we'd booked to stay in Boston, in the Longwood Medical Area, right near the hospital where Stella would be treated.

'It's one of those big chain budget hotels so you know what you're getting – comfort but not luxury,' she agreed. 'It sounds like your best option and then I expect Stella will have to convalesce before she can fly home, so you might want to move to a more central hotel later. I'll ask our Kevin where would be best.'

'Yes, I wondered about that, but it'll have to be economical, because there are more and more costs cropping up all the time.'

'I wouldn't worry, we're all going to raise a lot more than the ten thousand pounds anyway,' she said comfortably, helping herself to another slice of cake.

'Boston's a great city, with lots to do, and once Stella's well enough you'll want to see the sights. When Mum came out with me a few years ago she loved the Salem witch trail near our Kevin's; she couldn't get enough of it.'

I thought there were probably more suitable diversions for a convalescing four-year-old, even one as bright as Stella, but I didn't say so. Stella was flagging now and ready for her nap, so Jenny helped carry all the fuzzy creatures back into her bedroom, saw her settled and promised to see her again soon.

I wrapped up the last chunk of Battenburg cake for Florrie, since Jenny'd said earlier that it was her mother's favourite and this was the best she'd ever tasted, so she could drop it in at the Falling Star on her way home.

While I was clearing up the cups and plates I finally had a phone call from Jago, who said he was sorry he hadn't been in touch earlier, but he'd been really busy.

Then he added mysteriously that if we could have a coffee together at the Blue Dog tomorrow he'd talk it through with me. For a moment I wondered if he might be about to tell me he was moving back to London with Abominable Aimee, until he added, 'And thank you for writing to Miss Honey. I think that might just do the trick.'

So perhaps he wasn't going anywhere and I felt a little better, even though I wasn't entirely sure he was right about Miss Honey.

We had a hospital visit first next morning and they were quite pleased with Stella, though when I said that she seemed to get tired more and more easily, they said that was only to be expected . . .

But *I* don't expect it: in my heart what *I'm* expecting is a miraculous overnight recovery.

Then they stressed that I should avoid exposing her to any infections before she left for America in the autumn, as if I wasn't neurotic enough on the subject already! And come to think of it, most of the people with serious infections were probably the ones milling round inside the hospital with us on Thursdays.

Afterwards I pushed her buggy through the open market in Ormskirk and we got one or two bits of shopping, before finally heading for the Happy Macaroon. A woman I assumed was David's mother was serving behind the counter, while he was setting out freshly baked pink and green macaroons. Stella climbed out of the buggy and went to stare fixedly at Dorrie through the glass display cabinet, though I wasn't sure what was so fascinating about her, unless it was the unusual aubergine shade of her short, permed hair.

'Hi! Jago's in the back, I'll give him a shout,' David said, looking up and spotting me. Then coming closer and lowering his voice conspiratorially, he added, 'Aimee's been ringing him all the time, but I've deleted most of her messages. I finally picked up this morning, though, and told her exactly how little he won on the lottery, because she probably didn't believe Jago and thinks he's a millionaire.'

'Oh? What did she say?' I whispered back, fascinated.

'I don't think she really believed *me* either, because she knows I don't like her. But now she's looking about twice her age she's probably feeling a bit desperate, so she'll try and grab him anyway.'

'You're wicked, you are, and that's not very flattering to Jago, love,' his mother commented, having finished serving her customers and now unashamedly listening in. 'He's a lovely lad and deserves better.'

'This is my mother, Dorrie,' David introduced her. 'Dorrie – Cally Weston.'

'I've heard all about you and the kiddie,' she said.

'Did Jago tell you about Miss Honey taking against me and throwing us both out?' I asked, and David nodded.

'But he thought she'd come round and—' He broke off as the door to the bakery opened. 'Here he is. He'll tell you all about it himself in the Blue Dog.'

Stella abandoned her study of Dorrie the minute she saw Jago and ran across to him. Grinning, he swung her off her feet and then carried her up the stairs to the café next door, where she chatted away to him non-stop until she suddenly spotted her three elderly lady friends at a far table. They waved at her and she got down and went over to visit. I hoped they were braced for it.

'I'm so sorry about spoiling things with Miss Honey,' I apologised. 'I wrote to her straight away, but I don't know if that'll make any difference.'

'It already has, I think, because she had someone at Pinker's End ring the estate agent first thing this morning, to pass on a message.'

'Really?'

'She said she'd thought things over and she'd like to see us again.'

'*Us?*' I repeated, startled. 'Are you sure?'

'Yes, quite sure. Her message actually says "you both".'

'Well, I hoped she'd relent and let you buy Honey's when she'd read my letter, but I can't see why she wants to see *me* again, especially now I've found out from Ma why she hates the Almond family.'

I told him what Ma had said about my wicked great-uncle (or great-cousin, or whatever he was) Esau. 'It was very cruel of him to let his family and his fiancée think he was dead, wasn't it? I wonder what got into him.'

'Some people do just vanish and start again, and who knows what kind of war he'd had? Didn't you say he'd been evacuated from Dunkirk and then been sent back for the D-Day landings?'

'Yes, you're right, he might well have been so traumatised by that that he just wanted to get away and make a new start, and when the opportunity arose, seized it.'

'I suppose he can't have been that keen on his fiancée, though,' Jago said. 'So you can understand why Miss Honey was upset. Seeing you must have brought it all back.'

'Yes – so I really don't know why she wants to see me again. I explained in the letter that your business would be nothing to do with me and even promised never to set foot over the threshold if she sold it to you, though actually it would be hard to resist the temptation. Just as well I didn't tell her I've already been there.'

'I'd hate to think if I bought Honey's that you'd never visit me,' Jago said seriously, just as I was lifting Stella, who'd returned, back onto her chair.

'Where are you going?' Stella asked worriedly, catching the end of this.

'Jago hopes to come and live near Grandma's house soon, Stella,' I explained. 'That would be lovely, wouldn't it?'

'Can we come and live with you then, Daddy-Jago?' she asked, in her high, clear voice.

'Now, Stella, you know Jago isn't your daddy,' I said, feeling myself blushing.

'He *is* Daddy-Jago,' she insisted, sticking out her bottom lip, a bit like Ma when she was determined on some course of action.

Jago laughed. 'I don't mind being Daddy-Jago.'

'Good, because my other daddy is a penguin and he lives at the North Pole,' she told him seriously. '*He* doesn't count.'

Jago and I exchanged looks.

'So, Miss Honey definitely wants us both to see her again: did she say when?' I asked.

'Yes, the royal summons is for Saturday afternoon – *this* Saturday. I can do it, because Sarah will be up for the weekend, and now Dorrie's working full time in the shop they can manage perfectly well without me. But I hate to ask you if you could come with me again at such short notice.'

'I'll see what I can do, but I should be able to make it,

because on Saturdays Hal is around and will help keep an eye on Stella. Miss Honey probably just wants me to swear a solemn oath that I really won't ever cross the Honey threshold,' I suggested. 'You'd better sweeten her up by taking her some iced buns, since she said those were her favourite, and I'll make her a rich fruitcake.'

'Good thinking.'

'Actually, I've got an alternative baby-sitter now, too,' I said, and told him about Jenny's visit.

'That couldn't be better, could it?' he said. 'I remember Florrie suggesting that her daughter went with you to America.'

'You liked Jenny, didn't you?' I asked Stella, and she nodded.

'She said she loves to read stories and when I showed her all my families she was mazed. She said so.'

'I don't think she'd ever seen them before, and you do have an awful lot.'

'She's coming on the plane to America with us,' Stella confided. 'She says you can sleep on it, and when you wake up, you're there. Then I'll have another little sleep in the hospital while they mend my heart, so when I come back, I'll be just like new.'

'Sounds good to me,' Jago said. 'And by the time you do come home it'll be nearly Christmas, won't it? You'll have to write your list for Santa early, so he can be getting on with it.'

'I need a hotel, a campervan, a greenhouse, a little boat . . .' she began.

'Sylvanian ones?' he guessed, and she nodded.

'And a pink castle.'

'Santa's probably got sacks full of those,' Jago said, straight-faced.

'My birthday's first, isn't it, Mummy?' Stella said. 'I'll get presents from you and Grandma and Auntie Celia and Uncle Will.'

'She's four at the end of July,' I told Jago. 'Perhaps you should wait and see what you get for your birthday, Stella, before you send Santa your list.'

'That seems like a good plan to me,' Jago said.

'Mummy will make me a pink princess cake again for my birthday: that's my favourite,' Stella said.

'I have to make and deliver a croquembouche wedding cake on Saturday, but early and it's a local venue, so I'll pick you up afterwards, Cally.'

'I'd like to watch you create a croquembouche one day, so I can describe it in my "Cake Diaries" page.'

'You'd be welcome to watch, though you've probably made choux buns often enough yourself.'

'Yes, it's the putting together bit that really interests me. But not on Saturday, since I'm already going out with you later in the day. I expect that once Miss Honey's satisfied herself that we really are only friends, I'll have to go and wait in the car while you persuade her to sell you the place – and at a reasonable price, so you can afford to do it up. How are you going to do that? Any master plan?'

'Yes, actually,' he said to my surprise. 'I spent yesterday working on it out at Hemlock Mill.'

'*Hemlock Mill*?' I echoed.

'Yes, I suddenly remembered that when we looked round the mill manager's house they were appealing for donations of Victorian furniture and furnishings, so I thought they might like the heavy pieces from Miss Honey's house. I rang up the manager and ran the idea past him and he invited me up to discuss it.'

'Aren't you jumping the gun a bit?' I suggested. 'It isn't yours yet to dispose of!'

'I'm just sounding things out – *and* there's more. Honey's shop is full of stock, it's a time capsule of old haberdashery, so I thought it might be just what they were looking for when they start to recreate a couple of old shops in the courtyard behind the house.'

'What a brainwave!' I exclaimed, staring admiringly at him.

'That's what the manager, Tim Wesley, thought, too. I'm a genius,' he added modestly. 'They've lots of student volunteers who could move it all, lock, stock and barrel. So now there's just the matter of the old lady to talk round. Do you think she'll like the idea?'

'I suspect she'll *love* it, Jago. In fact, it may just clinch the deal,' I assured him.

'Well, we'll see the proof of the pudding on Saturday, won't we?'

'Afterwards you could come back to Ma's for early dinner with us?' I suggested. 'Then maybe watch a DVD.'

'Won't your mother mind?'

'No, she likes you.'

'How can you tell?'

'She didn't say you were a waste of space, which is how she describes most men.'

'I like you too,' Stella assured him drowsily. By now she was sitting on my lap, thumb in mouth. 'Mummy, can we watch *Mamma Mia!*?'

'That's one of my favourites,' Jago admitted.

'Who said we'd be watching the film before you went to bed?' I asked her. 'And speaking of bed, it's time we went home so you can have a little snooze,' I added, though I thought she'd be fast asleep the moment she got in the car.

Later, Jago sent me a text saying he'd find a pink castle for Stella's birthday as his gift, though I warned him that if it was the Barbie one they probably cost a fortune.

It got me thinking about what I was going to buy her and since she's taking more interest in the garden now she has Hal as a role model, I went online and ordered the toy greenhouse, vegetable plot and beehive sets for her birthday.

I asked Ma if she wanted me to order her anything while I was at it, but she told me that she and Hal already had it covered . . .

Jago

When Aimee finally managed to get Jago on his mobile, she immediately complained that he'd given her the wrong number. 'But I know what you're like, so I tried switching the last two numbers over and that worked.'

'Sorry,' he apologised. 'And I kept meaning to ring you back when I got your message on the shop answer phone, but I've been pretty busy.'

'*Messages*,' she snapped. 'I'd begun to think David was wiping them, since you never replied.'

'Oh, he wouldn't do that,' he protested, thinking she was so impatient that she probably hadn't even waited for the bleep before ordering him to ring her back.

'Well, at least I can get you now,' she said, and Jago's heart sank slightly.

'How is the new job?' he asked quickly.

'Loathsome. Organising events for corporate businessmen is *so* tedious. But maybe I won't have to do it for long, because now I've told Daddy that we're back together again, he's so pleased he's invited me down there for the weekend, so—'

'But we're not together, Aimee,' Jago interrupted hastily. 'Why on earth did you tell him that?'

'You've forgiven me, haven't you, Jago darling? You said you had,' she said in a little-girl voice.

'Of course I've forgiven you, but—'

'David's been trying to wind me up by dropping hints you'd met someone else, but I knew you'd still be too heart-broken over naughty little me to even think of it.'

'Actually, it's been over a year, Aimee, and—'

'Sorry, I'll have to go, darling,' she broke in. 'But don't worry, I'll ring you on Monday and tell you how the weekend with Daddy and the gold-digger went. I'm going to have to be *so* nice to their ghastly infant. I've even bought it a present.'

'*It*?' he questioned, only to discover he was speaking to empty air.

Chapter 21: Is There Honey Still for Tea?

Ever since the fundraising meeting, Hebe Winter had kept the Stella's Stars supporters in tight constellation by way of calls, printed leaflets pushed through doors (delivered by Effie Yatton on her bike – I saw her doing it), and emails efficiently filtered through her right-hand man, Laurence Yatton. These updated everyone on progress and with the arrangements for the fête which, despite the short notice, was being arranged with almost military efficiency for 7 August, with an auction pencilled in for mid-July.

A whole string of other events, both large and small, soon dotted my calendar for the coming weeks, ranging from Celia's Knitathon to sponsored anything-you-could-think-of. For instance, the local Scout pack were going to walk to Southport and back, which is quite a hike, the Middlemoss Infants' and Junior School were having a sponsored hop-on-the-spot, and for one week only, a pound from every admission ticket to Gregory Lyon's Museum of Witchcraft would be donated to the fund.

The events were to taper off in the autumn and I'd marked nothing at all on the calendar after we flew out to Boston in October. To all intents and purposes I might as well be going over Niagara in a barrel then, which come to think of it, would be much preferable to putting Stella through such a long and difficult operation . . .

When I ran into Sophy Winter in the Spar and told her how grateful I was that her great-aunt was organising all the fundraising, she said there was nothing Hebe liked better and her stillroom up at Winter's End now looked like a communications centre, with calendars, maps and flip charts.

Sophy had Alys, her little girl, with her, also in a buggy, but she was bigger than Stella even though quite a bit younger, being a robust child with dark curls and a look of her father, Seth Greenwood. She and Stella eyed each other silently and gravely, without speaking, though Stella did give her a sneaky peek at the Mummy Cat she had in her pocket.

Stella's Stars collection boxes have appeared in all the Sticklepond shops and, I'm told, in the villages of the Mosses and beyond. Jago and David had one in the Happy Macaroon, too, as if they weren't already doing enough. There was a growing buzz of activity around the village, as if someone had stirred up a hive of bees, and whenever we were out, everyone stopped to ask me how Stella was, or to exclaim over her pretty silvery curls and harebell-blue eyes, or tell me what they are making/doing/planning to raise their bit towards the fund.

It's all very touching . . . I was really starting to feel myself become slowly woven into the tapestry of the community, and my London life had begun to fade into a fuzzy memory.

When I'd asked Ma if she could mind Stella while I went with Jago to visit Miss Honey again, she'd said she couldn't because she was going to the Gardening Club with Hal. Then she said it didn't matter really and she'd cancel it, but since it was so nice to see her leave the house during daylight hours, I wouldn't let her. So now Jenny was going to do her first baby-sitting stint instead.

And actually, that was quite handy, because Celia and Will were coming over late on Sunday afternoon and we were going to book the plane tickets to America, so Jenny could bring her passport details with her.

Later, I made a rich, all-butter fruitcake for Miss Honey, and one for us at the same time, as well as some little cheese tartlets and a big chicken pie that could just be reheated for tomorrow's dinner.

When I rang Jago to say I'd definitely go with him to see Miss Honey and I'd already baked the cake, he said he'd made iced buns.

'Iced buns might be quite nice for "The Cake Diaries",' I said. 'But really, I ought to try and think up a few new twists on traditional Christmas recipes and file those, before I do anything else.'

'I'll give it some thought too, then, and see if I can suggest anything,' he said.

'I can repeat myself to a certain extent each year, but there has to be *some* new stuff. I mean, in every Christmas issue of "The Cake Diaries" there's the same recipe for home-made mincemeat and a potted history of how it came about, but I do need a new twist on a recipe using it.'

'I see what you mean . . .' he said thoughtfully. 'How about ice cream? I've seen recipes for Christmas pudding ice cream, so mincemeat ice cream should be possible. It's not cake, of course, strictly speaking.'

'Great thinking!' I exclaimed. 'I do wander off the cake

making into other recipes from time to time and I've got a little ice-cream maker. I'll experiment.'

'I'm utterly brilliant,' he said with mock modesty.

'Yes, you are,' I assured him sincerely, but he just laughed.

I was ready on Saturday when Jago's red Saab pulled up in the lane.

Jenny had arrived in good time so I'd already shown her where everything she might need was, and the cheese tartlets, little sandwiches and fruitcake for tea.

Then Stella had woken up from her afternoon nap, grumpy as usual, and Jenny had quickly settled her with a drink and her favourite book, so I knew she'd be OK . . . It didn't stop me from fussing, though. I must have asked Jenny three times if she had my mobile number before I finally got myself out of the door.

'How did the cake delivery go?' I asked Jago, sliding into the car next to him.

'Fine – once I found the place where the reception was, that is. It was out the other side of Prescot and I'd never been there before. I think I'd better get sat nav.'

'Good idea. *And* that van,' I reminded him.

'Yes, assuming Miss Honey lets me have the shop *and* with enough money left over for the renovations and everything else.'

When we arrived a cheery care assistant, who introduced herself as Charlene, went up in the lift with us and chatted all the way, but trepidation rendered Jago and me almost silent. I was clutching a biscuit tin containing the fruitcake and Jago carried a large silver Happy Macaroon box full of iced buns.

227

Miss Honey was sitting in the same high, wing-backed tapestry chair, looking like a malevolent pixie, her small sheepskin booties placed on the embroidered hassock. She had her glasses on and regarded us severely through them as Charlene announced unnecessarily, 'Here are your visitors, dear. Shall I bring the tea now?'

'I am *not* your dear,' Miss Honey told her acidly, but her eyes were on the biscuit tin I was clutching rather desperately to my more than ample bosom.

'Humph – what have you got there?'

'It's a rich fruitcake, to my own recipe. And Jago's made you some iced finger buns.'

'Trying to sweeten me up, eh?' she said. 'Well, Charlene, you can fetch up the tea now, but you'd better bring extra plates for the fruitcake and leave cook's rubbishy one downstairs.'

Charlene seemed be made of a less easily dented material than the assistant we'd met last time because she giggled, said Miss Honey was an old toot, and went to do her bidding.

'I suppose you'd better both sit down, hadn't you, unless you're going again?'

'I thought you might want me to wait in the car,' I suggested.

'Don't be daft,' she snapped, and we both sat hastily down on the nearest chairs.

Miss Honey gave me a glare and then to my surprise said, 'When I found you were an Almond, I was that overset I might have been a little hasty. Then when I got your letter, I could see how much you wanted your young man to get the shop.'

'Yes, but he's not—' I began to protest, but she ignored me.

228

'I suppose you've asked your mother about the Almonds and Honeys by now?' Her mouth worked a little and her expression became even more forbidding. 'My sister, Gladdie, said when she got engaged to Esau that Honey and Almonds went together . . .'

'Mum did tell me what she knew, and I *totally* understand how you feel. I'm so sorry about what happened to your sister.'

'Well, now I've thought it over, I don't see what *you've* got to feel sorry about. Your ma's father was only a cousin, wasn't he? So the Almond blood is well diluted when it gets to you, and in any case, I've never been one to think the sins of the fathers should be visited on the children.'

'That's very kind and generous of you,' I said, touched. 'But I'm sorry that seeing me brought back sad memories.'

'Well, it's all a long time ago, when all's said and done. There's no denying it hit Gladdie hard. When he was reported missing, believed killed, she still hoped he'd turn up after the war finished, but he didn't. The Almonds had his name put on the family memorial and there was a church service that Gladdie went to and she was terribly cut up when she came back from that. She went back to Scarborough afterwards, but she mourned him right up to the moment she found out he hadn't been killed, after all.'

'That must have been a huge shock,' Jago said sympathetically and she gave him a startled look. I think she'd been so lost in the past and he'd been so quiet, she'd forgotten he was there.

'You can say that again! You could have knocked us all down with a feather. Still, eventually she met her husband when he was staying at the hotel, and after that she never looked back. Happy as Larry, she was.'

Charlene crashed back into the room just then with the trolley and, while the cake was being decanted from the tin and slices cut and the pretty pink-iced buns arranged on a chintz china plate, we were otherwise occupied.

Now I knew the full story, I thought it was more than generous of Miss Honey to invite me back. And perhaps, since evidently she'd come to terms with it, she'd be ready to move on . . . once she'd loaded her plate with a cheese and tomato sandwich and an iced bun. For such a small and extremely elderly lady, she had a very healthy appetite.

'I had a word with that daft child at the estate agents. What's he called, Charlie?'

'That's the one who showed me round,' Jago agreed.

'He said yours was the best offer I could expect and you were a cash buyer, so there was no chain and it would go through quickly. When you're a hundred and two and settling your affairs, quick is good,' she added drily.

'It could be as quick as you liked,' Jago told her eagerly. 'I'm keen to start up my new business.'

'But if I let you have the place, what would you do about all the old stock? There's some furniture in the house too that I didn't want to part with, like Mother's organ, which she used to play hymns on, come Sundays.'

Jago pulled his chair a bit closer and prepared to play his ace. 'I had a great idea about how we could preserve Honey's Haberdasher's shop for ever, and share the history of it with everyone,' he said modestly, then outlined his plan for relocating the stock to a recreated Honey's up at the Hemlock Mill nature reserve.

'This is the old Hemlock Mill site? Isn't the mill there any more?'

'No, I'm afraid it was demolished years ago,' I told her gently. 'Only the mill owner's house and some attached outbuildings remain.'

'Everything's changing,' she said, shaking her head. 'It was a good mill, they'd no cause to knock it down. I remember many of my friends working there before the war . . . and the annual picnic, I went on that once, to Rivington Pike. I used to go to Blackpool with my friends for the August Bank Holiday week, too . . . Eh, you've seen nothing unless you've seen Blackpool on a bank holiday!'

She ordered me to pass her a slice of my cake with a piece of crumbly Lancashire cheese on the side, then resumed her inquisition.

'So, they'd display all the stock up at the mill?'

'They'd completely recreate the whole shop,' he assured her. 'It's exactly what they wanted, so they're really hoping you'll say yes to the idea.' He paused. 'The other thing is that they're furnishing the mill owner's house as it was in Victorian times and would love to have the organ and the other large pieces of furniture too. Of course, they'd look after it very well and it would all be labelled as coming from your family home.'

'Well, that's something to think on . . . everything being preserved as it was . . .' she murmured.

'People will be fascinated to learn all about your family, the Honeys, and how they built the business up.'

'I hadn't realised before what a museum piece *I* must be too,' she said with a sudden flash of humour. She handed me her now empty plate.

'As for you – well, it's still a pity that you're a relative of the Almonds, but you look a nice sort of girl and not the flighty type, despite having a little girl out of wedlock.'

'No, I'm certainly not flighty,' I said. 'And as I explained in my letter, I'm entirely focused on raising the money to take Stella to America for her operation, nothing else.'

'Poor little thing. You'll have to bring her to see me next time,' she suggested, and I shuddered at the thought.

'I'm sure she'd love that,' I said truthfully, even if I was *un*sure how Miss Honey would feel about being told she looked really, really old and asked why wasn't she dead yet?

'But it doesn't really matter what you think of *me*, does it? It's what you think of Jago that counts, because he's the one who's going to be living there.'

'I think your young man has his head screwed on the right way.'

'He isn't my young man, Miss Honey, I keep telling you!' I said slightly desperately. 'In fact, I don't even need to cross the threshold of Honey's at all, ever, if you don't want me to.'

'Don't be daft, you can't pull the wool over my eyes! Of course you'll be going over the threshold – in fact, your young man should carry you over it, when you get wed.'

Jago, instead of backing me up, laughed and said he would be more than happy to carry me over the threshold one day, but for the moment he was just focusing on getting his business up and running.

'Quite right,' she approved. 'I said you were a sensible boy.'

'So . . . will you let me buy Honey's?' he asked eagerly.

'I think . . .' She paused and her beady eyes examined us both. 'I think it's the best thing to do. I like the idea of the old Honey's shop being there at the mill for everyone to learn about for years to come. And I like the idea of you two raising a family behind the shop in the high street, just like my parents did, and generations of Honeys before them.'

'But . . .' I began to protest again, since I really didn't want to mislead her so that she sold the property under false pretences, but she was closing her eyes and murmuring, 'Happy days . . .'

Then she slipped into the light, sudden doze of old age, so we exchanged a glance, got up and tiptoed out.

Once we were outside on the gravelled drive Jago gave me a sudden hug, which I enthusiastically returned.

'Wonderful!' he said.

'Isn't it? I really didn't think after what Ma told me that Miss Honey would ever forgive me for being related to the Almonds – and even less so when I heard the rest of the story. But I'm so glad she did and you've got the place.'

'She really liked my idea about Hemlock Mill and *they* are really keen too. It's all going to turn out amazingly well,' he said optimistically.

He checked his phone before we drove off and said he had five messages. 'Aimee,' he muttered. 'Now she's got my mobile number she's texting me non-stop.' He looked down and added morosely, 'What's it got to do with her where I am and who with?'

'Is that what she wants to know?'

'Yes.' He messaged her back shortly and shoved the phone in his pocket. 'Not that it's any of her business, but I've said I'm out with a friend.'

I still wasn't entirely sure how he felt about his ex, even now: in his heart, did he really want her back, but found it hard to forgive her? Or was he, as he said, just trying to let her down gently?

Hal was cutting the front hedge when we got back, the cat Moses sitting nearby, observing things. Or maybe directing the operation?

I asked him if he'd like to join us for dinner tonight and he thanked me, but said he was taking Ma to the Green Man for sausage with mustard mash and a game of darts.

'Really? I mean, it's not like she doesn't go out walking at night, she always has – it used to petrify my father, when we lived in Hampstead – but she's never been much of a one for pubs.'

'It's generally just the Winter's End gardeners in the back where the dartboard is, and I've told her no one cares about the old stories about the family any more, because times have changed.'

'True,' I agreed.

I was still surprised though, and even more so when he added, 'Sometimes I go out walking with her nights, if I hear the gate squeak, though she's safe enough round here. I don't seem to sleep so much these days, I might as well be out walking.'

'How's the sciatica?'

'It comes and goes,' he said vaguely.

'Did you have a good time this afternoon at the Gardening Club?'

'Yes, but your ma's had enough of folk and she wanted to go up to the studio for a couple of hours on her own.'

He seemed to understand my mother very well, I thought, taking Jago into the house and introducing him to Jenny, who was in the sitting room with Stella and Toto.

Stella was pleased to see us, but said she'd had the best time ever and Jenny was her favourite person after Mummy, Grandma, Hal and Jago.

Then she counted us on her fingers and said, 'Five best.'

'Fifth,' I corrected automatically.

Jenny said, 'My, she's so sharp for her age she could cut herself!'

Then she got her coat and went home, saying she had a little job to do on the way back.

After she'd gone the three of us – four if you counted Toto – went into the kitchen and had an early dinner of the chicken pie I'd made yesterday, followed up by a sort of Eton mess made with microwave meringue, cream and tinned fruit.

Then we popped some corn and watched *Mamma Mia!* for the millionth time, followed by *While You Were Sleeping*, after Stella had gone to bed, which I suppose was apt.

Sitting on the sofa with the big bowl of popcorn between us, Jago said with a happy sigh, 'This is wonderful! I've had a really lovely evening and it's got me out of David and Sarah's way for a while, too . . . Are you and Stella still on for Rufford Old Hall tomorrow?'

'Yes, that would be lovely, though Stella might still be tired from today and need carrying round.'

'I can do that,' he volunteered. 'She's light as a feather.'

'I'd have to be back by mid-afternoon, because Celia and Will are coming over for a fundraising discussion and then dinner, but it would be lovely if you could stay for both, too.'

'If you're sure you don't mind an extra mouth to feed.'

'Roast beef and Yorkshire pudding,' I promised.

'I can't resist you!' he said, grinning. 'Especially since Sarah and David are starting to paint and decorate the flat tomorrow, ready for when she moves up here permanently.'

'Ah, an ulterior motive. Shouldn't you help them with that?'

'I think I'd rather eat roast beef and Yorkshire pudding, actually,' he said.

Jago

When Jago got back to the flat it already reeked of paint, so Sarah and David must have been unable to resist starting on the redecoration after the shop had shut. The fireplace alcoves had been papered in a bold retro dandelion-head design in shades of blue, black and grey, and one wall painted in experimental squares of grey ranging from soft dove to darkest battleship.

At least, Jago *thought* they were experimental squares . . .

He went into his bedroom, almost falling over the folded stepladder someone had stored there, and switched on his mobile, to find it full of missed messages from Aimee. It instantly rang again, as though she'd telepathically divined when he'd switched it back on.

'Hi, Aimee,' he sighed wearily.

'There you are at last!' she said, sounding exasperated. 'I tried to get you for ages earlier and then your phone went off.'

'Sorry, I was busy, though I did send you a message. Then the battery went dead,' he lied. 'Just got back to the flat and plugged the charger in. Was it anything urgent?' he asked, though he couldn't think of any emergency he could, or would, want to help her with.

237

'Not *urgent*, exactly, it's just that some friends of Daddy's are selling up their perfect little country house hotel and I had a brilliant idea – *we* could take it on.'

'*We?*' Jago said blankly.

'Yes, it would be ideal. You can cook and I'll be the hostess and manager – just think of the themed house parties I could organise!'

He did and shuddered.

'It's in the Cotswolds so it's near loads of friends as well as Daddy, but really accessible for London. I thought you could drive down here tomorrow and I'll take you to see it, before I go back to London. But if you can't, then next weekend you—'

'Whoa, hold it right there, Aimee!' Jago interrupted hastily. 'I'm a baker; I'm not remotely interested in becoming a hotel cook!'

'But it would be our own hotel and if you can bake, I don't see why you can't cook *anything*.'

'Aimee,' he said, with much more patience than he felt, 'I don't know what made you think I'd be interested in buying a hotel, or even living in the Cotswolds, but I've already told you I'm looking around here for premises to run my croquembouche business from. In fact, today I've had an offer on a property in a local village accepted – that's what I was doing earlier.'

'But I don't want to live up there,' she protested.

'That's all right, because you don't have to. We're not engaged any more, remember? We're just friends.'

'Oh, come on, Jago,' she wheedled. 'You know you don't mean that. I can understand that you want to punish me a bit, but you're the only man I've ever really loved and now I'm ready to settle down with you and—'

'I'm sorry, but I don't feel the same way any more, Aimee. It's not that I'm trying to punish you, because that never entered my head – and yes, I'm still fond of you and hope we'll stay friends, but that's as far as it goes. Now, it's late, so—'

'Wait, you can't possibly mean that,' she snapped, then paused and added in a more conciliating tone, 'I'm sorry, Jago, perhaps I've been a bit too quick off the mark and made assumptions . . . though I can't believe I've lost your love for ever.'

Jago thought that was a pretty trite line.

'I'm not absolutely set on the hotel idea,' she added. 'Maybe we could set up a party package business like the Middletons instead, but just for weddings, because they seem to have made a good thing out of it. Only I don't think the North of England would be a good base for that kind of thing.'

'I'm sure it wouldn't,' he said.

'I tell you what, I'll come up and see you next weekend and you can show me this place you want to buy,' she suggested magnanimously.

Jago had a horrible mental vision of Aimee in the cluttered, dusty, cobwebbed shop, clad in dirt-magnet taupe silk and linen, with teetering stilettos that would catch in the wooden floorboards.

'I'm sorry, that's not convenient because I'm going to be very busy all weekend.'

'You're just trying to put me off . . . unless you really have taken up with someone else, like your best buddy was hinting at?' she said more sharply.

'I have been seeing a lot of a local friend lately, that's who he meant,' Jago explained.

'A *female* friend?'

'Well, yes. She's got a little girl who's nearly four and has serious health problems, so I'm helping her to raise the money to take her to America for life-saving surgery.'

'Always the bleeding heart,' she said sarcastically. 'She hasn't persuaded you to give her all your winnings, has she?'

'No. In fact, she won't take a penny of them.'

'How long have you known this woman?'

'Oh, I met her years ago in London, when I was at Gilligan's. She's a cookery writer specialising in baking, so we've got loads in common,' he said enthusiastically, forgetting for the moment who he was speaking to. 'It was great to find she'd moved up here.'

'I bet it was!' Aimee snarled and from the sound of it, then hurled her phone at the wall. He turned his off quickly, in case she hadn't broken it and thought of anything else to add.

Chapter 22: Princess Possibilities

After Jago had gone I felt suddenly exhausted, but also strangely wide awake, so I tried out that mincemeat Eton mess idea I'd had. It came out well and I'd just roughly written up the recipe for *Sweet Home* on my laptop in the little breakfast nook, when Ma came back from the pub.

'Had a good time?' I asked, looking up.

'Yes. Ottie came down with Seth and Sophy, but Ottie's lethal with a dart so they banned her after the first go. What are these?' she added, picking up a tumbler of Eton mess.

'It's a Christmas dessert and it's come out quite well: I might make it again for pudding after dinner tomorrow. You've remembered Celia and Will are coming over in the afternoon and staying for dinner, haven't you?'

She nodded. 'And Hal has remembered he's invited to dinner, too. Is this mincemeat at the bottom?' Ma had fetched a spoon and was digging into the pudding, watched keenly by Moses and Toto.

'Yes. It's mincemeat, cream and crumbled meringue. I mixed a tiny bit of brandy in with the mincemeat. By the way,' I added, 'Jago's going to be here for dinner tomorrow too, because we're going out to Rufford Old Hall in the morning.'

'Right,' she said vaguely, putting down the empty pot and then wandering out of the room.

'Good night, Ma!' I called, before putting a bit of polish on the article for 'Tea & Cake'.

Individual Christmas Eton mess desserts are a refreshing twist for a seasonal dinner party. In a pan, gently warm one generous tablespoon of mincemeat per person, then stir in a tablespoon of brandy. Divide between small dishes or tumblers and allow to cool. Crumble up some meringue (microwave meringue works very well) and mix with whipped cream. Spoon this over the mincemeat and then sprinkle a little more crushed meringue onto the top. An edible gold or silver star adds the final touch.

Then, suddenly weary, I closed down the laptop and ate the other dessert. Toto and Moses had lost interest and were curled up together in front of the unlit stove, and Toto didn't even twitch when I asked him if he wanted to go out.

I opened the back door anyway and looked up at the velvety ultramarine sky, jewelled with sparkling stars, while nearby owls hooted.

When I could see the stars, I somehow felt comforted, as if they were a kind of sign from the heavens that I'd set the right course for Stella, my own little star.

The Three Wise Men, setting off to goodness-knew-where guided by their own particular star, must have felt very much the same.

*　*　*

The sky had changed to a delicious pale blueberry streaked with raspberry and vanilla when I got up on Sunday morning, and since I'd forgotten to put the used dessert tumblers in the dishwasher the night before, Moses had sneakily been up on the table and licked them out, knocking one over in the process, though luckily it hadn't broken.

'I know what you did last night,' I told him, but he turned his back on me and began washing Toto's face.

I needed a cup of strong coffee to get me going after my late night, but then I dug out my ice-cream recipe book and started trying to work out how I could make some Christmassy variations – mincemeat again, obviously, but also perhaps Christmas pudding or even brandy butter.

Having a big jar of mincemeat opened and partly used, I started with that, though first I put enough aside for tonight's desserts. I wished I had a separate ice-cream maker, not just the sort where you have to put the bowl into the freezer, but they're so expensive that I couldn't possibly justify one.

Stella slept quite late, but woke up surprisingly frisky, considering her busy day yesterday, and excited because Jago was coming out with us again. Or rather, we were going out with him, because when he arrived he told me he'd been to Halfords on the way and had a child seat fitted in the back of the Saab, so he could safely drive us out to places instead of always having to use my car.

'You're so kind and thoughtful,' I told him, and he looked embarrassed.

'I have ulterior motives. I enjoyed yesterday so much that I'm hoping you and Stella will take lots more trips with me.'

'Yes, we will,' Stella told him. 'Won't we, Mummy?'

'That would be fun, though there are plenty of free things we can do as well as look at old houses,' I suggested, 'like take a picnic to Hemlock Mill, Ashurst Beacon or some other beauty spot, go to the Botanical Gardens or the beach . . .'

'They all sound fun and we can mix a few treats like Chester Zoo or a run to North Wales to see a real castle, among the inexpensive days out,' he suggested. 'Come on then, Princess Stella: your carriage awaits.'

Stella was wearing a cardboard crown and was dressed in a Cinderella-style lilac net princess dress, while I held a clipboard.

'When we get there, we're going to check whether Rufford Old Hall is a suitable palace for Princess Stella,' I explained as we got in. 'It's a game. We tick off all the vital things as we go around, like it having at least one Rapunzel tower, for instance, and then if it has more than eight out of ten points, it goes on our Possible Palace list.'

'Right – I'd like to help with that.'

'Are we going to see a pink castle today, Mummy?' asked Stella.

'No, it's a princess house. I'm not sure there are any real pink castles – certainly not in Lancashire.'

'I saw a photo of Conwy Castle in Wales at sunset, and that was pink,' Jago said helpfully. 'But I don't think it's pink all the time. We'll have to go and see.'

As he headed out beyond the village I was still checking off a mental list of juice, little snacks, the all-important Bun (how many times had I had to turn back to fetch that blessed rabbit!) and other vital odds and ends.

Then, satisfied that nothing had been overlooked, I said, 'I didn't feel sleepy after you left last night, so I tried out a mincemeat Eton mess and it was really good. You'll see, because we're having it for dessert later.'

'I couldn't sleep either: I switched my phone on again when I got home and Aimee got me.' He sighed. 'She had some mad idea that I'd like to buy a country house hotel down in the Cotswolds, which would have been way out of my financial league even if I wanted to, which I didn't. So I told her I'd had an offer accepted on a property up here.'

'How did she take that?' I asked curiously.

'She suggested she come up next weekend and see it, but I told her I was too busy.'

'*Are* you busy?'

'I have another cake to make on Saturday morning and then I certainly *hope* I'll be busy going somewhere new with you and Stella on Sunday.'

'You don't need to worry about us, if you'd *rather* see Aimee,' I suggested, still uncertain about his real feelings.

'No, I don't,' he said, slanting an unreadable sideways glance at me.

'I want Jago always to come with us,' Stella piped up. 'Who's Aimee?'

'Just an old friend,' Jago told her. 'I'd much rather be with Princess Stella and Queen Cally.'

Stella giggled. 'Mummy's a queen bee. A big, fat, fuzzy bumble bee!'

'Thank you, darling,' I said, and Jago grinned.

'Before I went to bed last night I emailed my parents to tell them about Honey's. I told you they were in New Zealand, living near my brother and his family, didn't I?'

'Yes. What did they think?'

'They couldn't understand why I wanted to set up some

245

kind of bakery business in the first place and suggested I relocate to New Zealand. I'm not sure that New Zealand would want me, though, because I expect they have enough bakers already.'

'Go to New Zealand?' My heart sank at the thought. 'Well, I suppose that would be logical, what with all your family living over there.'

'Perhaps, but though I loved visiting them, after spending two weeks with my family we'd bored each other rigid. I think I'm a changeling.'

'Dad always said the same thing about me,' I said. 'I wasn't academic like him or even arty like Ma.'

'I'm glad they're happy in New Zealand, but I'm not emigrating, because everything I want is right here in West Lancashire.'

'Did you email them the online link to the shop and tell them how much potential it had?'

'Yes, though it doesn't show much of it. They liked the seventeenth-century overhanging quarry-glazed window, but they thought it all looked run down. They don't understand why I want to stay in Lancashire either, since they seem to think it's entirely covered in back-to-back houses with outside toilets and peopled by characters from *Coronation Street* and *Cotton Common*.'

'A lot of people in the south do, don't they? It's odd how these stereotypes linger on. But I suppose it would have seemed more natural to them if you'd gone back to your ancestral roots in Cornwall?'

'It's another lovely place, but when I've visited it I've never felt that connection that I do here. It's very odd.'

'I feel just the same about Sticklepond – but then, I do

vaguely remember coming here when I was little to see my grandmother, so I've always been familiar with the village and the area. And now, I feel even more part of the community, because I can't even walk through the village without people stopping me to ask how Stella is, or how the fund is going, or just to pass the time of day.'

'Let's hope they accept me into the community, too, when I move in,' he said.

'How quickly do you think you'll be able to take possession of Honey's?'

'Since I'm a cash buyer and there's no chain involved either end, theoretically it could go through in only a couple of weeks. I'd like to take Tim Wesley from the nature reserve round the place soon, to have a look at the shop and the pieces of Victorian furniture, so they can start planning out where everything's going, but I'll have to get Miss Honey's agreement first.'

'I suppose Miss Honey could sign the contents over to them right now? Or perhaps if the sale is going to be that quick you might just as well wait until it's gone through.'

'I'll see what my solicitor says tomorrow – there'll be searches and other legal stuff to sort out. I'd like to have an electrician and a builder in to get estimates as soon as possible, too, and one from a specialist firm who can make the sort of kitchen-preparation area I need for the croquembouche.'

'I expect you'd like another good look round the place anyway, because it's surprising how much you forget. Do you have any furniture from your last house?'

'Not a huge amount, because David and I were sharing a furnished flat with a couple of other friends in London, and my parents shipped all the family stuff out with them to New Zealand, so none of that's in storage. I think I'd like to furnish the house in Victorian style,' he said thoughtfully, 'though not with such huge, heavy pieces. With vintage and antique furniture, anyway.'

'Cottage-sized stuff, shabby-chic,' I suggested. 'We could start looking in second-hand and antique shops, which would be fun.'

'My mouse family want a tree house,' Stella remarked conversationally. 'But the penguins want a house boat.'

'Your little friends have expensive tastes,' I said. 'Didn't your rabbit family want a greenhouse, a vegetable bed and some beehives?'

'Yes, they *need* them.'

'Do the manufacturers make all those?' asked Jago, surprised.

'Oh, yes, there's a huge range – they've been going for years, after all. Stella, your list for Santa is going to be *pages* long.'

'I think all my families will have their own lists,' she said.

'Oh . . . right,' Jago said. 'But Santa won't be able to bring everything, or he wouldn't have enough presents left for all the other children.'

'He'll just have to do his very best,' she said seriously. 'Are we there yet?'

We were indeed, and since Rufford Old Hall was a lovely place with a wealth of history, we had a great time looking round it. Jago carried Stella and joined in the game of Palace for a Princess, while I wrote down the scores: it came out moderately well, though the lack of a moat and drawbridge marked it down.

I told Jago all about Rufford Old Hall and Winter's End having rival Shakespeare connections.

'Apparently the jury's still out on the authenticity of the document said to have been written by Shakespeare that they found there recently, partly because the family won't let it leave the premises and the experts have to go there – they won't even let them take a tiny sample of the parchment to analyse.'

'It's all very fascinating,' Jago said.

'We'll have to go there, too, but not a Sunday when they're closed, obviously. But Bank Holiday Monday is coming up and they'll be open for that.'

'Let's call it a date – if you don't mind seeing it again, that is?'

'I want to go with Jago,' declared Stella, though I'm sure she had no idea where he meant.

'If it's true about Shakespeare having written the poem and all the rest of it, it means all the Winters are descended from Shakespeare – Ottie and everyone, which is an odd thought, isn't it?' I said. 'I think there are descendants of Shakespeare's family down south, so they could compare DNA . . . though all of that would take away the magic a bit, wouldn't it?'

'I suppose it would. I'm looking forward to seeing these famous knot gardens too – now I know what a knot garden is.'

'The rest of the gardens are also lovely and there's an amazing yew maze.'

'Amazing maze,' repeated Stella, and then giggled.

'Ottie made a statue for the new rose garden and it's weird, but sort of fits in. She told Ma last night that she would donate one of her sketches to the auction.'

'That could possibly pay for the trip on its own,' he said. 'Doesn't her stuff sell for a fortune?'

'She's very well known, but it's not like she's donating a sculpture. It's very kind, though.'

Stella had a sleep in the car on the way back and was so zonked that when we got home she didn't wake. Jago carried her in and I put her straight to bed to finish her nap.

Then I left him listening out for her while I popped up to the studio with a plate of sandwiches and cake, because I was pretty sure from the state of the kitchen that Ma hadn't been near it for lunch. But Hal, who was potting up some seedlings with the shed door open to the sunshine, said he'd gone halves on his Cornish pasty.

'There's enough here for two, Hal, and dinner will be early, about five. I'll call you both if you don't appear!'

I put the plates on the table in the studio and left them to it. Ma was too absorbed in her painting even to glance up. And what a painting! I'm sure her pictures are getting odder and odder!

Chapter 23: Mincemeat Mess

Jago helped me to start dinner while Stella snoozed. Luckily she was still fathoms deep when Celia and Will arrived, because it made it easier to get down to a good fundraising discussion.

I gave Will Jenny's passport details and since he'd already checked out the best option, he booked our plane seats online then and there. We knew what date we wanted to fly out, but our return tickets needed to be open-ended, because of not knowing how long Stella would need to convalesce.

'I've been reading the literature they sent me and it says some children recover really quickly after major heart surgery,' I told them, 'but others take longer . . . even if the operation is a total success.'

'Stella's *will* be a total success,' Celia assured me, as if she had the power of second sight. 'But you're right, she may need extra time before she's fit to fly back.'

'You can stay on at the Great Western afterwards, or we could find you a hotel in a more central location,' Will suggested.

'I'm inclined to think we should just stay put. I'd certainly like to be near the hospital in the early days, at least. But

Jenny's son's family, who live near Salem, have kindly given us an open-ended invitation to stay with them once Stella's recovered enough, so we might go there for a few days.'

'Salem? Is that where the witch trials were?' Celia asked interestedly.

'That's the one. I think I'll give their tourist trail a miss, though: Stella has such a vivid imagination!'

'No, perhaps that's not exactly the soothing kind of day trip she'll need while convalescing,' Jago agreed.

Jago fitted in so well with my friends that it was as though he, Celia, Will and I had known each other for ever and I left the three of them chatting while I went to finish off the dinner. I make a good Yorkshire pudding, but it needs concentration.

Stella woke while I was still busy, but Celia got her up and she seemed revived by her long nap, so she must have needed it. She helped Celia and Will to lay the table while Jago went to the studio to fetch Ma and Hal.

No one needed to fetch Moses and Toto: the smell of the roasting beef had done that.

By an unspoken consensus over dinner we talked about everything but Stella's operation and the conversation was free ranging and interesting. I do love to look down a dinner table packed with family and friends!

Everyone voted the mincemeat Eton mess a huge hit but I didn't try them with the first batch of Christmas ice cream, because I'd tasted it and I didn't think I'd got it quite right yet.

Will and Celia left after coffee, because they wanted to get back to let the dogs out, but Will said he'd work on finalising our travel insurance and tying up all the other loose ends within the next few days.

Hal went earlier, right after his pudding: he'd thanked me and said it had been a grand dinner, but he was off home, because there was something on the box he wanted to watch. Ma must have felt the same, because she took her cup of coffee and vanished without a word into the garden room, from which faintly issued the theme music heralding the start of the *Cotton Common* omnibus. She's strangely addicted to this period locally set soap drama.

Stella and Jago helped me clear up and load the dishwasher, then we went into the sitting room and did a big alphabet floor jigsaw. But after her busy day, Stella soon started to flag again and I got her ready for bed.

Once she was tucked up she insisted on Jago reading her a bedtime story, even though he explained that with his dyslexia he was the world's worst reader. But in the event it didn't really matter because he'd barely got into her favourite Moomin book before she was fast asleep.

We tiptoed out, leaving the door ajar so we could hear her from the kitchen if she woke. I wanted to look up recipes for castle pudding, because I'd suddenly thought that little individual ones might be a nice recipe for 'Tea & Cake'. I actually had a little Victorian copper jelly mould shaped like a turret.

'I always worry Stella will be poisoned by copper things, so I don't use it,' I said, getting it off the dresser.

'I think that's only if they aren't thoroughly cleaned,' Jago suggested.

'I know, but I'm so neurotic about anything that might affect her health, however unlikely, that I wouldn't risk it.'

'That's only natural.' He was examining the old china and glass I'd displayed along the shelf and added, 'I like these three old glass rabbit moulds.'

'I got them from jumble sales. Stella likes chocolate blancmange rabbits and it's one way of getting milk into her. I make jelly ones with fruit juice sometimes, too.'

'Have you tried her with caramel custards?'

'No, but she might well like them. I haven't made those for ages . . . and I don't think I've done that recipe for "The Cake Diaries", either.'

'Good old-fashioned chocolate blancmange, served in individual ramekins, would be quick and simple for "Tea & Cake", too,' he suggested. 'A swirl of cream on the top and one of those mini chocolate flakes.'

'That's another good idea, and I might even stretch my "Tea & Cake" remit to include mini cheesecakes – at least that has *cake* in the title. They don't seem to mind at the magazine, so long as the recipe is quick and easy. Isn't it amazing what you get served as buffet food at London events these days?' I added. 'Little pots of this or that, or tiny portions of paella served on Chinese soup spoons. Once, I was even given a teeny paper cone of fish and chips.'

'I know, though I was usually on the other side of things setting up the cake display. I did go to some parties that Aimee organised but I felt like a fish out of water,' he added slightly morosely. 'Did I tell you that organising events for her friends was what she used to do for a living? But not *really* a living, because Daddy was still paying her a huge allowance then.'

'I think you did mention that she organised parties.'

'I went to one house party she organised as well, but it was all a bit wild and they played really silly games . . . it wasn't my kind of scene, at all.'

'It wouldn't be mine either; I like a peaceful life. I used to enjoy going to the theatre and museums in London, and Stella loved the zoo, but that's about all we miss.'

'Yes, me too. It made it a bit difficult when I was engaged to Aimee, because she'd never been short of money and she didn't seem able to grasp that I couldn't afford to go night-clubbing in the kind of place she and her friends did, even if I'd wanted to, which I didn't.'

'Funnily enough, my ex-fiancée was much the same and *he* had elderly, well-off parents to dole out a generous allow-ance, so he and Aimee would probably have been a better match for each other,' I said and then it suddenly occurred to me that Jago and I also suited each other, which I suppose is why we'd instantly hit it off . . . in a friendly way. Neither of us was looking for more than that and perhaps that was why we felt so comfortable together?

He sighed. 'Really, Aimee and I had nothing in common at all. I can't imagine what she saw in me and I certainly don't know why she wants me back.'

His thin, handsome face looked pensive and a lock of dark, shiny, curling hair fell forward over his forehead. I resisted the urge to reach out and smooth it back but it was a struggle.

Part of his charm was that he had no idea he was gorgeous and I could see exactly why Aimee would want him back, even if they *were* polar opposites!

And speaking of polar opposites, I didn't suppose mine had ever given me another thought after he'd waltzed off back to the Antarctic!

Stella was still tired on the Monday morning, which worried me so that I was in two minds about going to the playgroup, but in the end I drove her down and just popped in for half an hour.

One side of the huge room was slowly filling up with stacked boxes and bags of things for the jumble sale, which apparently Effie Yatton's Brownies would sort and then spirit across to the village hall on the day.

Stella just wanted to sit on my knee and didn't even look at the pink castle. Sophy's little girl, Alys, very sweetly and gravely came and held her hand out to Stella in an invitation to come and play, but she shook her head so that all her silvery curls danced, and carried on sucking her thumb.

Zoë and Rachel, the two young mothers who lived next to each other in the neat row of pebble-dashed council houses on the edge of the village, had both brought paperback copies of *Around the World in Eighty Cakes* for me to sign. Unlike all my own favourite cookbooks, they were pristine – entirely unmarked by greasy fingerprints or food stains, so I'm not sure they'd ever been opened.

We didn't stay long after that, but as we were leaving Poppy kindly invited us up on Friday to her riding school, Stirrups, to see the horses and the old donkey they had.

'Stella hasn't stopped talking about it since,' I told Jago later when he rang to say how much he'd enjoyed spending time with us at the weekend and to hope it hadn't been too much for Stella.

'She does seem very tired today, but it was probably the fresh air and excitement that did it, because you carried her round practically the whole time,' I said. 'When she's had another nap today, I think she'll be fine again – she's perked up already since Poppy told her about the donkey. No, I'm more worried about her catching coughs and colds, because she's so susceptible and one of the children at playgroup had the sniffles.'

'Weren't you supposed to be warned if there was any infection going round?'

'Chloe did promise to let me know, but obviously not everyone will tell her if their child's a bit off colour before they turn up.'

'If *I* catch anything, I promise not to come near either of you,' he said.

'Well, you could, but only wearing a surgical mask,' I suggested half-seriously. 'I think I'm going to get more and more worried about her catching something as the date to go to America gets closer. I might be terrified about the risks of the operation, but I couldn't bear for anything to prevent it, when I know it's her only chance of leading a long and normal life.'

'That's entirely understandable. I'll mask up like an extra from a medical soap any time you like,' he offered, and I laughed.

'If you hadn't been going to the stables, I'd have asked you if you'd like to meet me at Honey's on Friday,' he went on. 'Tim Wesley from Hemlock Mill is going to see it. The estate agent spoke to Miss Honey, and she gave permission.'

'I'd have loved to have seen it again, but hopefully before long you'll have the keys and I can come and be nosy.'

'You'll always be welcome – we'll nosy round together.'

'I've written up some of those dessert recipes you suggested for articles,' I told him, 'and early this morning I froze a batch of brandy butter ice cream.'

'How has that turned out?'

'Even weirder than the first mincemeat one, though Ma had a taste and said she thought it would be good served with Christmas pudding.'

'She's probably right, and you could spice up a basic Christmas pudding "Cake Diaries" page with it, couldn't you?'

'True,' I said, thinking that he had already spiced up both my life and my ideas no end . . .

Stella was still not quite herself by the time we went to the hospital for her check-up on Thursday. They said she had a slight temperature, though nothing to worry about and a little Calpol should take care of it. But of course, everything worries me and sends me into panic mode, so instead of going into Ormskirk, we went straight home.

That made Stella cross. 'I want to see Jago and I want my gingerbread piggy! And we might have seen the three Graces in the café too!'

'We'll go in next week, darling, I promise.'

'Jago will wonder where I am.'

'We'll tell him,' I assured her and rang his mobile. Luckily he answered and I said, 'Hi, Jago, it's me, Cally. We won't be in the shop today and Stella wants a word with you.'

I handed the receiver across.

'Mummy wouldn't bring me to see you, because I had a tiny tiny *tiny* little temperature, so I'm cross with her.'

I couldn't hear what Jago said in reply and obviously he couldn't see her nodding, but some kind of agreement must have been reached because she handed the phone back to me.

'That's all right now,' she said. 'Not as good, but all right.'

'What did you say?' I asked him as she wandered off towards her room, dragging Bun behind her by one threadbare ear.

'I said I'd pop out later and bring her a special gingerbread pig . . . if that's all right with you?'

'Of course. But aren't you way too busy?'

'Unless I've got a croquembouche to make or David's got a big order, I'm fairly redundant now Dorrie's here, actually. She's so capable and she keeps saying she doesn't want me under her feet. It'll be even worse when Sarah moves up at the end of June!'

'Let's hope you complete on the house in Sticklepond quickly then.'

'I'd settle for a bedroom of my own at the moment, now they seem to be storing the stepladders and pasting table in mine,' he replied ruefully.

Jago

Jago was about to leave for his appointment with Tim Wesley at Honey's when he made the mistake of popping his head into the shop to tell David and his mother that he was off.

'There you are!' Aimee exclaimed, with a triumphant look at the other two. 'They said you'd gone out and they didn't know where to, or even when you'd be back.'

'I *am* on my way out. What on earth are you doing here?'

'Oh, I've got to organise a ghastly lunch party at a race-course somewhere round here tomorrow – Haydock? Something-dock, anyway – I've got it in my sat nav. So since I had to come up today, I thought I'd drop in and see you. I've brought the estate agent's brochure for that hotel I told you about too, because I don't think you've thought this pit village thing through properly.'

'Aimee, it isn't in a pit village, and in any case, you're way too late,' Jago said impatiently. 'I've had my offer accepted and I'm just on my way to meet someone there, who's inter-ested in clearing the old stock out of the shop.'

Her mouth dropped open and for a minute she didn't look quite so pretty.

'So you see, I was quite serious and you've wasted your journey.'

She rallied and smiled sweetly at him. 'It's not too late until you've actually signed the contract, is it? And anyway, aren't you pleased to see little me?'

'Yes, but I'm afraid you've had a wasted journey, because I really will have to go now, or I'll be late.'

'Then I'll just have to come with you,' she said quickly, and his heart sank.

'Perhaps it has possibilities and I should at least *see* it,' she suggested. 'I mean, I'm not entirely fixed on the hotel idea because there's the other one I told you about.'

'Aimee, I already know what possibilities it has, so there's no point in you seeing it. And today is more of a business discussion than a viewing.'

She pouted. 'You mean you don't want little me to come with you?'

'Lord love a duck!' muttered Dorrie, and David made gagging noises.

'Nobody asked your opinion,' Aimee snapped in their direction, and Jago suddenly decided to give in and take her with him. He had a strong feeling she'd be horrified by the state of Honey's, even though he was pretty sure that the survey would say it was substantially sound and just in need of rewiring, replastering and a whole lot of updating.

'Come on, then. You'd better follow me. Where are you parked?'

'In a small car park right behind this road.'

'I know the one. You go and get in your car, and I'll drive through it in a minute and you can follow me.'

'What's the name of this village we're going to?'

'Sticklepond.'

'What the hell kind of a name is that?' she demanded.

'One that suits it,' he said.

He wasn't actually late for his meeting at Honey's, because he'd intended having a quick look round before Tim arrived, having got his hands on the keys.

Aimee ominously remarked that the village looked quaint as they walked from the car park of the nearby Green Man, but once Jago opened the front door and ushered her into the dusty time warp of the shop, she went silent. After that, she barely said a word as he led her all over the property and since he'd brought a large torch with him this time it tended to make it all look even worse. In the circumstances, he thought this was a good thing.

Finally, when she'd shudderingly declined any interest in looking at the garden and garage, he glanced at his watch. 'Well, that's the tour over then, and the man I'm meeting here will be arriving any second.'

'But, Jago,' she bleated, 'it's all so horrible! How can you possibly think of buying *this*?'

'Once it's renovated, it'll have everything I need.'

'But it's so far out in the sticks, too.'

'I thought you said Sticklepond was quaint? And there's a lot going on in the village; you'd be surprised. I know *I* was.'

But she was too busy angrily brushing off invisible dirt and cobwebs to listen. 'I feel filthy and I haven't even *touched* anything. And this dust is starting my asthma off – I have to get out of here!'

She scrabbled in her bag and produced an inhaler and he

suddenly realised that the faint creaking he'd been conscious of for several minutes was not, in fact, the old floorboards under their feet, but Aimee's increasingly laboured breathing.

'I'm so sorry,' he said contritely. 'How thoughtless of me! Look, why don't you go back to the Green Man and wait for me there? I shouldn't be too long.'

She agreed to this and tottered off in her spiky heels, wheezing histrionically. He felt a bit guilty . . . but then, if it finally put her off the place completely, perhaps it wasn't so bad!

Tim Wesley had brought a camera, a clipboard and his second-in-command, Candy. In marked contrast to Aimee they were absolutely bowled over by the shop and just as enthusiastic about the huge old dresser, heavy table and the organ in the living room.

'How wonderful! Maybe we could get a volunteer in to play hymns, occasionally, when we've got it up in the mill house,' Candy suggested.

'Miss Honey told me her mother used to play hymns on it on Sundays,' Jago said.

'Good idea, Candy, but we'll have to raise the money to have it renovated first,' Tim pointed out.

'That's OK, we can put it on display as it is for the present, with a special collection box for the restoration fund,' Candy said.

'Would you want all the fixtures and fittings from the shop too, the counter and stands and everything?' asked Jago as they took a few rough measurements, which Candy wrote down, though it was too dark to take any decent pictures.

'Yes, lock, stock and barrel, if that's OK with you? We want to recreate it as exactly as possible. It's lucky the space it's going into will be about the same size – maybe even slightly bigger.'

'Sorry the electric's off,' Jago apologised. 'I'll get it back on again as soon as I've completed on the place.'

'It's all right, we can come back to take more thorough measurements and some pictures with lights, if necessary. This is just to make sure it'll fit into the designated space. We want to move the gift shop out of the eco-lodge and put it next door to Honey's, so that visitors have to go through the haberdasher's to get to it, then exit into the courtyard again.'

'The counter and a couple of little rope barriers will keep visitors from touching anything,' Candy explained. 'Maybe there could be an audio history of the family and the shop playing, too.'

'Miss Honey is still alive and she's a hundred and two, but her mind is clear as crystal, especially about the past: you could ask her if she'd let you record her memories,' Jago suggested.

'Great idea. To have the voice of the last owner telling the history and any anecdotes would be marvellous! Do you think she'd let us?' Tim said eagerly.

'I'm pretty sure she'd love it.' Jago gave them the Pinker's End phone number.

He'd entirely forgotten Aimee until Tim and Candy had gone, when he realised it had all taken a lot longer than he'd expected.

He dashed off guiltily to the pub, hoping she was feeling better, but when he got there she not only looked perfectly well, but was deep in conversation at a corner table with a handsome, if slightly raffish, man.

She'd always had the ability to pick up strange men

and he was tempted to sneak off again in the hope she'd either pulled, or met an old flame. But unfortunately she looked up and spotted him, beckoning him over with a turquoise talon and he supposed he couldn't really have driven off and left her there, anyway, however tempting the prospect.

'There you are at last, Jago, darling! Jack, this is my fiancé.'

'*Ex*,' Jago qualified quickly and then his eye fell on the engagement ring he'd given her, which was now sparkling on her left hand.

'Silly! You're such a tease,' Aimee said playfully. 'This is Jack Lewis. He's related to the Winters up at the big house here and he's been telling me about the village. I hadn't realised how terribly trendy it is – I always thought Lancashire was all *Coronation Street* and too dim and dismal.'

Jago shook hands with Jack Lewis, who gave him a warm, open smile and said he had to go, but it was nice meeting them and they should stay in touch.

Jago, who was soft-hearted but not soft in the head, thought Jack Lewis looked both familiar and untrustworthy . . . and on the way out to the car park, he remembered where he'd seen him before.

'That Jack Lewis was on a TV show a year or two back,' he told Aimee. 'I knew I'd seen him before. I think it was *Dodgy Dealings*, the one where they expose all kinds of rogue tradesmen and scammers, and he'd been defrauding old people into selling him their homes cheaply.'

He suddenly hoped Aimee hadn't told him all about Honey's, or he might put in a higher offer! Mind you, he couldn't see Miss Honey taking a fancy to him: she was too sharp an old bird to be taken in.

'He's very nice, so I'm sure you are wrong,' Aimee said. 'Or maybe he was framed.'

She seemed so taken with him that Jago hoped she'd given him her number and lost any interest in himself, but no: suddenly her attention and all her charm was switched back onto him like a searchlight.

'Maybe Honey's won't be so bad when you've done it all up. I can't imagine what kind of social life I'd have up here, though!'

'Then it's just as well you won't have to find out, isn't it?' Jago said pointedly. 'I don't mean to be unkind, but would you stop telling people we're engaged when we're nothing of the kind? *And* wear your engagement ring on another finger.'

'But it fits so much better on that one, darling. I should never have taken it off in the first place.'

'But you did and it's too late to go back now, Aimee. There's no point in pretending we're engaged when we're not, because I just don't feel the same way about you any more.'

'You mean, you *haven't* forgiven me yet?' She faced him, her hand on his arm and that familiar little-girl pout on her face, an effect that didn't really come off when she was as tall as he was in her stiletto heels.

Jago couldn't imagine why he'd ever fallen for all this stuff in the first place . . . yet strangely, he also felt guilty that he'd tumbled so completely out of love with someone he'd once been prepared to love and cherish for ever.

'Look, Aimee, I have forgiven you, but that doesn't mean—'

'I knew you would,' she cried, and to his hideous embarrassment threw her arms around his neck, a feeling compounded

266

when over her shoulder he glimpsed Cally walking past, shopping bag in hand.

She spotted him at the same moment and must have misconstrued what she saw, for she turned away and hurried on.

He fended Aimee off with more force than tact and called urgently, 'Cally! Cally – wait.'

She turned back reluctantly. 'Oh – hi, Jago. I've just got back from the stables and left Ma looking after Stella while I popped to the Spar – she's out of sugar and I need to keep her sweet.' The joke seemed forced.

'Aren't you going to introduce me?' Aimee said, resting on his arm the possessive turquoise-taloned hand still sporting her engagement ring. 'But let me guess – this is your poor friend with the sick kiddie, right?'

'Cally Weston – Aimee Calthrop,' Jago said reluctantly.

'I've heard all about you. Jago's such a pushover for a sob story,' Aimee said bitchily. 'Just as well I'm back to make sure he doesn't give all his lovely winnings away!' Aimee laughed artificially.

Cally gave Jago a look of deep reproach from her harebell-blue eyes. 'Yes, isn't it?' she agreed. 'Well, I must get home, so I'll leave you both to it.'

'Cally, wait . . .' Jago began, but she hurried off without a backward glance.

'I've seen that face before,' mused Aimee. 'It's so wholesome, it could advertise soap.'

'That's better than looking so artificial you could advertise plastic,' he snapped back without thinking, and she gave him a dirty look.

'I hope that wasn't aimed at me? I don't know what's got into you lately, Jago, you used to be so sweet!'

267

'I keep telling you I've changed. And you've probably seen Cally's photograph on her newspaper recipe page, "The Cake Diaries".'

She shook her head. 'You know I loathe cooking, so I never read that kind of thing.'

'Except cooking up trouble and trying to give Cally the impression we were picking up our relationship?' he suggested. 'I'm not a fool, Aimee, though perhaps I was once.'

'Well, it doesn't matter anyway, does it? I can see now David was only winding me up when he hinted you were in a relationship with her. I mean, apart from looking such a mess, she's so fat!'

'Fat . . .?' he echoed. 'She's not fat! And David was quite right.' He hadn't meant to say that but the words had tumbled right out of his mouth and now hung, quivering, in the air between them.

Her mouth fell open. '*Right?* You mean . . . you *are* in a relationship with her?'

'We're seeing each other, but of course her first priority at the moment is to get her little girl to America for the operation, so we haven't planned ahead of that.'

'I don't believe you,' she said flatly. 'You're still paying me back for running off with Vann.'

'Aimee, I don't play that kind of tit-for-tat game. I told you I'd forgiven you and I'm willing to be friends, but that's all. I've moved on and found someone else. Now, can you find your way to Haydock from here? I've got to go.'

'But I've got time to have a coffee with you first – I'm only meeting my boss this evening at the hotel and—'

'Sorry,' he said firmly, and walked off to his car without another word.

In his rear-view mirror he saw that she was still standing there, looking both furious and frustrated.

Jago drove slowly round the block to make sure she wasn't following him and then, feeling like a not-very-good spy, stopped at the entrance to the lane leading up to Cally's cottage. But there was no sign of her and by now he'd thought better of bursting in and trying to explain that scene with Aimee anyway.

And why had he blurted out to Aimee that he and Cally were in a relationship? Was it because it was what, deep down, he really wanted . . . one day, when Stella was better? Though then, he supposed that she'd be off back to London again to pick up her career.

No, he was sure Cally only saw him as a friend and probably always would . . . and that was better than nothing. His own feelings might be changing and growing warmer, but he wouldn't risk losing what he had by pushing for something more.

When he got home he emailed her, explaining that Aimee had arrived unexpectedly just as he was leaving for Honey's and he was sorry she'd seen her at her worst, but he'd tell her all about it tomorrow, if she could meet him for lunch in the Blue Dog.

Then he added a recipe for sharp lemon curd tartlets and added: 'Friends?'

She didn't reply to say she'd meet him . . . but then, she didn't reply to say she *wouldn't*, either. But she did ask him about the recipe . . .

He took that as a good sign.

Chapter 24: Tart

Stella's temperature had been normal that morning and we'd had such a lovely time at Stirrups: she'd had a ride on the patient old donkey and met a pretty, fat little pony called Butterball that she loved so much she wanted to take it home with her.

I'd looked forward to telling Jago all about it later . . . and I don't know why seeing him and Aimee having a bit of a moment should spoil all that, but it did. I felt really upset . . . which I expect was because Jago must have discussed me and Stella with her, since she seemed to know all about us, and that somehow felt like a kind of betrayal.

Aimee's thinly veiled insinuation that I was after his lottery winnings really set my back up, too – what a bitch! *And* she was warning me off Jago, with all that possessive stuff, not to mention the great vulgar chunk of diamond on her ring finger. I can only assume they've got back together again, and actually, that feels like another betrayal, when all along he's been telling me that Aimee was a mistake and he wasn't going to give her another chance.

Not that it matters to me really, of course, because we're

just friends and that's all he's ever seen me as . . . which of course is exactly how I want it to be, too. We have such fun together, he's great with Stella and I just really, really like him and feel comfortable with him . . . or I did, till this afternoon.

If he succumbs to the Abominable Aimee, she'll whisk him back down south and make sure I never see him again . . .

Oh, but Aimee did make me feel fat and frumpy! She's as tall and thin as a model and totally beautiful, in an artificial and glossy way, with a private-school voice and that air of never having been denied a single thing she'd ever wanted.

In fact, she emanated such polished perfection that she was probably dipped bodily into a vat of wax weekly and then buffed up.

I'd walked – and even run – home so fast that I was pink and out of breath by the time I got there and had to cool down and then eat half a chocolate fudge cake before I was ready to go up to the studio.

There I found Stella fast asleep on the chaise longue with Moses wedged in between her and the back and Toto lying at her feet like a cut-price heraldic dog on a tomb.

She woke up as soon as she heard my voice and told me that she'd just seen a fairy in the garden.

'She's been away with the fairies since you left,' Ma said, scraping her palette off and then wiping it with an oily cloth.

'Mummy,' Stella said, ignoring this, 'I think that fairies are just very small angels.'

'As theories go, that seems a very good one to me,' I agreed.

'I'd rather have an economy-sized one than something that flits about faster than the eye can grasp, like a humming-bird,' Ma said.

'Well, let's flit down and have some tea,' I suggested, holding out my hand to Stella.

Jago sent me an email later apologising for Aimee and saying he was sorry I'd seen her at her worst. So was I, come to that, but I expect she can be much, much worse than that. Then he said he hoped I'd be in town tomorrow as usual and he'd tell me all about it then.

Tell me about *what*? About him and Aimee getting back together? Do I want to know all the details about that? I don't think so!

And why had he added a recipe for sharp lemon tarts at the end? I don't remember either of us mentioning them.

It was easier to go into town next morning than explain to Stella and Ma why I didn't really feel like it. The shopping still had to be done, after all (Ma proving surprisingly and illogically resistant to the idea of internet grocery shopping and home delivery) and I wanted a lot of lemons for curd, some waxed discs and jam pot covers. Stella also gave me to understand that there would be hell to pay if I didn't bring her back her gingerbread pig.

Dorrie and Sarah were in the shop when I went in and after saying hello and asking after Stella, Sarah called through the door to the bakery, 'Jago!'

He came in looking more like Captain Jack Sparrow than ever, his black headscarf tied pirate-fashion and long, black curling strands of hair showing beneath it.

His soft caramel eyes lit up when he saw me and there was no mistaking the warmth in them, so that my quick-frozen heart started to thaw a bit . . . until I wondered if he was so bubbling with happiness at his re-engagement that he wanted to share it!

We went up to the café, where Stella's three friends were already having lunch – I think they must come in every market day, like me. That, or they spend every day there.

We ordered lunch and then there was a little silence until I broke it by saying, as lightly as I could, 'So, that was the lovely Aimee – and you're back together again?'

'What – *no!*' he exclaimed, looking both startled and horrified. 'What gave you that idea . . .? Then he paused and added ruefully, 'Oh . . . I suppose it did look a bit like that, what with Aimee going into her "this is my man" routine.'

'*And* she was wearing an engagement ring,' I pointed out.

'Yes, she chose such a flashy great thing you could hardly miss it, though last time I saw her she was wearing it on the other hand. I think she's gone totally bananas, because she introduced me to someone in the pub as her fiancé and she's even told her father we're back together, though I've told her repeatedly there's no chance.'

'But . . . are you sure about that? I mean, now I've seen how beautiful she is, not to mention sophisticated and—'

'Bitchy as hell?' he finished for me. 'She was really nasty to you – and no, before you ask, I didn't tell her any more about you and Stella than everyone knows: that you're raising money to take her to America for an operation.'

'I should have known that,' I said contritely.

'By the way, after she'd met you, Aimee said she thought she'd seen you before somewhere.'

'I can't imagine where . . . though she's posh and so was Adam, so I suppose she could have been at one of the ghastly parties he dragged me to. Now, there was *another* fiancé on an entirely different wavelength.'

'Yes, we got matched up with the wrong people: he and Aimee were clearly made for each other,' he joked. 'I think David must have tried to get her off my back by telling her I was in a relationship with you and that's why she was so jealous.'

'Well, she's got no need to be jealous of me!' I said, astonished.

He put his warm hand over mine on the table. 'I really am finished with her, and she'll have to accept that, but I was sorry for her and trying to let her down gently and she seems to have got the wrong idea.'

'I don't think subtlety's her strong point,' I agreed.

'I'm going to be much more direct with her in future – in fact, I was brutally honest after she'd been so rude to you, so she's probably gone off in a hissy fit. Still, with a bit of luck she'll soon find someone else and lose interest in me,' he added hopefully. 'All *I* want is to make a new life up here – and help you to get Stella to America, of course. Those are the important things.'

His phone buzzed and he read the message, then looked up at me and grinned. 'No, it's not Aimee, before you ask! I should think she's at Haydock racecourse, knee-deep in businessmen. No, it's David reminding me that Sarah made us promise to paint all the flat ceilings this afternoon, while she and Dorrie mind the shop.'

'Are you painting tomorrow, too?' I asked. 'Only Celia and Will suggested you go over there with us and I said I'd ask.'

'No, I'm let off tomorrow because they're going to go to the Ikea store near Warrington. Sarah has a list about ten feet long and I only hope they don't expect me to put the flat pack stuff together when they get it back, because I can't even read the instructions on those things.'

'She sounds as if she has very definite ideas on how she wants the flat,' I commented.

'She certainly does, and it's not my taste at all. I'd love to come with you tomorrow – and are we still on for Winter's End on Monday or will Stella be too tired?'

'She should be OK. I'll take her buggy, but you'll probably end up carrying her round instead,' I warned him. 'I only want you to come as a beast of burden.'

'Neigh, never!' he said, and I hit him with the menu.

At Celia and Will's the men vanished to the coach house studio, leaving us to have a girly chat over coffee.

I told Celia all about meeting Abominable Aimee and thinking she and Jago were engaged again and then finding out they weren't.

'Of course they're not,' she said. 'She sounds totally the wrong kind of girl for him and I'm sure he realises that and is thanking his lucky stars for his escape.'

'She's very beautiful, though. But I think you're right – and I hope so, because he's so nice that she doesn't deserve him in the least!'

I'd taken Toto with me, though because he's quite small I worried at first that the greyhounds would suddenly decide he was a rabbit and chase him. I needn't have bothered, because they were intimidated by his cold stare as he stalked across the kitchen floor and ate their left-over dinner, before flopping down in the nearest comfy bed.

* * *

On Bank Holiday Monday Jago drove us up to Winter's End, even though it wasn't that far to walk, then we pushed Stella in her buggy up the long drive from the car park. The weather was bright and very warm for the end of May, so there were a lot of other visitors too.

Though Stella and I had been there before, she was always entranced by the maze and fascinated by the Friends of Winter's End, the volunteers who manned it on open days, dressed in Elizabethan costume. Some of them had been at the fundraising meeting and stopped to say hello to us and especially to Stella.

'I can't go anywhere these days without being stopped every five minutes,' I said after about the fifth time.

'But that's nice, isn't it?' Jago said. 'It's how things should be in a small community.'

'Yes, it is, you're quite right: I feel everyone *does* care and they're all working to help us.'

Stella got out of her buggy in the rose garden in order to examine more closely Ottie's *Spirit of the Garden* statue. It was more than a little strange, so I hoped it didn't give her bad dreams. Mind you, if Ma's paintings hadn't done that by now, she was probably immune.

Seth Greenwood came through one of the rose arches, accompanied by a timid-looking man dressed in ruff and tights and carrying a parchment with a big 'W. S.' inscribed on the back in flowing script, in case anyone didn't immediately guess who he was meant to be.

'Ah, a beautiful princess!' Seth said, picking a yellow rose and handing it to Stella with a courtly bow. You can do that kind of thing if it's your garden.

Then he gave me a fat, tight white rose with pale pink

edges to the petals, and I tucked it into the lapel button of my denim-coloured linen jacket. Shakespeare didn't say anything, though he did bow to me and give a twitch of a nervous half-smile, before scurrying off after Seth, who is a big man and tends to stride about as if he's wearing ten-league boots.

While we were heading for the fern grotto, Hebe sailed by in full Queen Elizabeth I regalia, but luckily she didn't spot us, because heaven knows what Stella would have said to her.

After we'd seen all the grounds and had tea in the café, we showed Jago the famous knot garden terraces at the back of the house and the Shakespeare wall with quotations from the Bard cut into the stones. Even the flowerbeds were filled with plants mentioned in his plays and poems.

'Lots of people have knot gardens round here, because that's Seth's speciality. He runs a company called Greenwood's Knots.'

'I think I like the true lover's knot best,' he said. 'I'd never really known much about them before, but now I want one.'

'Ma hasn't got one because she prefers a natural effect. In fact, her garden would be a total wilderness if it weren't for Hal. She's even let him put in a couple of formal flowerbeds, but she won't allow him to tame the whole garden.'

'It's great as it is, and I suppose a knot garden would be a lot of work, anyway. I think I'd better settle for a bit of lawn and a border, maybe a small fruit tree.'

'There's some kind of tree at the end of your garden; we'll have to see what that is when the jungle's been hacked down.'

We sat on a stone seat in the Shakespeare garden lazily chatting about whether apple pies were better with cream or ice cream, and the merits of honeycomb crunch versus cinder toffee, while the bees buzzed lazily round the flowerbeds and Stella slept in Jago's arms, still clutching Bun and a slightly moist fuzzy mouse.

She didn't wake up on the drive home, either. When we pulled up, Hal was weeding a flowerbed and Ma was sitting nearby, drawing and smoking a pink Sobranie. She said they were going to the pub again later, so her life is rapidly moving from a semi-hermitic existence to one of riotous dissipation.

We put Stella on her bed to have out her nap and Jago would have stayed for tea, except that David rang him and he had to go back to help him carry the last heavy boxes of flatpack furniture out of the hired van up to the flat.

It sounded as if he and Sarah had bought up the shop!

When Stella finally woke up she was well miffed to find that Jago had gone and was only cheered up when I suggested we made honeycomb crunch.

Aimee

The minute Aimee arrived at the hotel near the racecourse she'd suddenly realised who Cally Weston was: the nobody that Adam Scott had produced as his fiancée at some party *years* ago.

His parents lived near her father's house in the Cotswolds and she'd known Adam all her life, even if their paths hadn't crossed very much recently . . . and now she came to think of it, Adam's parents had been round to dinner when she was spending the weekend with Daddy and the gold digger.

In fact, Lydia Scott, who'd been sitting opposite, had told her Adam was back and working in London and then gone on and on about how he'd said he was ready finally to settle down and raise a family, and they hoped he did because they would so love grandchildren and they were getting on a bit . . .

They'd even said something about how they'd liked that nice girl he was engaged to once and how it was unfortunate that it didn't work out!

It was a pity she found the Scotts so boring that she hadn't really been listening properly.

Of course, Cally looked a lot better when she'd been

engaged to Adam – my God, she'd let herself go. No makeup, shabby but definitely not chic jeans, a baggy T-shirt, hair that hadn't been near a hairdresser forever – and *fat*!

Of course, when Jago had called out 'Cally!' in that soppy voice, as if she was something special, her instincts had been to demonstrate that Jago was hers and see her rival off. But once she'd really had a good look at her, she'd realised she actually wasn't any rival at all, so she'd annoyed Jago for nothing.

Mind you, with that soft heart of his, Cally might just manage to get her claws into him while he was helping her with all this fundraising for the little girl . . . had he said she was about three or four?

She cast her mind back, trying to remember how many years it was since she'd run into Adam and Cally . . . and thought it was about that long. Certainly long enough to drop a few hints and stir things up, anyway.

If the child was his, did he know about it, she mused. If he didn't, then he might be interested in a ready-made family if his parents were right and he was talking about settling down. And the Scotts were well off, old money, so Cally wouldn't need to worry about funding treatment abroad for the child. And that, in turn, would mean she wouldn't need Jago's help, either.

Cally would probably leap at the chance of getting Adam back again, though Aimee didn't exactly rate her chances unless she did something drastic with her face, her figure and her messy hair!

Later, armed with the Scotts' phone number, Aimee gave them a ring and asked them if they could give her Adam's

London contact details, because she'd love to catch up with him again.

Then she mentioned that funnily enough she'd bumped into his old fiancée, Cally Weston and added innocently how difficult it must be for them, not having any role in their granddaughter's life . . .

That had set the cat among the pigeons with a vengeance, though she'd immediately backtracked and said she must have got the wrong end of the stick, because if they didn't know anything about the child, then it couldn't be Adam's after all. Silly her . . .

Aimee was so pleased with her machinations that although she still felt furious with Jago, she was now *almost* ready to kiss and make up. After all, she was sure he wasn't really romantically interested in that Cally Weston – who could be? – and anyway, with a bit of luck Cally would soon be preoccupied elsewhere and Jago would be all hers again.

Meanwhile, she thought she should cut him a bit of slack until he came to his senses, so she left him to stew in his own juice for a few days.

Chapter 25: Horse Feathers

Jago and David spent hours assembling flat pack furniture and finishing the painting and decorating. Now new carpets were about to be laid throughout the flat and poor Jago was starting to feel like a lodger. He'd taken to popping in to see us just to get a bit of peace and quiet, which luckily didn't appear to bother Ma at all: in fact, he seemed to be wallpaper, like Hal.

'I'm thinking of finding somewhere to stay in Sticklepond before Sarah moves in permanently,' he told me one afternoon, on the way back from delivering one of David's macaroon cones to a children's party. 'The Green Man's a hotel, isn't it?'

'Yes, but I think their rooms are quite pricey.'

'Maybe not there, then, because I'll need everything I've got left after paying for Honey's for the renovations. I suppose really I ought to wait until I've exchanged contracts anyway, because I haven't even had the searches back yet. What if the property's built right on top of an old pit, or something?'

'Part of it goes back to the seventeenth century, so I think it's too old for that – and anyway, Sticklepond's never been a pit village. If the searches don't show up any major problems, then things should move very quickly, shouldn't they?'

'Yes, after that there's nothing to stop it being signed, sealed and delivered . . .'

'Bell, book and candle,' I said, which sparked an idea. 'The Falling Star, that old pub at the other end of the main street, lets rooms. Florrie Snowball and her son run it – do you remember Florrie from the fundraising meeting?'

'I'd find it a bit hard to forget her,' he said. 'She's quite a character.'

'I noticed the sign about accommodation when I took Stella there to see the meteorite – that's the Falling Star the pub's named after.'

'Really? Do I want to stay somewhere where rocks drop out of the sky?'

'Don't be daft, it was just the one. I don't know how comfortable the rooms are, though, because I think they mainly cater to sales reps rather than tourists.'

'That's OK, I'm not a tourist, and they couldn't be less comfortable than a flat where the carpets are being ripped up and mounds of flat pack furniture and boxes of stuff are everywhere. I'm dreading the moment when they start taking out the kitchen.'

'Does it really need replacing?'

'No, but Sarah has her own ideas about interior decorating. When she's finished making the flat perfect, she'll probably start organising an equally perfect wedding for next spring, so I certainly need to get out of there fast. David says he likes all those shades of grey and mustard she's decorating the flat in,' he added gloomily, 'but I'm finding it a bit depressing.'

'I'm sure I would, too. Maybe we should go down and have a word with Mrs Snowball some time?' I suggested, and Jago agreed.

It's lovely that we're comfortably back on our old friendly footing. In fact, now the air's been cleared between us and I can see he really *doesn't* want to get back with Aimee, we've become even firmer friends.

Meanwhile, he says the dreaded Aimee has apparently gone into a fit of the sulks and remains blessedly silent, so long may that continue . . .

Stella's last hospital check-up had been fine, so the next Thursday they let her off, though we had our usual little outing to Ormskirk anyway.

The first fundraising events had already started, like the Middlemoss Christmas Pudding Circle's 'Guess the weight of the pudding' competition, so donations were trickling into the fund by way of Raffy and needed to be paid into the bank.

As the summer went on and the major events took place, I hoped that the trickle would turn into a raging torrent, because the Stella's Stars account was pretty depleted after paying for the plane tickets and other major expenses.

We went for a coffee in the Blue Dog café with Jago and I wasn't entirely surprised to see the three Graces there, at their usual table.

'Cooee!' they called, waving at Stella. 'We're not dead yet, love!'

'I'm going to see my friends,' Stella announced, and while she was off paying her respects, Jago and I shared a huge chunk of chocolate fudge cake with our coffee, and he told me that David was going to branch out into making traditional wedding cakes to order.

'Only classic tiered horseshoe-shaped or round ones. You can get novelty ones anywhere these days,' he explained, 'and apparently there's someone out in one of the villages, Neatslake, specialising in unusual cakes.'

'I don't think I've ever seen a horseshoe-shaped cake, it sounds lovely! But is he going to have time to make wedding cakes as well as the macaroons?'

'I'll be able to help, even after I've moved into Honey's and got my own business going, but I think eventually he'll need to take on a full-time bakery assistant.'

When Stella finally came back, Jago told her he knew someone even older than her friends.

'She must be very, very old,' she breathed, impressed.

'She is. She's called Miss Honey, and Mummy and I have been to visit her. She said next time we go, she'd like it if you came too.'

'I was sort of hoping she'd forgotten about that,' I muttered, but Stella was very taken with the idea and immediately demanded more details.

Of course, once he'd put the idea into her head, she didn't stop pestering me to know when we were going to go and visit the very, very old lady. I'm not entirely sure that such a clash of the Titans would end happily, but if it does come off, then my money will be on Stella.

I was still trying to stockpile enough Christmas recipes, but very early the following morning, when the star sprinkled sky was still as dark as a blackcurrant puree and lit only by one

285

pale Promethean spark of light, I did think up an interesting new twist on an old favourite.

> When making your spiced Christmas star biscuits to hang on the tree, it's very easy to give them a stained-glass effect. Simply cut out a hole in the middle (you could use a star-shaped *petit four* cutter, if you have one), and then place a boiled sweet or two in the space before baking in the oven. They will melt to form little translucent coloured windows that look very effective
>
> Cally Weston: 'Tea & Cake'

On Saturday Stella seemed extra tired, so we had a quiet day. I did the shopping early, but I couldn't have seen Jago even if I hadn't wanted to dash straight home, because he had two croquembouche cakes to make and deliver, while David had party pyramids orders too, so they were both up before dawn baking and then out delivering.

He's started taking pictures of his cakes as he makes them, ready for a brochure when he's established in the new premises – and all this waiting until he exchanges contracts is really nail-biting, because he's set his heart on Honey's and I couldn't bear anything to go wrong at this stage.

He texted me a couple of times while he was out delivering the cakes, but then rang me later to say he'd spotted a nice small white van in a garage, and was going to buy it for the business, but keep his beloved Saab too.

'I'm really looking forward to tomorrow,' he added, because we were to go and meet Will and Celia at the Botanical Gardens in Churchtown, near Southport. 'I deserve a rest and with Sarah around the flat on Sundays till she goes for the last train back to London, I'm certainly not going to get that here.'

'You're hardly likely to get a rest with us, either, what with Stella bombarding you with questions and wanting to be carried about,' I pointed out, but he laughed and said that was a different kind of tired and he liked it.

Stella was hoping to get some more feathers for her collection at the Botanical Gardens and she did bag a long Golden Pheasant one, though the peacock huffily declined even to ruffle his lovely tail out for us.

When we'd looked at all the birds, rabbits and guinea pigs in their little enclosures, we had lunch in the café, though Stella's was mostly a couple of chips dipped in tomato sauce, and some ice cream. Though this was better than nothing, it was hardly a nutritious balanced meal.

When we came out into the warm June sunshine, Will put Stella on his shoulders and carried her off to feed the ducks on the pond, with Celia.

'I'm a big bold giant!' she was screaming excitedly as Jago and I strolled leisurely after them.

'I think she's a bit too overexcited,' I said.

'Maybe, but it's nice to see her having fun and I don't think it'll do her any harm, though she might sleep all the way home in the car.'

'Do you think I fuss over her too much?'

'No, you just want to keep her as well as possible and you know how easily she overtires. It's natural to be worried about her.'

'I'll have to go down to the Mother and Toddler group tomorrow morning even if she's still tired then, because I'm taking lots of stuff for the jumble sale. Did I tell you it's going to be on the fourteenth of June?'

'No, I don't think you mentioned that. Where are they having it?'

'In the village hall, from six o'clock onwards. I've already asked Jenny if she'll baby-sit while I help out.'

'I'll see if I have any jumble,' Jago promised. 'And I could come and help.'

'Would you have time?'

'Yes, no problem. I could sell the bric-a-brac, perhaps.'

'I'll ask, but I'm sure they'll be delighted. And if Stella's too tired to play tomorrow I'll just drop the things off. Unless Chloe rings me first thing to warn me that any germs are going round, in which case we won't go at all. I don't want any setbacks at this stage.'

'How's the fund doing now?'

'Slowly filling up again.'

'I'm sure they'll be well over the target by the end of the summer,' he said. 'Just as well, because I think you've under-estimated how much you'll need when you're out there.'

'That's what Raffy said when he popped in the other day with the cheque from the Witch Craft Gallery's "How many beans in a jar" competition,' I agreed. 'He said there'd be more than enough, but if there was any left over it could be donated to some other good cause, which would be a bonus.'

'Quite right, it would.'

Jago drove us home afterwards and stayed to dinner, though we didn't manage to get much down Stella before she zonked out and had to be put to bed, but not before she'd told me Will said that horses had feathers on their feet.

Afterwards Ma vanished into the garden room and we

watched an old film on telly and then messed about in the kitchen making rum truffles with white-iced tops like little Christmas puddings. I even found some miniature plastic sprigs of holly in the sweet tin where I store my cake decorations, to complete the effect.

When he had gone, it occurred to me that I hardly remembered any more what it was like *not* to know Jago and have his warm, friendly reassuring presence in my life.

Chapter 26: Jumbled

Jago rang later to tell me he'd exchanged contracts, though the searches had thrown up a couple of quirky things.

'I'm not allowed to have a bear pit in the garden,' he said.

'Did you want one?'

'Not really. I quite fancied having a few hens eventually, though, and it does say something about that. I think it was no cockerels.'

'Odd, but that doesn't mean any *hens*, does it? And you don't actually need a cockerel to get eggs.'

'That's true,' he said happily. 'I wonder if one of the original owners way back had a really noisy cockerel. There must be some reason for it.'

'Did the searches throw up anything else?'

'Well, rewiring, which I expected; no central heating, of course, so that will have to be put in with a new boiler; new plumbing . . . then there's some woodworm in the roof timbers, which needs treating. Other than that, it didn't sound so bad, but I wondered if you'd like to go through it with me and see if I've missed anything important? Only if you've got time, though.'

'Of course I have, and you know you can come over to

Ma's any time you like,' I said, because those forms are complicated even if you haven't got dyslexia.

'Completion should be quite quick now the searches are done, and as soon as I get the keys I'll start getting estimates for the work. I'm dying to get on with it, now,' he said, sounding really excited.

At her next hospital appointment, Stella told the consultant very firmly that she was quite fed up with hospitals and she would be glad when she'd been cured in America and didn't have to go there any more.

I didn't have the heart to tell her that she'd still need to have check-ups, to make sure everything was healing and working as it should – which, please God, it would be . . . and, though I'd never been religious, I had begun to send up a silent prayer whenever we went down to the church, which was quite often, given Stella's angel fixation. We lit a little candle, too, though Stella thought this was just a fun thing.

At that rate I thought I might revert back into a Strange Baptist, the sect Ma's family belonged to before they emigrated, though there weren't many of them left now, and the chapel in Ormskirk, where the Almonds once attended, had become a carpet warehouse.

Anyway, the consultant, Mrs Barrie, pretended to be very hurt and said she hoped Stella would pop in sometimes just to show her how well her new heart was working and Stella conceded graciously that she supposed she could, so long as they didn't stick needles in her arm.

Afterwards she seemed to flag, so since we knew Jago had a wedding cake to make and deliver that day, we just went straight home. Stella played quietly in Ma's studio with her mossy tabletop village, then after lunch and a nap, messed around in her sandpit while I lay on a travelling rug on the grass and contemplated the inside of my eyelids, though luckily Moses woke me by walking across my stomach just as I was falling asleep.

Ma had joined us and I'd just fetched out a tray of homemade lemonade and sliced and buttered fruit loaf for a little picnic, when Jago popped in on his way back from delivering his cake.

'Get on the magic carpet quick, before it takes off!' Stella told him and he dropped down beside me on the rug.

'Where are we going?' he asked her.

'Fairyland, where the little angels live.'

'Right,' he said, fending Moses off the fruit loaf. 'I was just on my way back from delivering that croquembouche and you were on the way home,' he added to me, though he must have intended to come, because he'd brought Stella her usual gingerbread pig and some macaroons from David for me and Ma.

'That was a late wedding,' I commented.

'It was, a bit, but the interesting thing was that the reception was in a converted barn and the woman who has it knows the weird and wonderful wedding cake maker I told you about.'

'Oh, yes, you said she lived in Neatslake. I wonder if she was miffed that she hadn't been asked to make the wedding cake, instead of you.'

'Actually, she turned up to have a quick look at the croquembouche, because she'd never seen one and we had a chat. She's called Josie and she's very nice – or she was once I'd explained that I was only going to be selling croquembouches, not encroaching on her territory.'

'I suppose David won't be either, really, since he's only going to make traditional wedding cakes,' I said. 'There's room for you all.'

Ma, who'd taken no notice of Jago's arrival other than adding him into her sketch, now laid her charcoal down. 'Isn't there a cold drink for me?'

'I offered you one, but you didn't reply,' I said, filling a tumbler and passing it across. 'David's sent us some macaroons. Do you want one of those or a piece of tea loaf?'

'Both,' she said decidedly.

When she'd finished those she insisted Jago go up to the studio with her because she wanted to draw him, and Stella took his hand and said she'd go with them.

I closed up her clamshell sand pit and took the tray back indoors away from an inquisitive wasp and even more inquisitive dog and cat, then followed them.

On the day of the jumble sale I felt perfectly OK about leaving Stella in Jenny's capable hands, sure that if there was any emergency, then she could cope better than I could. She said not to rush back, because she wasn't going anywhere until nine, when she was needed to give supper to an elderly lady and then put her to bed, because her usual carer was laid up with a broken ankle.

I'd never helped at a jumble sale, but the best bit was that when we were spreading the clothes out on the tables and lining up the shoes in pairs, we were allowed to keep anything we wanted, so long as we put twice as much as we'd charge anyone else in the box.

Jago and Raffy unpacked the bric-a-brac and toys and spread out a row of larger household items, like laundry baskets and lightshades, along the edge of the stage, and then we braced ourselves and opened the doors.

I immediately saw what Chloe had meant about a stampede! The first group in the room thundered down on Raffy and Jago, while everyone else crowded up to our tables along the sides of the room. Arms reached in and snatched, and soon people were clutching whole bundles of things to their chests without even really looking at them.

I did recognise quite a lot of locals, but people seemed to have come from miles around, too.

At the end, we bagged up the remaining clothes for rag collection and boxed the last bits of bric-a-brac for the charity shop. Raffy had saved for Chloe a Bakelite mould that made four chocolate watches, which she was highly delighted with – and so was I when Jago presented me with a long, green-tinged glass rolling pin that was probably Victorian.

Effie Yatton and a few of her Brownies were going to clear the rest away and Raffy said he would count up the takings and email me later to say how much the jumble had raised, so the rest of us could go home.

'I don't suppose you've got time for a quick drink before you go back?' Jago asked me. 'We could put our things in the car on the way, it's just outside,' he added, because he'd taken a fancy to a brass coal scuttle with a blue and white china handle and a pair of old wooden butter paddles, while I was carefully clutching my glass rolling pin and a pink My Little Pony, still in its original packaging, for Stella, because it had reminded me of Butterball, the little pony at the stables.

'I could do. Jenny did say not to rush back.'

We put our finds in the boot and then he said, 'Let's go to the Falling Star. We've got something to celebrate – I completed on the property today.'

'You kept that quiet!'

'I thought I'd wait until after the jumble sale, but I get the keys in the morning so I think it's safe enough to celebrate now, don't you?'

'Of course it is!' Impulsively I stopped and hugged him and he picked me up off my feet and swung me round, grinning.

'Isn't it great?' he said. 'And the sooner I get my hands on the keys the better, so the stuff for Hemlock Mill can be removed and all the rubbish cleared, especially those tons of old newspapers in the attic. I can't get workmen in until that's done. They're a fire hazard, too.'

'After that, doing it up will be fun, won't it? And I'll help as much as I can,' I promised. 'I don't want to expose Stella to all that dust, though.'

'No, you certainly don't want to bring her until it's cleaned and painted. But I'll need your help planning out the layout and I'd love your input on colour schemes and stuff like that, because I'm useless at it.'

'Anything but grey or mustard?' I suggested, and he laughed as he held open the door to the Falling Star for me.

'That's about right. I know what I *don't* like.'

'I'd love to help and the other day Hal said he wouldn't mind looking at the garden for you, to see if there's anything in there worth keeping.'

'That's kind, but the garden might have to take a backseat until the house is sorted out, because I won't have a huge amount of time. I'll have to beat a path to the back, though, because the bins are there somewhere, and if I can get the double gates to hang properly I'll be able to park at the back.'

'Maybe just the hinges?' I suggested.

'We'll see. The garage probably wants pulling down and replacing, but if it does then that might have to wait a while, too.'

'Yes, getting the basic renovations done to the house and equipping the cake workshop have to be the priorities, don't they?' I said. 'But now it's all happening, it's very exciting.'

Florrie Snowball came into the snug and, seeing us there, came over to ask how Stella was. 'And don't you fret about rushing back home, because she's safe enough with our Jenny.'

Then she said she'd got a grand new winter coat from the jumble sale.

'Navy-blue wool, it is, military style and down to my ankles, so that'll keep me warm. Our Clive says I look like I just got back from the Russian front, the cheeky monkey.'

Jago seized the opportunity to ask her about booking a room there while Honey's was being renovated, and though by now I think the whole village knew that he was buying it, she was very interested in what he meant to do with it.

She gave him her terms for weekly boarders, which seemed more than reasonable, and agreed he could move in at the end of June.

When we walked back to the car Jago stopped to look with proprietorial eyes at Honey's, tucked shyly back between its neighbours like a wallflower at a dance.

'I can't wait to get the keys and have a good poke around tomorrow.'

'Oh, I'd love another look at it, too.'

'Well, you could, if you can get away?'

'I could ask Ma if she'd keep an eye on Stella – or maybe Jenny might pop round again. What time?'

'Any time you like.'

Back at the cottage, Stella was already fast asleep in bed, and Jenny and Ma were in the sitting room having a lively discussion about the *Cotton Common* TV soap, having found a mutual passion.

Jenny had to go and minister to her elderly lady and when I got back from seeing her off, Jago had already told Ma that he'd completed on the house and would be living at the Falling Star while it was being renovated.

'There's a lot to do; it could be Christmas before you're in there,' Ma said pessimistically.

'It will be a long job, but I'm certainly hoping to be living and working at Honey's before then.'

'What will you do for Christmas this year?' I asked. 'Will you go out to your parents in New Zealand?'

'No, I don't want to be away that long, and anyway, I'd rather stay here.'

'You can come and spend Christmas with us, then,' I offered, before belatedly remembering the house was Ma's and adding to her, 'can't he?'

'Yes, why not?' she agreed. 'Though you can't *stay* here, because we're crammed full as it is.'

'But this is going to be a very special Christmas,' Jago pointed out. 'Wouldn't you prefer to be just family?'

'You practically *are* family,' Ma said cryptically.

'I'd love you to be here,' I assured him. 'And so would Stella . . .' I tailed off as my mind for a moment threw up a darker image of a Christmas that was not celebrated at all . . . then I pushed it firmly away.

'Do come: this will be the best Christmas ever!' I said. I refused to dwell on any alternative scenarios: we'd follow our star and the miracle *would* happen.

Aimee

When Aimee finally decided to make her next move, she thought it would be best to rehearse the sob stuff and leave a message that was bound to appeal to that soft and soppy heart of his . . . but she'd send it to his mobile voicemail, so that that interfering friend of his wouldn't delete it if he got to it first!

'Jago darling . . . it's me, Aimee,' she said in a hesitant, little-girl voice. 'I just wanted to say I'm so sorry if I seemed to be rushing you into our engagement again and taking too much for granted, only . . .' here she allowed a break in her voice and a stifled sob, '. . . only as soon as I saw you again I realised what a *huge* mistake I'd made and it was you I loved all along. When you said you'd forgiven me, I just sort of assumed that you meant we'd be back together . . .'

Another break in her voice. Aimee thought she really should have been an actress.

'Let's just be friends, because I'd hate to think I'd never see you again . . . and it seems as though I'm constantly going to be sent to organise events at all the racecourses near you.'

Aimee, forgetting her role for a moment, added more unguardedly, 'This job is *so* ghastly! I hope to God they don't start sending me to run corporate events at rugby and football matches too, because that would be the last straw and—' She caught herself up and resumed her little-girl voice. 'Oh, well, perhaps something more interesting will come up soon,' she said. Like maybe he'd come to his senses and they could set some kind of business up together back in London . . .

'By the way, I apologise if I was a bit rude to that friend of yours, but I was jealous, sweetie-pie.' Aimee pulled a rude face at the phone. 'I remembered where I'd met her before too, at a party when she got engaged to Adam Scott. His parents live in the same village as Daddy, so I've known him for ever. Small world, isn't it?

'Anyway, I hope you forgive me, darling, because I'm so, so sorry. Speak to you soon, by-eee!' She ended the message and sat back, feeling satisfied that his soft heart would be softened to treacle by what she'd said.

When her mobile rang only a few minutes later, she snatched it up eagerly.

'Hello?'

'Aimee? Tracked you down at last,' Adam Scott said.

Chapter 27: Nearer, My God, to Thee

Ma was listening out for Stella while I looked over Honey's and then later she was going up to Winter's End to talk to Ottie about the joint exhibition they were holding in the autumn.

Jago was already in the shop when I got there, poking around by the light of a large torch. He had another for me, too, since he daren't pull up the worn blind in case the whole thing fell down.

'I'm going to arrange for the utilities to be reconnected later, but I expect it'll take a while before they are,' he said, rummaging around under one side of the counter. 'Look, a whole drawer of knitted baby jackets, though the moths seem to have had a field day.'

'What a shame! I expect they've had a good go at every-thing, unfortunately. I read somewhere that you can stop a moth infestation by freezing clothes for twenty-four hours,' I added, and he said he'd pass that tip on to Tim Wesley.

'It's hard to see what else is in here without the electricity on, but I suppose I'd better give everything a quick dust before Tim comes back again or it might put him off.'

'Oh, I don't think it would. He's already seen it at its

worst and you might find treasure trove when the lights are back on. These hatpins are pretty, aren't they?' I said, though I discovered that they were also firmly rusted into the pincushion. 'But if I can get away, I'll come and help you clean.'

'Despite the spiders?'

'Yes – if you brush the cobwebs down first!'

He stood in the middle of the shop and looked around him. 'I think I'll have a little office and reception area for customers at the front of the shop here, with an inner door and a glass window onto the preparation room.'

'There's something like that at one of the swish London hotels,' I said. 'You can see them making patisserie. Even with the front bit missing, you'd still have a huge kitchen-preparation area.'

We went through the rotting baize curtain at the back into the living room.

'The fireplace is nice, isn't it?' Jago said. 'I love those old turquoise and lilacy-pink tiles round the edge.'

'Yes, you could pick those shades up in some of the soft furnishings, later.'

We went and had a good poke round the rest of the house and he told me his plans for throwing it all back into one big family home, though he didn't mention who he hoped to start the big family with . . .

'The annexe cottage would make a great guest suite eventually,' he said. 'And I think it would be easy to turn the bit of paving between the kitchen and the annexe into a conservatory, to link them.'

'That's a good idea, because if it had a glass roof and front, then you wouldn't lose any light in the living room.

In fact, you could put a glazed door from the living room into the conservatory,' I suggested, and he thought that was a great idea.

Upstairs he intended upgrading the large but Spartan Victorian bathroom with modern fittings and a walk in shower. 'I might squeeze an en suite shower room into the main bedroom too, so this could be the family one.'

'What are you going to do with the flat upstairs?'

'Eventually turn it into two more en suite bedrooms.'

'Gosh, a three bathroom home – how posh!' I said, impressed.

'It'll be four; you've forgotten the one in the annexe,' he said, grinning.

'Oh, yes – there may even be an outside one at the bottom of the garden, you never know. If there is, you'll go down in local history as Five-Loos Tremayne.'

'I think five might be a toilet too far,' he said. 'Do you think I should go all out for a Victorian look through the house?'

'No, I think I'd just give a nod to Victorian. Maybe have light, warm shades on the walls, but William Morris curtains, and make a feature of the lovely fireplaces in every room.'

'That upstairs little front bedroom over the shop is pure seventeenth century,' he said.

'Yes, it could be lovely if the panelling and wooden floorboards were polished, and it's got a window seat and that cute little stone fireplace, too. I'm not sure how you would double-glaze that old diamond-paned window, though.'

'I'll have to find out, but it might have to be just secondary glazing in there. Most of the rest are sash windows, and I'm pretty sure you can get double-glazed versions of those.'

We were back downstairs now and he asked, 'What sort of a kitchen do you think I should have?'

The quarry-tiled room was bare, apart from some painted wall shelves and a deep, chipped sink set in a wooden draining board.

'I don't know. It's a bit of a blank slate, so you can start from scratch. Maybe you should get some brochures, or we could go and look at kitchen showrooms and get some ideas?'

'That would be fun.'

'The redecoration and furnishing bit will *all* be great fun,' I promised him, 'you just have to get the basic renovation done first.'

'Just,' he repeated.

'I know there's a lot to do, but I can imagine how it's going to look in the end – amazing.'

'That's more than Aimee could when she had a look round,' he said. 'I knew she'd hate it because she likes everything modern, minimal and open plan.'

He paused, then added awkwardly, 'She finally left a message on my phone yesterday, apologising for being bitchy to you and for getting hold of the wrong side of the stick. She sounded really sorry and said she understood I just want to be friends now.'

'How nice,' I said, and he grinned.

'Well, it had been so long that I was sort of hoping she'd found someone else and forgotten about me.' The smile suddenly vanished. 'I'm afraid she remembered where she'd seen you before – at your engagement party to your ex. Apparently his parents and her father live in the same village in the Cotswolds, so she's known him all her life.'

'Oh, right! She did look vaguely familiar and a lot of his

posh crowd of friends were at the party, though they only talked to each other, not to me.'

'Polite!' he commented. 'Aimee's friends were always like that too, when I was out with her.'

I had to go back and relieve Ma then, but we bounced ideas around by text later and then Jago relayed yet another summons to tea from Miss Honey – this time with Stella.

'It's for Friday, but I can tell her it's not convenient if you like?' he suggested.

'No, I expect she doesn't get a lot of visitors and she'd be disappointed if we didn't go. I only hope Stella doesn't finish her off, though.'

Jago hoped to have the electricity and water reconnected to Honey's the following week, so our fingers were crossed it didn't all go up in a blue light before it was rewired. He kept bringing round brochures for kitchens and wallpaper brochures, and paint charts.

'I think I'm turning into Sarah,' he said ruefully, one evening.

'But with better taste, from the sound of it. Have they finished putting carpets in the flat now?'

'Yes – and guess what, *they're* grey too.'

'I think we can safely say there won't be any hint of grey at Honey's.'

He told me that the people from the mill were coming the following Saturday to measure, photograph and then pack the contents of the shop up, but since Jago had a cake to make and deliver to somewhere the other side of Bolton that morning, I said I'd go and let them in.

'Celia and Will are having Stella for most of the day

anyway, did I tell you? It's the first time I've ever left her with them for so long, but she really wanted to go when they suggested it. They're having a picnic in the garden if it's fine, in the middle of that giant stone mushroom circle. Stella thinks it's enchanted.'

'She'll love that and I'm sure she'll be fine,' he said reassuringly. 'And anyway, she's only fifteen or twenty minutes away there, isn't she?' His eyes met mine and we both smiled. His crinkled up endearingly at the corners.

Jago did a bit of sneaky enquiring and discovered that Miss Honey's favourite tipple was Harveys medium dry sherry, so we took a bottle of that with us when we went to visit her on Friday, along with an assortment of sticky iced buns that Jago made specially, and my contribution of fairy cakes and mini meringues.

Stella, excited by the prospect of meeting yet another old lady, brought Bun and the mummy from her ginger cat family.

'Be very polite to Miss Honey,' I warned her.

'Yes, Mummy.'

'She's very old, so she gets tired easily. She might even just fall asleep in her chair in the middle of talking to us.'

'Awesome!' she said, and Jago laughed.

The assistant we'd seen last time, Charlène, took us up in the lift and ushered us into Miss Honey's suite.

'Here are your visitors, love, and one of them's a sweet little girl – pretty as an angel, she is.'

'I'm a big girl, nearly four,' Stella told her gravely. 'And I'm not an angel, because I'm not dead.'

Then she let go of my hand and went to stare closely at

Miss Honey's netted skin and knotted, blue-veined hands. 'You're very, very old – even older than the Graces,' she remarked admiringly.

'Which graces?' demanded Miss Honey.

'My three Graces and they're three hundred years old.'

'No, darling,' I broke in, 'they said *between* them they were that old, but actually, I think they were exaggerating and it's more like two hundred and fifty. Miss Honey is only a hundred and two.'

'Hah! *Only*,' said Miss Honey tartly.

'Your neck looks just like the tortoise's neck at the Botanical Gardens,' Stella observed.

Instead of taking umbrage at Stella's frankness, Miss Honey seemed to relish it. 'And you're so skinny it's a wonder you don't blow away.'

'I know, but when my heart's all better I'll suddenly grow and grow.'

'Well, that'll be good, so long as you don't sprout like Alice and fill the whole house.'

'Alys isn't very big yet,' Stella said, puzzled.

'She means her friend, Alys – Sophy Winter's little girl. We haven't got as far as reading *Alice in Wonderland* yet.'

'*I* can read,' Stella said.

'Can you indeed?' Miss Honey said, and then added, 'I don't know Sophy. Hebe and Ottie, now, I know them . . .'

'Ottie's a friend of my mum's.'

'It's a funny old world . . . and what's that you're both holding?'

'Sherry,' I said. 'I thought we should celebrate Jago buying Honey's.'

'And cakes,' Jago added, just as Charlene came back with

the tea trolley, to which she'd thoughtfully added a jug of rather synthetic-looking squash for Stella: clearly no oranges were harmed in the making of the product.

'Good: you can take that moth-eaten jam sponge away then, Charlene, but leave the plates.'

She watched Jago set out the goodies on the chintz-patterned china, which Stella admired.

'It's my own tea set. I'll leave it to you when I pop my clogs,' she told her.

'Thank you,' said Stella, and I think, though the expression was unknown to her, she still got the meaning because she asked, 'Are you going to die soon?'

'I expect so, but it depends when my Maker wants me. Sometimes I wonder if he's forgotten me and that's why I'm still here. I get tired.'

'So do I,' Stella said.

'After your operation you'll be full of beans, don't you worry,' Miss Honey said.

'Boston beans,' Jago suggested. 'That's where the hospital in America is.'

Stella nodded, though her thumb was back in her mouth and she had to remove it to speak. 'I'm glad you're still here,' she told Miss Honey, then showed her the ginger mummy cat in her pocket, and Bun, which Miss Honey kindly admired, though a more threadbare object you never saw in your life. Then she came and sat on my knee.

We toasted Jago's purchase of Honey's in sherry, though I hate the stuff and I was pretty sure from his heroic expression as he sipped that Jago felt the same.

Then I said, cautiously, 'You *did* understand that Jago and I aren't engaged, didn't you, Miss Honey?'

She nodded. 'Oh, yes, I understood all right, though I don't condone modern manners and having children out of wedlock. Still, there have always been little mistakes . . .'

She brooded for a few moments and then went on, 'It's sensible of your young man to get his bakery up and running before you think of anything more than walking out.'

We seemed to have hit an insurmountable barrier and Jago and I exchanged glances. Luckily Stella seemed to be too drowsy to be taking in what we were saying now, especially when Miss Honey added her clincher.

'When the time is right, I hope you'll invite me to the wedding. Though if you do, I wouldn't leave it too long, because at my age you never know when your number's up.'

'If we do get married, you'll be our guest of honour,' Jago assured her, straight-faced, then started enthusiastically describing his plans for the shop and house.

'The people from the mill are going to photograph the interior of the shop tomorrow and measure it up before they pack everything, so they can recreate it exactly up there. Everything will be just as it was, right down to the original shop sign, because I'll have a new one made that says "Honey's Croquembouche Cakes".'

'That's a mouthful,' she observed.

'So are the cakes,' I said.

'They'll be taking most of the furniture straight up to the mill house, though the organ's now going to a restorer first, because Hebe Winter offered to pay for it. Apparently one of the people who volunteers to help up at the mill plays, and is looking forward to striking up a hymn or two for the visitors.'

Miss Honey was very keen on that idea. 'I always liked

"Nearer, my God, to Thee", she said. 'Apt, given my age, nowadays. When will it all be open?'

'The mill owner's house is already open, though it's only partly furnished. I'm not sure how long the shop will take to set up, but there are lots of student volunteers to help so it could be quite quick.'

'I might live to see it yet, then,' she said. 'And even if I don't, the visitors will hear my voice, because they sent some of those students up here to start recording my memories.'

'Yes, the visitors will love that,' Jago said.

'There's some woman from the Middlemoss Living History Archive wanting to come and record me, too,' she said. 'I'm a living fossil. Or maybe,' she added, her eyes softening as they rested on Stella, 'the oldest tortoise in the world.'

From the way Miss Honey had perked up again and was wolfing iced buns, washed down with another glass of sherry, I didn't think she'd be going anywhere fast.

'Now, Jago,' Miss Honey said, sitting upright. 'Fetch some more glasses from that little corner cupboard, because I've invited a few friends round to celebrate and I can hear Annie's walking frame thumping.'

Chapter 28: Taking Stock

On Saturday Stella woke up very excited about her day with Celia and Will, and they arrived early to collect her, since part of the treat was going to be a McDonald's breakfast, a prospect that she found very exciting, since it wasn't something she'd ever had before. I tried my best not to fuss and Celia assured me they'd ring my mobile at the least sign that Stella wasn't feeling well, or wanted to come home.

When I went down to open up Honey's, the village was still quiet and I barely saw a soul. Inside the shop it didn't look that bright even with the light on, so I gingerly tried raising the blind. It got almost all the way up, but then the cord at one side snapped and it hung down at an angle like a bird with a broken wing, though at least we now got a little light, revealing that Jago didn't seem to have done more than swipe down the cobwebs from the ceiling and scrape off the top furring of grey dust.

Jago would be arriving later, after he'd delivered his croquembouche to a wedding reception venue, but Tim Wesley and a whole bunch of students got to Honey's soon after I did. They swarmed over everything like ants, photographing and measuring and noting the position of every last thing. Easy-peel labels were slapped all over the place and then they started to pack.

I was more of a hindrance than a help, really, since the contents of the drawers were such a fascinating jumble: button hooks and buttons of all kinds, papers of rusting pins, darning wool, knitting needles, hanks of pale blue and pink silk, button-up leggings for toddlers, hairbrushes, rattles, matinée jackets, silk socks and yellowing leather booties for babies. There were hand-crocheted dressing table mat sets, hairpins, fifties-style crepe dresses and flowered cotton pinafores, nylons, rayon scarves and bits of costume jewellery . . . The list went on and on.

All the price tickets were in pounds, shillings and pence, and candy-striped paper bags with pinked tops and gussets hung from a string under the counter.

I made a little selection of the buttons, lace, trimmings and hatpins before they were packed up, because I thought that if they were displayed in a deep frame, it would make a nice memento for Miss Honey.

The students had a short break outside the back door, washing the dust out of their throats with cola or the kind of energy drinks that would have had me bouncing off the walls in minutes. Then a small hired removal van came for the dresser, organ and the hefty pedestal table, which were carefully packed in hessian as if they were very precious, which was something Miss Honey would appreciate. The organ went in last, since it was to be delivered to the restorers on the way to the mill.

There was still no sign of Jago even after the van returned to ferry the first consignment of shop contents up to the mill – the counter, stands and mannequins, along with as many boxes as would fit around them.

I'd started to worry about Jago's non-arrival till he texted me again to say he was stuck in a traffic jam caused by an accident. He only finally arrived just as the students were packing the final boxes of stock for the last load.

'It's been an absolute treasure trove,' Tim told him, enthusiastically describing some of the things they'd unearthed. 'Thanks so much for letting us have it. I know you could have sold a lot of it off – some of it is very collectable.'

'I didn't feel any of it really belonged to me: it's the Honeys' heritage. But I'm looking forward to seeing it all set up again at the mill house and so is Miss Honey.'

'We'll have a special opening ceremony when it's finished and see if she feels up to coming along and cutting the ribbon,' Tim suggested. 'She's a very lively old lady for her years, so she might well.'

'I'm sure she wouldn't miss it for the world,' I said. 'How are the tape recording sessions going along? She said some students had been up.'

'Oh, we've got hours of reminiscence and it's being edited down for a short permanent audio loop for the shop. I told someone from the Middlemoss Living History Archive about her – that's an ongoing project to record the memories of people living in the borough of Middlemoss – and they asked for a copy of the tapes. I think they were going to see if Miss Honey would let them tape some reminiscences of her life for them too, since ours is mostly about the shop.'

'Yes, she mentioned that, and I think they've already started. All this excitement has given her a new lease of life!' Jago said.

Tim drove off back to the mill, ready to supervise the van when it arrived with the last load, and Jago and I watched the final boxes carried out, leaving only light patches on the wooden floor where things had stood. The long empty room seemed to stretch back like a dark cave.

'I'll need loads of lights in here when it's my preparation area,' Jago said thoughtfully. 'I must have a think about that before the electricians come in.'

He went out to have a word with the students before they departed, but it turned out he wasn't just thanking them: he was arranging for some of them to come back next Saturday, when they were free, to clear out all the rubbish from the house into a skip he was going to order for the weekend.

'It'll cost me a few quid but it will be worth it. So, all in all, a pretty good day,' he said with satisfaction.

'Yes, but I'd better go now, because Celia and Will will be bringing Stella home soon. They called earlier to say they'd picnicked in the garden and then she had an afternoon snooze on the swinging seat – it was too warm to stay in.'

'I'm sure she's had a lovely time,' Jago said.

'Actually, I feel quite guilty, because it's all been so interesting today that I'd quite forgotten about her until they rang!' I confessed.

He laughed. 'I think that's pretty healthy.'

'I'm desperate for a shower before they bring her back. I feel filthy.'

'Me too, even though I haven't been here that long,' he agreed, and said he'd go back to the flat to shower and change, then return later with a Chinese takeaway, since Ma and Hal were going out again – this was getting to be a habit!

And the following day we'd *all* be at Honey's, since Ma and Hal wanted to look at the garden and see what – if anything other than weeds – was in there.

* * *

When Stella got home she excitedly showed me the toy-families-sized quilt she'd made out of a snippet of silk and a little thin wadding. Actually, I'm sure Celia had made the whole thing, but since Stella had directed the operation, she felt that she'd had a major part in it.

Before Celia and Will went home again, I showed them my treasure trove of buttons, bows, lace, hatpins and tiny wooden cotton reels, and Celia offered to construct a sort of little three-dimensional collage out of them for Miss Honey, which Will would put in a deep box frame. In fact, she said there was enough there for two, so I think one would be nice for Jago to display somewhere, maybe in the office/reception area he was going to make at the front of the shop.

Stella had tea and then was so tired she went willingly to bed, though with the promise that when he came, Jago would come and say good night to her.

Next morning we were all at Honey's for the great garden inspection, Hal armed with a giant Strimmer and me carrying a picnic basket with refreshments and a rug.

I wouldn't let Stella go into the house because of all the dust, though I thought Ma and Hal might be curious to see it. But Ma refused, because she didn't feel Miss Honey would approve, and Hal was disinterested in anything except the garden.

He and Ma waded about in waist-high weeds – practically head-height on Ma – and then he cut a path to the far end by the garage, which we all trooped down in single file, like a strange Famous Five.

Actually, the garage was in better condition than you might have expected, apart from the paint having peeled away from

315

the wood like silver birch bark. Inside, there was nothing except some dubious heaps of sacking, a rusty jerry can and a few ancient oil stains on the cracked concrete.

'Perhaps the lodger, or whoever rented the annexe, had a car and used it at one time?' I suggested.

'Not for ages, though,' Ma said. 'The gates to the lane are nearly off their hinges too.'

'Corrugated iron never looks good, even when it isn't rusty,' Hal observed. He was chewing a long piece of grass, though Ma had told him it would give him liver fluke. I hoped not, but I expect it was just an old wives' tale.

'It seems a strange thing to make gates of,' agreed Jago. 'I'll have them replaced to make the back access more secure. What's that small stone building for, over the other side of the gate?'

'Oh, that was a midden, for putting the rubbish in,' Hal explained, then peered into the small door at the back of it. 'Looks like they blocked up the other side and used the midden to keep chickens in at some time: there's nesting boxes.'

'There you are, see – you *can* have your hens. Just not cockerels,' I said to Jago, and then had to explain the covenant on the property to the others.

'I like hens,' Stella said, peeping in at the nesting boxes.

'You can help me look after them, if I get some, then,' promised Jago. 'It won't be for a while yet, though.'

'Perhaps Santa will bring you some?' she suggested seriously. 'You'd better write him a letter.'

'Lots of people keep hens in the village and you don't notice a cock crowing if you've been brought up to it,' Hal said. 'I wouldn't take no notice of any covenant.'

'I suppose it's only newcomers who notice that kind of thing,' Jago said.

Hal began wading about in the weeds with his Strimmer, the modern-day machete-wielding explorer in the jungle, while we watched him from the paved area near the back door.

'Anything worth saving?' Ma called when he finally turned it off and could hear us again.

'Not a lot. That tree there's an apple – clear it around and feed it some good muck, then prune it back hard and see if it does anything. And there's some quince up the dividing wall that look all right. I doubt there's anything else worth keeping.'

'I'm not a great gardener, so I'm thinking mainly lawn and maybe a herb bed?' Jago said.

'You liked the knot gardens up at the hall,' I reminded him.

'I know, but I don't think I've got the patience to keep one trimmed into shape.'

Hal said that now he'd started he might as well finish Strimming all the weeds down, so we all had a little picnic with cake and cold drinks, and then Ma, Stella and I left them to it and went home.

It was ages before they turned up at the cottage, hot and tired, just as it started to rain in big, splashy drops, and a late roast Sunday lunch was nearly ready. Over it, Jago said Hal was going to knock the garden into shape for him.

'Moonlighting from your moonlighting here?' Ma said, but I don't think she minded and anyway, it seemed unlikely to take up much of his time, since he was going to get a couple of the other Winter's End gardeners down next

Sunday to clear it ready for turfing and to dig out a herb bed at one end.

'Oh, good,' Ma said, 'because this lady's not for turfing.'

Stella was half asleep in bed and I'd just got to a mention of Moominpappa in her favourite storybook when she suddenly opened her eyes and said, 'Where's *my* daddy?'

'At the North Pole, counting penguins,' I said, as I always did. 'There are an awful lot of them and they keep moving around, so it's taking him a very long time.'

'No,' she said crossly, 'Daddy-*Jago*. I want him to read my book. I bet he can do the Moominpappa voice better than you can.'

'Maybe,' I conceded, not reminding her that Jago tended to stumble his way through unfamiliar books, due to his dyslexia. 'But he had to go home. He did say goodbye, don't you remember?'

'He should live with us and be my Moominpappa,' she said, her eyes closing again, so that I abandoned my half-formed notion of trying to explain to her a little more about why her real daddy had never been around because she was way too tired tonight to take it in.

'Jago will read your bedtime story next time he's here,' I promised rashly, and then carried on until she was fast asleep, which took about a minute.

Chapter 29: Nesting

Next morning the weather had changed and the sky was a soggy, fuzzy grey blanket lying heavily across the landscape.

I'd had an Easter idea for a 'Tea & Cake' recipe, carrying on from the little nests that Stella and I made the previous day, and created a big one using a ring mould, lots of melted chocolate and twiggy cereal. I decorated it with little sugar eggs stuck on with dabs of icing and tiny sugar flowers I had left over from something else. The effect was very pretty.

I arranged my collection of painted wooden eggs in the middle and then sent Jago some pics, though he didn't reply straight away so he and David must have been baking.

When I'd cleared up, assisted by Toto, who was under the table hoovering up any fallen scraps, I checked on Stella and found her still fast asleep. So I turned on the laptop, meaning to type up the Easter ring recipe, though first, as usual, I checked the donations to the Stella's Stars fund and then my email inbox.

And there, in the inbox, was a once-familiar name . . . Adam Scott's.

In case my short-term memory was really bad, he'd put 'From Adam Scott' in the subject line, too.

I deleted it before I knew what I was doing, and then sat there, my hands shaking, my nerves twanging and my heart pounding. Then I took a couple of deep breaths and fished the email back out again.

Another intake of breath and it was open in front of me.

Hi Cally, it's me, Adam, it began, followed by a smiley face emoticon.

A smiley face? I stared at the screen blankly. Not a word during the years of trauma his child had suffered and he'd sent me a *smiley face*?

Creep! The air turned bluer than Gauloise smoke.

Heard from a friend that you had a little girl and I assume she's mine? Have been thinking about you a lot lately and I know I behaved badly, but I'd really like to meet up and say I'm sorry.

Bit late, Adam, I thought.

I did two tours of Antarctica, then I was based on a small island near the Falklands, but I'm back now. Got a job in London with Wesley Marine and ready to settle down.

Another smiley face.

Had all that exposure to extreme cold done something to his brain? And why would he think I had any interest in what he'd been doing, or was doing now? I wished I'd changed my email address as well as blocked him on Facebook!

Please reply, if this gets to you,

Adam x

His last kiss had turned out to be a Judas one. I stared at that kiss for so long that the screensaver kicked in.

It was a bit pat that he should suddenly pop back up so soon after Aimee had seen and recognised me, so I had to assume she was the 'friend'. Jago might have managed to forgive Aimee for jilting him, but how much more did I have to forgive Adam for!

Ma, entering the kitchen and seeing me sitting there, said, 'What's up? You look as if you've seen a ghost.'

'I have – I've just had an email from Adam.'

'What, Scott of the Antarctic?' she said incredulously, her precious jade cigarette holder coming perilously close to falling on the kitchen floor.

'The very same.'

'What on earth does *he* want?'

'He was politely enquiring if he was Stella's father, since someone had helpfully mentioned to him that I have a little girl. I think it's Aimee, trying to stir things up – remember I told you Jago's ex recognised me?'

'Sort of. All these exes popping back up again is a bit complicated.'

'He says he'd like to see me again and presumably also Stella, but only if she really is his, of course.'

'Are you going to reply?'

'No,' I said, but I was thoroughly unsettled and didn't even protest when she broke off a big chunk of the giant chocolate bird's nest and munched it while popping bread into the toaster. 'Mmm, chewy,' she said.

'It was meant more as a table decoration,' I told her. Then Stella woke and called me, so I quickly deleted the email again and decided to put Adam right out of my head. Perhaps if I ignored him, he'd go away.

Unfortunately, putting it out of my head proved impossible, so I rang Celia later when I was on my own to talk it through, though at first she thought I was calling about the cakes I was making for the Knitathon tomorrow. She chatted away quite happily until it suddenly dawned on her that she wasn't getting much response and asked what was up.

'I had an email from Adam!'

'What, Adam your ex, Adam?'

'That's the one,' I agreed, and then told her what he'd said. 'I'm not answering it, of course.'

'Oh . . . I don't know about that, Cally. I mean, he is Stella's father, so—'

'Only biologically,' I broke in, 'not any other way. And I don't want him in our lives, especially at this stage.'

'I know you wouldn't want Stella upset or unsettled, but she doesn't have to be. I mean, perhaps he's changed,' she suggested. 'If he's heard about Stella's problems from this Aimee, then he might feel guilty and want to help now.'

'We've managed perfectly well without his help all these years, so he can keep it,' I snapped.

'Well, don't entirely close the door on the possibility,' she advised, and I wondered if Elizabeth Bennet ever felt like murdering her lovely, sweet-natured sister Jane?

Later Adam sent me another 'Dear Cally' email which, after a profound inner struggle, I opened. It said he hoped I'd got his first email and would I now give him my mobile number so we could talk and arrange to meet.

I did answer that one, but no 'Dear Adam' in *my* reply:

I was surprised to hear from you, I wrote without any preamble. *My daughter is nearly four so you can do the maths yourself if you want to. We have managed perfectly well without you so far – and long may that continue.*

Cally

322

I hoped that would do the trick, but I felt so ruffled that I phoned Jago when Stella was in bed that night and told *him* all about Adam's contacting me, too, and his sudden interest in Stella. Actually, I'd been dying to tell him all day, but I didn't like to unload *all* my troubles onto his shoulders.

But he said I should have called him earlier. 'It must have been such a shock suddenly hearing from him – and I'm sure you're right and he got to know about Stella through Aimee, and I feel that it's my fault.'

'Maybe he'll think better of it now and that'll be the last I hear from him,' I said optimistically. 'I told him straight that we'd managed fine without him all these years.'

'I don't know . . .' he said doubtfully. 'Perhaps he genuinely does want to apologise and to be part of Stella's life, even if it took him a long while to get there?'

'That's more or less what Celia said,' I admitted, 'but I don't want him to suddenly appear and then vanish again, which would upset Stella for no reason. I mean, she's used to the idea that he lives at the North Pole and that's why she's never seen him.'

I didn't add that Jago was fast becoming the dependable father figure in her young life, so any sudden attempt by Adam to assert himself in that role would just confuse her.

'You're right, it's tricky, and your instinct as a mother is to do what's best for Stella, whatever that is. We are a pair, with our exes trying to muscle back into our lives as if nothing ever happened!' he said ruefully.

'But unlike you and Aimee, I don't even want to be friends with him. I don't want to *see* him, come to that.'

'Actually, I'm fast starting to feel the same way about Aimee,' he confessed. 'I began by feeling sorry for her, but now I'd prefer it if she forgot all about me. She hasn't rung me, apart from that message asking me to forgive her, but she keeps sending little text messages.'

'They aren't covered in smiley emoticons, are they?'

'How did you know?' he asked, surprised.

'She and Adam seem to have come from the same mould. A shallow one, with chipped edges. Oh, well,' I sighed, 'I'll just have to wait and see what happens with Adam.'

'But do tell me straight away if you hear from him again. You don't have to worry about anything on your own, when you can share it with me,' he said, and I felt a warm and fuzzy glow round my heart.

I hoped to discuss things with Celia a bit more next day, but the Knitathon event was such a success that there was little opportunity to talk.

The garden was full of people sitting crocheting on the grass, on garden chairs, on fold-up ones borrowed from the church hall up the road, and even perched on the stone toadstools like terribly domestic fairies. They were all sponsored for every square they produced, but lots of other people had simply paid their entrance to sit about under the shady trees and have tea.

The sun shone on the righteous. Will had put up a gazebo with trestle tables near the house, where my home-made cakes and scones were spread out, and volunteers trotted in and out with fresh pots of tea and coffee and jugs of cold drinks.

Stella spent most of her time with Jenny and Mrs Snowball

under a shady tree, eventually falling asleep on Jenny's lap, and only woke up when everyone was going.

Long shadows moved across the grass as the volunteers folded the chairs ready for collection and carried dirty crockery and cups into the house. The day had produced a great mound of crocheted squares in a rainbow of colours and I asked Celia what she was going to do with them.

'The ladies at the church up the road that we borrowed the chairs from are going to sew them into blankets and then distribute them among the elderly locally just before Christmas,' she said, which seemed a lovely idea.

'We must have made loads of money just from the entrance fee,' Will said, staggering past under a mound of multi-hued wool. 'Then there's the sponsorship money to come in, too. I'd say it's been a *huge* success.'

'Yes, me too,' I agreed. 'Thank you so much, both of you!'

'We're only a small part of the fundraising programme, going by Hebe Winter's constant updates,' Celia said. 'There seems to be some event or other now practically every day till autumn!'

'I think that might be a slight exaggeration, but a lot is happening and we still have the biggest events, the fête and the auction, to go.'

'I confidently predict you'll double your target and so you can stop worrying about any new expenses that crop up,' she said. 'Will's sorted your tickets, visas, hotel booking, insurance . . .' she ticked off each on her fingers. 'All the arrangements are made at this end and the hospital here is in contact with the one in Boston, isn't it?'

I shivered suddenly, though it was still warm. 'Yes, they update them constantly on Stella's condition, and Boston has just emailed me all kinds of information about the treatments she'll receive and about how children recover after major heart surgery.'

Celia gave me a hug. 'It will all go well and she'll bounce back to health, you'll see. And never mind what I said about Adam: you were right and I was wrong, because he's a complication you don't need at the moment. Maybe when Stella's fit and well again you might let him visit her and play some small future role in her life, if that's what she wants, but don't worry about it till then.'

'So long as *he* doesn't worry *me*,' I said with a wry smile.

Chapter 30: Plagued

It wasn't surprising that Stella was tired and fractious during her next hospital appointment, though they were a little concerned about her so we went straight home afterwards instead of into Ormskirk.

But Jago came out for tea, bringing her a gingerbread pig, which she said was even more fun, even if she didn't get to see her friends the Graces . . . and actually, I thought so too.

By Saturday she was herself again, her small reserves of energy restored and so when we took Toto out for a walk we went by way of Honey's to see how the students were doing with the big clear-out. Jago didn't have a wedding cake to make, luckily, so was going to be there all day, supervising.

There was no sign of life at the front, so we went round the corner and up the unmade bit of lane at the back, where the rusted corrugated iron gates had been wrenched wide open to allow entry for an enormous skip.

Already it was half full of flattened cartons, rotted curtains and carpets and crumbling lino. A line of students carrying stacks of old newspapers were scurrying down the metal staircase from the flat like a procession of ants.

Jago came out of the garage holding a bundle of old sacking and the rusty jerry can and tossed those into the skip, too.

'Hi,' he said, then as Stella clambered out and would have run to him, added quickly, 'No, don't touch me, Stella – I'm filthy!'

'Do you need a bath?' she asked, stopping dead.

'Yes, but I'll have it when we've finished the clearing.'

'How's it going?' I asked.

'We've emptied the house and annexe and they're just starting on all those newspapers in the flat, so pretty well, actually. I'm going to break up and bring out the kitchen units in the annexe in a minute, and when I can get near the ones in the flat, I'll do the same with those. Then that should be it.'

'You haven't thrown out that lovely Belfast sink from the kitchen, have you?'

'No, I'm leaving all the sinks and the baths and stuff until I get a plumber in.'

'Good, because when you turn the washhouse into your utility room it'll be really handy. Or if you don't want it there, then they make nice planters in the garden.'

'I'll probably have it in the utility room, then, if you think it's a good idea,' he promised. 'The good news is that now I've had a better look at the garage, it's not as bad as I first thought, so I'll have it repaired and painted when I have the gates replaced, and a gravel hard parking area, too.'

Then he went off to rip out cupboards, but promised to come round later when he'd been back to the flat and showered off the grime.

'Come for dinner,' I invited.

Stella nodded, so that her silvery curls bounced. 'Pink fish,' she offered enticingly.

'Salmon *en croute*,' I said, 'salad, then raspberries and ice cream. It'll be just us, because Ma's off to the pub again with Hal – it's getting to be a habit.'

'OK, that sounds irresistible!' he said, and so was the smile that went with it.

Stella obviously felt the same because she beamed at him and said, 'I love you, Daddy-Jago!'

He was exhausted when he arrived but pleased with the day's progress and updated us about it over dinner.

'What will you do with the shop window?' I asked.

'Display a model croquembouche in it, like the one at the Happy Macaroon, and probably one of David's party pyramids too, since we'll take orders for each other.'

'You'll need a new blind, that one's never going to rise again.'

'It certainly won't – I put it in the skip,' he said with a grin. 'But the next thing on the agenda once the cleaning service has been in is to get the woodworm treated. Because of all the chemicals they use it'll need to air for a few days before the other workmen go in.'

'There's an awful lot to think about.'

'I know, and I've also had to apply for change of use from a haberdasher's shop to a bakery, so there'll be various checks, certificates and health and safety hoops to jump through before I finally open my doors. Still, I've been through all that with David when he opened the Happy Macaroon, though that's a shop open to the public, of course, and mine will only be open by appointment.'

He'd brought more paint charts and some wallpaper samples and we pored over those later, after Stella was in bed.

To keep the house light, we decided that most walls should be emulsioned in a warm cream shade called Linen, with the occasional feature wall in a Morris print of fruit and foliage to give a nod towards the house's Victorian features.

'I'll keep the stained wooden floor in the seventeenth-century bedroom, and the panelling, of course,' he said. 'But we can paint the walls above and I can put down a couple of rugs to warm the room up.'

He sighed, shuffling the brochures together. 'There seems a long way to go before I get to the redecoration stage!'

'I suppose it will take ages, but meanwhile you can start getting adverts ready to go into the wedding magazines and brochures, and order business cards . . .' I began.

'And have leaflets printed to leave in local shops,' he continued. 'I must get onto the Sticklepond Saunter tourist trail leaflet too. Then I want the name of the business painted on the side of the van – I've ordered a new shop sign already.'

'The people in the Witch Craft Gallery next door to Honey's seem friendly, so perhaps you could ask them if you could fix a sign on their side wall, so people don't walk by without seeing you're there?'

'Good idea, and I wondered if I could have some tubs of flowers and maybe a stone bench outside the shop too.'

'I don't see why not, and it would look very enticing,' I said.

'Well, until I move in I'll be dividing my time between earning a living at David's and overseeing the renovation,' he said. 'This could be a very busy summer!'

*   *   *

330

Stella and I took another picnic down to Honey's for everyone on Sunday while the garden clearance was going on and, with three gardeners plus Jago's inexpert help, they soon had it all cleared and dug ready for turf to be laid over most of it, though they left flowerbeds down the sides, where the quince bushes were, and an area for the herb garden near the house.

Eventually, when the space between the kitchen and annexe was glazed over and turned into a conservatory, there would be a small patio in front of it, but Jago said that could be done when he had the gravelled parking area made later.

We sat under the old apple tree and after a while Stella fell asleep on the rug, looking quite rosy. I felt her forehead in case it was a fever: but no, it was just a healthy glow.

On the way home later, I thought what a lovely day we'd had – a lovely weekend, in fact.

Although the recollection of Adam's making contact had impinged from time to time, it had been immediately banished – as, apparently was Aimee from Jago's mind, because he'd never mentioned her once.

Jago began packing ready to move to the Falling Star, but he couldn't take all his things with him so I'd suggested he store a few boxes in Ma's garage temporarily, since now all my smart clothes had gone there was a bit of space.

So on Thursday, after we'd been to the hospital, we parked right behind the Happy Macaroon, squeezing into the left-over space in their yard between the Saab and the van, so Jago could load up the boot with boxes for us to take back.

We had a peep at the flat, too – and Jago hadn't been exaggerating about all that grey and mustard! It was immaculate, but not my cup of tea in the least.

There were only a few boxes, so once he'd loaded the car we left it there and had lunch in the Blue Dog, to Stella's delight. This was tempered somewhat by discovering that her friends were not there, though luckily they soon came in and sunshine was restored.

Then on the Friday Sarah moved into the flat for good and Jago moved out to the Falling Star. It felt odd but nice having him only a few minutes' walk away in the village, though Ma said he was around so much she didn't see that it would make a lot of difference. She didn't seem to mind, though. Really, I was only surprised she'd noticed.

But I'll tell you something that *I* noticed very early on Saturday morning, just as I was about to switch on the kitchen light: a Hal-shaped figure moving rapidly past the window followed by the squeak of the garden gate . . .

Have we been cramping Ma's style all this time?

After breakfast, while Ma was smoking a sneaky Sobranie in the garden, I asked her if there was anything she'd like to tell me.

She regarded me thoughtfully over the rings of smoke. 'No, actually, I don't think so. Is there anything *you'd* like to tell *me*?'

'Like what?' I asked, puzzled.

'Well, I don't know – you started this conversation!' she said crossly, then ground the stub of her Sobranie out under her heel and went off up to the studio.

We had a change of scene this Sunday when Jago and I took Stella to picnic on the Lido field, which was on the outskirts of the village where a safe bathing area had been created by cordoning off a bit of the river Ches with a half-circle of huge stones.

We read the information board, which said the field was the site of a plague pit, where the unfortunate villagers who succumbed to the Black Death had been buried in mass graves. This felt sort of odd as you sat on it eating your sandwiches.

'It must have been scary, not knowing who'd get the Black Death next when it popped up mysteriously everywhere,' Jago said.

'A bit like Aimee and Adam,' I said tartly, 'only without the buboes.'

He grinned. 'We do seem to be plagued by our pasts, though as with the Black Death I hope the worst has now passed. Aimee still texts me a lot, but hasn't rung again and you haven't heard from Adam again at all, have you?'

'No, I'm happy to say.'

'What's a bubo?' asked Stella, looking up from her egg sandwich.

'A big spot,' I said. 'But if you sing "Ring a Ring o' Roses", you won't get one.'

'You too then, Mummy,' she urged, so we had to do the song with actions, watched with amusement by all the other families picnicking on the field.

It was the hottest day of the year and I let Stella paddle, though kept a careful eye on her since she had a tendency to turn blue even in warm water. But she was fine, splashing about with one or two of the toddlers from the playgroup. Then an ice-cream van arrived, heralded by a jangling rendition of 'Greensleeves' and we all ate cones with chocolate flakes in them.

Stella went to sleep on the picnic rug under the shade of an elderberry tree and I asked Jago what it was like living at the Falling Star.

He said the coffee was excellent, breakfast was a limp microwaved bacon bap, and if he wanted an evening meal he had a choice of microwaved sausage rolls, meat pies, or scampi and chips served in a plastic wicker-effect basket lined with a paper napkin.

'You can come and eat with us whenever you like, because I always make too much. Ma won't mind.'

Ma probably wouldn't even notice.

On our way back, Jago carried a sleepy Stella and I had the picnic bag. In a blissful moment of unalloyed happiness I thought what a lovely day we'd had . . . and wondered at what point we'd started holding hands while we were out? I couldn't remember, but it seemed *very* natural.

Chapter 31: Cooking Up a Storm

I quickly got used to having Jago actually living in the village and, even though we were both very busy, it was lovely to be able to compare notes at the end of each day, if he came round to Ma's, which he usually did.

Apart from being occupied with Stella, I was cooking up a positive storm of recipe articles which, with the Christmas ones I'd already filed, I hoped would last from autumn to late the following year when, please God, Stella would be fully recovered and leading a normal life. Then I could work a few months in advance of publication, instead of stockpiling what seems like several years' worth.

Given that Stella's operation hovered on the distant horizon like a pewter-dark cloud that we all hoped would prove to have a Sterling silver lining, the summer days passed in a sort of sunny idyll, strangely unaffected by the changeable weather.

Hebe continued her tireless fundraising scheduling and twice I was called on to be photographed receiving a cheque for a local paper article. Raffy dropped in to tell me about some of the promised lots for the auction, which was coming up later in July: the first of the biggest fundraising events. Ma has promised a painting, of course, and Ottie has already given him a framed sketch for a sculpture. I suggested I could offer to make a Swedish celebration cake for any occasion and when I told Jago about it, he generously said he'd do the same with a croquembouche.

The renovations at Honey's were in full swing and Jago was dashing about between overseeing them, helping out David with cake and macaroon orders at the Happy Macaroon and making and delivering his own croquembouche, orders for which seemed to be steadily coming in, despite his not having advertised them other than in David's shop window. I thought this boded well for when he did have his own premises and publicised Honey's Croquembouche Cakes.

By now he was popping in and out of Ma's cottage as easily as if he was a member of the family, largely unnoticed by Ma.

The hospital have been quite pleased with Stella, although she had to have another going-over at Alder Hey Children's Hospital, which she hated until they assured her they were not going to stick big needles into her arm. Jago had made time to come with us and I was glad he had because he seemed to have such a calming influence on both of us that I wished he was coming to America!

But on the whole, everything in the garden was rosy . . . apart from the odd aphid, like Abominable Aimee. She was back in the area and called in to see him one day, though he only had time for a quick cup of coffee with her in the Blue Dog. From the sound of it she was being as sweet as pie and he said she was very contrite about having accidentally let fall to Adam's parents about Stella – not that I thought it was innocent and nor, I'm sure, did Jago really.

Aimee had also professed great interest in the interior of

Honey's and offered her help with the décor. 'She wanted to have another look round, but I said even if I had time, it was unsafe because there were workmen in,' he told me.

'Quick thinking,' I said admiringly.

'She was still wearing her ring, but on the other hand, and she didn't say anything else about getting together, so it was all right, really. I think she's finally accepted that it's not going to happen.'

I thought she was probably just regrouping before her next major move, but I hoped I was wrong!

'At least I've heard no more from Adam,' I said. 'Maybe he just emailed on impulse when Aimee told him about Stella and now he's had second thoughts and lost interest again.'

I could but hope.

Stella had obviously been a big hit with Miss Honey, for we were summoned again, the invitation expressly including her.

We took cake and sherry, these seeming to have been very acceptable, and Stella had some more animals in her pocket to show to her new and interestingly ancient friend.

When the goodies had been handed over and the niceties observed, Miss Honey wanted a full description of what was being done to the shop and the house, so Jago got his camera out and showed her some pictures of the new 'Honey's Croquembouche Cakes' sign over the window, and some shots of the garden at the back, where the Winter's End gardeners had unrolled new turf like so much green carpet, and it was all so neat and tidy it looked like a minor diversion in *Homes & Gardens*.

'I've had "Honey's Croquembouche Cakes" painted in the same green and gold as the shop sign on the sides of my delivery van, too,' he told her, 'and it's on my leaflets and business cards. I'll bring you some when they arrive; they're being printed.'

'You seem to be getting organised,' Miss Honey approved, and then switched her attention to me and started to quiz me about Stella's health and the operation in America. Luckily Stella was on the other side of the room, engrossed by a table covered in snow globes all featuring Blackpool Tower.

'She's fine, and the fundraising is going amazingly well. The surgeon in Boston, Dr Beems, kindly waived his fee, but we still have huge medical expenses to cover and we're not sure how long afterwards we'll need to stay before we can fly back.'

'You can come to America with me if you want to,' Stella told her, coming back and catching the last bit. 'I don't mind.'

'Eh, I'm not flying at my time of life!' she said. 'In fact, I don't get out much at all now and that Tim Wesley needs to get a shift on and finish the shop at the mill if he wants me to open it.'

'He rang me the other day and said it was coming along quickly,' Jago told her, but didn't mention all the cleaning, restoration and moth treatment that had been going on!

'Those students came back and did another recording,' she said. 'I assumed they'd finished, but they said they thought I needed a break before they did the final one.'

It sounded more to me as if *they* were the ones who'd been tired and needed a break!

'They were nice young things and that interested in what

I had to tell them, I could have gone on for hours. I've loaned them my family photos so they can copy them to display in the house near the furniture. I expect I'll see it all, if the Lord spares me long enough.'

'And the new Honey's, if you'd like to,' Jago suggested.

'We'll see . . .' she said non-committally, and I thought perhaps she realised she'd find it difficult to see it so transformed.

'With the mill, it's just a question of being wheeled into the van and wheeled out at the other end,' she said. 'I don't see why I shouldn't go, because if my time's up, then it's up and it doesn't matter where I am, does it?'

Then she said she was about to start a whole new series of recordings for the Middlemoss Living History Archive and that seemed to perk her up no end. She could live for ever!

Stella asked Miss Honey suddenly if she was called Grace, seemingly now assuming that every elderly lady she met might be called by the same name.

'No, I'm Queenie.'

'Are you the queen, then?' Stella asked, impressed.

'I'm only queen of this nursing home,' Miss Honey said.

'In your dreams,' said Charlene cheerfully as she wheeled in the tea trolley.

'Take no notice,' Miss Honey told us. 'The peasants are revolting.'

Then she cackled with laughter and I thought whatever they were paying good-natured Charlene, it should be doubled.

After that visit, life rolled along merrily until one Thursday after lunch, when the phone rang just as Stella had gone down for a nap.

When I answered, a once-familiar voice said, 'Cally? Is that you? It's Adam.'

'How did you get this number?' I demanded.

'I've got a flat in Pimlico and I was unpacking my stuff when I remembered I still had your mother's number in an old address book.'

'Well done, Sherlock,' I said sarcastically. 'What do you want?'

'To see you, like I said in my emails. We've got a lot to talk about.'

'Haven't you left it a little late for that?'

'I hope not: I thought about you a lot while I was out near the Falklands and as soon as I got back, I tried to find you, only there was someone else in the flat. It was a lucky break when an old friend told me you were living up there with your mother.'

'Not for me, it wasn't. I'd much rather you kept out of our lives.'

'But I want to see you – and my daughter. Stella, is it?'

'It is,' I said drily.

'Come on, Cally,' he coaxed. 'I know I behaved very badly, but I've matured over the last few years and I'm ready to play a part in your lives.'

'Not in mine, you're not: you don't get two bites at *this* cherry,' I told him straight.

'But don't you see, Cally: I loved you all along, it was just that I met you at the wrong time in my life, when I wasn't ready to start a family.'

'I understood the second part of that all right.'

'I'm only surprised it took me so long to realise what I'd thrown away,' he continued, seemingly oblivious to my unresponsiveness. 'I must have been snow-blind not to see it before, but I've turned my life around. I've got a permanent job, a new flat and I'm ready to settle down.'

'I'm so pleased for you,' I said. 'Better late than never, I suppose.'

'I assume you haven't found anyone else, or you wouldn't have moved back in with your mother?'

'You assume too much,' I said tightly.

'Aimee did say you were friendly with her fiancé.'

'Yes, I thought Aimee must be the little bird who'd been tweeting in your ear,' I said. 'And Jago is her *ex*-fiancé.'

'That's not what she says.'

'She's wrong: Jago's moved on. In fact, he and I are now *more* than friends.' The words simply slipped out, I really hadn't meant to say that!

There was a pause. 'Look, please let me come and see you and we can talk everything through. What have you told Stella about me?'

'She thinks you live at the North Pole, counting penguins, and you can only come home when you've finished.'

'But – there aren't any penguins at the North Pole,' he said blankly.

'I know: it's one of those never-ending mythical tasks.'

'Perhaps you'd better tell her I've finished counting them, then,' he suggested.

'I'd rather you didn't meet at all, when we both know playing daddy will just be another short-lived fad until the novelty wears off.'

'You're wrong, and anyway, you can't deny me the right to see her.'

'Actually, I think you forfeited those rights when you dumped me before she was even born,' I said coldly.

'I think I probably could apply for visiting rights, but I really don't want to do that. Come on, Cally,' he wheedled, softening his tone. 'If she finds out when she's older that I wanted to meet her but you prevented it, what will she think?'

That gave me pause and I was quiet for a few moments, weighing up what he'd said, which pretty much tallied with what Celia thought. I didn't ever want to see him again, but would I be doing the right thing if I prevented Stella from meeting her father?

'I suppose I'll have to let you meet her at some point, but—'

'Great!' he broke in, before I could explain that I thought any meeting should be delayed until after Stella had recovered from her operation.

'The sooner the better. Is there anywhere to stay locally?'

'Well, there's the Green Man but—'

'I'll come this weekend.'

'That's not possible,' I said quickly. 'We've got things planned.'

'The one after, then,' he said impatiently, then added, 'How's your mother? Weird as ever?'

'My mother is not weird,' I said icily. 'She always said you were a total waste of space, and I should have listened to her.'

'See you soon,' he said obliviously, and put the phone down.

How do I loathe thee? Let me count the ways . . .

Chapter 32: A Random Lot

I was in such a state of turmoil after Adam's call that it was just as well Celia rang me only a few minutes later so I could pour it all out to her.

'I didn't want him to come here, but he steamrollered right over me before I could explain why that wouldn't be a good idea just now for Stella,' I said. 'I don't suppose he's got over his phobia of illness and hospitals, for a start, so when he realises the seriousness of her condition he'll probably run a mile.'

'But if he does, then it's probably going to be all for the best, so long as it doesn't upset Stella,' Celia pointed out.

'He'd better not upset her,' I said fiercely. 'But the other thing that freaked me out was the way he kept saying he'd missed me and he'd got a job in London and was ready to settle down, as if he'd just remembered he had a ready-made family he could pick up whenever he wanted one!'

'That *is* a bit odd,' she admitted. 'Absence probably made the heart grow fonder when he was stuck out in some icy wasteland and he realised what he'd thrown away.'

'If he's been cherishing a rosy dream of how I used to look, then he's going to get a bit of a shock when he sees me, isn't he?' I grinned. 'I'm a couple of stone heavier, for a start.'

'Only a little bit, and the extra weight suits you.'

'It's more than a little, Celia: I'd certainly be the last survivor in any famine. Unless the others ate me, of course,' I added. 'And apart from that, I'm not exactly the polished girl-about-town that he was engaged to. That'll shatter his illusions!'

'You look like a mum and a country girl now – glowing with health, in fact, so he might prefer the new version.'

'I don't think so – heaven forbid!' I paused. 'I told him me and Jago were in a relationship.'

'You are?' she demanded excitedly.

'No, no, of course we're not,' I said hastily, 'I just said it on the spur of the moment to put him off. Jago and I are only friends, nothing complicated: that's all we want.'

'Right . . .' she said doubtfully. 'Oh, well, it doesn't sound as if you can stop Adam turning up and I suppose he was right, in that you can't deny Stella a chance to meet him.'

'Even if he's so horrified by her health that he vanishes again?'

'Oh, I expect he'd still keep in touch, if only to send her a Christmas card or something.'

'Whoopee-do,' I said sourly.

'You'll have to prepare Stella before he comes, won't you?'

'I know, and I'm not looking forward to it . . . but I'm not going to worry about it till after the fundraising auction; that's way too important.'

Since Stella was still sound asleep I impulsively rang Jago and told him everything, too. Or *almost* everything. He seemed to think Celia was right and Adam should have a chance to make amends.

When Ma came in and heard the news, she said at first she wouldn't have Adam in the house, but I persuaded her that it would be better to let him meet Stella here, on home ground.

Ma was babysitting on the night of the auction and Hal was fetching in a fish-and-chip supper for the three of them, though what Stella would make of mushy peas was anyone's guess.

When Jago and I arrived at the hall it looked like the whole village, plus lots of people I didn't recognise, were crammed in there. Celia and Will had come over and were saving us seats.

There were printed lists of the lots on each chair, though Hebe had helpfully sent round an advance one, so Stella's Stars had a good idea what was coming up. Various lots were ranged on a table at the side of the room and printed cards with the promises were propped up, some with photographs.

We all stopped chatting and turned to the stage when the curtain was drawn back with a swoosh. Raffy appeared, reminded us of the purpose of the auction, and then left our auctioneer for the evening, Mr Yatton, to start the bidding on the first lot.

'Right, we'll begin with the food lots and two amazing cakes,' he said. 'Now, most of you will have seen the photograph of lot one, Cally Weston's amazing Swedish celebration cake, and this is your opportunity to have one specially made for any celebration – birthday, anniversary . . . whatever you like.'

The bidding was surprisingly brisk and won by Zoë, the girl I knew from the playgroup. She waved triumphantly at me over the crowd.

Next was Jago's croquembouche – there was a big photo in case the assembled throng didn't know what that was, either. It was successfully bid for by the young couple sitting right behind us, who said they wanted it for their wedding.

Mr Yatton called us to order and carried on. There was a food hamper supplied by the Middlemoss Christmas Pudding Circle, who Mr Yatton said made Christmas hampers up for the senior citizens in their parish.

'It's an idea we could maybe adopt here, too,' Raffy called out. 'I hadn't thought of it before.'

'We can discuss it on another occasion,' Hebe Winter said regally from her chair at the front and Mr Yatton carried on to the next lot, which was a large box of macaroons from David and Sarah.

'You are all being so kind,' I whispered to Jago. 'You and David have already done enough, just selling the gingerbread stars.'

'We want to help,' he said. 'Oh, look, we're on to the main lots now and here's your mother's painting!'

Raffy bought it. I'm not sure if he liked it, but I wouldn't put it past him. He also bid for Ottie's sketch, but there was a brisk bidding war between two determined strangers and one of them secured it for a thousand pounds. I think we were all stunned: I mean, she's quite a famous sculptor, but this was just a little scribble of an idea in pencil.

'Ottie will be delighted,' Hebe said, before Laurence led the bidding on the rest of the lots.

I made the final one on a tea-leaf reading with Zillah

Smith, though actually, I'd only intended to push my hair behind my ears. I didn't really mind, though I wasn't quite sure how I felt about having a reading done. Could she really tell my fortune in tea leaves? And even if she could, did I want to know what the future held?

Hebe Winter paid a ridiculous amount for a reading by the reluctant Shakespearian actor, Ivo Hawksley, who looked resigned to his fate.

'I would like you to perform a reading from Shakespeare up at the hall on August Bank Holiday,' Miss Winter told him triumphantly.

'All right,' he said, 'I suspected as much when I put myself up for this.'

'He was a leading Shakespearian actor,' I whispered to Jago, 'but he's retired now and just writes his bestselling crime novels as Christopher Marlow.'

'I know, I remembered you'd said so and I bought one from Marked Pages,' Jago whispered back. 'The owner – Felix, is it? – reminded me about the fundraising event he's holding in early September, when you and some of the other local writers will be signing your books.'

'Yes – it'll be Ivo's wife, Tansy, with her *Slipper Monkeys* books, Gregory Lyon's supernatural novels, Seth Greenwood's gardening book . . .'

'And your *Round the World in Eighty Cakes* and the first volume of *The Cake Diaries*,' he finished.

I nodded. 'The proofs of the second volume should arrive any minute . . .'

Then my attention was distracted as Raffy got knocked down at a good price to a couple who wanted him to come and sing their special song at their ruby wedding anniversary.

'What *is* your special song?' he asked.

'"Love me Tender",' they chorused back, and he looked relieved: I suppose it could have been *anything*.

There was a short break for refreshments after the promises, before the rest of the lots came up, which ranged from a brass coalscuttle to one of those hideously uncomfortable stools made out of a leather camel saddle.

Zoë, who'd won my cake, explained that it was for her sister, who had had a premature baby. It had been touch and go but now that the baby was home and thriving they were going to have a big christening in the church and they wanted a pink prinsesstårta as the christening cake. I thought that was lovely and promised the prettiest cake ever.

Fortified by tea and seed cake, Mr Yatton galloped along with the bidding on the last lots.

'Lot Forty-two, donated by Florrie Snowball: a charm to ward off evil. Hold it up, Effie,' he ordered his sister, and she held aloft a murky green glass bottle full of indistinct objects. 'Every home should have one placed above the door,' he added.

'That's right,' Florrie agreed, piping up from nearby. She's so diminutive, I hadn't even realised she was there. 'House or shop.'

'I've noticed quite a few local shops do have one of those over the door,' I whispered to Jago, and then when he didn't answer I looked at him to discover he was bidding by waving his brochure in the air.

He won it, too. 'Just what I need when I open Honey's,' he said, then seeing my surprised expression, added that Mrs Snowball had told him about it over his breakfast bap, so it hadn't been an impulse bid, he'd *meant* to get it.

At the end there was more tea, coffee and cake, and before we left Raffy announced that with tonight's takings, he expected we would already have exceeded the ten thousand pounds we'd originally set out to raise.

There was a round of applause.

'It's just as well, because I think two times that is more realistic and anyway, a little leeway is a good thing,' Raffy observed when the noise had died down again. 'There are always unforeseen expenses and since Jenny Snowball, who as you know is a qualified nurse, is accompanying them, it's only right that we pay her air fare.'

'Not at all,' said Jenny, who was clutching an outsize green furry dragon. 'I'd be going to Boston anyway, to visit our Kevin and the family, so I wish you'd let me pay for my own ticket.'

'Even so,' Raffy said. 'Then Stella will have to convalesce afterwards for some time until she's fit to fly home, won't she, Cally?'

'Yes. But if there's any cash left over when we get back, I'm sure you'll be able to find another worthy cause for it.'

I was still stunned by how much everyone had raised so quickly and when I tried to add a few heartfelt words of thanks to everyone, I choked up. Jago put his arm around me and gave me a hug.

'I think we all know what Cally's trying to say,' Raffy said. 'Keep up the good work, everyone!' he added, and then declared the evening over.

Zillah Smith tapped me on the back as we were leaving and gave me her business card: 'Your future in my hands' it said, 'Zillah Smith: tarot or tea leaves'.

'You give me a bell when you're ready for your reading,' she told me. Then she gave Jago a wicked glinting gold smile and told him that *he* could give her a ring any time and she'd do him for free.

Chapter 33: Up the Pole

I tried gently explaining to Stella that Penguin Daddy was coming to visit her soon, but she didn't seem terribly interested.

'Is he coming for my birthday, with a present?' she suggested.

'No, it'll be a little before that, and I don't know if he'll bring you a present or not. He's really looking forward to seeing you, though.'

'Is he?' she said absently, wandering off, so I thought he'd been a storybook person for so long, she couldn't take in that he was real and about to appear.

I wasn't sure *I* could, either, and the thought of him turning up was making me feel really edgy . . .

Not that I didn't already feel edgy anyway since I'd started arranging Stella's birthday celebrations, because it had brought back memories of when I wasn't entirely sure she'd even make it to her first birthday. I was so thankful that she had and that this time next year, if all went well, she'd finally have started school and be running round with the rest of the children, even if I had to scale a mountain of emotions to get her there.

*   *   *

Zillah Smith accosted me in the street one day, when I was heading home from a walk with Stella and Toto, and reminded me about my tea-leaf-reading prize, then said tomorrow was as good a day as any and she'd expect to see me then. So I decided to go once Stella was in bed, with Ma to listen out for her. Ma even said she'd watch the telly in the sitting room for a bit so I needn't hurry back, if I didn't want to, so I arranged to meet Jago in the Falling Star for a drink afterwards.

The house attached to the Witchcraft Museum, where Zillah kept house for Gregory Lyon, was Victorian and decorated in period style, though in the kitchen there was a bright red Aga and one of those huge American-style fridges to match. They were incongruous but yet sort of fitted, and Zillah's taste obviously held sway in there, because the tablecloth and soft furnishings were very bright and there was a huge TV at one end of the room with a comfy chair covered by a patchwork throw.

Zillah made me drink tea from a wide, fine porcelain cup and then swirled the dregs about a bit before informing me that someone from the past would turn up, but it wouldn't make any difference to the course I'd set.

That was pretty spot on for Adam's coming visit, which she couldn't possibly know about. Then she said difficult times were drawing to a close and the future was all rosy, with wedding bells.

'Do you think that means Stella will be cured and she'll get married one day?' I asked eagerly

'This is *your* fortune, not hers,' she pointed out. 'Though of course, her future is bound with yours to some extent, so it wouldn't be bright if she *didn't* make a full recovery after the operation, would it?'

'No, that's true,' I said, relieved and wanting now to believe that she really could foretell the future.

'Is a tall, dark stranger about to come into my life?' I asked half-seriously.

'Not unless you bumped into my great-nephew Jasper on the way in?'

I shook my head.

'Tall, black hair, Goth, glooms about a lot with his girl-friend when he's home in the university holidays,' she said. 'But he's a good boy and a great help to Gregory in the museum. The girl, Cat, lives with her parents in that converted barn up past your mum's cottage.'

'Really? I haven't seen them to talk to, only driving past, because they never seem to walk anywhere.'

'That's townies for you,' she said, and then we had another cup of tea and a chat, without any more fortunes, before I walked up to the Falling Star and told Jago all about it.

Adam emailed to say he was driving up on the Saturday morning, so would be with me just after lunch. He's booked himself into the Green Man for the night.

I felt really on edge and unsettled, despite Zillah's comforting predictions, but I tried to carry on as usual, going to the supermarket early that day, leaving Ma with Stella. I'd told her her Penguin Daddy might pop in later, but she only asked me if Jago was coming too.

'Later, probably for dinner,' I said, because he'd told me he'd wait until I rang him to say the coast was clear before coming round.

Stella went down for her nap after lunch and Ma went up to the studio with instructions to tell her when Adam had cleared off.

'Can you take Toto with you? He hated Adam and I don't want him to bark and wake Stella up before she's ready.'

'All right. What are you going to do while you're waiting for him to turn up?' she asked.

'Send off that article for "The Cake Diaries" about Summer Puddings and then finish making the prinsesstårta for Zoë, which I started yesterday, because she's coming round for it later. Raffy's going to christen her sister's baby after one of the services tomorrow and then they're having a bit of a party. I've baked the cake, now I just have to layer on the confectioner's cream and cover it in marzipan.'

'That should keep you occupied, then.'

'Adam'll probably be here any minute so he'll have to talk to me while I'm working,' I said, but in the event it was ages before he rang to say he'd arrived at the Green Man.

'It's Adam – I'm here. Can I come round and see you now?'

'I suppose so,' I said. 'But I'm up to the elbows in cake, so you'd better walk round the side of the house to the kitchen door and let yourself in.'

I gave him directions, then wiped a blob of confectioner's cream off the phone with a bit of kitchen towel before carrying on with what I was doing, though there was a sick churning feeling in the pit of my stomach and my heart was doing ominous little flips.

I was just about to smooth the pale pink marzipan over the domed cake when some sixth sense made me look up and spot him through the top of the glass door, just before he turned the handle and let himself in. It was like a snapshot from the past.

'Hi, Cally,' he said with a smile, as if we'd only parted the day before.

I think he'd have come and kissed me if I hadn't pointed my wooden rolling pin at him and said, 'Just sit there while I finish covering this cake: it's special and I want only good thoughts to go into it.'

One side of his mouth twitched in amusement in a way I remembered, and he obediently sat down on the chair opposite.

'Same old Cally – and you look cute even with flour on your nose.'

'Icing sugar,' I said, rubbing it off with a corner of my apron.

'What kind of cake is that? It looks weird.'

'It's a prinsesstårta and it's going to be the christening cake for a very special baby – she was premature and so tiny it's a miracle she's made it.'

'Well, I'm sure that's great, but do you think you could stop and give me your full attention for five minutes?' he said

'No, because I want to get this finished before Stella wakes up. But I'll listen while I'm working.' I smoothed down the pale pink marzipan covering and then began creating a little crown to sit on the top.

'Stella's still asleep? Isn't she a bit old for a nap?'

The marzipan crown in place, I looked at him properly

for the first time and noticed that his boyish good looks now sat oddly on the face of a man in his forties, like an ageing Peter Pan.

'Stella's not quite four and lots of children still have a nap in the afternoon at that age. But in Stella's case, of course, she gets tired really easily because of her medical condition and needs lots of rest.'

He looked blank. '*What* medical condition?'

'You mean . . . Aimee didn't tell you that Stella had a heart condition?' I said, startled.

'No, she never mentioned there was anything wrong with her,' he said, looking totally taken aback. 'I mean, is she . . .?'

'She was born with a complex condition affecting the heart and one of the arteries going into it,' I said. 'She was operated on right after she was born and then she had another operation later, but I'll spare you the details because you're going green.' I added unkindly.

'Well, it's a bit of a shock.'

'Yes, well, considering all that *Stella* has suffered with it, I think you could brace up and listen to me tell you about it without keeling over,' I said tartly. 'Perhaps it's time you grew out of your phobia about illness and hospitals?'

'So, didn't the operations cure it?' he said, ignoring that.

'No, they were more of a temporary fix while she got stronger. I hoped they'd be able to do something more, but then just before last Christmas they said they'd run out of options other than palliative care and as she got older and her growing body put more strain on her organs, she'd eventually succumb to some infection and . . .' I stopped and turned back to my cake, carefully positioning a tiny baby in a cradle inside the marzipan crown.

356

'Oh my God!'

'But just because they couldn't do anything more in this country didn't mean that no one could, and there's a surgeon in the USA who's successfully pioneered an operation for rare cases like Stella's. He's agreed to treat her.'

Adam was still looking faintly green, but I had to give it to him, he persevered. 'So when is this operation?'

'It was supposed to be just before she turned five . . . and really I hoped by then there would be something in this country and we wouldn't have to go to Boston. But she had a serious infection that weakened her in January and they brought the date of the operation forward to the start of November this year. I've been raising money to fund the trip and the treatment ever since.'

He got up and paced about a bit, brow furrowed. 'This isn't quite how I thought it would be . . .' he muttered.

'It isn't quite how I thought it would be, either!'

Looking down at my slightly trembling hands, I found that quite without realising what I was doing, I'd neatly trimmed the edges of the cake. I popped it under a cover in Ma's larder, in case Moses decided to investigate when my back was turned.

When I came back, Adam had regained some of his colour. 'The thing is, Cally,' he began portentously, 'I've already told my parents that I'm mad keen to get back with you and that I hope you'll give me another chance so we can slowly become a family.'

'You've *what*?'

'I told you I'd got a job and a flat and I was looking for you,' he pointed out. 'They're desperate for grandchildren, so when Aimee let fall that they already had one, they were delighted. I mean, they realised it would take time for you to forgive me, and for Stella to get to know me, but—'

I was dumbfounded! How could he possibly assume that I'd welcome him back with open arms after what he'd done? He'd been so disinterested in the outcome of my pregnancy that he hadn't even known if I'd had a boy or a girl, let alone about her illness. But because he'd suddenly decided he wanted to play Happy Families, he'd assumed I'd just fall in line at his command.

'You must be quite mad!' I told him, incredulously. 'I didn't even want to *see* you, let alone get back with you. You weren't there when I needed you and now you're a stranger to me and to Stella. The baby you didn't want, remember?'

'That was then and this is now: I told you I'd changed.'

'You didn't tell me you'd gone gaga, though,' I said.

'You should have told me about Stella's problems when she was born.'

'I might have done, if you hadn't changed your email address.'

'You could have got in touch through work or my parents.'

'You'd made it plain that if I went on with the pregnancy, I was on my own. *And* you were sharing an igloo with someone else.'

'I had a right to know,' he said stubbornly.

'You would have known if you'd stayed in touch and been supportive. It's entirely your own fault.'

'Well, I suppose there's no point in splitting hairs at this point, and at least now I can help you raise the money for the operation.'

'There's no need, because I'm doing fine without you. I

raised the bulk of it by selling my flat, and the whole village is rallying round to get the rest. Everything's planned and I – we – don't need you. And I don't *want* you either, especially if you upset Stella in any way.'

As if on cue, I heard Stella crying. Sometimes she woke up a bit grumpy and sad, though it didn't last long.

'There's Stella, I'll go and get her up,' I said, fetching her beaker of juice out of the fridge. 'Come on, you'd better wait in the sitting room.'

'Why is she crying?' he asked, looking slightly alarmed and as if he'd rather fly the country than follow me.

'She'll be fine when she's up and has had a drink.'

'Perhaps I should come back later . . .' he was saying, but I ignored him. He could please himself.

I gave Stella a cuddle and then told her she had a visitor.

'I'll just brush your hair while you have a drink,' I suggested.

'Is it Daddy-Jago?' she asked eagerly.

'No, not Jago. Do you remember I said your real daddy was coming to see you?'

'Penguin Daddy?' she said doubtfully.

'That's the one,' I said with a cheerfulness I didn't feel. 'All the way from the North Pole just to say hello.'

I carried her through to where Adam was now sitting on the edge of a chair and looking as if he was in the dentist's waiting room.

'Here's Stella,' I said, sitting opposite on the sofa with her on my knee. She was not normally a shy child, but after one quick look at him, she turned her face to me and sucked her thumb, while fingering a strand of my hair.

'Hello, Stella,' he said. 'Aren't you too big to suck your

thumb? And aren't you going to come and say hello to your daddy?'

Stella stopped sucking and turned to give him a comprehensive but silent stare, from top to toe.

'Mummy, I think he should go back and finish counting the penguins,' she told me finally. 'I don't need another daddy.'

'What did she say?' he demanded.

'Nothing,' I said hastily.

'I love Daddy-Jago,' Stella explained helpfully. 'He's my Moominpappa.'

'Jago? Isn't that the man Aimee's just got back together with?'

'In her dreams,' I said rudely. 'We're seeing each other, I told you.'

Well, that was certainly true because we'd barely been apart since he'd moved to the village . . .

'I think you're just trying to put me off,' he said shrewdly, 'because Aimee definitely said she and this Jago were engaged again, and you and he were just friends – and frankly,' he added, 'you seem to have put on a bit of weight and let yourself go, which is quite understandable in the circumstances, I suppose, but—'

'Thanks,' I said. 'Jago thinks I look just right.'

'Jago says you're pretty as a princess,' Stella said unexpectedly

'What? When did he say that?' I asked, flattered.

'When we were putting the meerkat family in their caravan and I said Mummy meerkat could be a princess.'

Adam was looking baffled. 'Meerkats in caravans? Is she all right in the head . . .?'

'The man's an idiot,' Stella said distinctly.

'That's one of Ma's sayings,' I explained.

To give him his due, after this unpromising start Adam did make an awkward attempt to get her to talk to him, but she just gave him a look and went back into her bedroom.

'I think I'd better go,' he said ruefully. 'I suppose she's too young to expect her to accept me that quickly. Perhaps you could have dinner with me tonight, though?' he suggested.

'Stella doesn't stay up that late.'

'I meant just you and me, at the pub. It looks OK.'

'I don't think so,' I said shortly.

'Then maybe in the morning we could—'

'I'm going out tomorrow,' I said.

'I suppose . . .' He looked uncertain, then ran his fingers through his hair distractedly. 'This is all a bit difficult. My parents will be ringing me wanting to know all about Stella and to be honest, she looks so frail and small that I need to think what to say to them . . . I mean, there's no point in them getting attached to her if she's having high risk surgery soon and—'

He stopped dead, warned by my furious, stunned face.

'Sorry, it's all been such a shock I don't know what I'm saying. Look, perhaps I'll just go straight back to London tonight and think things through a bit, get back in touch with you later.'

'You do that,' I said. 'The later the better!'

When Zoë had collected the prinsesstårta, which she adored, I sent Jago a text to say the coast was clear and he came round.

Stella told him all about Penguin Daddy. 'He was silly and his face crinkled in the wrong places,' she said critically. 'I told him I didn't want him so he's gone again.'

'I expect he was glad to see you, though.'

'I don't think so, he didn't even bring me a present,' she said thoughtfully, 'and he made Mummy cross.'

Jago, who'd looked gloomy since his arrival, seemed to brighten up at this.

'Mrs Snowball's invited us down to the pub for scampi in a basket – are you up for it?'

'What, Stella too?'

'Especially Stella. She said she'd cook early just for us.'

'Do you want to go and eat your dinner in the Falling Star, Stella?' I asked.

She nodded. 'Jago, you're my best daddy!'

Later, when we were back at Ma's, with Stella tucked up asleep, I described Adam's visit in more detail.

'It sounds a bit of a disaster from beginning to end,' he said, 'though suddenly finding out about Stella's medical condition must have been a shock.'

'Yes: I'm hoping it shocked him right back to London and out of our lives, but I suppose if he decides he does want to try and build some kind of relationship with Stella, I'll have to let him . . . but after the operation. Perhaps he could just write to her before then, to get her used to the idea.'

'That sounds like a good option,' he agreed, and then, since we were sitting together on the sofa, put his arm around me and gave me a comforting hug.

I was inspired by Adam's visit to experiment with baked Alaska, which has a cold heart and a warm exterior, but found it quite tricky.

The man himself didn't ring for several days, though he

362

emailed to ask me a few questions about Stella's condition and the operation in America. I suppose he felt better able to cope with it that way.

Then finally he phoned me again.

'Look, I admit I didn't handle it very well, but it was a shock finding out about Stella's problems like that. I'd like to come back when I've got a weekend free and perhaps the three of us can go out somewhere together and make a new start?'

'I don't think there's much point at the moment, Adam. She didn't really take to you very much and it might upset her if you come back again so soon.'

'I'm sure you've been poisoning her mind against me, that's why she wouldn't come to me.'

'I've done no such thing!' I exclaimed indignantly. 'In fact, considering how you treated us, I think I've been jolly fair spinning her nice stories about you living at the North Pole.'

'Well, I'm not in the North Pole now and she's going to have to get used to me being back again – you both will,' he said stubbornly. 'I'm not free this weekend but I am the one after, so I'll come up then.'

'That would be a waste of time, because I'll be too busy with the village fête. It's the major fundraising event for Stella, so it's really important.'

'Then all the more reason to come and support you.'

'I'm going to it with Jago.'

'Come on, Cally, I know you're not going out with him, so you can drop the pretence.'

'You're quite wrong – we *are* in a relationship,' I insisted. 'We're just taking things slowly till after Stella's had her operation, that's all. And that's what I'd like you to do, too

– back off until she's well enough to cope with having an absentee father popping in and out of her life.'

'But I am her father and I've got rights,' he said, as if that was some kind of clincher.

'You've never been more than a sperm donor,' I said, and put the phone down.

Aimee

Adam rang Aimee when he'd thought things over and said accusingly, 'You didn't tell me the little girl was ill.'

'Oh, didn't I?' she said vaguely. 'I could have sworn I had.'

'Well, you didn't and it was quite a shock. I had to tell my parents about it too, so I wish you'd never mentioned her existence to them in the first place.'

'Yes, but she's going to have an operation to fix whatever she's got, according to Jago.'

'It sounds so serious it could go either way. And there's another thing: Cally insists Jago hasn't got engaged to you and that they're seeing each other.'

'That is *so* not true!' Aimee exclaimed angrily. 'She's just an old friend he's helping out with the fundraising for the little girl, because he's so soft-hearted he's a sucker for any good cause. There's nothing more to it than that, whatever she told you.'

'Maybe you've got it wrong, Aimee? The little girl was going on about "Daddy-Jago" too,' he added broodingly.

'Look, Jago's been playing hot and cold about forgiving me, just to pay me back for ditching him, but it's time he got over it – and I'm going to make sure he does.'

'Are you sure about that? I wanted to go down and see Cally and Stella again next weekend, but she put me off because it's some big fundraising fête and she's going to it with him.'

'Well, Jago put *me* off seeing him this weekend because it's the little girl's birthday party!' she said.

'What? Cally didn't mention that – and I *am* her father, after all.'

'Yes, you've a right to know,' Aimee agreed.

Adam suddenly felt jealous: he'd been so convinced he only had to click his fingers and Cally would come running back to him. And the little girl . . . well, he hadn't thought that one through. He knew nothing about children, but he'd assumed she was so small she'd probably soon forget he hadn't always been around.

He'd always had what he wanted – and now he'd decided that that was Cally and Stella, he wasn't inclined to give up that easily.

Neither was Aimee. 'You know,' she said thoughtfully. 'I think it's time I went down there and showed Cally Weston just who Jago belongs to.'

'And I'll go down for this fête, whether she wants me to, or not,' Adam said.

'So – we might as well go together then?' she suggested.

'OK, but I'll pick you up – I remember your driving. We can stay in that pub in the village overnight, the Green Man.'

'Agreed,' Aimee said, thinking that all she had to do now was pick out her most stunning outfit and dazzle Jago back into adoring enslavement, while Cally's attention was otherwise engaged . . .

Chapter 34: Babes in the Wood

The Swedish celebration cake called a prinsesstårta is a domed, layered confection of sponge and cream, with a marzipan covering, Making it is time-consuming, but you can bake the cake part of it the day before, and the end result is stunning.

Cally Weston: 'The Cake Diaries'

Thankfully there was no more from Adam, and I tried to put him out of my mind while I finalised the arrangements for Stella's birthday.

She'd been getting more and more excited as the day approached and anxiously supervised every stage of the making of her special prinsesstårta cake, which she wanted a traditional pale frog green. For some reason she's rather into frogs just now, though this interest has not superseded her angel (and fairies, their miniature brethren) fixation.

All her favourite people were invited to the birthday tea: myself, Ma, Jago, Hal, Celia and Will. She'd wanted Jenny too, but she was otherwise engaged at the time, though she'd already left a card and little gift for her. In fact, since Stella had been telling every person she met for at least a week that her birthday was on Saturday, it was no surprise that an avalanche of cards and presents had already landed on the doorstep.

Jago was being rather mysterious about *his* present and went off the day before to collect it, so I only hoped he hadn't ordered something hugely expensive, because goodness knew, the renovations at Honey's were likely to take every last penny of his lottery winnings at the rate they were going.

Ma was also being secretive, but suddenly demanded acres of gift-wrap when Stella was in bed on the eve of the big day, so I had to dash down to the Spar and buy more. I'd already carefully wrapped up my presents, including the toy narrow boat that had been high on Stella's wish list, but also a cottage hospital, ambulance and a paramedic rabbit with a patient. I thought a bit of role-playing leading up to her operation might be a good idea, especially since in this case she'd be in charge of the outcome.

Next morning I made sure Stella had some breakfast inside her before letting her loose on her cards and presents.

I knew she'd love mine, especially the whole new family of hedgehogs I'd put inside the narrow boat, and she was also delighted with Ma and Hal's joint gift of a child-sized wheelbarrow, set of gardening tools, watering can and small blue rubber gardening clogs with pink spots.

Ma, in an inspired moment, had also bought her a bright red ladybird Trunki suitcase, the sort that children can sit on and ride.

'You can take some of your toys and books in it when you go to America,' she explained to Stella, 'and it can go in the cabin with you as hand luggage: I checked.'

'Brilliant idea, Ma!' I said, and Stella happily played at packing various combinations of her new toys in the Trunki, then pushing it round the room, until the arrival of Jago, the first of the birthday guests.

He came in carrying a huge parcel and when I said I hoped he hadn't spent a fortune he looked faintly guilty. 'Not really,' he muttered.

But he had, because inside was a beautifully made animal family-sized pink castle in the style of a doll's house, so that the front hinged open and so did the turrets in each corner.

'Oh, Jago, you shouldn't have!'

'Yes, he should, it's *mazing*,' Stella said. 'You're my most favourite Daddy-Jago ever.'

'I'm your only Daddy-Jago,' he said, with a grin.

And as if that wasn't enough, Celia and Will turned up with a big antique rocking horse.

'Good grief!' I said, when Will staggered in with it and put it down in the window, then set Stella onto the saddle, still wearing the white feather angel wings that Sarah and David had sent her.

'It's not quite as extravagant as it looks, because we found it in a junk shop without its rockers and in a bit of a state and we've done it up ourselves,' Celia explained. 'It didn't really cost much, it just took time. I made the leather saddle and bridle.'

'Stella, what do you say to everyone for all their lovely gifts?' I prompted.

'Thank you and I love you all,' she said very seriously, though a little like a queen to her courtiers.

We had the birthday tea and with much huffing she blew out the four candles inside the crown on her prinsesstårta.

Stella was starting to flag soon after tea and happy to sit quietly on Ma's knee watching a new Disney film, until she suddenly fell deeply asleep and we decided just to put her straight to bed early . . . though without the wings, of course.

She didn't stir while I popped her into her pyjamas and tucked her up with Bun, so I tiptoed out, leaving her toadstool light on and the door slightly ajar.

Ma and Hal had already disappeared when I went back to the sitting room, and Will and Celia were just waiting to say goodbye and give me a hug.

Left to ourselves, Jago and I tided up and put all the shredded wrapping paper in the recycling bag, loaded the dishwasher, and then sank limply onto the sofa with a glass of Prosecco apiece.

'It's been a wonderful day – thanks to you and everyone who've made it so,' I said gratefully. 'You know, when she was born I didn't even know if she'd make it to her first birthday; I just hoped for a miracle. And now she's four and we need another . . . How many miracles can one little girl expect?'

'As many as it takes,' he said, putting his arm around me comfortingly. I gave a long sigh and rested my head on his shoulder, quite exhausted . . .

We must have both been so tired we just zonked out after that, because the next thing I knew we were lying in each other's arms on the sofa and I was blinking up at the dazzling ceiling light.

Ma was standing in the doorway looking slightly startled. 'Good heavens, it's the Babes in the Wood . . . or the Babes on the Sofa, at any rate,' she said, as we scrambled stiffly to our feet.

'We fell asleep,' I explained. 'We were almost as tired out by all the excitement as Stella!'

'It was a pity I disturbed you really, but I didn't realise you were here.'

'It's probably just as well. I'd better get back to the pub before they shut me out for the night,' Jago said, stretching the kinks out of his tall frame, but I gave him a bit of the leftover party food to take with him before he left, since we'd never got round to any kind of supper.

The weather was a bit iffy for the first week of August but we all crossed our fingers and hoped for a fine day on Sunday for the fête. Apart from the book signing at Marked Pages in September, this would be the last fundraising event and I was now sure we'd greatly exceed, if not double, the ten thousand pounds I'd originally needed. The proceeds of the other smaller events kept trickling in too, in a small but steady stream.

Stella had a bit of a temperature at the check-up on the Thursday before the fête, though I thought it was probably because she was excited about it. She'd taken her cottage hospital and the doctor rabbit and patient with her to show them and re-enacted her favourite scenario.

'You're going to go to sleep now, little mouse,' she said, doing the doctor bunny's voice in a low, gruff tone. 'And when you wake up again, your heart will be all mended and you can go home.'

Then she looked up at the real consultant and nurse and said chattily, 'In America, they don't stick big needles in your arm.'

'I think they do if they have to, Stella,' I said, 'but with the magic cream on first so it doesn't hurt.'

Stella gave me a look that expressed what she thought of this remark, but I didn't want to lie to her . . . though on the other hand, I didn't want to frighten her, either. I shivered suddenly, realising how close October seemed now, when we would be leaving for Boston. It seemed only days ago that I was worried I'd never manage to get her there, and now it was hurtling towards us like a train.

I'd arranged for Jenny to come round early to baby-sit on the Saturday morning, so I could get to Ormskirk in time to see Jago put a croquembouche together. It didn't matter that he'd already made the choux buns before I arrived, because I've made those myself several times.

When I got there he was neatly piping patisserie cream into each one through a small hole he'd made at one end, while David was also working away, since the couple who'd ordered the croquembouche wanted two macaroon cones to flank it.

I sat down quietly with my notebook and watched as Jago began to form the base of the croquembouche around a huge special cone. The choux buns were dipped in melted caramel to stick them together and each layer built up until he reached the top.

Then he began expertly flicking long sugar strands over the cake, using two forks held back to back and dipped in the liquid caramel. He made it look terribly easy but I was quite sure it wasn't!

When it was finished it looked stunning, and Jago made us all a cup of coffee while I wrote up my notes. I'd taken a couple of pictures, too, but I hoped before the article appeared in 'The Cake Diaries' they'd send a photographer to Honey's, which should be up and running by then.

Dorrie arrived to open up the shop and Jago walked out with me to my car for a bit of fresh air. Because I'd arrived so early I'd managed to get into the tiny car park right behind the main street, but I needed to go down to the supermarket before I went home.

'I'll be off to deliver the cakes in a bit,' he said, 'or the ones for the wedding, anyway. I think David has another macaroon cone to make for this afternoon, but he'll probably take that himself.'

'It was great watching you making the croquembouche,' I told him. 'I'm going to have a go, on a smaller scale, but I'm very sure it's a lot harder than you made it look.'

'Oh, it's not so bad. Getting the sugar strands round it is probably the only dicey bit and that's just practice,' he said, then added, 'I'm really looking forward to the fête tomorrow.'

'Yes, me too. I told you Adam wanted to come up this weekend, but I hoped I'd put him off, didn't I?' I paused and then went for a full confession. 'He was a bit persistent, actually, so I'm afraid I've told him we're in a relationship so I'd be going to the fête with you.'

'You did?' He looked down at me and grinned. 'Well, funnily enough, I'd already told Aimee the same thing to put *her* off, though I don't think she believed me.'

I laughed. 'Great minds think alike! And let's hope that finally does the trick, because neither of them seems very good at taking no for an answer.'

Driving back through Sticklepond later I saw that bunting was already strung up everywhere ready for the fête and was in time to glimpse a bride and groom coming out of All Angels in a cloud of pink rose petals.

That could have been me and Adam . . . but how glad I was now that we *hadn't* married, because it would have been the mistake of my life.

Chapter 35: Fêted

I woke up very early on the day of the fête, though when I went into the kitchen already a few weak rays of sunshine were fingering the plant pots on the windowsill like a doubtful shopper.

I hadn't noticed Hal passing the window again early in the morning, so I was starting to think I'd jumped to conclusions and he'd merely been taking an early stroll, or perhaps fetching something from his shed . . .

There was no sign of Toto or Moses in the kitchen, but when I opened the back door to admire the cloudless pale azure sky, there they were, sitting side by side staring at me.

I've no idea why, because if they could get out of the catflap, then there was nothing to stop them coming back in again.

I'd already baked a cake for another prinsesstårta, which was to be sold by the slice at the fête, so now I set to work and created the domed shape of the top, then covered the whole thing in traditional pale green marzipan, finished off with the usual little crown.

Once it was in the cake box I went to get Stella up, and by the time we got back to the kitchen Ma was also down and toasting slices of the fruit loaf that had baked overnight and made the kitchen smell wonderful, so we all had some of that.

Stella was excited, but I made sure she had a quiet morning and then Jago came to collect us after an early lunch and we pushed Stella down to the fête in the buggy. Ma and Hal said they would follow us down, because there were to be one or two plant stalls, not to mention candyfloss, another of Ma's not-so-secret passions.

Already cars had overflowed the car park and were lining the streets, and people were making their way towards the green where all kinds of booths had been set up – hoop-la stands and coconut shies, roll-a-penny stalls and one where you tossed a coin into a ring. They all looked ancient and sun faded, as if they came out every year, but the acres of bunting festooned everywhere was bright and fresh, and fluttered in the warm breeze.

The village hall, which was on the edge of the green, had the big double doors at the front and the side door open to show more stalls inside. I left Jago with Stella for a moment while I popped over and handed my prinsesstårta to Effie Yatton.

I got back just in time to watch Hebe Winter, who was dressed entirely in white, which was, I'd been told, her usual garb on Sundays, graciously remind everyone why they were there, exhort them to spend lots of money and declare the fête open. With a cut-glass voice that could carry for miles, she didn't need a megaphone.

There was polite applause and then her place was taken by a sort of folk-rock group from a nearby village that, going by the banner across the front of the stage, was called the Mummers of Invention. They were quite good.

'Chloe's in the hall, running a chocolate stall,' Raffy said. 'Her grandfather's got Grace – they're over at the pony petting.' He pointed to the corner of the field near the church wall.

'Pony?' echoed Stella, clambering out of the buggy and seizing my hand, which she tugged imperatively.

'Now you've done it,' I said, and we all headed across to where Poppy from Stirrups riding stables had created a My Little Pony experience in an enclosure made of hay bales. There, for a pound, children could groom, brush and generally play with the small golden-brown pony we'd seen up at the stables when we visited.

'It's Butterball,' Stella said.

As we neared I heard Poppy say to a worried parent, 'Oh, no, Butterball's totally safe,' as the pony's tail was plaited for probably the tenth time. 'He's about as intelligent as a cushion and his idea of bliss is to be stroked, petted and brushed – he can take any amount of it. In fact, I'll have to keep an eye on him, because he can sometimes get so chilled out from being groomed that he falls asleep and starts to topple over.'

I was glad to hear this, since Stella was now demanding to be allowed to go and play with him and my mother was already getting out her purse to pay Poppy.

'You let her,' advised Jago. 'Poppy's obviously keeping a close watch and she'll enjoy it.'

'Grace seems happy enough,' Raffy commented. Gregory Lyon, tall and with his long white hair and blue cloak blowing in the breeze, was holding his great- granddaughter on Butterball's back. The pony's eyes seemed to be half-closing . . .

Poppy gave his fat round butterscotch-coloured rump a little slap and he opened his eyes and looked at her reproachfully.

I wondered how you made butterscotch flavouring . . .

'Cally?' Ma said, recalling my wandering attention. 'I'll stay here until our Stella's had enough. Leave me the buggy and we'll come and find you.'

So Jago and I made our way round the field, trying our hand at all the stalls, which was a lot of fun, even if my aim was terrible. Jago was a bit better and won a rainbow-coloured teddy bear and a bag of pink candyfloss, which he said he was going to give to Ma. Then, just as we were about to make for the hall, something made me look across the field to the entrance.

I clutched Jago's arm. 'Oh God, it's Adam!'

'*And* Aimee – and they've seen *us*, too,' he said as the two horribly familiar figures headed determinedly in our direction. Aimee was hanging onto Adam's arm and had to stop to wrench one of her stiletto heels out of the soft grass.

We turned to each other. 'Too late to hide,' he said ruefully.

'I know, there's only one thing to be done: quick, *kiss* me!' I ordered.

'*Kiss* you?'

'Yes, and let's make this look convincing,' I said, winding my arms around his neck. He looked faintly startled but gathered me close and obliged. I shut my eyes and . . . blissed out. The kiss went on and on . . . and on. In fact, I'd entirely forgotten where I was until someone jostled us in passing and our lips finally parted. I stared up at Jago dazedly.

'That was realistic,' I murmured weakly.

'I did my best,' he said modestly, though he looked slightly

378

shaken: probably because I'd fallen on him like a desperate woman after a kiss famine. He kept his arm around my waist holding me close to his side as we scanned the crowd for Aimee and Adam.

'Can you see them?' I asked.

'No . . . or is that them, right over there, heading away?'

'Yes, it is. Well, that worked.'

'I don't mind doing it again, if you like,' he offered with a grin, 'but we seem to have attracted a small audience already.'

We had indeed and, my cheeks glowing slightly, I suggested we make for the hall, though he didn't remove his arm from my waist in case, he explained, Aimee and Adam came back.

'I don't think they will; we seem to have fooled them,' I told him, but unfortunately we also seemed to have fooled everyone else, because we were on the receiving end of a lot of knowing looks and kind smiles.

We joined the flow of people round the hall after buying raffle tickets, past a booth with a sign saying, 'Visit Gypsy Zillah Smith at the end of the pier', Chloe's chocolate stall and trestle tables laden with plants and home-made goods of all kinds, including some donated by Celia and her Crafty Knitters. She and Will hadn't been able to make it today, but I was pretty sure I'd recognised one or two of the people who'd been at the Knitathon. Mrs Snowball was doing a roaring trade selling Jago's gingerbread stars.

Stella must have exhausted her small reserves of energy, because Ma brought her back to us before wandering over to examine the plant stall. It was so crowded in the hall that we folded up the buggy and I parked it in a corner behind a screen while Jago carried Stella.

'Come on,' I said, 'Raffy told me that when he announces the tea and coffee are ready, he's also going to tell them they can buy my cake by the slice and I can see the urns have been brought out.'

My cake was on a table to itself next to the refreshments, along with a stack of paper plates and napkins. I took up my place behind it and one of the ladies at the next stall handed me a cake knife.

'Wow,' Jago said. 'That one's even better than the last – it could have been professionally made.'

I blushed with pleasure. 'Thank you – and I took your advice and wrote it up for "The Cake Diaries".'

'You know, a prinsesstårta would make an excellent alternative wedding cake, alongside my croquembouche,' he said thoughtfully. 'If you ever want a job, I'll take you onto the payroll.'

'Actually, I'd love that, because I think I enjoy making them as much as you do the croquembouche. Perhaps one day, when Stella's well enough to start school, I'll take you up on it . . .'

I looked at my now-sleeping daughter, whose arms were linked in a fond stranglehold around Jago's neck. 'If all goes well, that is,' I added, a lump suddenly forming in my throat.

'Of course it will, but I do wish you'd change your mind and let me go to America with you,' he said, continuing an argument we'd been having off and on for a few days. 'I'd pay my own way, and come back as soon as Stella was starting to recover after the operation.'

'Absolutely not, you know you've got to get your business up and running by Christmas and you've already got croquembouche orders to fulfil for autumn,' I said firmly. 'Anyway, you've done enough, and I'll have Jenny and Ma.'

'You'll at least let me drive you to the airport and see you off, though, won't you?'

'Of course *and*, God willing, meet us again when we come back.'

'"All shall be well, and all shall be well," to quote Dame Julian of Norwich,' Raffy assured us, arriving in time to overhear this last sentiment.

'I'm just about to announce that the tea and coffee is being served, along with slices of your very excellent cake, Cally, so would you like to take up your station with the cake knife and paper plates? George from the local newspaper is going to take a picture or two of you cutting it.'

'Oh, yes, I've met George before,' I said, seeing the familiar figure of the local reporter bob up, camera in hand.

'I'll buy the first slice,' Jago said. 'I want to test if it tastes as good as it looks.'

Stella was still fast asleep against his shoulder and he glanced down at her and added, 'Make that two pieces: we'd better save one for Stella when she wakes up.'

I'd teamed a pretty, flowery, floaty tea dress that I'd got from the jumble sale with a pink cashmere cardi, so I hoped I'd look all right in the photographs, even if my hair had been tangled by the breeze. I thought my lipstick had probably vanished after that kiss, too . . .

When the cake had all gone and the cups were empty, Raffy announced that everything remaining on the stalls was half price, and he wasn't going to close the fête until they'd all been bought, so there was a minor stampede. Ma must have been in the mêlée somewhere, because she came back with a carton full of foliage, which she parked by the push-chair behind the screen.

'Have to do my bit,' she said bravely, before diving back into the fray, only to return with two jars of blackcurrant jam, her favourite.

'Where did Hal get to?' I asked.

'He was here for a bit, but he's not really one for crowds,' she said. 'He got you some herbs for your garden, Jago – you owe him four pounds fifty.'

'That was kind of him,' Jago said.

She eyed us both closely. 'I saw that Scott of the Antarctic earlier, he was heading out of the exit gate with some skinny tall blonde woman in ridiculously high heels.'

'The Abominable Aimee, Jago's ex,' I explained.

Jago, as was his casually friendly habit, had draped the arm that wasn't holding Stella around my shoulders and I suppose we must have suddenly looked to Ma like the perfect family unit.

'Anything you want to tell me?' she asked, as I had once asked her, and I blushed slightly.

'No.'

'Oh? Only someone told me they saw the pair of you having a bit of a moment in the middle of the field.'

'We were just trying to convince Adam and Aimee that we're a couple, so they leave us alone,' I explained.

'Fair enough. From the sound of it, you did that all right.'

'I hope so, then maybe they'll head straight back to London.'

Knowing the coast was now clear, I thought I'd better do my bit, so I left Jago with Stella and bought one of those peg bags shaped like a little flowered dress on a coat hanger, a knitted pink mouse with black cross-stitch woollen eyes, and a lot of tasselled bookmarks made out of old birthday cards.

I wasn't entirely sure what I would do with any of them, but Ma said she thought she could find a use for the peg bag up in the studio, because a hanging pocket had to be handy for *something*, and she wandered off holding it as well as the bag of candyfloss with which Jago had presented her.

Stella chose that moment to wake up, sleep-creased and grumpy, demanding another session with Butterball the pony.

'I'm afraid my mother's taken him home,' Poppy explained, overhearing. She was holding her own little girl in her arms, wrapped in what looked suspiciously like one of those sheep-skin pads you put under saddles to cushion them. 'But when you come back from America, perhaps you could come to the stables again and ride him?'

'Oh, yes and you could have riding lessons when you're well enough,' I suggested.

Stella's face lit up. 'The doctors are mending me, so I can run around and go to school,' she told Poppy. 'I won't be all wobbly or tired any more.'

She wriggled a bit and Jago set her carefully down on her feet.

'Gingerbread piggie?' she said, looking up at him hopefully.

'I just brought stars today, but I saved you one, and a piece of Mummy's princess cake.'

Stella took hold of his hand. 'Now.'

'Now, *please*,' I corrected automatically, thinking how quickly Stella had grown fond of Jago . . . as had I. I'd willingly shouldered the heavy burden of her medical problems alone all these years, but how much easier life had been since I'd had Jago to share my innermost thoughts and worries with!

'Are you crying, Mummy?' Stella asked worriedly.

'Yes, but only because I'm really happy,' I told her, managing a smile.

Stella, having missed her long nap, was still sleepy when we got back to the cottage, but I kept her awake to eat some tea before tucking her up for an early night. There was no sign of Ma, so she was either in the studio or had gone to the Green Man.

It turned out to be the latter, because she rang me later, while we were in the kitchen looking up recipes for butterscotch sauce, to tell me Adam and Aimee were in the bar, drunk as skunks.

I think they must have gone straight there from the fête and presumably would stay the night, rather than drive home in that condition. I hoped so, for the sake of other road users.

I was glad Ma had warned us, though, because we both got inebriated calls on our mobiles before Jago went back to the Falling Star.

First Aimee rang Jago and he said she'd told him he'd ruined her life, shattered her dreams and broken her heart, followed by a lot of gusty sobbing that I'd been able to hear myself from across the kitchen.

Then only a few minutes later Adam informed me that he didn't think Stella was really his daughter, but Jago's! Aimee had told him that we'd known each other for years, so unless I could produce a DNA test proving he was her father, he was no longer interested in either of us.

'Oh, well, it's probably all for the best,' Jago said when I relayed this unsavoury little nugget. 'I expect we've heard the end of them.'

I could only hope he was right.

I lay awake for ages that night, thinking about that kiss . . . and finally, I admitted to myself that I was in love with Jago. I probably had been from the moment our eyes met across the croquembouche in the window of the Happy Macaroon.

I think since Stella's birth I simply had never perceived myself in any light other than that of mother . . . and even if I had, I'd had no time or spare emotion left for any other kind of relationship.

But that long, tingling kiss had lit a slow fuse that still burned, though unfortunately not one that was likely to lead to a big bang in the distant future, for Jago obviously saw me as a friend. A close friend, a loving friend, but a friend.

Aimee

Aimee, who'd ended up in bed at the Green Man with Adam, said sleepily, slurring her words slightly, 'I simply don't know how it's taken us this long to get together.'

'Yeah, blindingly obvious,' he agreed, his voice muffled since he was lying limply face down in the feather pillows.

'We've a lot more in common than we ever had with Cally and Jago, haven't we?'

'I could never see you living in a dead-and-alive hole like this village,' he agreed.

'Or you playing the nine-to-five family man for ever – sooo boring.'

'Especially when the family isn't mine after all,' he said bitterly, having been convinced by now, with a little assistance from Aimee, that Stella was Jago's child. He rolled over and pushed the hair out of his eyes. 'And I'd already started wondering how long I could stick my job.'

'I absolutely *loathe* mine,' Aimee said with deep feeling. 'Life used to be much more fun! I'd love to simply throw everything up and go globe-trotting for a year. Daddy'd cut my allowance off again, but I could let my flat.'

'Me too – and what's to stop us?' he said slowly.

Chapter 36: Surprise Package

Stella, unsurprisingly, was too tired for playgroup on the Monday, so we gave it a miss. I'd assumed a hungover Aimee and Adam would have set off at dawn in order to get back to London, but when we had a little walk later we avoided the village, just in case they were still hanging about.

I'd made some choux buns early that morning and, once they were cold, piped patisserie cream filling into them, so I could experiment with my own croquembouche later, though mine would be tiny compared to Jago's.

So in the afternoon while Stella was napping, I made a cone out of a piece of cardboard taped together and covered in baking paper and then, dipping the buns in liquid caramel, began to build my cake around it. This is not the easiest of things to do, even if Jago had made it look that way!

Still, by the time Stella woke again I had a slightly loppy little tower, plus a kitchen covered in sticky strands of caramel. I must have flicked some over Toto and Moses too, because they spent ages frantically licking first themselves, and then each other.

At teatime Ma came down from the studio and we all had a piece or two of the croquembouche – or three, in Ma's case

– which pretty well finished it off, though I did save a bit for Jago to try when he popped in on his way back from the Happy Macaroon.

He couldn't stop, because he'd managed to find a reconditioned red Aga and it was about to be delivered.

'And it was just as well I had an excuse handy to get away,' he added, 'because Sarah tried to rope me into helping David retile the bathroom tonight, as if I hadn't got enough to do with my own place.'

If Stella hadn't still been a bit wan I might have taken her down to watch them manoeuvre the Aga up the garden and into the kitchen, which would probably be quite a performance, but since the new kitchen units I helped Jago to choose are being fitted soon, perhaps we'll wait and see the whole effect.

> The croquembouche, or *pièce montée*, is a very spectacular French wedding cake, consisting of a tall tower of patisserie-cream-filled choux buns, held together with melted caramel and decorated with fine sugar strands. It is time-consuming, but well worth the effort for a special occasion . . .
>
> Cally Weston: 'The Cake Diaries'

I mentioned at Stella's next hospital appointment that she didn't seem to have recovered her energy after our busy weekend, as she usually did and they gave me to understand that this was part of an expected slow decline in her health. Then they stressed that the important thing was to try to keep her clear of any illnesses and infections that might hasten that downward trend, before her operation at the start of November.

This unfortunately had the effect of making me even more anxious about her health, as well as causing me to step up my cake intake drastically and I continued to keep her quiet for the rest of the week. We didn't even go to Celia and Will's Crafty Garden Party and Selling Exhibition, though I did lots of baking and sent it over with Jenny, who reported that the event was another great fundraising success.

Over the ensuing days, which were blessed by warm sunshine, Stella and I took lots of lazy summer walks up the country lanes towards Winter's End with Toto, or to the village to feed the ducks and see the angels.

But whenever we visited any of the local shops, I now had to run the gauntlet of well-meaning banter about me and Jago. Rumours spread fast in a village, and by choosing to share a kiss in the middle of the fête, I suppose we were hardly going to go unnoticed or untalked about.

Jago told me it was happening to him too, and Mrs Snowball had asked him if she should get her wedding hat out of storage yet.

'What did you say?'

'That we were just close friends. She said, "Pull the other one, it's got bells on," so I suspect she wasn't entirely convinced.'

'Oh, well, I suppose we let ourselves in for it, but we had to make it convincing to fool Adam and Aimee,' I said, though I could feel my face burning slightly.

'We seem to have managed that, all right – there's been a total silence from both of them since they called us, hasn't there?'

'Yes, so mission accomplished – and I expect everyone else will realise we're not really a couple when they see we don't make a habit of snogging at village functions,' I suggested.

Though come to think of it, due to the casual way we held hands whenever we were out together, or Jago draped his free arm around my shoulders if he was carrying Stella, perhaps not . . .

One hot Sunday afternoon we took a picnic down to the Lido field, so Stella could paddle in the rock pool. It being a day that Winter's End was closed to the public, Sophy and Seth were there, too, with Alys in a little swimming costume and arm bands, splashing about at the edge of the river. I wished Stella could have joined in, but despite the heat of the day, I knew it would still be too cold for her.

Afterwards we walked back to Honey's, so I could see how the half-wheel herb garden that Hal had created and planted up was looking. The turf had settled in well and Jago, having discovered the joys of internet sites devoted to the free recycling of unwanted items, had installed a small, brightly coloured plastic slide and swing under the apple tree, as a surprise for Stella.

'I wiped them down with disinfectant, so no germs,' he assured me, and I told him he was getting as neurotic as I was.

'No, I just knew you'd ask,' he said. 'I'm recycling a couple of things that I don't want any more and I'll start pouncing on anything that would do for the house that comes up. The Snowballs said if I bought anything big I could store it in one of the disused stables at the back of the Falling Star, till the house is ready.'

'That was kind of them,' I said.

Inside, most of the house was still an empty shell, though the conservatory was finished and the double glazing put in. Jago would be moving in as soon as he'd finished painting his bedroom and tiling the en suite shower room, so he could get on with the rest of the redecoration while he was on the spot.

Currently the only finished room was the kitchen, which was so beautiful I want it for my own. The red Aga looked lovely and he'd splashed out on a big, retro fridge to match.

He may not so far have collected much in the way of furniture but, like me, he does have an awful lot of kitchen equipment!

I'd been so inspired by finding that the supermarket now stocked those delicious American Reese's Peanut Butter Cups, that I'd bought a huge jar of peanut butter and begun a whole new series of recipes using it.

Unfortunately, my cake consumption was taking on an even steeper upward curve as we moved through summer towards autumn and what it would bring, though for much of the time I managed to push my worries to the back of my mind and enjoy the moment. Some moments, especially those involving cake *and* Jago, I enjoyed more than others . . .

Aimee and Adam seemed to have vanished from our lives as if they'd merely been figures from a long nightmare and I'd almost managed to forget about them.

Then one day I answered a knock on the door and opened it to find an elderly couple standing on the doorstep. They were smartly dressed and vaguely familiar . . .

'Hello, Cally,' said the woman, in a frightfully posh voice.

She had elegantly coiffed silver hair and was clutching a blue cashmere coat around her thin frame as if she was cold, though the day was warm and even slightly sticky.

The man, bald but with a flourishing white moustache, smiled hopefully and said, 'Hello, my dear.'

Then it clicked – Adam's parents! We'd only met once before, in London, and they'd aged noticeably since then . . . but then, Adam *had* been a late and unexpected only child.

'Mr and Mrs Scott. Well – this is a surprise,' I exclaimed. Then I remembered my manners and showed them into the sitting room, which was littered with toys. The rainbow teddy bear that Jago had won at the fête was sitting on the rocking horse in the window.

'Do sit down and I'll just pop into the kitchen and make tea. My mother's out with my little girl at the moment, but I expect they'll be back soon,' I added.

Ma had taken Stella up to Winter's End in the car, because Ottie was back and wanted to check over the leaflet for that joint exhibition they were having in early October.

While I made the tea and arranged some peanut biscuits that I'd made that morning onto a nice china plate, I was wondering what on earth they were going to say when I went back in, because I'd assumed that by now Adam would have shared with them his view that Stella was not his after all.

They'd seemed a bit nervous . . .

'I hope you don't mind our calling in unannounced, but we wanted to talk to you . . . and to see the little girl, Stella, if that is possible,' Mrs Scott explained as I poured tea. 'We're feeling very confused . . . so driving up today was a sudden impulse.'

I nodded, thinking that it was a very strong impulse to have brought them all the way up from the Cotswolds.

'When Aimee Calthrop first told us about Stella, we thought she might be mistaken,' Mr Scott put in. 'But then when Adam contacted you and found out it was true, we were very excited.'

'Of course, poor Adam was terribly upset when you broke up with him before he went back to the Antarctic,' put in his wife.

'*I* broke up with Adam?' I interrupted.

'Yes . . . I expect you felt very bitter when he signed up for another eighteen months, but when you found out you were pregnant, you really should have told him *and* us. We'd have helped you and been delighted to hear we had a grandchild.'

'Look, I don't know what Adam's been saying, but he'd left me for someone else before I discovered I was pregnant,' I told them. 'I didn't end the relationship just because he had signed another contract for Antarctica. When I found out I was expecting, I rang him up, but he wasn't interested.'

They gazed at me, puzzled.

'I don't think he can have understood,' Mrs Scott said doubtfully. 'Surely if you'd said—'

'I told him I was pregnant and he said if I carried on with it I was on my own.'

'Well, I don't know what to think now,' Mr Scott said. 'Perhaps it was all just a misunderstanding? He certainly hoped when he came up here to see you that you'd give him a second chance.'

'Perhaps he did, but he could hardly expect to walk back

into my life as if nothing had happened,' I said. 'I felt I had to agree to let him meet Stella, though it wasn't a great success. Aimee hadn't warned him that she had health issues.'

'Yes, and he is a little difficult over things like that,' his mother said indulgently. 'He warned us that there was no point in our meeting Stella and getting attached to her, because she had a very serious heart condition and might not get through her next operation. We felt so worried about the poor little thing.'

'He said that? But the operation in America this autumn has every chance of being a huge success!'

'We do hope so,' said Mr Scott.

They exchanged a glance, as if urging each other on, and Mrs Scott said, 'He called in after he'd seen Stella for the second time and told us he'd discovered that not only were you involved with someone else, but you'd known this man for years, so he didn't think Stella was his, any more!'

'But we thought you were a very nice girl when we met you and you both seemed very much in love then, so we were sure he was wrong,' Mr Scott finished.

'He *is* wrong,' I said. 'I am seeing someone else, and yes, I did briefly meet him in London years ago, but it's only in the last few months that I've really got to know him. He's helping me to raise the money to take Stella to America for her operation.'

Mr Scott said, 'I thought he might have got hold of the wrong end of the stick, because that Aimee Calthrop was with him, egging him on, and she's always seemed to me to be a bit of a mischief maker.'

'Jago, the man I'm seeing, is her ex-fiancé, so she has an axe to grind.'

'Oh . . . right,' he said. 'Modern relationships are very difficult to understand . . . But did you say you'd been fund-raising for the operation Stella needs?'

'Yes, because it's in America. Everyone locally has been very kind, so I'm sure we'll have exceeded the target by the end of the summer.'

'If not, you must tell us, my dear, and we will make it up,' Mr Scott offered.

They wanted to know details of Stella's condition and the operation, which I told them, and also about how successful Dr Beems had been with it, even though the programme was still experimental.

Then the kitchen door slammed and Stella herself trotted in, calling excitedly, 'Mummy, Ottie gave me a stick of rock from Cornwall with words all the way through it!' Then she spotted the visitors and stopped dead, putting her thumb in her mouth.

'I have a nice surprise for you,' I said, picking her up and giving her a cuddle, though due to the half-sucked stick of rock I soon slightly regretted that. 'Your other grandma and grandpa have come to meet you.'

'Oh, she's the image of Adam at the same age!' cried Mrs Scott. 'What a darling!'

'Is she?' I asked, surprised, because she'd never looked remotely like him so far as I could see, but very much took after the Almond side of the family. I supposed Mrs Scott had just seen what she truly wanted to.

'This is Grandma Scott,' I told Stella.

'Do call me Granny, darling,' she said. 'And this is Grandpa Ralph. We're so happy to meet you, Stella – and we've brought you some presents to make up for all the birthdays and Christmases we've missed.'

I'd wondered what was in the big Hamleys bag Mr Scott had carried in with him.

Stella revived now that the first surprise was over. She scrambled down and went across to stare at them. I braced myself.

'You're quite old, aren't you?'

'I'm afraid so,' Mr Scott said.

'That's all right, I like old people,' Stella assured them, and then cut to the chase. 'Are my presents in the bag?'

They'd brought her a musical jewellery box with a fairy inside who danced, and Stella explained her theory about fairies being small angels, which seemed to fascinate them. In fact, Stella herself seemed to fascinate them and I warmed to them, just as she was doing. There was a huge floor jigsaw of zoo animals in the bag, too, which she got out and started to assemble on the rug.

'Where's Grandma?' I asked her.

Stella looked up. 'She said it looked like you had visitors, Mummy, and she couldn't be bothered so she was going up to the studio.'

'We hope we can meet your mother another time,' Mrs Scott said to me. 'I don't think we will be back again before you go to America, though, because it was rather a long drive here – and in fact, I suppose we ought to be setting off home again.'

'You'll always be welcome,' I assured them.

'Well, Stella,' Mrs Scott said, putting her hand on Stella's silky curls and stroking them, 'when you come back from America, we'll send you a very special Christmas present, so perhaps Mummy will help you write to Santa later on and tell him what you'd like?'

'Her list already runs to about three pages,' I said.

'But I got some things for my birthday, so I can cross those off,' Stella said. She paused from assembling her jigsaw for long enough to say goodbye to the Scotts, then we left her to it while I showed them out.

'I feel everything will go well in America,' Mrs Scott said, squeezing my hands in her two little bony bird claws. 'I love Adam, but I'm not so blinded by that not to see that he hasn't behaved quite as well as he should have. I'm so sorry, my dear.'

'It isn't your fault,' I assured her, wondering how such nice parents had managed to produce a son like Adam.

'I'm sure when he's had time to think things over and Stella's well again, he'll see sense,' Mr Scott said.

I didn't reply to that, because what use was a father who couldn't cope with his own child's pain?

'But we would like to keep in touch with you and write to Stella,' Mr Scott said.

'Yes, and then perhaps you could both come down to us for a holiday in spring, when Stella is well enough: that *would* be something for us to look forward to. We'd love to see as much of Stella as we can, as she grows up,' said his wife.

'Of course . . . if all goes well,' I added involuntarily.

'It will. In fact, I'm so confident that we will go right home and set up a university fund for her,' Mr Scott declared.

'That's very kind of you, especially since Adam hasn't even accepted that she's his daughter and I'm certainly not doing a DNA test to prove it.'

'You don't need to: we are quite sure Stella is our grandchild.'

'If he was serious about settling down, you may well get some more grandchildren before long,' I pointed out.

'But Stella would always be our precious first-born one . . . and actually, we both thought he and the Calthrop girl were hitting it off quite well,' she said. 'Though she's not really a girl, she's the same age he is, so I don't know that there'd be any more grandchildren if they got together.'

'You know, I think they'd be the perfect match, apart from that,' I said. 'They have such a lot in common.'

And when later I told Ma, she said they'd be a perfect couple, because they wouldn't spoil two families.

She was only mildly interested in the sudden advent of the Scotts into our lives, but said they sounded sensible and it certainly wasn't in her nature to be jealous of a new grandmother on the scene.

When Stella grows up, I think she'll be glad that she knew her other grandparents, but though I explained that they're Daddy Penguin's mummy and daddy, I'm not sure she believed me.

Chapter 37: Nuts

These peanut butter and chocolate cups are quick and easy to make. You can either put the mixture straight into small foil sweet cases to set, or use to fill ready-made dark chocolate shells.

Cally Weston: 'Tea & Cake'

Raffy was summoned to Pinker's End, where Miss Honey presented him with a thousand pounds for the Stella's Stars fund and told him that we should use it for any extras that would make our trip to the States more comfortable. It was so kind of her that I was very touched.

Raffy also reported that she hadn't been well, which would explain why Jago and I haven't been asked there for a while, but she was now full of beans and had said she hoped to see us at Pinker's End again before too long.

I wrote to her to thank her for the donation and in return received an old postcard of Blackpool pier. At least, I assumed it was from Miss Honey, because although the card was addressed and stamped, she'd forgotten to write a message.

Tim Wesley and his staff must have moved mountains up at Hemlock Mill, because the reconstructed Honey's shop and the next-door gift shop were ready to open by the end of August. He explained to Jago that it was because Miss Honey was keen to see it and they thought the original official opening day at half-term would be a bit late in the year for her to brave the weather.

But in any case, when you're a hundred and two, the sooner the better. It was arranged that she would perform the official opening ceremony on the Saturday of the Bank Holiday weekend. Jago and I thought we'd take Stella to watch.

Meanwhile, we tried to ignore the faint dark cloud on the horizon that was the operation and enjoy the gentle, peaceful summer days. Stella's health seemed to be on an even keel again, so that we made it to a couple of the play-group sessions, had days out to her favourite places, spent time with Celia and Will in Southport, and even went out to the riding stables, Stirrups, to visit the old donkey and Butterball.

In the evenings, Jago and I have now added scouring the internet sites for free furniture to our old hobbies of trying out new recipes and watching films. We've found all kinds of things, including a lovely old dining table and a mismatched assortment of chairs to go with it, which he commissioned Celia to cover in the same William Morris fabric as the curtains so they all sort of go together.

By the time Jago finally moved into Honey's he'd almost filled the outbuilding loaned to him by the Snowballs, and it took him several trips in the van, helped by David, to transfer it all across. Two battered and ancient leather sofas wouldn't fit in the van at all, so they had to carry them from the pub to the shop in the late evening, one at a time, though

Jago said since they had big brass castors, they managed to push them up the road for part of the way even if they had, according to Mrs Snowball, squealed fit to raise the dead.

Mrs Scott has written two or three times to Stella by now, in tiny lettering inside cards with old-fashioned fairy pictures on the front, which Stella found enchanting. They were little chatty notes, saying how much her new granny and grandpa enjoyed meeting her and how they hoped she and her mummy would come to stay for a little holiday next year, when she was all better.

There was no word from, or about, Adam.

Stella seemed fine for the Bank Holiday weekend and it was a lovely day for the opening of the restored and recreated Honey's shop at the mill.

Miss Honey arrived in her wheelchair encased in a kind of sheepskin body muff that would have had me expiring with the heat, and all you could really see of her was her face topped by a red turban hat with a Scottish Celtic circle brooch pinned to it.

The wheelchair was trundled directly from the van down a ramp and straight through the arch into the courtyard, where Tim and various Trust members and local dignitaries, including Hebe Winter, awaited her.

There was a good crowd there to watch her cut the ribbon, too.

'God Bless the good ship Honey and all who sail in her,' she announced clearly, grinning, and there was a ripple of laughter and then applause.

She was taken inside to view the new shop and emerged

some time later from the other end of the building via the gift shop, clutching a bunch of yellow roses, which she waved at Florrie Snowball, who was standing near us with Jenny.

'Is that you, young Florrie?' she called, having herself propelled in our direction.

'Not dead yet then, Queenie?' replied Mrs Snowball, and then they both cackled with laughter as though this was a joke of high order.

'I'm glad you're not dead,' Stella told her, and then Miss Honey insisted we all go and have tea with her in the eco-centre before she was, as she put it, incarcerated at Pinker's End again.

Bank Holiday Monday was Ivo Hawksley's Shakespeare reading up at Winter's End, but we thought yesterday had been excitement enough for Stella, so we left her with Ma and went on our own.

David and Sarah, and Celia and Will had also said they were going, and Miss Winter had certainly made the most of the publicity leading up to it because there was a crowd of people heading up there.

It was a warm day with a heavy, sultry sky that threatened a thunderstorm later. Ivo performed from the lowest of the three terraces behind the house, which was very appropriate because the Shakespeare garden and the wall incised with quotations from the Bard were both on that level. His audience were grouped on the terraces above and it made quite a natural auditorium.

He performed three pieces, at first funny, then sad and moving, his beautiful voice carrying clearly up to the highest point without him seeming to raise it, which I suspect will

402

give Hebe Winter ideas about having whole performances of Shakespeare there in future.

We were all so gripped and mesmerised that when he'd finished, there was a short silence and then a thunder of applause and cheering. He was persuaded to do an encore and, appropriately, given the gathering storm clouds, it was a piece from *The Tempest*.

But luckily the weather must have read the stage directions, for it held off until we were almost home again afterwards, when the rain started to splash down in big, hard drops that exploded onto the car windscreen.

'Good timing,' Jago said. 'And the gardens need it, after this dry spell. I'm glad it didn't start while Ivo was still reading, though – great, wasn't it?'

'Yes, amazing. The theatre's the only thing I've really missed since I had Stella . . . and do you know, I was thinking earlier that despite all the worry over her health, I've had more fun since moving to Sticklepond than I've ever had in my entire life before!'

'Me too, and I feel more a part of your family than I ever did my own. Now they're in New Zealand, I think they forget I exist most of the time,' he added ruefully.

'Ma says you don't bother her and she doesn't mind whether you're there or not.'

'Maybe she'd like to adopt me?' he suggested, which I thought showed just how brotherly a light he saw me in.

Unfortunately, that was not how I was increasingly coming to think of him.

I should have seen that storm after the spell of lovely weather as an omen, for on the following Thursday morning Stella

403

slept so late that in the end I had to wake her up and I could see at once that she was heavy-eyed and running a slight temperature.

Luckily her hospital appointment was an early one, because by the time we got there she was burning up and tearful, and I wasn't surprised when they decided to admit her overnight, so they could give her antibiotics intravenously, the quickest way of getting them into her system.

This did not go down well with Stella. It was hard being a mother and having to watch doctors do something that will hurt your child, even if the result was for the best. The last time she had an operation she wasn't really old enough to understand what was happening and that was bad enough . . .

Once she was settled in bed with Bun tucked up beside her, I rang Ma to tell her what was happening.

'They don't know what's causing the temperature yet, but they've taken some blood for tests and they're giving her antibiotics intravenously in the hope it will stop any infection taking hold. They'll see if that's had any effect tomorrow and hopefully it will do the trick. If not, they'll probably send her across to Alder Hey . . .'

'Then let's hope they've caught it in time, whatever it is,' Ma said. 'Shall I come in now and do you want me to bring anything?'

'She's in a small side room on her own, and I'm staying here overnight,' I said, and told her where the emergency bags I always keep packed were. She said she'd be in shortly with them. 'What about your car?'

'They don't have overnight car parks; I'll have to move it somewhere.'

'We'll work something out, don't worry about it.'

'Stella told the consultant he was a bad Dr Rabbit and the nurse that she wouldn't let her work in her cottage hospital,' I said, managing a laugh, despite my worry.

But when I was talking to Jago a few minutes later and he said he'd be in as soon as he could get there, I began to cry, which is not like me in the least.

'But it's always busy at the Happy Macaroon on market days and, anyway, haven't you and David got orders to make?' I protested, sniffling.

'Nothing he can't handle on his own,' he assured me. 'Dorrie and Sarah are covering the shop, and although I'll have to deliver a macaroon party cone order first, it's in Ormskirk so it won't take long.'

Ma arrived first with Hal in tow, but he'd just come to take my car back home and went off with the keys, so that was one thing fewer to worry about. She'd brought both our overnight bags, too.

Stella had fallen asleep and Ma tiptoed in and stroked her hot forehead as she slept whispering, 'Poor little mite!'

'I think we caught it quickly – I hope so,' I said devoutly.

After a while she went home again to feed the animals and I said I'd ring her if there was any change; then soon afterwards, Jago arrived.

Stella was still asleep, though I thought she didn't look as flushed, just very small and frail in the big white expanse of bed.

'Oh, Jago!' I said, running straight into his arms. He folded me into a strong, reassuring hug.

'It's going to be all right, Cally.'

'I think she's starting to look better already . . . or I could just be fooling myself,' I told him.

He looked down on her tenderly. 'She's certainly fast asleep and that's probably the best thing for her. She doesn't look very flushed, either, so you're probably right about that.'

'She hated it when they put the line in her arm and . . . well, it really brought home to me what I'll be putting her through in Boston now she's old enough to know what's happening.'

'I know, but at least this should be the last time she has to face an operation.'

'But what if it all goes wrong and—'

'It won't,' he broke in firmly. 'It's all going to be fine.'

We sat on either side of her bed talking in whispers until she woke. She was much more her usual self and pleased to see him, though she told him indignantly what the doctors and nurses had done and showed him the drip in her arm.

'Do they do this in America?'

'I think they might put *one* needle in your arm, but then you'll be fast asleep after that while they mend your heart and when you wake up you'll soon start to feel much better.'

'Huh!' she said. 'I'll believe it when I see it.'

'Who says that?' I asked, startled.

'You do, Mummy,' she told me. 'You say it all the time.'

'Well then, you'd better believe it,' Jago told her, grinning.

Ma returned bearing a special present from Hal – an angel feather.

Stella was enchanted by the lovely plume of purest silky white and wanted to know how he had got it, but Ma told her it was a big secret.

She sat with her while Jago and I went and had something to eat in the hospital cafeteria, though I don't think either of

406

us noticed what was on our plates. When we got back to Stella's room the nurse had been in in our absence and said her temperature *was* coming down, so I felt a little less fraught.

Ma went home but Stella didn't want Jago to go; she wanted us *both* there . . . and in the morning when I awoke in the chair by the bed he was fast asleep in the one opposite, unshaven and uncomfortable, and I felt a strong stirring of that deep and entirely un-sisterly love . . .

Then Stella opened her eyes and murmured querulously, 'Mummy?'

Stella made a rapid recovery and they said the tests they'd done were inconclusive, so it was probably some anonymous infection she'd picked up, which luckily they'd stopped in its tracks before it had a chance to properly take hold.

They kept her in for another night to be sure and then released her with a warning to me to be careful and make sure she took things very easy. But I could already see that the stuffing had been knocked out of her by the episode and I didn't need the warning – I wanted to wrap her up in cotton wool and keep her safe . . .

It only occurred to me to tell Adam's parents what had happened when we got her home – I wasn't used to having anyone other than Ma and my friends to consider. Still, it was probably better that they only got to know when she was feeling better, so they were spared some of the worry.

'We'll try and tell Adam,' Mrs Scott said, 'but I'm afraid we're a little cross with him because he's thrown up his job, and he and the Calthrop girl have left the country. They're travelling round the world for a year, but he only told me after they'd left.'

'Really? That was a bit sudden,' I said.

'He says they're engaged, too,' she told me.

'I think they'll be perfect for each other,' I assured her. They were shallow, selfish and thoughtless: the perfect match.

Jago wasn't all that surprised either, and said drily, 'I don't somehow think they'll be inviting us to the wedding.'

Jago tried again to persuade me to let him go to America with us, but I was adamant he shouldn't, because he really needed to get Honey's Croquembouche Cakes going before his winnings ran out.

It was quite likely we'd be in the States for weeks, too, and he simply couldn't take all that time off: it would be selfish of me to let him, especially when he'd already done so much for us . . .

Chapter 38: On the Edge

After this scare, and with less than a month to go before we flew out to Boston, I became even more terrified that Stella would get another infection and this time be too ill to travel.

And now the realities of the operation had *really* come home to me – that they would stop her heart beating and hook her up to all kinds of machines that would keep her alive while the delicate surgery was performed. The prospect terrified me and gave me sleepless nights. But I could also see that even this small setback had taken its toll on Stella and, without the operation, she'd continue her steady decline, her resistance to any further infections weakening. I couldn't bear to think of that alternative, either.

Ormskirk were keeping the Boston hospital updated and they'd emailed me all kinds of information about children's heart surgery and how long I could expect Stella's recovery to take afterwards. So long as there *is* an afterwards . . .

Stella was now worried too, since she was old enough and certainly smart enough to guess that more of the same as she'd just had awaited her in Boston, even though we kept reminding her that this would be the last time she had to face an operation like this and assuring her that she would be fine afterwards. Please God we were not all going to be proved liars.

I was now totally Little Miss Neurotic: I'd told Chloe we were not going to playgroup till after the operation, and I turned tail and fled if I was anywhere with Stella and someone started to cough, sneeze or just looked vaguely diseased. I'd even wondered if I should make Stella wear a facemask on the flight, because we'd be cooped up over the Atlantic for hours with a lot of germy people, but Jenny talked me out of that one.

So we carried on quietly, our social circle limited to home, Celia and Will, who were busily sorting out any last-minute arrangements for the trip as they came up, and Jago, who luckily seemed resistant to coughs and colds. We still had little trips out to our favourite places and often went down to Honey's, where a state-of-the-art croquembouche preparation area was being installed.

The house was looking much more like a home now and Jago had found an old dresser on which to display a collection of antique moulds, dishes and jugs to rival my own.

The last of the Stella's Stars fundraising events was the book signing at Marked Pages with Ivo Hawksley and his wife, Tansy, Gregory Lyon and Seth Greenwood.

The event was a distraction and surprisingly busy – in fact, at one point people were queuing out of the door, though that was mostly for Ivo, who had loads of fans for his Elizabethan crime novels. Lots of parents had brought their children to have their *Slipper Monkey* books signed by Tansy, too.

Gregory Lyon was most popular with the photographers

from the local papers, since he was dressed in a flowing green velvet cloak and, with his long silver hair and piercing blue eyes, he looked sort of alarming but splendid. I noticed that once he'd fixed his gaze on a customer, they didn't go away without buying at least one of his books, so that the most unlikely people left clutching lurid supernatural thrillers.

After the event we all had a cup of coffee together, and Gregory said Zillah had told him that my little one had a glowing future and he himself would perform a rite to ensure the best outcome, which was sort of comforting even if I wasn't sure if I believed in that kind of thing.

Raffy had stayed for coffee at the end too, and he added that his whole congregation were going to pray for Stella when she was in America, so it looked as though all my bases were covered.

'It'll be the meeting to wind the fundraising up soon,' he added, 'and I confidently expect we'll have more than double the amount we set out to raise. In fact, the money from today's event will just be the final cherry on top of the icing on top of the cake.'

'I'm so grateful to everyone for their help. It's been wonderful and I really do feel part of the community now.'

'You *are* part of the community and will always be, whatever your plans are for the future. But I don't suppose you've given that much thought yet.'

I shook my head. 'No, I suppose I'm like one of those brides who are so busy planning their perfect wedding day that they don't give a thought to what life will be like afterwards. When I sold the flat, I imagined that as soon as we could we'd be back to London again . . . but now, I don't know.'

'I wouldn't worry about it. Things have a way of working themselves out,' he said kindly.

Stir a good tablespoon of peanut butter into the flapjack mixture. After baking, the flapjacks taste extra delicious with a thick layer of dark chocolate on top . . .

Cally Weston: 'Tea & Cake'

Miss Honey invited us up for tea again, though I thought Stella seemed a little off colour and left her behind in Jenny's capable hands. I'd made peanut butter and chocolate flapjacks that morning and she'd eaten part of one, so I was suddenly afraid she might have developed a peanut allergy.

Jenny told me not to be daft, because she wasn't likely to suddenly get one at four if there'd been no sign of it before, and I supposed she was right.

Miss Honey looked frailer but cheerful, and although she was disappointed that Stella hadn't come, she wished her well for the operation.

'Perhaps, if I'm spared, you'll bring her to see me when you get back,' she said, then sighed. 'Livens us all up no end, when children visit. It's a pity poor Gladdie didn't have any more.'

'Any . . . *more*?' I repeated blankly, as this sunk in. 'You can't mean—'

'Ah, so your mother didn't know all of the story, did she?' Miss Honey said. 'I don't think it got round the village, but I thought the Almonds would be sure to talk about it.'

'Apparently not. But if the Almonds knew, then does that mean your sister . . .' I paused, wondering how to phrase this with least offence.

'That Esau Almond got Gladdie pregnant on his last leave. She wrote to him as soon as she found out and so did Father – well, he was furious! Esau wrote back saying he'd put in for compassionate leave and they'd get married. But of course, that was just before D-Day, so that was the last she ever heard from him.'

'Well . . . that makes more sense of the whole thing,' I said thoughtfully. 'But poor Gladys!'

'Having a baby out of wedlock was a huge scandal at the time, though others in the village were rumoured to have been caught the same way – things were a bit different in the war. To go by the carryings-on on the telly, you'd find it hard to believe anyone ever bothered about these things. Sodom and Gomorrah, that's what the world's coming to.'

'You're probably right,' I said diplomatically. 'What happened to your sister – and the baby?'

'She kept it quiet because she hoped he'd get leave quickly so they'd be married before it showed, but when he didn't, Father sent her up to his cousins in Scarborough, who had a small hotel. She was there when she heard he'd gone missing and then she lost the baby – stillbirth.'

'How awful,' I said. 'I'm so sorry.'

'It took her a while to get over it and then she was knocked for six when she found out he hadn't been killed in action after all. But after a while she met her husband and they were happy as Larry, so in the end it all worked out for the best.'

After this final revelation I was even more amazed that Miss Honey had been so forgiving towards one of the hated Almond clan, and so was Ma when I told her. In fact, a few days later she went up there to see Miss Honey herself and

413

I don't know what they said to each other, but she seemed cheerful when she came back so I expect it cleared the air.

Ma looked after Stella while I went to the village meeting to officially wind up the Stella's Stars fundraising. Raffy was right – we'd raised well over twenty thousand pounds!

I thanked everyone all over again, though Hebe Winter assured me there was no need.

'We have all enjoyed it – and perhaps we should have a welcome back party when you come home? You will return by December, won't you, so the party can be Christmas-themed, since the hall will be decorated ready by then anyway.'

'Oh, yes,' Florrie Snowball piped up eagerly, 'I always like a good Christmas party, with mince pies and a bowl of hot punch. The Falling Star will provide that.'

'We usually have a Christmas party for the kiddies,' Jenny said, 'so we could combine them and have it a little earlier this year.'

'That would be lovely, but I think *I* should be throwing a party for all of you, to thank you for your help, not the other way round,' I said. 'If all goes well, we'll be home long before Christmas . . .'

My voice broke, because now the time to leave was so close, I was starting to panic at the thought of the difficult surgery that lay ahead for my little girl, and the chances of a good outcome . . . Though of course, there was no real alternative, for without it Stella would simply fade away.

'Don't worry, the surgery will go well,' Hebe said, as if she had a direct line to the future.

'Yes – I saw it in the leaves,' Zillah Smith agreed firmly.

'And the Angel cards said so too,' Chloe Lyon said.

'You see, all the omens are good, so there's no need to fret,' said Hebe Winter.

'And we'll all be praying for you,' Raffy assured me.

'Not perhaps *all*,' interrupted Gregory Lyon, 'but ceremonies will be performed and our good wishes and thoughts will be directed towards you.'

'The party will be something for Stella to look forward to when she's recovering after the operation, won't it?' Jago suggested. 'You can tell her that Santa will drop in, with a very special Christmas present.'

'Laurence will be contacting you all soon, then, to arrange the first of a series of meetings to organise the Christmas party,' Hebe said. 'The usual people and any extra volunteers.'

'I'll volunteer,' Jago offered immediately.

'Good man,' she said.

'Jonah from up at the hall is always the local Father Christmas,' Mrs Snowball told me. 'He loves to do it. There'll be a gift for every child in the village, so we usually start to organise that around now anyway.'

Suddenly I had a shining vision of a twinkling Christmas star beckoning to me from the other side of the dark chasm in which lay the dreaded operation, and I felt heartened.

Stella had her final hospital check-up and suddenly, it was almost time to leave.

The last-minute details had been sorted out: Hal was to look after Toto and Moses, and keep an eye on the cottage, and Jenny, by now a seasoned traveller, kept us calm and gave us sensible advice – not to mention describing to Stella all the fun places in Boston she'd be able to visit.

Stella packed and repacked her favourite toys in her Trunki ladybird suitcase until she'd made her choice, though Bun was always a given, of course.

And then soon, too soon, it was the night before our flight and the cases were lined up in the hall. It took me hours to get to sleep and no sooner than I had, the alarm went off.

Jenny had met us at the airport, the luggage was checked in and Ma and Jenny had said their goodbyes and were waiting for us to join them. But Stella was clinging round Jago's neck, her face hidden, and didn't want to let him go.

'I wish you were coming with us,' she said.

'I wish I was too,' Jago said, 'but I'll be thinking about you all the time and we'll talk on the phone a lot. And when the doctors have made you better and you've had a lovely holiday, I'll be waiting right here for you when you get back.'

'With a gingerbread piggy?'

'Yes – and then you and I and Mummy will make a gingerbread castle together for Christmas.'

'Promise?'

'Promise. And it'll be the best Christmas ever, because you'll be well again.'

'Come on, our Stella,' Ma called, and Stella finally released her stranglehold on Jago's neck and ran to Ma, who took one hand and Jenny the other.

I looked at Jago hopelessly. 'I keep going hot and cold and I feel I'm moving through a dream-like trance – or a nightmare. It's all so unreal, I can't believe I'm doing this.'

'I know it must seem surreal but you have to take this chance for Stella's sake. There's no going back. Only I want you to keep in contact and tell me what's happening every step of the way, because I'm going to be thinking about you all the time. And just say the word and I'll fly out.'

'Oh, Jago!' I said, feeling my lip trembling, and then somehow our goodbye kiss turned into a reprise of the epic kiss we'd had at the fête and time stopped in its tracks.

Then we broke apart, and he touched my cheek and smiled. 'Boldly go, as they used to say in *Star Trek*.'

I grinned weakly: 'Oh, beam me up, Scotty!'

Jago

Jago sat in his car in the airport car park, his head resting on the steering wheel and his heart winging its way towards Boston with Cally.

Logically he knew Cally was right and he needed to stay and get his business up and running, but he still would have dropped everything and gone with them, if she had only given the word.

Not that he had any rights in the matter, despite loving them both, of course.

Then he thought about that last kiss . . . whatever scale that was on, it was so far away from platonic it had probably dropped off the end. Had that been just a need for comfort, or was she beginning to care for him? Only time would tell.

But she certainly hadn't given much thought to what would happen after they returned and it would probably be some time before she would be in a position to move back to London . . . if she still wanted to.

Then and there, Jago hatched a plan to offer them the annexe at Honey's to live in after Christmas, for as long as they needed it. He'd put off finishing the attic and the annexe till a later date, but now the task of turning the annexe into a wonderful guest suite in the hope Cally would agree would give him something to occupy his mind with.

Chapter 39: To Infinity and Beyond

I'd never flown business class before and neither had Jenny, but it was so much more comfortable than tourist class. They gave Stella a special child's goodie bag and then seemed to be constantly offering us food or drink, though Stella, exhausted by excitement, was soon fast asleep in her reclining seat, thumb in mouth and Bun tucked in under her cheek. Ma soon followed suit and could be heard gently snoring.

It was a long flight, but due to the five hours difference we arrived at Logan International airport outside Boston practically before we set out, though of course it didn't feel like that.

I staggered off the plane well and truly jetlagged, but Stella and Ma seemed surprisingly fresh and Jenny said it had all been so comfortable compared to her usual flight over that it had been a complete pleasure.

Jenny's family met us at the airport, bringing with them the buggy they were kindly loaning me for Stella. Jenny had already given me their address and phone number and promised Stella she'd come to visit her soon.

We got into a yellow cab with a friendly driver who told

Stella she could call him George and then chatted with her all the way out to the Best Western in the Longwood Medical Area, where we were staying.

She told him she was going to the hospital to have her heart mended and he assured her that he'd driven lots of much sicker children than her to the hospital and when he took them back to the airport to go home, they were all as good as new.

I could have kissed him, because Stella took this as gospel, though why she should have believed a cabbie over me or anyone else, I've no idea. But I was just grateful she did.

The hotel was literally next to the hospital, so it couldn't be handier, and they'd given us a two-bedroom suite, which was much swisher than anything I'd stayed in in the UK. Ma had one room and Stella and I shared the other, twin-bedded one.

We unpacked while Stella had a nap on the bed, and then went out for a little stroll around the area and an early dinner in the hotel.

We had the weekend free and had already planned to go to see the New England Aquarium and perhaps the Children's Museum on Sunday, if Stella wasn't too tired.

Ma came to the aquarium with us, bringing her sketch-book and making lots of drawings, because it was the most amazing place with seals and penguins, and a vast tank with a coral reef in it, which riveted Stella.

Stella tired first, so we left Ma there and went to find lunch – and discovered the delights of Boston cream pie. Why had no one ever told me about this wonderful creation before?

*　　*　　*

Boston cream pie is local speciality, I texted Jago. *But it's a cake.*

Trust you to find local cake on first day in Boston! he texted back. *Bring recipe.*

Jago and I had been exchanging texts and emails since we landed, but I was already missing the sound of his voice.

Come to that, I was desperately missing everything about him!

Ma and Stella were both so enchanted with the aquarium that we went back again next morning, which I didn't mind so long as I got to eat more cake afterwards. I needed it to calm my nerves, along with any variety of Reese's Peanut Butter goodies I could get my hands on. Stella had developed a liking for Reese's Pieces, which are candy coated and a little like a peanut butter version of Smarties, though unlike me, she made a bag last her all day.

Ma came out to lunch with us this time, then went off to some art gallery, and Stella and I went back to the hotel so she could rest. Later on, when Ma had returned and she and Stella were in her room drawing very strange angel fish, Jago called and I can't tell you how wonderful it was to hear his voice.

He seemed to feel the same, because he said, 'You're so far away, but you *sound* close. How's the hotel?'

'Really comfortable and very handy for the hospital and everything else. We've been to the aquarium twice – it's huge, much bigger than any I've ever seen.'

'And you've found the Boston cream pie!'

'Yes, though like I said, it's not a pie at all, it's a big sponge cake with a vanilla patisserie cream filling and a chocolate ganache topping. Apparently you can get mini ones too, and Boston doughnuts, which sound a bit like those Krispy Kreme ones . . .'

I paused. 'Tomorrow we go into the hospital to meet Dr Beems and then Stella will be admitted the day after . . . There was a letter waiting at the reception when we arrived, with a map and some leaflets.'

'How's she doing?'

'She seems pretty well, considering the flight, though she did sleep for most of it. I was the one who got off the plane like a zombie. We've been concentrating on having a fun weekend and not thinking about anything else.'

Stella came in from Ma's room and I said, 'Hello, darling, do you want to speak to Jago?'

She nodded and I handed her the mobile, though I held her close so I could still hear him. She told him that the cab driver had taken lots of little girls and boys to the hospital and they'd all come out as good as new, because they had the best doctors there in the whole wide world.

'Of course they do,' I could hear him saying.

'And they have the best red socks too,' Stella added, which she'd seemed to find so impressive that I hadn't yet had the heart to explain that they were a local baseball team. '*And* a huge 'quarium. But I wish I could come home now and not go to hospital.'

'I wish you could, too. But the special doctor there will make you better while you're having a little sleep and when you're well again, you and Mummy can have a holiday.'

'Jenny says I have to be brave and then she's going to bring me a Salem witch doll.'

'You *are* brave, Stella, and when you get home, we're going to make that gingerbread castle with Mummy and there's going to be a *huge* Christmas party.'

'Do you think Father Christmas got my list?'

'I'm sure he did and he's got the elves working on it right now,' he said.

'I asked him for snow, too. I've never seen snow.'

'Yes, you have,' I put in.

'Well, I don't remember,' she said crossly. 'And I *want* snow.'

Then she handed me the phone back and inserting her thumb into her mouth, started sucking furiously.

'Come on, our Stella,' Ma said, coming in and summing up the situation. 'We'll go and see if we can find a half-decent cup of tea somewhere in this place.'

When the door had closed behind them I confessed, 'I'm getting terrified, Jago, but I'm trying not to show it, because she's already nervous. She's cross and very clingy too, and that's just not like her.'

'She's bound to feel frightened, however reassuring you are. I'll ring you again tomorrow, to see how the first appointment went.'

'I should phone you – it's going to cost a fortune.'

'It doesn't matter,' he said, 'at a time like this, it really, really doesn't matter.'

Ma went with us to the appointment with Dr Beems next day and I think we all felt better once we'd met him. He was a small, plump and friendly man. Stella told him that he looked just like a penguin she'd seen the day before at the 'quarium.

'I'll take that as a compliment,' he said, and admired the penguin family she'd taken in her pocket for comfort.

'I've got a doctor rabbit, too,' she said, warming to him. 'But there should be a doctor penguin, shouldn't there?'

Then she informed him that she didn't like having big needles stuck in her arm and he assured her they weren't going to do that today. I think he realised how bright she was for her age, because he explained to her in simple terms that while she was having a sleep, they were going to make her heart work just like everyone else's and then a friendly nurse took her out and he went into a lot more detail about what he was going to do.

I'd been trying not think too much in advance about how machines would take over the work of keeping Stella's little body going while they performed their miracle of surgery . . . but suddenly now I knew too much. My head throbbed and my palms went clammy as I signed the forms.

'It's a bigger operation than she's ever had before,' Ma said. 'But pray God it all goes well and it's the last.'

'Amen to that,' the doctor echoed. 'I promise to do my very best.'

Back at the hotel I gave Stella the new polar bear family I'd brought with me especially for this moment, which proved a good distraction. She told them that they would be right at home when they got back to Sticklepond, because it was going to snow, so I started to hope we'd have a hard winter!

But later she was clingy and tearful and I had to lie down on the bed with her before she would fall asleep for her nap. That evening, after an early dinner, it seemed easiest to let her watch cartoons on the huge TV in bed until she fell asleep.

Then I sneaked into Ma's room and rang Jago to describe the hospital visit.

'Dr Beems is very nice, though he made sure we realised the dangers of the surgery. But he seemed confident that she had a very good chance of coming through and making a good recovery.'

'And she goes in tomorrow, ready for the operation the next day?'

'Yes, and I can stay with her. They showed us the room and there's a chair that folds down to a bed, and a shower and stuff – it's not like in the UK.'

'I'm glad you have Martha with you, but I wish I could be there too, even if they wouldn't let me stay with you.'

'Ma will come back to the hotel after the operation, as soon as we know she's out of danger. Stella will be in intensive care right afterwards, but I'll be able to stay with her then, too, until they move her back into her ordinary room. Everyone's very nice and friendly, but the hospital is so big and bustling and . . . well, *different* from our hospitals.'

'I suppose they are – I only really know what they're like from watching series like *House* and *Scrubs*,' he said.

'I haven't seen either of those.'

'That's probably just as well,' he assured me.

It was another surreal moment taking Stella to the hospital next day, as though we were in some film with a life-and-death drama and it wasn't really happening at all.

Jago said later that he felt exactly the same, that none of it could be happening. Then he passed on messages of love and support from lots of people in the village and David and Sarah.

'It's lovely to know they're all thinking of us, and Celia and Will keep emailing and texting, too. There was already a bouquet of flowers and a message from Adam's parents at the hotel when we arrived.'

'How's Stella coping now?'

'She's gone very quiet. Ma's with her and then I'll stay the night and she'll go back to the hotel. Stella's going down for the operation first thing in the morning and it'll be a long one, they won't know how long until they're doing it.'

'Can you let me know as soon as you can when it's over?'

'I will – if I can't leave her, then I'll get Ma to ring you.' I sighed. 'You feel like my lifeline; talking to you is the only thing keeping me grounded. Stella mentions you all the time, too – and no, before you ask, not just about the gingerbread pigs.'

He laughed. 'I'd better make her a princess pig to go into the gingerbread castle we're going to make when she comes home.'

'I only hope we get a little bit of snow before Christmas too, because she's convinced there's going to be some.'

'That's out of our hands, unless we can hire a snow blower? Do they actually make snow, or just blow it about?'

'I don't know, but I forbid you to hire one if they do make snow, because it would be way too expensive,' I told him firmly. 'By the way how was that Goth croquembouche order you were making?'

'Well, the wedding reception was in a marquee, though it was a bit late in the year. Still, often they're too humid in summer for the croquembouche, so I suppose that's better. I decorated the cake with red and black hearts and sugar strands to match the décor in the marquee and I thought it looked weird, but it went down well.'

'I don't think I'd fancy a Goth croquembouche, but each to their own,' I said.

'We'll have to try out that Boston cream pie when you get home, and then you can write it up for your "Cake Diaries".'

'Yes, I'm hoping to come back with a few new recipes . . . There's a lovely nurse – though actually, she said she was some kind of volunteer called a candy-striper – and she's going to give me her recipe for key lime pie. The receptionist at the hotel's writing down her grandmother's Mississippi mud pie recipe too . . . it all seems to be pies, so far, even when they aren't actually pies, but cake.'

I stopped, then asked despairingly, 'How can I be so interested in cake when my child is about to have a major operation?'

'Because we find comfort where we can,' he said understandingly. 'I know the more you talk about cake, the more stressed and worried you are.'

'Cake's my comfort food of choice – but *you* seem to be my comfort blanket of choice,' I confessed. 'I miss you.'

'I miss you too and I love you both. In fact, I even love your mother,' he added, which made me laugh despite everything.

I didn't want to end the call and I don't think he did, either, but I had to get back in case Stella woke up.

I hardly slept at all that night because every instinct of a mother was telling me to scoop Stella up and run away with her; yet my brain accepted that this had to be done. It was the only way she would have a future.

Jago

Cally rang Jago when Stella went down to theatre and then texted him once or twice after that, but then there ensued long hours of agonising silence during which Jago imagined her pacing up and down the waiting area.

He was fit for nothing except to sit by his phone and wait, but when after what seemed like several lifetimes it rang, it was Martha.

'Jago? Our Cally asked me to call you to tell you that Stella's back from the operating theatre and she's sitting in intensive care with her.'

'Did it go . . . well?' he asked nervously.

'They said the surgery was a complete success, though of course it's early days yet and the next twenty-four hours are critical. She's hooked up to all kinds of machines and still right out of it, poor little thing, though that's probably all for the best.'

'Thank God she came through it well!' Jago said devoutly, and he wasn't ashamed of the tears that pricked at the backs of his eyes.

'That Dr Beems came out afterwards and told Cally and me that unless there are any setbacks, he expects her to make a full recovery, though she'll need monitoring, of course, as she grows.'

'That's the best Christmas present anyone could ever give me,' Jago said, feeling like a chewed rag from an excess of strain and emotion. 'I'll pass on the news to Raffy, so he can tell everyone in the village, shall I?'

'Do, and Cally said she'd given you Adam's parents' number so you could let them know, too.'

'Yes, I'll ring them, don't worry.'

'I'd better go – I want to give Celia and Hal a quick call, but then I need to get back to them. Poor little mite – she does look as if she's been in the wars.'

'She's got through it, that's the main thing,' Jago said. 'Now we just all have to will her on to recover quickly.'

'I'll give Cally your love, shall I?' she asked slightly drily.

'I hope she knows she's already got it,' Jago said. '*All* of it.'

Chapter 40: Flying Pigs

The next few days passed in a daze. Stella stabilised and woke up, uncomfortable and disorientated. Then, as she began the process of recovery, the machines sustaining her were removed, one by one.

For some reason it reminded me of that piece of music where all the musicians vanish, one by one, though I couldn't remember what it was called. Jago said he'd Google it and let me know.

By the end of the week she was weepy and clingy and lacked appetite, though after reading the literature on what I might expect post-op, that didn't come as a surprise. They *were* pleased with her progress, but seemed worried that she hadn't yet perked up and started to show more interest in getting better.

I'd been sharing my worries with Jago, of course, but one day Ma suggested it might help Stella if we let her talk to him on the phone – in fact, she picked my mobile up and rang him then and there.

'Our Stella's been asking for you, Jago, and wanting to know why you haven't brought her a gingerbread pig,' she told him, carrying the phone into Stella's room when he answered. 'But I told her, you're in a different country, you can't just pop in and visit. Here she is now,' she added, and gave the phone into Stella's eager little hands.

'Daddy-Jago?'

I couldn't hear his side of the conversation but Stella listened carefully, then took her thumb out of her mouth and said, 'But I don't *feel* mended.'

Then she listened again. 'I thought it would just happen straight away. I want to come home.'

She stuck her thumb back in her mouth and didn't say anything else, though she nodded a few times and smiled around her thumb. Then she passed the phone back to me and I went outside with it.

'What did you say?' I asked him.

'That she had to *try* to get better; it wouldn't happen on its own. But if she did, then she'd soon be coming home again and I'd be waiting at the airport to meet her.'

'Thank you, that might spur her on a bit,' I said gratefully. 'She *is* making physical progress, because her heart is working and her colour is better. They took the line out of her arm this morning too, thank goodness. It's just that she seems to lack any spirit.'

'Did Jenny come over to see her?'

'Yes, and she brought Stella a rag doll in a witch's costume, which she loved. She's got it tucked in bed with her alongside Bun. But even Jenny couldn't get her to eat much,' I told him worriedly. 'Still, perhaps now she's talked to you, she'll try a bit harder.'

The next afternoon Jago suddenly went quiet for hours, after sending me a text saying he'd catch up with me in the morning. I felt as if my lifeline had been cut.

'The lad's got to sleep sometime; he must be exhausted,' Ma said. 'He can't have had much rest since Stella came out of theatre, because he's been on the phone to you every five minutes.'

'I expect you're right,' I said guiltily, 'and since it must be evening there, he's probably crashed out, what with no sleep and working such long hours.'

But when there was still no word from him next morning and I only got his messaging service, I started to get seriously worried . . . until on my way back from a meal I didn't want in the cafeteria a familiar voice called, 'Cally!'

'*Jago?*' I swung round, my heart thumping wildly, thinking I must be dreaming, or that I'd longed for him so much that I'd conjured him up from my yearnings.

But no – it was the man himself, rumpled, unshaven and tired. In two quick strides he reached me and enfolded me in a rib-cracking embrace. Then he kissed me . . . and kissed me again.

'Oh God, I've missed you so much!' he said finally, laying his cheek against my hair.

'I've missed you too,' I said shakily. 'But I'm stunned – what on earth are you doing here? I was getting really worried because I hadn't heard from you for hours and hours.'

'Well, I hadn't got a cake order till Saturday and David could manage without me, so I managed to get on a flight. And this literally *is* a flying visit, because I've got to go back tomorrow.'

'You're quite mad,' I told him. 'But – oh, I am glad to see you!'

'How's Stella?'

'Still not perking up as much as we'd like, but she's going

to be so pleased to see you! She keeps asking for you because she can't seem to grasp how far away we are from home, probably because she slept through most of the flight.'

'Will they let me see her?' He flourished a familiar silver box. 'I've brought a trio of gingerbread pigs: mother, father and little piglet. And this bag is full of cards and presents from your friends and well-wishers. You wouldn't *believe* how long it took me to persuade Customs just to X-ray them and not make me unwrap everything.'

'Of course you can see her,' I said, leading the way back to her room, and Stella's face lit up when she saw him.

'Daddy-Jago!'

Our favourite candy-striper, Opal, was just on her way out and gave me a strange look, there having so far been no mention of Stella's father.

'This is our friend Jago, who's flown in specially to see Stella,' I introduced her.

'I told you you should come,' Stella told him. 'I'm *trying* to get better, like you said.'

'Jesus saved her, because he doesn't want her yet,' Opal said. 'I hope you're going to get that little girl to eat something, because she's taken no more lunch than would keep a sparrow alive.'

'I've got some magic gingerbread pigs in this box,' he promised. 'She'll eat every meal after one of those.'

Opal said she hoped so and went out, but Stella giggled. 'I'll try. The food is funny here, but I liked the wafflies with maple syrup at the hotel. Can I have a gingerbread piggie?'

'Of course you can,' he said, handing over the silver box. 'You nibble one of those while I get all the presents out that your friends at home have sent you.'

433

She started gnawing on the smallest pig while together they opened everything and by then all of the biscuit had vanished.

'Are you staying with me, Daddy-Jago?' she asked suddenly.

'No, I'm afraid I'll have to go back tomorrow, Stella, because I have a wedding cake to make and it'll spoil the bride's special day if I don't get it there for the reception, won't it?'

Stella nodded, reluctantly, and put her thumb back in her mouth.

'But all you have to do is eat lots so you get well quickly and Mummy can bring you home.'

'All right,' she said, removing her thumb and holding her arms out for a hug, which he returned as if she was made of glass.

'As soon as Mummy says you're on your way home, I'll bake all the pieces of gingerbread to make our princess castle and then we can build it together and cover it in icing and Smarties.'

'They have peanut butter Smarties here,' she said. 'But they're a funny shape.'

'Reese's Pieces,' I explained.

'I'll have to take some of those back with me for the gingerbread castle, then.'

'I'm going to save a bit of gingerbread pig for Opal,' announced Stella.

'Everyone's been so kind here,' I told Jago. 'And Opal, the hospital volunteer you just met, prayed for Stella every day, so what with Raffy doing the same in Sticklepond, God was clearly on our side.'

'And the angel. I saw it when I was going to sleep,' Stella said. 'It wasn't in my head, because Grandma saw it too.'

'That figures,' I said, though this was the first I'd heard of any heavenly visitation. 'It wasn't one of those angel fish from the aquarium she keeps drawing, was it?'

Stella giggled. 'No, it was a *real* angel. Opal said it was my guardian angel, telling me everything would be fine.'

'I think she was probably right.'

'Grandma does too – look, we've been drawing angels.' There was a scattering of paper on the bed, under all the get-well cards they'd just opened.

'Where *is* Grandma?' I asked, realising I hadn't seen her for ages.

'She popped out for five minutes when Opal came in. I bet she's smoking outside,' Stella said disapprovingly.

'That's quite likely,' I admitted, because the stress seemed to have upped Ma's Sobranie consumption, just as it had upped my cake one to whole new levels of gluttony, but I hoped her habit would soon revert back to two a day.

Jago had booked himself into our hotel, and later in the afternoon we left Ma in charge at the hospital, while I went back with him to change and then have dinner, the first time in a week I hadn't just dashed to the hospital cafeteria for something.

Then we walked back to the hospital to relieve Ma, holding hands just as we used to, and I felt warmed, comforted and heartened.

I'd slept in Stella's hospital room since the operation, in a chair that folded down into a bed, so Jago went back to the hotel later when Stella had gone to sleep, though not before she'd made a valiant attempt to eat all her dinner for him and then extracted a promise that he'd come back early next morning to say goodbye, before jetting off home again.

I hesitated to think what state he would be in by early Saturday, when he had that croquembouche to make!

When Jago popped in to say goodbye, he said he'd had an idea for the Christmas/Welcome Home party. 'What if I baked lots and lots of gingerbread stars and hung them on ribbons, one for each of the people who helped you to get better, Stella's Hundred Stars?'

She nodded. 'I'd like that.'

'That's a lot of work,' I said.

'Not really, and you can both help me thread the ribbons through them when you're home, can't you?'

'Of course,' I agreed.

'I'd better make lots of smaller ones to hang on the tree, too, so everyone who comes can have one.'

'And one for Father Christmas,' Stella said seriously.

'Definitely – a special one,' he agreed solemnly. 'It's going to be a great party.'

'This year we'll have the *best* Christmas ever,' I agreed, because now I was sure that Stella had turned a corner and suddenly there was a future for her, beckoning star bright.

'Are those happy tears, Mummy?' Stella asked worriedly.

'Yes, *very* happy,' I assured her.

She was sad after Jago had gone, but she already seemed brighter and more alert.

When Dr Beems came in to see her, she told him, 'I have to get better quickly, because I can't go home until I do. But I've eaten a magic gingerbread pig now, so it should be *soon*.'

'Those magic pigs, they always do the trick,' Dr Beems agreed gravely.

*   *   *

Jago hadn't been gone an hour before I was missing his comforting presence. I said as much to Ma later when Stella was having a little doze.

'It's as if I've always known him and he's been part of my life, like the brother I never had. I'm sure he feels the same way.'

'You daft ha'porth!' Ma said. 'There's nothing brotherly about the way he looks at you – or you at him. I wasn't born yesterday.'

I looked at her doubtfully. 'But . . . I mean he never ever makes any kind of move to show he wants anything other than friendship.'

'I don't know, there seems to have been a lot of kissing and cuddling going on.'

'That was mostly me,' I confessed.

'From what I heard about the pair of you at the fête, he didn't exactly fight you off.'

'Well, he is very kind, he probably wouldn't want to hurt my feelings,' I told her, though it had to be said that he put a lot of enthusiasm into his kisses . . .

'He's in love with you,' she said. 'I expect he thinks you've been too taken up with Stella to say anything.'

I wasn't sure she was right . . . but yet, I began to hope she was. And if Jago didn't realise that I'd fallen in love with him . . . well, he was probably assuming I'd be heading straight back for London as soon as Stella was well enough, so he wouldn't say anything even after we got home . . . unless I gave him a bit of encouragement!

'So, that was your daddy?' asked Opal when she came in later with a vase for the flowers that had just been delivered, along with a teddy bear from Adam's parents.

'No, Jago's just a friend,' I explained quickly. 'Stella calls him Daddy-Jago and he doesn't mind.'

'He likes it,' Stella said.

'It's clear he thinks a lot of Stella – of both of you.'

I grinned. 'He makes a mean croquembouche wedding cake, too.'

'What's that?' she asked. 'Never heard of one of those.'

I described the huge pyramids of airy patisserie cream-filled choux buns, held together by caramel and decorated with gossamer fine sugar strands and she said she was going to look them up on the internet.

'So you both love cake – that's something you have in common.'

'Mummy has a special cake she makes for birthdays,' Stella said, 'a princess cake.'

So then I had to describe that too, and once she found out about my books on cakes Opal said she was going to order them. But I told her no, she should just write down her address and we'd send her copies in return for all that praying.

'I like to pray,' she said. 'I like to talk to God; I do it a lot.'

'I talked to an angel in my dream,' Stella put in.

'I know, darlin', you told me,' Opal said.

'That was her guardian angel,' Ma said, arriving in time to overhear the last bit of conversation.

'Angels seem to be a recurring theme in our lives,' I said.

'And angel fish,' Stella suggested. 'I wonder why there isn't an angel fish family?'

'They'd be fish out of water,' I said, but when I looked at her she'd fallen suddenly asleep, a half-chewed relic of ginger-bread pig in one hand.

'I think she's saved the bum end for you again, Ma,' I said.

Jago had had about two hours' sleep before he started making that croquembouche and he told me he did it on automatic pilot.

'Actually, if anything, it's better than my usual ones,' he said, when he rang me from Honey's once he'd got back from delivering it. 'I'm going to crash out in a minute, but when I wake up I'll call Raffy and Hal and Stella's grand-parents again.'

'You're an angel.'

'It's because I love you both,' he said.

'We love you too,' I assured him (little did he know how *much* I loved him!), 'and Stella's a changed child since you left: she really *has* turned a corner.'

Jenny visited again. Her family wanted us to stay with them in their guest suite for a few days once Stella was well enough, which was very kind, though I felt for the first few days I'd like to move back to the hotel, to be near the hospital even though Jenny's daughter-in-law was a nurse, too.

But Dr Beems didn't anticipate any emergencies and was very pleased with Stella now. He told me her long-term outlook was good, and though she'd continue to need regular check-ups, they should be less frequent as she got older.

'So . . . she can start school in spring and live a normal life?'

'Yes, that shouldn't be a problem, and she should also start with moderate exercise and build up her strength.'

'When do you think we might be able to go home?'

'If all progresses well, I'd suggest the beginning of December,' he said.

So we moved back into the Great Western, and though at first Stella was still a bit clingy and whiny, unlike her old self, I knew from the literature they'd given me that that was only to be expected. I introduced her old routine as much as possible and let her act out what had happened with her doctor rabbit and a whole string of other unfortunate little creatures. That poor polar bear family were the sickest animals on the planet, until she made them all better.

Her physical recovery, though, went in leaps and bounds so that Ma, who'd always intended if all went well to come home earlier than us, decided to fly back with Jenny the following week.

'Stella hardly stops talking about you and says she misses you,' I told Jago next time he rang. 'She's counting down the days till we can come home.'

'Absence makes the heart grow fonder, they say.' He paused, then asked lightly, 'Do *you* miss me too, Cally?'

'All the time,' I admitted truthfully, 'and if I'd realised how much I'd been relying on your support, I'd have let you come with us in the first place, however selfish that would have been! It seems like ages until we'll be able to come home.'

'Just concentrate on Stella's convalescence and having a rest yourself, and I'll be waiting at the airport to meet you,' he said, sounding as if he was smiling.

'Mum'll be home on Tuesday,' I said. 'Now we know Stella's going to be fine, there didn't seem to be any reason for her to stay and she wanted to get back again, so she managed to get on the same flight as Jenny.'

'I'll pick her up at the airport, if you tell me when her plane gets in, and drive her home. I must see Raffy about the party too, now we know when you'll be getting back. It's going to be quite an event. I hadn't realised how much the villagers liked a good party.'

'Ma said they'd take it over, but I'd still like to do something special to thank everyone.'

'Oh, I think they'll all appreciate their special gingerbread stars, and I'll make a Christmas croquembouche, too. David said he was going to send a macaroon cone in red and green.'

'Sounds lovely,' I said appreciatively. 'But it doesn't seem fair that you've got to make your *own* thank you star *and* a cake!'

'I don't need a thank you. Seeing Stella well and running around like any other four-year-old will be the best present I could ever have.'

'Me too,' I sighed happily. 'I know it will take some time until she's fully recovered and there are lots of check-ups still to come, but already I feel as if all my birthdays and Christmas presents have been rolled into one.'

Jenny saw us installed with her family near Salem, and then she and Ma caught their flight home, though Ma had a slight wobble just before she left.

'I don't like to leave you. Maybe I should wait and come back with you.'

But I knew she'd really had enough of people and was desperate to get back to Sticklepond and her work – and, I suspected, Hal – so I assured her we'd be perfectly OK without her.

'We'll be fine, we're in good hands here, and then we'll

move back to the hotel for the last few days when Stella has more bounce and maybe have some little trips out . . . I'd like to find a good bakery and arrange to have a special Boston cream pie sent to the staff at the Heart Centre. I've heard of a really good chocolate shop too, so I'm going to get something for Opal; she's been so good.'

'*And* given you her Mississippi mud pie recipe,' Ma said.

'That's a point,' I said. 'That recipe and the one for key lime pie, which the hotel receptionist gave me, both need Graham crackers and I don't think I can get them back home. I'll put some in my luggage, just in case.'

Jago

Jago collected Martha at the airport and drove her home, once she'd said goodbye to Jenny, who'd been met by her brother, Clive Snowball.

'Well, I'm that glad to be home again,' Martha said with a sigh, sitting back in the front seat of the Saab as Jago headed back to Sticklepond. 'Being cooped up in an aeroplane with a lot of strangers is my idea of hell, even if we did have return flights in business class.'

'I can imagine,' he said sympathetically. 'But I'm sure Cally and Stella must be missing you already.'

'Not as much as they're missing *you* – or not in Cally's case, anyway,' she said pointedly, and he glanced across at her.

'I'm very fond of Cally – of them both. And I'm sure Cally loves me like a brother,' he said gloomily.

'Well, you're right out there, and you're a pair of daft ha'porths who can't see what's under your noses!' she said forthrightly.

He looked across at her, startled. 'Do you mean . . . you think she really—'

'For goodness' sake – yes!' Ma snapped impatiently, then

she shut her eyes and refused to be drawn for the rest of the journey back.

'I've just dropped Martha off, and Moses and Toto were really glad to see her,' Jago told Cally. 'Hal was at work, but he'd left a bottle of whisky and a note on the kitchen table saying he'd be round later, so she'll be fine.'

'She's always fine on her own,' she said. 'Was the house warm?'

'Yes, the heating had been going on and off and Hal had been keeping an eye on things. I'd better get back to work – I've got a bride and her mother coming in a little while to talk about ordering a cake for spring. The orders for the next wedding season are really starting to snowball already.'

'Well, that's what you need, so you can see how it will pan out over the first year of trading.'

'I've got a new order book and I've worked out how many croquembouche I can make in a day, though if I'm very busy I may have to train up someone to deliver and set them up. I miss you helping me with the paperwork, too.'

'I'll be back before long and I'll sort you out if you've got in a muddle,' she promised.

'I *am* in a total muddle,' he confessed ruefully, though not to the fact that she was the cause of his confusion, 'a mess that only you can get me out of.'

He dropped in to see if Martha was all right once or twice, but he could see that she was perfectly happy on her own. Hal was often around, of course, but somehow he didn't seem to count . . . except that he was sure there was a hint of romance there because late one evening, driving through the village, he'd spotted them walking back from the Green Man, hand in hand.

He'd carried on with Plan A and almost finished turning the annexe behind Honey's into a guest suite, so as soon as Cally got home he'd unroll before her his master plan that she and Stella live there after Christmas until they were ready to pick up their old lives in London . . . though, encouraged by what Martha had said, he really hoped that when Cally had had time to think about it, she'd change her mind about that part.

'I'm counting down the days till you get back. I've got something I want to show you,' he told her, but then refused to be drawn on what the surprise might be.

'I don't suppose you've seen any long-term weather forecasts for snow when we get home, have you?' she asked. 'Stella seems to think because she mentioned it to Father Christmas, it's going to happen.'

'Martha's told Hal about it and he says not to worry, he's on the case.'

'What, he can do a little snow dance and it falls from the sky to order, or something?'

'I've no idea, but maybe he'll rope in a witch or two to help,' he suggested, and then they got giggly over the idea of Hebe Winter, Florrie Snowball and Gregory Lyon all joining hands and frolicking under the full moon.

Later, Jago woke up in the middle of the night with a start, hoping none of those three had *really* got second sight or he might find in the morning he'd been turned into a little white mouse . . .

Chapter 41: Boston Beans

Stella was like a different child after being spoiled by Jenny's family in Salem during our relaxing stay, and then when we went back to the Great Western for the last few days she greeted the staff like old friends.

We had a couple of little trips out, back to the aquarium and to the wonderful Children's Museum and ate Boston baked beans at a place called Durgin-Park in the market, which the hotel receptionist told us about. Of course, we sampled variations of Boston cream pies, cupcakes and doughnuts everywhere else too . . . I kept scribbling down recipes and I was looking forward to trying some of them out at home with Jago.

I'd eaten so much cake in America that I was now about the same shape as a Christmas pudding and all my clothes were too tight. But luckily Ma said my payment on publication of the second *Cake Diaries* book had come, so I treated both of us to some new clothes – trousers, mittens and hats, warm socks and thick, fleecy sweatshirts – and a lovely dress for me that I thought would be nice for the welcome home party. It had a deep cross-over neckline that flattered my curvy figure and if Ma was right about Jago being in love with me – well, my gorgeous new dress might just do the trick!

The shops were all Christmassy by now and irresistible, so we did a little present buying, too . . .

Stella had her final hospital check-up and was passed fit to fly home. Jenny's family collected us and saw us off at the airport, which was just as well, considering how much extra baggage we had. But Stella was deeply disappointed not to see the friendly yellow cab driver who'd taken us to the hotel when we'd arrived in Boston, and only cheered up when Kevin promised to go and find him after our flight left, to tell him she was fine. I'd have been worried if I'd thought he really meant it, because it wouldn't be an easy task, seeing he had no idea what he looked like or, in fact, anything about him except that his name was George. However, Stella went off to the departure lounge perfectly happy.

I got on that plane feeling relieved, relaxed and rested, but by the time I got off in Manchester, I felt like a puppet with its strings cut. I don't know why, but it was all I could do to collect our stuff together and get through into the arrivals hall.

So it was a huge relief when I spotted Jago waiting to meet us, looking darkly and delectably handsome. His caramel-brown eyes lit up at the sight of us, and Stella woke enough to transfer her hot, sticky cross self from my arms to his. He hugged me with his free arm and kissed me – not one of our never-ending kisses, but warm and sweet, for all that – and then we went out into the cold air. And it *was* cold.

'Is it cold enough for snow?' I asked, as we drove home,

the heaters pumping out warmth. 'Are we going to have a white Christmas?'

'I don't know; the forecast's a bit ambiguous. Still, Christmas seems to be such a big deal one way or another right across the borough of Middlemoss, that maybe Stella won't notice if it *doesn't* snow,' he said. 'The party is next Saturday: do you think you and Stella will be up to it? I know you'll need some time to settle back and get Stella into her usual routine again.'

'Oh, yes, she's full of beans now – Boston beans – and she's really looking forward to it. She'll be having a check-up in a couple of days in Ormskirk, when I think the physio-therapist is going to give her some exercises to do, too.'

'I've baked and iced the stars ready for her to hand out at the party, and I'll buy a few metres of narrow ribbon from the market on Thursday to make the loops.'

'We'll help you to thread them up, it'll be fun,' I said. 'Everyone must have gone to a lot of trouble.'

'Yes, but they're all having a great time,' he assured me.

Ma's cottage looked strangely small after the hotel – and Kevin's home had been on the large side, too. A brief moment of claustrophobia swept over me, which was probably how poor Ma felt most of the time – and I thought how bravely she'd put up with the crowded house for so long.

'She's got a tree and lights on it already!' I exclaimed, seeing it flashing on and off through the window.

'I came over yesterday and helped her put the tree up: she said she wanted it all ready for when you got home.'

'She doesn't usually remember things like that, but Stella will be so excited,' I said, touched.

Stella woke up enough to exclaim sleepily over the tree

and then was put into her own warm bed, surrounded by Bun and so many stuffed toys that it was a wonder there was enough room for her in there, too.

Looking down at her, before I turned off the light, I thought already my changeling child had begun the metamorphosis from fairy to human, for she'd definitely grown and that transparent, other-worldly look had been replaced by a healthy, rosy flush.

The Boston cream pie isn't really a pie at all, but a very rich and delicious cake. I found several variations of it while I was over there recently, but they are all basically similar: a cream-filled chocolate sponge covered with a thick layer of rich chocolate ganache.

Cally Weston: 'The Cake Diaries'

The sky was a cold but limpid blue next morning when I was up early and baking as if I'd never been away, and there wasn't a single snow cloud on the horizon.

When I said as much to Ma later, while she was eating endless rounds of toast and Marmite, a delicacy she'd missed in Boston and was now trying to catch up on, she said you never knew, it could just blow up out of nowhere in an instant.

Then she followed me into Stella's room and wandered over to the window to draw the curtains, while I was getting her up.

Out of the corner of my eye I saw her start histrionically and then she exclaimed, 'Well, I never! I'm sure those are flakes of snow!'

'Where? Show me, Grandma!' Stella demanded, rushing

449

to see, and Ma's eyes, blue and wide with innocence, met mine over her head.

'Mummy – look! It *is* snowing,' Stella cried.

'So it is,' I agreed, for the first few drifting, lazy, feathery flakes had now become a thick, whirling swirl of purest white . . .

'Feathers? Snow is feathers?' Stella said, enchanted.

'Yes,' Ma said. 'Hal says snow is the feathers from angels' wings, so it always melts away eventually . . . unless some very special little girl has asked for snow; then sometimes it doesn't vanish at all.'

Stella stood on tiptoe and looked down at the ground as a last solitary, downy feather drifted and landed light as a whisper on top of the white scattering that lay on the grass beneath the window.

'It's magic!' she breathed.

'It certainly is,' I agreed.

And later, when she'd been bundled up warmly so she could go out and collect every last precious snowflake and then gone up to the studio with Ma to put them in a special jar of their own, I sought Hal out in his shed and thanked him.

'Nothing to thank me for,' he said, absently brushing a tell-tale fragment of fluffy whiteness from his tweed sleeve, and then refused to be drawn on the matter.

'Some things are better if you don't think about them too much,' he said.

In future, I might adopt that as my philosophy for life.

Stella showed her angel feathers to Jago when he came round, but by then she'd thought of something that troubled her.

However, he assured her that the angels weren't feeling cold because they'd lost all their feathers, they just naturally moulted, like birds, from time to time as the new ones came through, so they could easily spare Stella a few.

We settled in as if we'd never been away, except, of course, that Stella seemed to grow in energy every day. And Jago and I picked up our old relationship as if there had never been an interval too, so I began to doubt if Ma had been right . . . I mean, Stella was well and we were home, so what was he waiting for?

Over the following week we gently eased back into village life and went for walks, well wrapped up. Although I still took the buggy in case Stella tired, I could see that one day soon she wouldn't want it at all – which would be just as well, because by then she wouldn't fit in it any more!

She quite cheerfully visited her old friends at Ormskirk Hospital and showed off her battle wounds, but was more interested in telling them about the angel snow. And afterwards, when we went to the Blue Dog with Jago, she told the three Graces, too.

Soon, I don't think there was anyone within a radius of about ten miles from Sticklepond who *didn't* know that snow was angels' feathers.

We had lots of visitors. Raffy and Chloe came together, and Jenny with Mrs Snowball. And Celia and Will came over, of course. Raffy was going to meet up with me, Celia and Will before Christmas to do a final reckoning and discuss where to donate the money left over in the Stella's Stars fund.

There was a card from Miss Honey, who said she'd been invited to the party but to tell Stella that she was going into hibernation for the winter like a tortoise, though if the Lord spared her, she'd see us in spring.

The November *Sweet Home* magazine, which had just come out, had slipped in my stained-glass star biscuit recipe, instead of the one I thought they were going to use and 'The Cake Diaries' featured my own mincemeat recipe and one for open iced mincemeat tartlets. A box of author's copies of my second *Cake Diaries* book arrived too, most of which I would wrap up and give as Christmas presents to local friends, though I sent both volumes to Opal in Boston straight away, with a letter thanking her for all her kindness and telling her about the angel snow. I knew she'd love that.

I hadn't been down to Honey's since we returned, because Jago went all mysterious and said he wanted to give something a final touch before he showed me whatever this surprise was, so goodness knew what he'd been up to.

But of course he'd been at Ma's a lot, and I'd already sorted out his bookkeeping and helped him with some complicated forms. Now we had resumed our evenings of baking, film watching and snoozing on the sofa, as if we'd never been apart – and it was lovely, though suddenly not quite enough . . .

But I had my plans, and Christmas was now hurtling towards us, a joyful one, destined to be the best ever. We made a Christmas pudding the size of a cannonball and the cake, too – both later than usual, but none the worse for that. Then Jago and Stella built the most stupendous gingerbread castle, covered in icing snow and decorated with brightly coloured Reese's Pieces, which I took lots of pictures of before it got nibbled. There was no chance it would last till Christmas.

We threaded red and green silk ribbon through the hundred big gingerbread stars and all the smaller ones for the party, then, the day before, it was a mad rush to make cakes, pack the star biscuits and, in Stella's case, try to decide what to wear.

Luckily a fairy outfit large enough to fit over a warm dress and leggings arrived from the Scotts just in time and, teamed with the angel wings that Sarah and David had given her for her birthday, she decided she had the perfect outfit.

I'd be wearing the blue and grey dress I'd found in Boston with cowboy boots, ditto, and declined Stella's offer of a pair of gauzy fairy wings. I told her I was so happy, I could probably fly to the party without them.

Jago

Stella and Cally, as guests of honour, were forbidden to arrive early at the party, but Jago was there, delivering one of his most magnificent croquembouche cakes, decorated with sugar strands and a myriad of silver sugared almonds and stars: his feelings always tended to express themselves edibly. He'd made a little sugar angel to go on top, too, using a chocolate mould.

The village hall looked very festive, with a 'Happy Christmas and Welcome Home Stella!' banner over the door. Inside, an army of helpers had erected the Christmas tree brought by Seth Greenwood, along with armfuls of holly and mistletoe from the Winter's End estate, and were draping it with twinkling lights.

Jago deposited his croquembouche in the centre of the refreshment tables and then carried in the two macaroon pyramids that he'd brought from David and Sarah, and the boxes of gingerbread stars.

There was a separate table for the special Stella's Stars biscuits, under the watchful eye of the WI ladies, who were busy putting out covered plates of triangular sandwiches, mini pork pies, jellies in paper cases, mince pies, and little cheese and tomato tartlets.

Jago, helped by Effie Yatton and a posse of Brownies, hung all the smaller gingerbread stars on the lower branches of the Christmas tree and by the time this was finished practically the entire village – not to mention Will and Celia – had arrived, the bright paper garlands festooned from the wooden beams of the ceiling swaying and rustling every time the door was opened.

Cally, Stella and Martha came in last, as arranged, looking self-conscious, especially when everyone applauded. But soon the babble of conversation resumed and Raffy turned on a CD of carols in the background.

Cally was wearing a dress patterned in the same pure harebell-blue shade as her eyes and she looked to Jago stunningly beautiful – and, when she spotted him and smiled, very happy. Stella ran straight to him and he picked her up, then put his free arm around Cally when she caught up.

Her eyes shone like stars when she looked up at him and he felt such a deep joy and happiness that he thought his heart might burst, realising that whatever happened after this, he'd always treasure this one precious moment.

Chapter 42: Piece of Cake

When we walked into the village hall and everyone went quiet and stared at us, then suddenly burst into a storm of clapping and cheers, it was both moving and hideously embarrassing at the same time.

It was a relief when I spotted Jago, looking handsome with his dark curling hair shining under the lights, my very own Captain Jack Sparrow . . . Did he have any idea at all that he made my timbers shiver?

Then our eyes met and I thought maybe the dress had had the desired effect, because for a moment he looked quite stunned. I followed Stella across to him and he looked down at me and said with a heart-melting smile, 'You look beautiful! And this is great, isn't it? Stella, Father Christmas is just getting warmed up in the other room and he'll be in in a minute.'

He was too, and possibly the smallest Santa I'd ever seen! There was a tissue-paper-draped throne ready for him and he had a sack full of presents for all the children, though Stella's was very special – a fairy wand that lit up and then sparkled in a rainbow of colours.

Raffy called for a moment's silence after that and reminded

us that we were here to celebrate both Christmas and to welcome home Stella after her successful operation in America.

'So please could everyone involved in the fundraising, all of Stella's Hundred Stars, come forward and get their very own gingerbread star of merit. And there are lots more hanging on the tree for everyone else.'

Stella and I started handing the special ones out while Jago went to help get down the biscuits from the lower branches of the tree. By the time he returned the stars had all vanished and so, too, had Stella, though I could see her fairy wand twinkling like a firefly at the other end of the room. Celia and Will had gone in pursuit to make sure she didn't overtire herself.

'This is yours,' I said, handing over the very last gingerbread star. 'I thought it would look a bit suspicious if you didn't eat your own baking.'

'I think I'd like to keep it, actually,' Jago said. 'I might have a bit of croquembouche shortly, though, because that's not something that'll last long.'

'Stella said it looked like a fairy wedding cake, which is a good thing, since she's still convinced that they're small angels . . . and I assume that lovely wand that Santa gave her was your idea?'

Before Jago could reply, Raffy, who had his star pinned to his chest like a slightly crumbly medal, stopped and said how delighted he was to see Stella looking so well. Then he added to Jago, with a twinkle, 'Have you shown Cally what you've been doing at the Honey's yet? Jago gave me a guided tour yesterday,' he added to me.

'That's more than I've had since I got back!' I said. 'What have you been up to, Jago?'

'Just finishing touches,' he said vaguely, though he looked a little self-conscious . . . and strangely nervous.

'We're delighted you're part of the community now and I hope Honey's will be a huge success,' Raffy told him.

When he'd gone I said firmly to Jago, 'Now I'm dying to see what you've been doing! Have you been holding out on me? Added a turret or put a pool in the back garden, or something?'

'No . . . well, not really,' he qualified, still looking suspiciously shifty.

'Which, the turret or the pool?'

'Neither.' He seemed to come to a decision and said, 'Look, if Celia and Will are keeping an eye on Stella, then we could sneak off for ten minutes and you can see for yourself – it's only across the road, after all.'

'Oh, yes – let's! I can't wait any longer, and I'll tell Ma where we're going as well, on the way out,' I agreed. 'Come on, show me all your secrets!'

Nothing looked much different, except he'd installed a small log-burning stove on the hearth in the living room.

'That's new,' I said. 'Is that the surprise? It does make the whole room look really warm and cosy.'

'No, of course that's not it! Come on,' he added with resolution, 'come and see what I've done with the annexe.'

'The annexe . . .?' I echoed, following him through the glass doors into the new conservatory and then into the annexe, which I saw had now been totally transformed.

It was decorated in the soft pastel shades I loved, with a child's bed in the small room and a pretty, wrought-iron white-painted one in the main bedroom. It was all very feminine and pretty . . .

'Oh, it looks lovely!' I cried. 'Fairy-tale beautiful!'

'Do you really like it? I asked Celia's advice on the colour scheme and she helped me pick out the furniture.'

'Did she? So you've both been holding out on me!' I said. 'But . . . I thought you were going to leave decorating and furnishing in here and the flat for much later?'

'I was,' he admitted, 'but then I decided I really wanted to get it done before you came back, because—'

'But if you'd waited, I could have helped you do it up. You know I'll always give you a hand with anything that needs doing.'

He gave me a look I found hard to interpret. 'Well, I did mean what I said about your prinsesstårte making a lovely alternative wedding cake and that I'd employ you – and I wasn't entirely joking,' he said slowly.

'Neither was I, when I said it would be a good idea – and I don't suppose there would be that many orders, so I could still write my articles.'

'True – if you're still here,' he pointed out. 'What I really wanted to say was, even if you and Stella eventually head off back to London, you might like to move in here until you've got everything arranged and you're ready to go.'

'You mean, you made this so beautiful for *us*?' I said, stunned. 'And are you *mad*? I wouldn't pick up my old life if it was gilded by Cartier and had a ribbon round it!'

'You wouldn't?' he asked hopefully.

'No, of course not. I realised ages ago that Sticklepond's where I want to live and bring up Stella . . . and if you're serious, we'll not only move in, but I'll work for you, too.'

'Actually, I had a cunning plan,' he said, raising one dark eyebrow quizzically in his best pirate fashion. 'I was hoping that once I'd got you under my roof, I might persuade you into some kind of *permanent* partnership . . .'

His soft brown eyes were so unmistakably full of warmth and love that my heart did a backflip.

'What exactly did you have in mind?' I asked, as I went willingly into his arms.

'Wedding bells, our own croquembouche cake and Stella in a bridesmaid's dress and angel wings?' he suggested.

'One thing at a time,' I said severely, but laughing. And then we kissed with the usual result, so that when we finally surfaced some considerable time had passed and we had to dash back to the party.

We were just about to go into the village hall when Jago's phone buzzed and he stopped and checked it to find a message – from Aimee!

It said she was stuck in Colombia and to urgently send money, because hers had all been stolen.

'I've heard about this kind of thing: it's just a scam,' he told me.

'Really? I mean, I suppose it could be real, though she doesn't mention Adam.'

'No, definitely a scam,' he said, deleting it. Then he slipped it back into his pocket and reached for me for one final kiss before we went back in.

Chapter 43: Celestial Bliss

I suppose when we went back into the hall hand in hand, our expressions gave us away.

'Well, that's five quid you owe me,' Florrie said audibly to Jenny as we passed, and Raffy congratulated us both.

'It's like I said: nothing ventured, nothing gained,' he told Jago.

'He could have saved himself a lot of money on furnishings by asking me earlier,' I pointed out.

'You weren't ready to think of the future earlier, though,' Jago said.

'No, that's true: not when I was afraid that Stella might not have one. No one understands me the way you do, Jago.'

I looked up into his warm brown eyes and then completely forgot we were surrounded by people . . . Our lips were closing in fast, when luckily Stella suddenly bobbed up and said excitedly, 'Mummy! Grandma kissed Hal under the mistletoe – I saw them!'

'Did you?' I said, not altogether surprised.

'She says I need to go home now, or its tears before bedtime. Can I give Daddy-Jago his present, first?'

'Of course – I'd quite forgotten.' I quickly delved into my

shoulder bag and handed Stella a silver-tissue-covered parcel. 'Don't drop it.'

'I chose this for you in Boston,' she said, giving it to him. 'You mustn't drop it, either.'

'For me?' Jago took the parcel and unwrapped it, revealing a moulded amber glass starfish, pierced to hang in a window. 'That is *so* beautiful – the nicest present I've ever had.'

Stella looked lovingly up at him. 'It's because you're my starriest star of all,' she said.

Will Holly Brown get more than
she bargained for this Christmas?

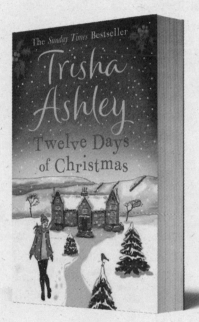

A charming romantic comedy about a
single mum who inherits a stately home…
and a whole lot more besides!

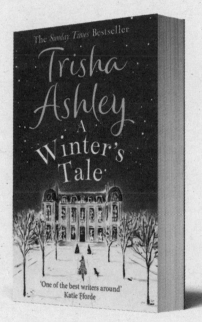

Available in all good bookshops now.

This Christmas is about to
go off with a bang!

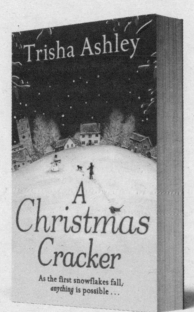

Home is where the heart is…
and Izzy is heading back to the village
of Halfhidden in search of hers.

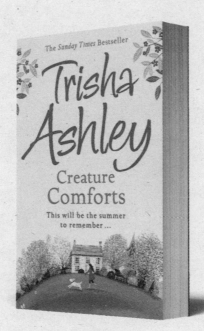

Available in all good bookshops now.

First comes marriage. Then comes divorce.
Then it's every woman for herself...

Available in all good bookshops now.